Made in Heaven

Also by Adèle Geras

Facing the Light
Hester's Story

Made in Heaven

ADÈLE GERAS

1 3 5 7 9 10 8 6 4 2

First published in Great Britain in 2006 by Orion, an imprint of the Orion Publishing Group Ltd.

A CIP catalogue record for this book is available from the British Library.

ISBN-13: (hardback) 978 07528 7246 9
(trade paperback) 978 07528 7247 6
ISBN-10: (hardback) 0 7528 7246 X
(trade paperback) 0 7528 7247 8

Typeset by Deltatype Ltd, Birkenhead, Merseyside

Set in Perpetua

Printed in Great Britain by Clays Ltd, St Ives plc

The Orion Publishing Group's policy is to use papers that are natural, renewable and recyclable products and made from wood grown in sustainable forests. The logging and manufacturing processes are expected to conform to the environmental regulations of the country of origin.

The Orion Publishing Group Ltd
Orion House
5 Upper Saint Martin's Lane
London, WC2H 9EA
www.orionbooks.co.uk

This one is for Jenny Geras and Ben Jones

Acknowledgements

Many people have helped me in the writing of this novel, either by sending me their notions of an ideal wedding, or in various other ways. I'd like to thank every one of them. In alphabetical order, then: Marianne Adey, Annie Ashworth, Rachel Benson, Caroline Bentley-Davies, Bespoke Events, Victoria Blashford-Snell, Sue Bush, Laura Cecil, Rebecca Cooper, Jo Dawson, Dianne Drymoussis, Susan Hill, Alice Hudson, Nicolette Jones, Morag Joss, Roger Judd, Joan Keating (and her children), Sara McDonald, Sarah Margolis, Katharine Martin, Sophie Masson, Geraldine McCaughrean, Gus Mills, Claire Morris, Sue Neale, Linda Newbery (and Hamish), Claire O'Grady, Janet Parr, Bella Pearson, Margaret Powling, Sally Prue, Edward Russell-Walling, Jessica Ruston, Linda Sargent (and Mister), Philippa Shepherd, Alison Stanley, Hazel Townson, Jean Ure, Gill Vickery, Anne Weale and Tara Wood.

Very special thanks to Kate Merrigan for bringing the wedding dress and the bridesmaids' dresses so beautifully to life in her sketches.
Anyone who's been on an Arvon Course will recognize Fairford Hall, but it is a fictional recreation of one of the Arvon Foundation's centres and not the real thing. Some people may also know the original of the Shipwreck Café , which is not in Dorset.

Jane Wood, Emma Dunford and Jane Gregory were a great support throughout. Finally, many thanks as always to Norm Geras, and to Sophie Hannah who read every page before anyone else and whose excellent advice I have, as usual, relied on.

May / June

Saturday

'Parents of the bride meet parents of the groom. It's a ritual that goes on in every society and has done for centuries.'

'We're not first-year archaeology students, Pa,' said Zannah from the back seat of the car. 'You're in professor mode and you shouldn't be. Just be normal.'

Bob Gratrix smiled. 'What if professor mode *is* normal? What then? No, I'm only joking, Zannah. I'll behave, I promise.'

Joss considered her husband's profile. After thirty-one years of marriage, it was easy not to look properly at a person who had become completely familiar. One flesh ... that was what they said and it was almost true. Joss didn't feel as though she was fifty-two, and wondered how different she was now from the woman she used to be, years ago. It was hard to tell, when it came to judging yourself. Bob, with his sharp nose, thick, white hair and skin that had, after years of exposure to the sun, turned rather dry and leathery, was still reasonably good-looking. Perhaps it was his cheerful manner, too, which made him seem younger than fifty-six. So why, Joss wondered, do I feel so ... so *unmoved* by him? He could be pompous at times ... all that stuff about rituals in every society, but she loved him. I must do, she reasoned, or I wouldn't have stayed married to him for so long. She refused to admit the possibility that remaining with Bob was tantamount to a kind of inertia; a lack of courage.

It was true that Gray had never, while they'd been writing to one another, suggested that she might leave her husband to come and live with him. He'd never said: *I can't bear to spend a single day without you. Leave your whole life and start again with me.* Not once. Would she have left Bob, with a bit of encouragement? Probably not. Her life was too settled, too comfortable, too much bound up with her daughters and her grandchild. Joss was not, and never had been, a rocker of boats. Perhaps, she told herself, I don't quite believe in Gray, but I mustn't think about him today, and I won't. Because he was in her thoughts most of the time, putting Gray aside and out of her mind could be almost pleasurable: like denying yourself a piece of chocolate when you were longing for one. I'll leave that till later. Today is Zannah's day.

Charlotte, Joss's aunt, was hosting the engagement party at her house in Clapham because Adrian's parents could get to it easily from Guildford, and she and Bob were always happy to come down and visit Zannah and Emily and Zannah's eight-year-old daughter, Isis. Everybody, she knew, regarded a trip up north as a 'trek'. That was how they put it: *a trek up north*, as though the Gratrixes lived in an igloo in the middle of a snowfield and not a spacious Edwardian semi outside Altrincham, on a suburban street that was proud of its fine trees. Also, (and this was more important even than the location of her house) Charlotte was on Zannah's side where wedding arrangements were concerned and eager to be involved in every phase of the planning. This was not quite true of Joss herself. Her feelings about the forthcoming bridal palaver ... perhaps campaign might be a better word ... were mixed, to say the least, but the one thing you did need for a proper family wedding was family – a grandma for instance. Joss felt a little guilty that she hadn't managed to provide one for her daughters, but, she reasoned, it isn't my fault my parents died so young. Bob was no better. His parents had been buried within months of one another just before Zannah was born. Charlotte, although technically a great-aunt, was, according to Zannah and Emily, better than any grandmother. She always knew how to provide precisely the right mixture of adoration and supervision, just as she had done when Joss was a girl.

Isis was filling the car with her chatter, telling her grandfather more than he could possibly take in.

'I'm going to be a bridesmaid, Grandpa,' she said. 'I'm going to have a pink dress with bows on and the skirt'll stick out really far and I'll twirl in it.'

'You don't know what colour your dress'll be, Icicle!' Zannah said. 'I haven't even picked a colour scheme yet.'

'You sound like one of those glossy bridal mags.' Joss turned round to smile at her daughter.

'Don't start on me, Ma,' Zannah sighed. 'I get the anti-big-wedding propaganda constantly from Em. I try not to listen. I'm the one getting married and this time, it'll be just the way I decide to have it. I've been dreaming about it since I was Icepop's age.'

'*Icepop. Icicle*. You shouldn't let them call you such things, Isis,' Bob snorted in disgust.

'I know,' said Isis. 'I'm named for an Egyptian goddess.'

'Quite right,' said Bob. '*Icepop* indeed.'

Joss looked out of the car window and marvelled at how little her daughters had changed since childhood. She could still remember a colleague of Bob's from the university asking the girls what they wanted to be when they grew up. Emily was about seven and Zannah eleven.

'An archaeologist like Pa,' Em answered immediately.

Zannah took a few moments to think. Then she smiled and said, 'When I grow up, I'm going to be a bride.'

'But that's not …' Bob had started to say, and Joss remembered ssshing him. *Leave her alone, Bob. Not now*.

'We're nearly there,' said Zannah. 'Come out of your daydream, Ma. You're about to meet my in-laws to be, but they're mine, not yours, so there's nothing for you to be nervous about.'

'I'm not nervous.'

'You look a bit pale, though.'

'Do I? Well, I can't help that. It's not nerves, honestly.'

Because of the way Zannah's marriage to Cal Ford had ended, and because of the agonies her daughter had gone through when it had, Joss didn't feel she could confess her misgivings; the pangs of regret she was feeling now. When Cal and Zannah had married, in a register office, with almost no one there and no pomp or ceremony whatsoever, she and Bob hadn't minded a bit. Cal was … still is … a darling, Joss thought, and no one else, not even the handsome and thoroughly eligible Adrian, could change her opinion of him. Zannah still saw him often because he shared custody of Isis, but that wasn't the same. Joss had always secretly felt she had a son while Zannah had been married to Cal. Perhaps she'd grow to feel more maternal towards Adrian Whittaker when she knew him better. He and Zannah had been together for a mere six months and Joss had only met him twice before today and never really spoken to him properly. She also wondered what the chances were of her getting on as well with the Ashtons as she did with Cal's mother, even now after the divorce. They still exchanged Christmas cards and Joss never thought of her without wishing that they were still connected. There was also the matter of Adrian's relationship with Isis. Joss made a mental note to question Zannah carefully about that, and to watch out today to see how they got on with one another.

They were nearly there. The flowerbeds all round the circular drive in front of Charlotte's front door were particularly neat and the lawn looked as though it had been recently brushed and combed. Mauve swags of wisteria blossom drooped languidly around the front door. Camellias seemed to flower earlier and earlier and here they were in May with most of their blossoms already gone. The pink and white petals and dead heads had been swept away. The peonies looked as though they had every intention of being spectacular this year and Joss wondered whether Zannah was going to set a date that would allow her to include them in her bouquet. July? Was that the best peony month? Did peonies ever figure in bouquets? She realized that she was quite ignorant about such things. They hadn't seemed to be of the least importance when she and Bob had married. A pleasant ceremony in the local register office and a pretty bouquet to hold. As far as she remembered, she and Charlotte had simply gone into the florist's shop in the next street and ordered one to be sent to the house on the morning of the wedding. This was going to be quite different: another sort of wedding altogether.

Charlotte's house (detached, Edwardian, double-fronted, with an elegant porch) was imposing without being overwhelming; and when she had lived there as a teenager, Joss used to think the windows gazed out at the world in a friendly and welcoming manner. She still liked them. There was something about the way they'd been set into the surrounding brickwork that pleased her. The proportions were right. She gathered up the filmy dark-green skirts of her dress to get out of the car. This whole wedding thing was going to be, in the hideous modern phrase, a steep learning curve.. Joss tried to imagine the slope of a hillside, or the sweep of a wave running to the shore, but that didn't work and the image of a graph on squared paper … exactly the sort of thing that used to terrify her when she was at school … wouldn't go away.

Zannah was doing rather well with the introductions. Emily, her younger sister (not exactly hiding away but observing from the window seat) was quite impressed. That sort of thing was always like a dance where no one was sure of the steps. She looked good too, in a dark red linen trouser suit with her reddish-gold hair piled up on top of her head and long, jade earrings a delicious undersea green against the pale skin of her neck. Emily, with her short, spiky dark hair, and her habit of wearing only black or white clothes, knew she wasn't a patch on Zannah in the looks department. I've never minded her being prettier, she reflected. Didn't really mind her being much thinner than me, or taller, or having the kind of small breasts that made clothes hang so well. I must have spent hours, Emily thought, helping her to work out good ways of stuffing her bras even before I was wearing them myself. There's only one thing I envied her for and that was Cal. And they're divorced now, so I'm not even jealous about that any longer. She was determined not to think about her ex-brother-in-law today if she could help it. There was too much going on and she needed her wits about her. Zannah would interrogate her about everything once they were alone at home and Isis had gone to bed. This was something they'd always done, even though she was four years younger than her sister. Emily remembered many nights when Zannah had crept into her room after Pa and Ma were in bed. She used to push back the duvet and say: *You're not asleep, are you?* The standard, jokey answer was: *Not any more.* Emily smiled when she thought now about how they used to sit up for hours discussing this or that young man's kissing technique, or whether someone's dandruff made them unkissable. And I thought it didn't and Zannah thought it did. Considering how fussy she is, it's a major puzzle to work out why she's got a second fiancé in tow and I've not had a bite of one. Emily wondered whether she was on the shelf. She was twenty-six, for Heaven's sake! Well, if she was on the shelf, she wasn't too steamed up about it. Maybe being on the shelf was the new black. Or whatever.

The big round table from the dining room had been set up here in the drawing room, which had been cleared of both armchairs and sofa, leaving only a few hard-backed chairs pushed up against the wall. It was a good idea, Emily thought. This room was the biggest in the house, with a bay window facing the drive and more than twenty feet away, French windows open on to the terrace and the garden on this sparkling day. The damasked cloth, the glasses and cutlery and vases of cream and pale pink roses were good enough to be in a photoshoot. Since she'd started working for a PR firm, she'd become much more aware of the appearance of everything.

Ma, for instance, was looking pretty but flustered. She very often did. Today, Emily could tell, she'd made a special effort to be smart in clothes that wouldn't let down the future mother of the bride. If they were a little on the hippyish side, if she wasn't in the same league as the groom's mother when it came to gloss and polish, her bones were finer and she was more instinctively elegant.

'Ma, this is Adrian's mother, Mrs ...'

'Maureen, please. We can't be formal if Suzannah's to be my daughter-in-law, can we?' She pronounced her own name in the melodious Irish fashion, with the emphasis on the 'een', Emily noticed. She insisted on it, according to Zannah. Emphasising the first syllable of the name, she'd decreed, made it sound common.

'Jocelyn,' Emily heard her mother say, 'but please call me Joss. Everyone does. And this is Bob, my husband.'

'Delighted,' said Bob. Emily felt proud of her father, who was not exactly pushing sixty but sort of waving at it as it came closer. He was still quite good-looking, with, as he put it, 'all my own hair and teeth.' He was getting a bit thick around the waist, and no one could call him really handsome, but he had a pleasant face and Emily noticed that Maureen was one of those women who turn up the wattage when they have a man in front of them at whom they can direct their smiles.

'I must apologize for my husband,' she purred. 'You're at the mercy of the system in his work. He's an anaesthetist in a big hospital. I always think that's such a terrifying responsibility.'

'Yes, indeed,' said Bob, and then, 'I'll go and get us a glass of wine, shall I? Shan't be long. And I'm sure you two have a great deal to talk about.'

Emily caught the panic in her mother's eyes, but she needn't have worried. Maureen had turned her attention to what was outside the open French window.

'This is a really amazing house and garden, isn't it? For Clapham …' Was there a suggestion in her voice that Clapham was some kind of shanty town, Emily thought, or am I being uncharitable and imagining it? No, it was there all right: a badly disguised astonishment that an urban house could be so relatively spacious and have such a huge garden.

'Charlotte inherited it from her husband, who died about ten years ago. They were devoted.'

Emily noticed that Ma wasn't going into detail about how that husband had been Charlotte's second, and wondered whether Adrian had said anything to his mother. She assumed that Zannah must have told him about Charlotte's past, but maybe not. I'll ask her tonight, she thought. Surely even Adrian with the 'high standards' he kept going on about wouldn't let something that was so far in the past and of so little relevance to anything, make a difference to his marriage plans?

'How very sad!' said Maureen. 'But this is a splendid house. And so well-maintained …'

She was fishing. Emily could see it in the way she was bending her head, as if she wanted to absorb any information that might be forthcoming. How, it was clear she was longing to ask, did a woman of over seventy manage? The pristine state of the decoration in Charlotte's house had always been a topic of amusement in the Gratrix family. Ma and Pa, Emily thought, believed in basic cleanliness and Ma wanted beautiful things around her and sort of believed in tidiness, but any kind of painting, wallpapering, carpet-laying skills; any d-i-y know-how whatsoever, had passed them by. The 'make your house gorgeous' gene was totally missing from their DNA.

Her father had an excuse. He was a professor. Papers and books over every surface was part of the job description. Sheets of notes and tottering piles of books obscured almost the entire surface of his desk. His computer was covered with dust even though it was constantly in use. The joke at home was: you couldn't see Pa when he was typing furiously for the clouds rising from the keyboard. His study had been a no-go area for years. But her mother … well, Joss had very strong views about what was beautiful (she was a poet, wasn't she?) but she could easily get carried away gazing at the heavenliness of a vase of tulips on the kitchen dresser and miss entirely the fact that the whole place could do with a coat of paint. Artistic, imaginative, dreamy but impractical: that was Ma.

'Charlotte has a lot of help in the house,' she was saying now. 'One of her lodgers . . . well, friends really . . . she has two friends who live here with her, both a little younger than she is. Anyway, one of them, Edie, has a son who's very good with his hands and that's been useful. And Val...that's her other friend, Valerie . . . is a passionate gardener herself and gets help with the heavy work.'

'What a stroke of luck!'

Emily thought she detected a note of rather grudging envy in Maureen's voice but perhaps, she conceded, she wasn't being fair. Joss was busy explaining Charlotte's domestic arrangements and making a muddle of it. Emily longed to interrupt and say something along the lines of: *She's got a chap who helps Val in the garden and someone else who comes to clean and Edie's son helps in all sorts of ways. And she manages very nicely thank you, with the money Gus left her and what the others pay her to live here. They play bridge with Nadia who lives down the road and have a whale of a time. So there!*

Maureen and Joss had now stepped out on to the terrace, which was always called that and not the patio. Patio, Zannah declared, was too *Brookside* for words. In Emily's opinion, this flagged space was rather small for a terrace but definitely bigger than a patio. Three steps led down to the lawn, which was smooth and unmarked and stretched for quite a long way to the hawthorn bushes blossoming into clouds of pink near the high wall at the end of the garden. The borders were crowded with plants whose names Emily didn't know, interspersed with rose bushes, just on the point of blooming, ceanothus (fluffy flowers exactly the same colour as a blue liquorice allsort) and camellia bushes (some with the odd cluster of pink petals still hanging on but mostly just glossy leaves). It was hard to tell from Maureen's back whether this sight was impressing her. All Emily could see was the rear view of the blue silk jacket she was wearing, and the almost helmet-like perfection of her hair, swept up into a French pleat of totally non-brassy and almost insufferably subtle blondeness. This signalled a fortune spent at some salon that you had to put your name down for practically at birth. Her own mother's thick, dark, short hair, which was beginning to show grey in places, shone in the sun. It was well, if unimaginatively, cut by Maggie, who'd been doing it in exactly the same style for years and years. From behind, though, Ma seemed much younger than Maureen: almost like a girl with her slim figure and her rather Bohemian style. Maureen looked definitely middle-aged. I'm glad she's not going to be my mother-in-law, Emily thought and longed for the party to be over so that she could discuss her with Zannah.

'You all right, Chick?'

'Pa! Stop it!' Emily grinned at her father, who, she knew, had come to her in refugee mode: fleeing the social chitchat he would have had to make with other people. 'I'm too old for Chick.'

'Not for me you're not. You're my baby and always will be. How d'you feel about Zannah's wedding faradiddle? Is your nose even the least bit out of joint? Your secret is safe with me.'

'I'd rather be put in the oven with an apple in my mouth, if you want the honest truth. It's not my thing, but Zannah likes it, so ...' She let her voice fade away.

'You're being kind and supportive. Good for you.'

'Well, only up to a point. I'm enjoying my role as Devil's Advocate. I'm the one who points out other things she might do instead of pouring large quantities of money into this wedding. Does she listen? Three guesses. She might look pretty and wafty but you know how stubborn she is. Not in a nasty way, but like a cat. They never do what you want them to do either, do they? But they're so elegant and lovely that you indulge them while they pursue their own furry agendas. That's what Zannah's like. She does what *she* wants, but in the nicest possible way.'

'She relies on you a lot, you know. So do I. Who else would sit and sort out bits of old pottery with me for hours?'

'I don't do that much any more, though, do I? It's hard to sort pottery long-distance.'

'I know you're with me in spirit,' said Pa. 'That's the main thing. I'd better go and socialize, I suppose. Much rather stay here with you, but needs must.'

Emily was watching him make his way towards Charlotte (another easy conversational option) when someone touched her shoulder.

'You're miles away, Em,' Adrian said, smiling at her, 'but I'm about to make an announcement I'm sure you won't want to miss.'

He was holding out a glass of champagne and Emily took it obediently, then went to stand with everyone else on the terrace. She remembered, with a small twinge of pain, the rowdy evening in the local pub when Cal had told a gang of friends that he and Zannah were about to get married. No fuss, no parents around, and an unassuming agate ring bought from the local health-food shop, which did a cool line in semi-precious stones set in silver. Friends, pints of beer and cider, laughter, casual clothes. Zannah was radiantly happy and I was miserable because I knew that Cal would be out of reach for ever. How awful it had been having to act ecstatic because of not wanting to hurt Zannah.

'Okay, everyone,' Adrian said. 'I'll ask you all to drink a toast to Suzannah, who has made me the happiest man in the whole world by agreeing to marry me.'

Cliché watch, Emily thought. Let's count 'em. She knew she was being unkind. If you couldn't use clichés on an occasion like this, when could you? Everyone did it, so why should Adrian be any different?

'It's a shame Doc's not here yet, but I'm sure he'll be along as soon as he can and, meanwhile, I know everyone's getting hungrier and hungrier, so I'd just like to say, Zannah and I are going to be married and we've all been invited by Mrs Parrish ... sorry, Charlotte,' (with a graceful nod and smile at her) 'to celebrate the occasion. I did try to persuade my lovely bride to accept a diamond or two but she wasn't having that. She's more determined than she looks, which you all know, of course, and this is what she chose.'

He took Zannah's hand in his, and slid a ring on to her finger. Emily had seen it but everyone sighed to indicate how lovely they thought it was, and how well it suited her. It was a large antique ruby in a simple gold setting: square and plain and just right with Zannah's colouring. She held out her hand and turned it so that the stone caught the sunlight and Isis, Emily noticed, was struck into uncharacteristic silence, her eyes wide at the sight of such splendour.

'We've agreed on a date,' Adrian went on, 'and I hope it suits everyone. The first Saturday of the May half-term, next year. In other words, a year from today. It'll be May the twenty-seventh and Zannah will have a week away from school to go off with me on a short honeymoon. I'm not saying a word about where that's going to be, but plans are afoot.'

Everyone laughed. They raised their glasses and drank to what Emily was afraid would be known, from this day forward, as *the happy couple*.

'Zannah and Adrian!' everyone said and Emily joined in the toast, smiling with the others. 'Congratulations!'

'Look, Mum,' said Isis. 'I put those bits of parsley round the mousse. Those ones.'

'Lovely, darling,' said Zannah.

'And the strawberries. I helped put the strawberries on top of the lemon tart. That's fiddly work, Charlotte says. You'll see when it's time for pudding.'

'I'm sure they'll look terrific, sweetheart,' said Adrian, leaning across Zannah slightly and smiling, then starting to speak to Zannah before Isis could come back with another remark. She made a face and turned her attention to the food on the plate in front of her, which was much nicer than school food and nicer than Mum's food too, though Isis decided not to say so because she didn't want to hurt Mum's feelings. They'd had green soup first, with cream swirled into it. Charlotte said it was made out of watercress. There were big plates covered with slices of ham and chicken decorated with green leafy bits that weren't parsley, and the salmon mousse, which was what Isis liked best. In the kitchen, waiting to be brought in, were two huge round tarts in enormous glass dishes. One was apple and the other was the lemon one Isis had helped to decorate. The knives and forks were heavy to hold, but they were silver and probably the sort of things you'd have on your table if you were a princess.

Adrian and Mum had their heads very close together. Mum was blushing. She loved Adrian. Isis remembered how upset she'd been when Mum first told her this.

'But you loved Dad once,' she'd pointed out. 'Maybe you could love him again, if you really tried.'

'It doesn't work like that, Isis,' Mum said. She sounded sad. 'You can't help falling in love with someone. Adrian and I love one another. And we love you too, of course.'

'Adrian doesn't. He's not my dad. How can he love me?'

'He loves you because you're my daughter and he loves me. After we're married, we'll be a family.'

'What about Dad?' A sudden terror seized Isis.

'He'll always be your dad. He'll always love you best in the world. That won't change. And you'll still see him a lot, just as you do now.'

'And will Granny Ford still be my granny, even though you and Dad aren't together?'

'Of course she will. Dad'll take you to see her, don't worry.'

Isis felt a little better after that, and remembered those words whenever Adrian annoyed her, which he did sometimes, even though mostly he was nice to her and brought her small presents practically every time he came to the flat. She'd noticed that when they were alone together, he didn't speak to her. Not properly. He just made a remark about something he thought she might be interested in, but he never waited to see what she said back and he never went on with the conversation for longer than he could help. He found things to do: reading the paper till Mum was ready to go out with him, or turning on the TV and watching something boring like sport. Isis didn't know if he did this because he was dying to see what was in the paper, or because he didn't want to talk to her for any longer than he had to. As soon as Mum came into the room, he changed and became all smiley and friendly. He even told her how pretty she was looking sometimes.

The main good thing about Adrian was that he wanted the wedding to be a real, proper wedding with flowers and lovely dresses and best of all, a bridesmaid. That was what Isis was going to be and she was so excited by the idea that she'd long ago stopped worrying about whether she really liked Adrian or not. When Mum or Grandma asked her how she and Adrian were getting on, Isis always said that everything was fine. Which it mostly was.

All the grown-ups were talking: Em to Grandpa, Grandma to Adrian's mother, who'd asked to be called Auntie Maureen, which was stupid, because she wasn't an auntie, and also to Charlotte (who was Grandma's auntie but liked to be called Charlotte) and Mum to Adrian. Adrian's dad was late. Isis didn't know his name but supposed he'd be Uncle Something. She picked up the heavy silver fork and began to eat the salmon mousse which was delicious and a really mega-cool colour. Perhaps, she thought, I could have a salmon-mousse-pink bridesmaid's dress.

Zannah glanced round the table and recognized what she was feeling as happiness. She closed her eyes briefly, wanting to hold the moment in her mind; wanting to be able to bring it back and remember it over and over again. Darling Isis, Ma and Pa, Charlotte, Em, even Maureen ... they all seemed absorbed in harmonious and delightful conversations. They'd have to get down to business later on; after coffee perhaps. This lunch was not just to get the two families together, but also to start a discussion about the venue for the wedding. Everyone agreed that this was the most important decision of all, and Zannah was determined that every arrangement should be made in an unhurried and unflustered state, where options could be rationally debated. She'd heard enough stories about families practically coming to blows over wedding plans and she was determined to avoid unpleasantness. Everyone, she was sure, would go out of their way to be helpful, but Em's reaction when she'd told her this had dismayed her.

'What you mean is,' she had said 'you're sure that everyone will roll over and do exactly what you want them to do. You don't see how they could fail to agree with you. I reckon you might get a rude shock.'

'I do not mean that!' Zannah had retorted, but now, thinking it over, she could see there was something in what Em said. She *had* made up her mind about certain things and anyone wanting to change it was going to have their work cut out.

I won't worry about that now, she told herself. The food is perfect, the house is beautiful. And Adrian. Thinking about him made Zannah feel faint. She remembered him beside her in bed last night and felt heat rising to her face. Sometimes, when a darker mood came over her, a tiny voice whispered in her ear saying, *the sex is so good, Zannah. Are you sure you're not being overwhelmed by it? Have you lost your critical faculties in a tide of lust?* The answers, of course, were always the same: no, and no.

Adrian Whittaker was handsome, clever, and he worked for an investment bank in the City at a job he enjoyed. He was, he told her from time to time, 'doing rather well considering I'm only thirty-one.'

Zannah thought he earned a ridiculous amount of money. 'It's not fair,' she'd told Adrian, early in their relationship. 'Teachers work far harder than bankers, plus we're dealing with kids, real people, all day long. You do nothing but stare at a computer and move notional sums of money around. You go out for a boozy lunch most days. I should be the one with a silly salary.'

'When we're married, darling,' Adrian answered, 'what's mine will be yours. You can leave your school and become a lady of leisure.'

The offer, Zannah was sure, was kindly meant but at once she felt a prickle of resentment. 'I'll do no such thing,' she said. 'I love my job. I love being a teacher and I'd be a useless lady of leisure.'

'You could paint. You're always saying you wish you had time for that.'

That was true, Zannah reflected. She'd married Cal even before she graduated from St Martin's School of Art, and had then become pregnant with Isis before she'd had a chance to try being an artist. She was pretty sure she didn't have the talent to make it, but it would be good, she sometimes thought, to have the luxury of trying. Still, as things turned out, she found she *did* have a talent for teaching, and a genuine liking for the children in her care. What she'd said to Adrian was no more than the truth. Her college friends were in advertising, and PR and some even teaching art, just like her. There wasn't, as far as she knew, a single full-time artist among them. Only the Tracey Emins of the world actually made a living from Art, which, when she thought of it in this context, always had a capital letter.

Now, she looked at Adrian's dark, soft hair and his beautiful blue eyes and remembered how that conversation had come to an end: with him pulling her into his arms and with her forgetting everything, as she always did when she was near him. I'm useless, she thought. However high-minded and principled I'm being, I become soft and giddy when he touches me. I wish we could go upstairs right now. I wish we were both naked. She took a deep breath and pulled herself together. This is not the time. This is my engagement party. I'm going to have the best wedding anyone's ever had. I'm happy. I wish this moment could last.

The royal wedding had been thoroughly discussed, and Camilla's dress at the Blessing pronounced both elegant and flattering.

'And a gorgeous colour,' Maureen added, 'though I wonder whether it wasn't perhaps a little tactless of the Queen to dress in cream, when she must have known, mustn't she, what her new daughter-in-law was going to wear to the register office? And,' she went on, 'didn't you just adore those blossoming trees in St. George's Chapel? If you two got married in the spring, Zannah, you could copy that idea, couldn't you? I thought it looked wonderful.'

'We've set the date, Mum,' said Adrian, smiling at his mother. 'Too late for blossom! You'll have to have some other bright idea. I'm sure you'll come up with something.'

Charlotte caught the look that Zannah sent in her fiancé's direction and smiled to herself. Adrian was tucking in to his food and missed it entirely but she'd have bet good money on her great-niece putting him straight as soon as she could. Zannah wasn't someone who'd allow Maureen to decide on the floral arrangements for the wedding, wherever it took place. We haven't even begun to discuss the venue, Charlotte was thinking, when the doorbell rang.

'That must be my husband,' Maureen announced. 'Better late than never!'

She'd had a couple of glasses of wine and was smiling a great deal, Charlotte noticed.

'I'll go,' she said. She pushed back her chair, and put her napkin near the plate that now held no more than a few crumbs of pastry from the really rather good *tarte au citron*. She hurried across the hall to the front door and opened it. Standing on the doorstep was a tall, thin man with wavy, browny-grey hair flopping over his forehead and a smile that, with the hair and his horn-rimmed glasses, made him look boyish.

'I'm so sorry. I'm Graham Ashton. I expect you've all finished lunch ages ago. My apologies.'

He took the glasses off and put them away and Charlotte saw that his brown eyes were flecked with green.

'Do come in, Dr Ashton. It's quite all right, really. We've kept you some food, of course. I'm Charlotte Parrish, Suzannah's great-aunt.'

'It's good to meet you.'

Charlotte said, 'We're all in here,' and smiled over her shoulder at him as she led him into the dining-room.

'Darling, at last,' said Maureen, wiggling her fingers in her husband's direction, sketching out a sort of wave and at the same time calling him to her side. 'Where on earth have you been? This is my husband, everyone, Graham Ashton.'

Bob, whose chair was nearest to the door, rose to his feet and extended a hand.

'Very glad to meet you. Do come and sit down. We've left room, and I'm sure there's some food. You know Zannah, of course, and this is my wife, Jocelyn. Joss.'

Charlotte saw what happened next, and yet, later on, when she told Edie and Val about it, and then lay in bed going over the events of the day, she was at a loss to understand the way one thing led to another. Joss's face: that was what she noticed first. She'd turned quite white, and both her hands were up in front of her mouth. She stood up and muttered something. *I must go. I can't.* Charlotte hadn't quite caught the words.

'Joss?' That was Bob.

'Ma? What's the matter? What's wrong?' Zannah and Em, getting up and moving towards their mother.

Isis sat quite still and stared. Maureen clutched Adrian's sleeve. Graham Ashton remained near the door as though he was never going to move again. He, too, was staring as though he'd seen a ghost. Joss got up from her chair. The French window was open behind her and she ran out on to the terrace and sat down on the top step of the flight leading down to the lawn. Bob moved quickly to follow her, indicating to Zannah and Em that he was in charge; had the situation under control.

Around the table, everyone hovered, uncertain what to do next. Charlotte could see that if she didn't say something, if she didn't restore order, everything she'd wanted this day to be was in danger of disintegrating. She said, with a great deal more confidence than she felt, 'Please sit down, Dr Ashton. And everyone . . . I'm sure we'll be back to normal in a minute. Let me get the coffee. Bob will take care of Joss. Don't worry.'

No one spoke. Maureen whispered to her husband, who had moved stiffly to sit beside her, looking trapped and uncomfortable. Zannah and Em, you could see, were longing to go and find out what was wrong with their mother. Isis said, 'Is Grandma ill?' and Charlotte, glad of the distraction, had answered, 'I'm not sure, dear. Just sit still and finish your tart.'

Then Joss came into the dining-room again. Bob stood next to her, with one hand on her elbow. She said, 'I'm terribly sorry, everyone. I have to go home. I . . . have a migraine. I must go. Charlotte, thank you so much for everything . . . I . . .'

'Are you sure you don't want to go upstairs and lie down, Joss?' Charlotte said.

'Or I could take you home to the flat,' said Zannah. 'You could rest there.'

'No, really, I can't. I couldn't. Thank you, but I have to leave now. I can't . . . I want to go home. Now, please. At once. I can't tell you how sorry . . . how sad . . .'

Her eyes filled with tears and she seemed to be having some difficulty in breathing. She was still white, but now two red patches had appeared on her cheeks. Bob put an arm around her and led her out of the room. Charlotte followed them to the front door, and watched as they stumbled down the drive. As soon as the car door slammed behind her, Joss collapsed against the seat and threw her arm over her face, as though she wanted to hide, or not to see, or both. Charlotte waited till the car turned out of the gate and then she made her way slowly inside again. Joss had hardly ever had even a mild headache as far as she knew. The migraine was a lie. Why, Charlotte wondered, did she feel she had to run away? Because that was what she'd done. What could possibly have happened to make her flee her own daughter's engagement party? It wasn't a *what*, she realized, but a *who*. Joss had been fine till Graham Ashton appeared. She'd been better than fine. Her distress must have something to do with him. I'll ask her, Charlotte decided, when she's feeling better. I'm sure there's a perfectly rational explanation. She went back to the dining room, ready to make light of the whole thing: ready to corroborate the migraine story Joss had produced. She had never suffered from migraines as a child, but must have had a good reason for lying. Charlotte wondered what that could possibly be.

Joss was aware of Bob being aware of her, even though he was supposed to be concentrating on the road. She hadn't opened her eyes since she got into the car and was determined not to speak or move till they reached home. I don't care if he's worried, she thought. I'll pretend to be sleeping. She heard his words as though he were speaking from a very long way away, instead of from right beside her, as though her ears were full of a thick mist.

'Jossie, darling.' Years and years since he'd called her that. It made her feel queasy. 'Don't worry about anything. You're tired. We'll talk later. You sleep.'

He was so kind, so loving, that she felt as though something inside her was being wrenched apart. Now, now would be such a good time to stop everything: to say: *there's nothing wrong with me. I'm fine. I don't know what happened back there* and end all the speculation that must, she knew, be preoccupying Zannah, Emily and Charlotte, and probably Maureen and Adrian too. *Whatever was the matter with that woman?* she imagined Maureen asking her husband and could visualize her expression as she spoke: a combination of curiosity, distaste and an undercurrent of glee at the sight of someone else making a *faux pas*, putting a social foot spectacularly wrong. Maureen's husband. Gray. *My Gray*. More than any other feeling: more than embarrassment, or shame, or sorrow at wrecking her own daughter's engagement party was the anguish she felt at his betrayal. He'd lied to her.

Almost as soon as they met, the strange rules that were to govern their dealings with one another had been set out. Other people embarking on a relationship of any kind wouldn't have hedged it about with such conditions, Joss knew that. And yet for her it was part of the magic, part of the *separateness* of her feelings for Gray from anything else in her life. She remembered the night she had met him, at Fairford Hall. She'd decided, even before she went on her first course there, that day-to-day Joss would be left behind and Lydia Quentin the poet would expand and grow for once. She'd decided that, apart from the very basic information, married, with children, etc. she wouldn't tell anyone the details of her life. As it turned out, Gray was the first person to take an interest, to ask her about herself.

After dinner on the first night, a group of them had sat round the fire. Outside, November frost had iced the grass. They'd drunk a couple of bottles of wine between them, laughed and exchanged gossip and opinions. Then, one by one, the others had gone to bed. A single lamp shed a yellowish light and filled every corner with black shadows. The flames had died into a cluster of embers, which glowed faintly pink. She was on the sofa, and Gray was sitting across from her on a low armchair. When they found themselves alone, he came and sat beside her, closing the distance between them, and Joss could still remember the tremor that ran through her as she looked at him. His thin face was half in darkness. She noticed his long eyelashes, how white and slender his hands were, and that the hair falling on to his forehead was glossy and dark and scarcely touched with grey.

'Tell me something about yourself,' he said.

'I don't do that,' she'd answered. 'I'm anonymous, when I'm here. I like being . . . well, not myself in some way. Lydia Quentin isn't my name.'

'But I like it. I'm afraid Graham Ashton *is* my name.'

What had made her say what she'd said next? Sitting so close to him on the sofa? The knowledge that he liked her? Admired her? The daring conferred by not being Joss Gratrix but someone freer, braver, more forward in every way? Anyway, she'd said it: 'I'm going to call you Gray. That suits you much better than Graham.'

It was hard to see in the dim light but Joss thought he blushed when she told him that. He said, 'Right. No one's called me that before. And it's a good word, isn't it? *Gray*. All sorts of associations and a colour I like as well. It can be yours alone.' He bent his head, and Joss could see that he, too, was embarrassed. He went on, 'What I mean is: I won't let anyone else call me that.'

A silence fell then. He broke it. 'Are you married?'

'Yes, I am. I'm fifty years old. I've got two daughters. I'm a librarian. I live up North.'

'Tell me their names. I want to know about you.'

Joss could still remember how vehemently she'd shaken her head. 'No, I'm sorry, Gray. I'm not going to say anything. I can't. This . . .' she gestured to include the whole room, indicating Fairford Hall, everything it stood for, 'this place is far away from my daily life and I want to keep it separate. I'm so sorry.'

He said, 'No need to apologize, as long as . . .'

'As long as what?'

'As long as the important things about you aren't part of what you call your daily life.'

'Oh, they aren't,' Joss said. The wine had made her feel light-headed, reckless. 'They really aren't. This, the way I am here, that's the real me, I promise. My thoughts, my dreams, my ambitions, my opinions, the whole of my childhood, my memories, my work ... everything. I'm happy to ...' Her courage failed her then. She had to pause to get her breath back before going on. 'Happy to share all those,' she said finally, almost whispering out of embarrassment at what she'd just done. What had possessed her? Why did she think this handsome man might be interested in – had she truly said it? How toe-curlingly *awful!* – her childhood memories?

She began to stand up, confused and wanting suddenly to go, to be in her room and away from his disturbing presence. He took her left hand and held it between both of his. Joss found herself sitting down again, every nerve-end charged with a kind of electricity, wondering what would happen next. The silence was unbearable. She turned to Gray and asked: 'What about you? Are you married?'

'No, I'm not,' he said. 'I'm going to do what you're doing and keep my real life out of this as well. I'm fifty-one. I live in the south. I work in a hospital. That's it. We're going to be friends, aren't we? Tell one another everything?'

'Except the facts of our lives,' Joss answered.

'Facts! Who needs them?' Gray said, and smiled at her so fondly, so lovingly that she felt an odd, liquefying sensation in her stomach. She stood up then, needing to be alone.

'I don't,' she said. Then, sounding much too brisk and schoolmarmish to herself, she added, 'I'm off to bed. See you tomorrow.'

'Good night,' he said, and she felt his eyes on her back as she left the room.

The sound of the car's engine brought her back to the present. She half opened her eyes, glanced at Bob's profile without moving her head and decided to keep on pretending to sleep. She couldn't think of anything except Gray.

He'd lied to her. He'd deceived her from the start, from that first night. All through the time they'd known one another, he'd never said a single word about a wife or a son. He was single. He'd said as much. Perhaps she should have been more sceptical, asked more questions. Perhaps she ought to have wondered how a man as attractive as Gray had escaped marriage. I didn't want to look into it too closely, she told herself. His being single was the one thing that kept me going. She realized it now: she'd relied on the knowledge that should she ever dare to go to him, or need to run away and find him, he'd be there for her. He would be waiting and wanting nothing but her. How many times had he said so? Words he had written over and over again came back to her. *You're the only one. There's no one else. My only only love. For ever*. God, how stupid she'd been. Now, her heart was breaking. She fancied she could feel it literally splintering into fragments, just there, under her ribcage, but for the moment everything else was obliterated by the force of a rage of such intensity that she was breathless. She could deal with the pain later on, and there'd be plenty of time to do that, because she had no reason to suppose it would ever stop. Her life, all the various strands of it that she'd managed to keep nicely separated, had come to resemble a mass of knotted threads, like the contents of an old tapestry bag that hadn't been touched for years. I wish I could cry, she thought, as she listened to the deafening shriek of her husband, her poor Bob, not speaking to her. Not asking her for an explanation. What was she going to tell him? She couldn't maintain silence for ever.

'You heard what Charlotte said. How she used to have migraines when she was a kid.' Zannah was lying on the sofa, still wearing what she'd worn at lunch.

'Then why,' said Emily, who'd changed into jeans and a sweatshirt the second they'd got home, 'haven't we ever seen her having one? Don't migraines keep happening over and over?'

'Well, what else could it have been? Ma'd rather die than make a fuss. It must be true.'

'It'd help if she answered her mobile. They must be home by now, surely. Even stopping off on the way up there.' Emily stood by the window, looking out at the London roofscape. Zannah knew her sister didn't think much of the view, even though if you leaned out far enough you got a glimpse of Highgate Wood. Emily didn't think things were beautiful unless they were deserts or mountains or countryside. And she'd picked up a love of anything ancient from Pa.

They were very lucky to be living in this flat. It belonged to one of their father's colleagues, Dr Farraday, who'd bought it more than thirty years ago. He'd arranged to let Zannah rent it after her divorce for a nominal sum while he lived in a whitewashed cottage on a Greek island, enjoying his early retirement. It was much larger than the usual London cubbyhole: an enormous four-bedroomed apartment on two levels in a converted Victorian townhouse. When Emily arrived in London, shortly after Zannah's divorce, she had moved in to keep her sister company, and each was glad the other was there, even though they occasionally disagreed about how the place was run.

'Slut and control freak living together,' Emily used to say. 'Bound to be a problem.'

Zannah knew that Em was far from a slut and she certainly didn't think of herself as a control freak but basically that was the way it was: Em was messy and she was tidy and between them they were just right.

But she doesn't realize, Zannah thought, that I mean it when I say I like what I see out of that window, especially at night. Twilight had washed the sky in mauve and apricot and the edges of the buildings across the road were sharp and black against the pale background. It looked like the paper cutouts she'd helped Year Six to make before half-term: silhouettes of houses and people and animals that she'd spent ages sticking on to a background of orange paper to make a mural for the classroom.

Isis was kneeling beside the coffee table in her pyjamas, drawing on bits of rough paper with her felt tips, and keeping very quiet so as not to draw attention to her presence in case she was told she had to go to bed. She wasn't interested in what was outside the window, but had covered her paper with more and more elaborate dresses of the bridal variety. Let her stay there, Zannah thought. I'm too worried about Ma to think about bedtime. And it's Sunday tomorrow. No school and none the next day either or for a whole week. Lovely, lovely half-term.

She, Emily and Isis had been back in the flat for a couple of hours. Adrian had wanted to stay for supper, but Zannah had managed to persuade him to go out to dinner with his mother and Dr Ashton instead. Adrian always referred to him, rather disparagingly, as *my stepdad,* or sometimes *my mother's husband* or *Doc*.

'I can see you don't want me around,' Adrian had sounded a little petulant. He'd walked with her to her car, as they all left Charlotte's house.

Zannah said, 'It's not that, really. Only we're so preoccupied with Ma, it'll be boring for you.'

'I could come and pick you up later,' he whispered. 'Em's there for Isis, isn't she? I could bring you back to my lair.'

He leaned over and as he whispered these last words, he kissed her, just below her ear. Zannah shivered and pushed him away. 'No, honestly. I'll phone you tomorrow.'

'Hope your mother's all right. Let me know what you hear.'

All she and Emily had talked about since they got home was Joss and her flight from the lunch-table. They'd both tried phoning her mobile at half-hourly intervals, only to be met with her voice telling them to leave a message and she'd get back to them. Bob never used his mobile in the car and he was driving.

Emily said, 'Let's phone home. You try.'

Zannah dialled the number and almost dropped the handset when she heard her father's voice.

'Pa! You're back. We've been so worried! How's Ma? Can she speak?'

'I'll put her on,' said Bob.

Zannah tucked the phone into the crook of her shoulder and said to Emily, ' Go and listen on the extension. Then you can talk as well.'

Emily ran into her sister's bedroom as Zannah said, 'Ma? Is that you? Are you okay?'

'I'm fine, darling. I'm so sorry. I wrecked your party.'

'Nonsense. It's nothing to be sorry about. We'd had lunch. You'd met Maureen at least and you can meet Graham another time. No worries.'

Silence. Emily said, 'Ma, are you still there?'

'Yes, Em. I'm here. I'm going to bed now.'

'Was it really a migraine?'

'What do you mean?' Joss's voice sounded thin and wavery to Zannah, listening to her younger, braver sister questioning their mother's excuse and thinking that she'd never dare to do such a thing.

'Well, I can't remember you having one ever before.'

'I haven't had one for ages, that's true. I used to get them as a child.'

Zannah interrupted. 'Yes, that's what Charlotte said.'

'There you are, then.' Joss's voice was beginning to sound stronger. Perhaps there wasn't anything really wrong. 'Don't worry about it, you two. I'll be in touch in a couple of days. I've got to ring Charlotte now and apologize to her, so I'll say good night, darlings.'

'G'night, Ma,' said Zannah.

'Phone tomorrow,' said Emily. 'I want to speak to Pa as well, only I haven't the energy now.'

'Right,' said Joss. 'Kiss Isis for us.'

'Will do.'

Emily came out of Zannah's bedroom and flung herself back on to the sofa. She picked up the TV remote and started to fiddle with it. 'I don't believe her,' she said. 'D'you think she sounded convincing?'

'Yes,' said Zannah. 'I think she did, on the whole.'

'You just don't like trouble.'

'What trouble? What're you talking about?'

'Never mind. We'll see soon enough who's right. And I meant to ask you . . . have you told Adrian about Charlotte?'

'No, not yet.'

'Why not? You don't think it'd put him off you?'

'Don't be ridiculous. It just hasn't come up, that's all.'

Emily made a face that meant: *I don't believe you but I can't be arsed to argue.* Zannah continued, 'We've had other stuff to discuss. I'll tell him. Or Charlotte will. You know she doesn't hide it particularly.'

'I don't see dear Maureen taking something like that calmly, do you? She looks like someone who might care about her son marrying into a family with an ex-con in it.'

'Charlotte is *not* an ex-con. She was innocent. Everyone knows that.'

'Nevertheless, six months in jail makes you a con.'

'Nonsense. And anyway it was years and years ago.' She paused. 'I'll tell Adrian in time, don't worry. I just want to choose my moment.'

Emily made an explosive sound halfway between a laugh and a snort and pointed the remote at the television. A picture flickered into life on the screen. Isis left her drawing and came to sit next to her. She put an arm round her niece and squeezed her tight. Zannah stood up and went into the kitchen to see about supper. Charlotte's lunch had been delicious but she felt as though they'd eaten it ages ago. Perhaps, she thought, as she searched the fridge for anything remotely tempting, Em's right and I ought to talk to Adrian about Charlotte soon. She was probably also right about Ma covering something up. Tomorrow, she thought. I don't want to think about all that tonight.

'How about a cup of tea, darling?' Bob was at his most solicitous. Joss, sitting across from him at the kitchen table, wondered when he'd stop being kind and start asking questions. He wasn't a fool. He must know the migraine story was nonsense. She'd never been so glad to come home. Her house had gathered itself comfortingly around her as she moved through the hall into the kitchen. She'd spoken to the girls and reassured them that she was all right and now she was seized by a longing to run upstairs and hide in her study. She wanted to be the person who worked there. She wanted to be the other half of herself – the one whose work had appeared in magazines, who was about to produce her first collection, and who was acquiring a reputation for elegant and precise poems. Lydia Quentin was the poet. Because this was the name Gray used, it was the one she loved. She wanted to stop being Jocelyn Gratrix and hide for ever behind her pseudonym. She wished she could stare into the lighted window of her laptop and write to him. What would she say? How could she express her anger? He wouldn't have had a chance to write to her, but there was the secret phone, which she regarded as her most precious possession.

Last year, on her birthday, Gray had sent her a tiny Pay As You Go mobile. She kept it among the papers in one of the compartments of a plastic concertina file in the bottom drawer of her locked filing cabinet. He had an identical phone, which he used, he told her, for the calls he made to her and for nothing else. She felt weak with wanting to press the only number keyed into its memory and hear his voice. She couldn't. She had to stay in the kitchen and she knew what was coming. Bob had always been someone who *thrashed things out*. That was how he'd put it. Joss sometimes felt that he must have been the kind of child who poked and prodded at things to see how they worked. It wasn't just the physical world he was interested in, either. He sought the truth.

He wanted to know about motivation, reasons for actions, ideas and where they came from: all the things that Joss thought were probably better unexamined if you wanted to remain unhurt in life. Bob had never been able to leave anything alone. He believed in discussion. He believed in sorting stuff out, getting to the bottom of problems, making everything better. He was known among his students as someone who wouldn't be shocked whatever you confessed; someone who had answers to the more unanswerable questions. Good old Bob.

I mustn't be nasty about him, she told herself. He's doing his best. She could hear him putting their suitcase at the bottom of the stairs, and now he was in the doorway, asking whether she wanted tea. 'Yes, that'd be good. Earl Grey, please.'

Joss watched him as he moved around, taking the blue teapot from its place on the kitchen dresser and reaching up to find the packet of teabags in the cupboard. He poured the milk into a pretty jug and put it in front of her and, in spite of herself, she felt touched at this attempt to please her. On an ordinary day, on an unfraught occasion, he'd have put the milk bottle on the table and the teabags straight into the mugs. He was making an effort. Something, some moment, was coming towards her and she wouldn't be able to avoid it for much longer. Maybe it would be better to pre-empt his questions. No, she couldn't. What would she say?

Bob pushed one of the mugs towards her and Joss picked it up. She had no desire whatsoever to drink tea but it would give her something to do with her hands.

'Jossie . . .' How she wished he wouldn't call her that! She'd stopped being *Jossie* long ago. 'You do know I love you, don't you?'

She nodded, unable to answer. This was her cue to say, *Yes and I love you too* and she couldn't. The words wouldn't come. He went on, 'I know that something happened back there at Charlotte's and all the way home I've been trying to work out what it could have been. The migraine was just an excuse.'

He wasn't asking her. He was telling her. Still, she said nothing.

'It began when you saw Graham Ashton. I've gone over and over it in my head all the way home and I've come to the conclusion that you must have met him before. That's the only thing that would make any sense. You know him. Am I right?'

Joss looked down. If she kept on being silent, was it possible he'd get to the truth by himself?

'Where d'you know him from?'

'I met him on a creative writing course. Three years ago.'

'But he's a doctor. How come he's at a creative writing course?'

'He wanted to learn to write poetry. Lots of people do, you know.'

Bob didn't snort, but Joss knew that if this conversation had not been so serious, he would have done. He had a strange relationship with poetry, believing that it had come to a full stop around the end of the nineteenth century. He was suspicious of anything remotely modern and there were times when Joss half agreed with him. Towards her own poems, he maintained a loyal approval, although Joss was sure he rarely understood them, even when he did get round to casting an eye over them. He'd have been deeply shocked if he knew what some were about. He didn't exactly bust a gut begging to see them and she only showed him the more easily explicable ones and then rarely. She read his essays, but that, she knew, was only because Egypt and the ancient world interested her. She would certainly, she often told herself, not have been so dutiful if Bob were a physicist or a chemist. He regarded her writing, Joss knew, as something she did and which he didn't need to worry about. Lately, she hadn't minded this at all because she had had Gray to tell her how much he loved her poems; how much they meant to him. Gray claimed to know almost all of her work by heart. Perhaps he was lying about that too. Would she be able to trust him ever again?

'Okay,' Bob said. 'You met him three years ago. On a course. Have you seen him since?'

A chill had appeared in his voice. Joss said, 'He was at Fairford again two years ago as well. A bit more than two years. September 2002.'

'Bit of a coincidence, wasn't it?'

How could she answer? 'No, that time we arranged it. We booked to be on the same course.'

'So you'd been seeing one another? Between one course and the next?'

Joss shook her head. 'No. No, we never met. We corresponded. By email, mostly. We swapped poems. That's all.'

'I don't believe you, Joss. You're lying. Why on earth wouldn't you meet, when you had a husband who was away conveniently so much of the time? A fool, you no doubt thought me, not seeing what was under my nose. And I was. Can't deny it.'

'You can believe what you like but it's true. The reason I didn't see him was so as not to hurt *you*. Not to hurt our marriage. I'd have thought you'd give me credit for that. We didn't lay eyes on one another for more than a year. I did it because I loved you, you bloody fool.'

But he's right in a way, she chided herself. I was unfaithful. Not seeing Gray didn't make any difference. She realized that part of the illusion she preserved of her own innocence was the fact that Gray didn't know her name. He's in love with Lydia Quentin, she told herself sometimes. That's not me. Not me in this house with a husband. That's another woman altogether. A woman with feelings Joss doesn't even acknowledge.

Would Bob know what *'correspondence'* meant? She'd emphasized the email, but Gray wrote her proper letters too sometimes, sent to the library, which was the only address she'd given him. The only address she had for him was his hospital. He gave her gifts. Most of the small objects on her desk, her precious things, had come from Gray. She answered him on the most beautiful postcards she could find, always enclosed in an envelope. She used to picture him holding what she said in his hand, touching the card she'd touched, kissing it and then sitting down to answer her. When she read his letters, she could feel how much he loved her. *We didn't need to meet,* she wanted to tell Bob now. *There was so much emotion. So much passion.* That was what had gone from her relationship with her own husband. She'd been at a strange time of her life, at the beginning of 2000. Zannah had left home and going through all the trouble with Cal and Isis, darling Isis, was a toddler. When Zannah had got over the worst effects of her divorce and returned to London, Emily went with her, just about to start work. Suddenly, the house was empty and Joss turned more and more to her poetry.

She'd been writing it for years, but now, with more time and the house so often echoingly empty in the evenings and at weekends, she began to submit her poems to magazines and to enter competitions, which, to her surprise, she sometimes won. Then, she went to Fairford for the first time, and her life changed completely. She realized almost as soon as she met Gray that her love for Bob, though it was still there, had turned into something different from what she was feeling now. She'd forgotten what that kind of mad, exhilarated, lifted-in-the-air feeling was like. Looking at Bob now, she thought that perhaps their love had been buried: covered up by layer upon layer of habit which was probably normal after so many years of marriage.

With Gray, the padding of domestic life was missing, and passion was all she had. Every morning, she would hurry through getting the breakfast ready, making sure that Bob remembered to take his brief-case, his lecture notes, his car keys and then, when he'd gone, she'd rush upstairs to her study, turn on the computer and read the email she knew had been waiting there since the early hours. Gray always wrote very late at night. She always printed out the email and kept all the messages at the back of one of the drawers of her filing-cabinet. She read them so often that she could recite whole paragraphs by heart. As she worked at the library, as she walked through the rest of her life, she found herself unable to concentrate on anything but Gray, and having to make a huge effort to keep the real world – the world she lived in, the library where she worked, the shops she went to – everything else but him somewhere in a mental landscape that had become nothing but his face, his words, his love for her and hers for him. And yet she told herself that she was being good. She wasn't being unfaithful, not really, and she congratulated herself on behaving well and not jumping into bed with someone she'd only just met.

'What about the second time?' Bob brought her back to the present. 'Have you seen him since then?'

'No, of course not.'

'Why not? Most people who're unfaithful to their spouses manage to get away for a dirty weekend or even a quick shag in a hotel on the odd occasion, don't they? Bit of illicit nookie in a motorway motel.'

Joss stared into her teacup. 'I'm not most people.'

'But you don't deny you're unfaithful, I notice.' Bob pushed his fingers through his hair. 'Did you sleep with him?'

She almost told another lie. Then the words came out before she had time to consider what she was saying. 'Yes. Yes I did.'

Bob stood up and walked over to the window. Joss knew him well enough to realize that he was hurt. His back, his shoulders, slumped in a kind of defeat. He looked suddenly much older. Should she say something? What could she say? If she kept quiet, would he ask her something she didn't want to answer? She took a deep breath and spoke as gently as she could. Damage limitation. 'It happened *once*, Bob. Only once, I promise. It was one night, more than two years ago. It didn't mean anything.'

Oh God forgive me for such a lie. It had meant everything. It means everything. It's governed every single thought in my head since it happened. She glanced at her husband to see whether he believed her. He was still staring out of the window. A silence stretched between them and Joss wondered what he'd say next. He couldn't really object. There was the time, very soon after they were married when he'd confessed, tearfully and full of anguish, to a one-night stand while he'd been away at a conference in Istanbul. She'd almost, but not quite, forgotten the pain she'd felt at the time. She'd forgiven him because he'd begged for forgiveness and she was pregnant with Zannah and had a terror of her life, whose elements she'd constructed with such devotion, coming to pieces around her. She was someone who needed to keep things as they were. In the past, she'd regarded this as a positive quality, but now she considered it a character defect; a sort of cowardice.

'If that's the case,' Bob said now, coming to sit beside her and taking her hand, 'why were you so shocked to see him? How come you didn't know his son was engaged to Zannah?'

How to explain their rules? Not knowing such basic things about one another would seem crazy if she were to try to explain it. She said, 'Adrian's surname is different. We just ... we never discussed our home lives.'

'Would have made you feel guilty, right? Okay, but if sleeping with him didn't mean anything when it happened, then surely it has to mean *less* than nothing after all this time, right?'

'It was the shock, that's all. I never thought I'd see him again and then there he is, and his son's going to marry Zannah. Adrian must be a stepson, I suppose. He's going to be ... he's going to be family. I just ... I couldn't take it in.'

'We don't have to see them much, I shouldn't have thought. I don't ever want to see him again, to tell you the truth. Not after what you've told me. They're down there in Guildford and we're up here. We'll just keep out of the way.'

'But what about Zannah's wedding? We'll have to see them for that.'

'Fuck the wedding!' Bob stood up, red in the face with the fury he'd managed to suppress till that moment. 'I don't know what you want from me, Joss. You seem to think that I'm meant to get over this in a civilized manner and move swiftly on to thinking about Zannah. Well, I'm sorry. I refuse to worry about that now. Of course we'll go through the motions. I'm not going to mess up Zannah's day, but let's just say it won't be a barrel of laughs. Nothing strange about that. They say that many weddings end in a fight. Punch-up between the families.'

'Stop it! This isn't a time to be frivolous.'

'I'm not being frivolous.'

Joss said, 'I'm exhausted, Bob. I think I'm going up to bed, if you don't mind. We can unpack tomorrow.'

'Joss, sit down. You can't go to bed now ... I'm still ...' Bob ran his hands over his face, as though he were trying to wipe away the stress of the day. 'What you've said ... it's knocked me out. I've always thought we had ... I thought we were ... well, I've never said as much, I suppose, but I'd always taken it for granted that we were ... are ... happy. Aren't we happy, Joss? Haven't things been okay?'

Joss thought for a long time before she answered him. Okay ... yes, things had been that. How long had it been since they'd spoken of anything more serious than family matters? How long since Bob had been impulsive in any way? Taken her out on a whim, brought her flowers? That wasn't quite fair. Their relationship hadn't been a flowery one, even in the beginning, but in those days, he'd regale her for hours about this or that interesting aspect of his work, and she still read the articles he wrote even though she didn't understand the fine detail. But they didn't laugh as much as they used to. She'd assumed it was simply that they had been together so long that they each knew one another's opinions backwards. Briefly, she remembered a meal at Fairford with Gray, and how they were so happy that anything seemed funny. She'd described a well-known poet as being *like a cross between a geography teacher and a vampire* and Gray had snatched up his knife and fork and made a rudimentary cross with his arms out in front of him at chest-height as he intoned, in a good imitation of every geography teacher Joss had met: *The main tributaries of the Nile, Dulcie ... what are they? Pay attention, gel!* It had been completely silly but it still made her smile to think of him with his eyes crossed, leaning sideways in his chair as he spoke. Bob was staring at her, waiting for her answer.

'Of course we're happy. I've explained what happened. I'm sorry if you're hurt. Truly.'

'Then you must promise me something.'

'What?'

'Promise me you won't see this Ashton except on family occasions ever again. Can you do that?'

'Yes. I don't want to see him. That's the last thing I want, honestly.'

'And we'll be okay?'

'Yes, Bob,' Joss said and allowed herself to be held. She let him kiss the top of her head then hurried out of the room and up the stairs to her study. She knew he wouldn't follow her at once. His own study was in the basement and he'd check his computer before he came to bed and quite possibly become absorbed in reading something or other. He thought the crisis was over. He thought everything was at least on the way to being *shipshape and tickety-boo*, as he used to say to the girls when they were small. He didn't like it when things were troublesome for too long and always moved straight on after a row or a crisis. She was safe for a while.

She closed the door and went to the filing-cabinet. She unlocked it, found the little phone and her hands trembled as she touched the keys. Three messages. She listened to each one over and over again, drinking in the voice, feeling warmth return to her heart.

'Lydia, my darling ... I know what you're thinking. I can explain everything. Call me. Whatever time it is. Call me.'

'Are you there? Ring me, Lydia. How could I possibly know you were Zannah's mother? Please, please phone me.'

The last message had come in only a few minutes ago.

'Are you there? Please call me now. I'm alone. I must speak to you.'

Joss sent a text message: *Can't speak now. Will phone you in the morning. Time?*

Almost instantly, the answer came back: *11.30. I love you.*

And I love you too, Joss thought, but what's going to happen now? I've promised Bob I won't see you. You lied to me. You've been lying to me since I met you. She hid the phone again and sat at her desk, looking at the small tokens of his love all around her and seeing none of them. She was remembering a conversation from their first and last, their only night together.

'You with someone else,' Gray was staring at the ceiling. 'I don't think I could live with that. What's going to happen to us?' They'd made love for the second time and Joss felt as though her body was being pressed down against the sheets by something huge and overwhelming: a weight of love so consuming that she didn't know how to breathe. Before they'd kissed, before they'd gone this far, she'd told him this was all there would be, ever. They couldn't do this again. This was never going to happen again.

'I can't leave my husband,' she'd said. 'I can't do it to the girls. To my granddaughter. This is not something I can do again. I shouldn't be doing it now, but I can't help it. D'you understand, Gray?'

'I'm not asking you to leave your husband. I just want you to stay tonight. To be here now.'

'I could go now. I can still leave.'

'No, I want you, Lydia. What do *you* want?'

'You. Oh Gray, I want you.'

At that moment, she would have stepped on hot coals to touch him. She couldn't stop herself. She leaned towards him and they clung to one another, touching, breathing, panting, and Joss could feel herself plunging into sensations that she'd never been even close to imagining before.

Those were the conditions, she told herself. Everything that happened that night was something I wanted and I've been remembering it and reliving it and inhabiting it ever since. I was the one who laid down the terms. I was the one who said we must never meet again, and not because I didn't love him. He knows how much. I've told him over and over again: in words, in poems, in thoughts, in everything but my presence. He's had the best part of me. It's only my body that's here with Bob. I've been thinking of him, dreaming of him, wanting him every day and every night. He's never asked me to leave Bob. Joss felt blind fury all over again. I thought he was being unselfish, not making me give up my life, when all the time it was him, his life, his career, that he was worried about. We're as bad as one another: happy to keep our love in a sort of secret drawer. But he knew my circumstances and I didn't know his. Would it have made any difference to anything? It might. Perhaps if I'd known he was married I'd have felt guilty. Was he trying to spare me that? That's the kind interpretation.

Tomorrow, she'd go out for a long walk and phone him and let him know it was over over over. Really and truly. No phone calls. No emails. Nothing any more ever again. It was the only way she'd be able to deal with this new situation. There was a telephone kiosk about a mile from the house from which she made the calls she knew would take a long time. This one would be hard. Gray would try to persuade her . . . try to change her mind. She picked up the tiny silver phone and listened to his messages again, before deleting them carefully. By the time she left the study, there were tears in her eyes. She wiped them away and took a deep breath, preparing herself to face Bob, who was making his way up the stairs to their bedroom.

Sunday

Order was important to Graham Ashton. He'd succeeded in organizing every part of his existence to his entire satisfaction, and what had happened yesterday when he caught sight of Lydia sitting in a chair outlined against the light coming through the French windows was something he couldn't begin to describe. A wave of emotion swept suddenly up and over and into his everyday concerns and he wasn't sure how to deal with it.

His life. It was bit like a filing-cabinet and he had a talent for keeping the various bits of it nicely separate and tidy: Maureen, their house, their friends and children in one drawer, his work and colleagues in another, and Lydia in a locked compartment all of her own, just above the one in which he kept everything to do with his poetry. He didn't hide the fact that he wrote it, but he didn't mention it either. Graham Ashton was a common name and he hadn't published enough to alert anyone in the medical establishment. No one he knew in the hospital was into poetry, as far as he was aware. What he liked about it was the pleasure of finding the right words, and organizing them into sequences that could illuminate something: make the reader see better. He liked the limitations of poetry, too: the rules. He didn't approve of those who blurted stuff out without even counting the syllables or worrying about the form. Lydia wasn't one of those. One of the things he loved about her was the way she paid attention to every word she wrote, and managed to express deep feelings without a hint of soppiness, or veering into the *hello clouds hello sky* school of verse which he hated.

On his desk, within reach of his hand was his secret phone. He picked it up and went downstairs. Only Lydia knew the number. It was a *pay as you go* mobile: the twin of one he'd sent her for her birthday last year. Every call between them went from one silver handset to the other and he took care to delete not only any messages, but the entire call history, so that if anyone happened to come across it, there'd be no trace of her. Nothing would remain of the thousands of words of love and desire that flew between them.

Seeing Lydia there, after so long, looking so beautiful, so like the woman he'd dreamed about, turned him for a few moments into a kind of statue. He'd stood there and tried to take in that she was Zannah's mother. Everything they'd said to one another, everything he'd been fantasizing about in the privacy of his mind night after night came back to him. Maureen had stared at him as though he were ill, and he was in a way. He'd pulled himself together eventually, and Lydia had left the party at once, which made things easier, but all through the evening, during a meal that seemed never to end, with Adrian and Maureen discussing what had happened, he'd sat there wanting to hit both of them.

He thought back to that first course at Fairford Hall. Although they'd done poetry workshops and cooked the communal meals together, he'd circled round her from some distance till the second evening, when they'd talked alone for the first time. The following day, they went for a walk through the wintry landscape. Later, it occurred to him that he should have said something at the beginning of the walk. It would have altered what they said to one another, how they were with each other. Gray cringed now to recall how shy he'd been. They'd discussed that morning's poems, the tutors, a couple of course-members who were more than usually annoying: trivial things. I didn't care. I just wanted to listen to her voice. I would have gone on chatting like that for a long time. But then it had started to rain. They'd taken shelter in the porch of a small, grey, architecturally undistinguished church. There was no one around.

'I knew I ought to have brought an umbrella,' he said. 'We're stuck here for a bit, I'm afraid. It should clear up quite soon.' He had no idea how soon it would or wouldn't clear up.

'Never mind,' she said. 'At least there's a bench. And maybe we can go in and have a look. Do they lock churches round here? It's such a shame when they do.'

He tried the heavy wooden door and it opened. The interior of the church wasn't memorable in any way, but there was the hush and the chill; the stained glass, the smell of winter greenery in the vases near the altar, and the unexpectedly fine carvings on the lectern. They spoke softly as they went round, and he took her hand. She didn't pull it away. They walked down the nave together and sat in the front pew.

'I never go to church,' he told her. 'Are you religious? Am I allowed to ask you that?'

Lydia shook her head. 'Not religious at all, but I do love churches. I love the thickness of the silence. I like organ music, too.'

When they emerged, the rain had stopped.

'We can go back now,' he said.

If she'd said, *Okay, let's go*, it was entirely possible that he wouldn't have kissed her just at that moment. But she hesitated, peering out at the graveyard as though reluctant to go back, and turned to him. She started to say something and he stopped her. He simply leaned forward and took her face between his hands and kissed her. His first thought was how different it was from kissing his wife. Maureen smelled of make-up and tasted of lipstick. She often giggled when they kissed; wriggled herself up to him in a suggestive way, almost forcing him to respond. And he did, too. No one could accuse Maureen of not being sexy. Lydia wore lipstick too, but that first time, all he could taste was *her,* her skin, her mouth. The kiss went on for a long time, and she didn't move, didn't step forward. He had the feeling that she was a source of something he needed, like water, like breath. When she took a step back at last, he couldn't think what to say. He was profoundly grateful for the thigh-length jacket that hid his erection. Was she aware of that? He was blushing again. What would happen now? He wasn't used to such intensity of feeling and therefore said nothing. Neither did she. They began to walk in the direction of Fairford Hall, not speaking. What am I going to do if there are people around when we get there? he thought. I want to kiss her again.

No one was in the entrance hall when they reached the house.

'Lydia?' he said, not knowing how to ask, suddenly awkward.

She reached up to gather him into her arms. She pulled him down to her, her hands on his neck, in his hair. He could feel how much she wanted the kiss. If she hadn't done that, hadn't reached out to him, would he have stepped back? No, no way, but things wouldn't have turned out the way they did, perhaps. I'll never know, he thought, as he stared out at the road unrolling in front of the car and tried to ignore what Maureen was saying.

She obviously couldn't leave the subject of Lydia alone. She'd chattered on till his teeth hurt. 'Whatever d'you think was the matter with her? Menopause, I shouldn't wonder. She's quite nice, isn't she? I wish I had the dressing of her, though. Somehow unfinished. And like Zannah, a little too thin. But very pretty, really. And I like her husband. And Adrian likes them.'

Sometimes he wondered why he'd married her, but now, looking around the morning room, he recognised that her love of order matched his. Her gift for household management, her capacity for seeking out the very best, the exactly right thing for whatever they needed in the house or garden was something he admired and appreciated. And she'd been a knockout when he first met her. Naturally blonde in those days, and with breasts that she managed to display to their fullest advantage while at the same time being dressed as soberly and neatly as befitted a hospital receptionist, she'd made no secret of her attraction to him and he ... well, as someone once said: she threw herself at him and he didn't exactly step out of the way. She'd made him feel drunk with lust. He hadn't even minded Adrian then. At the time, he was a toddler whose father had walked out. Gray was moved by the plight of the gallant single mother, (struggling alone to keep up standards and get her life together) and her pretty son. He thought of himself as their rescuer and it felt good.

Maureen had been so lovely as a young woman. And she flirted with him in a way he liked. You had to hand it to her. As soon as she saw he was keen, she'd started inviting him round to her house. Adrian was only a little kid then, and Maureen made much of how good he was and how much he needed a father. They used to go to the cinema and snog their way through the films. No question of going back to her place, and his room in the hospital wasn't much better.

'It's not exactly home from home,' Maureen used to say.

He didn't mind. They'd start taking their clothes off as soon as the door closed and he couldn't have cared less where they were. Maureen was so enthusiastic, such fun, so full of laughter and so uninhibited that he wanted to make love to her all the time. He'd slept with a few women before he met Maureen, but no one who enjoyed it so much, and responded so quickly.

'Oh,' she'd say, and her eyes would roll back in her head, 'oh my God, I can't get enough of you, my darling. I wish I could gobble you all up!'

Afterwards, her talk often turned to her little boy. She started to drop hints about how ghastly it was living where she did. And she began to paint pictures of what life could be like if they moved in together.

He'd soon fallen out of love with Adrian, but Maureen was a different matter. What he felt for her now was complicated, but some sort of love was still bound up in there somewhere, and denying it wasn't going to help matters.

Their wedding had been very low-key. A couple of the nurses from the hospital as witnesses and that was it. Maureen had worn a blue suit with a wide-brimmed hat to the register office. He'd bought her some flowers. Nothing as grand as a bouquet, but a small bunch of yellow and white roses. There were a few photos of the occasion, taken by one of the witnesses on his very basic camera and that was it. Where were those photos now? He had no idea. Maureen would know but he had no desire to look at them again.

For the honeymoon, they'd sent Adrian to Maureen's mother and gone to Paris for the weekend. Maureen found fault with the hotel in the short intervals between fucks. *We'll stay at the Ritz one day, darling, won't we?* she'd asked him. He'd agreed. He'd have agreed to fly to Mars, just to get her to stop talking. Just to see her waiting for him, opening herself, legs, mouth, arms, everything, wanting him and nothing else. Remembering those days, he felt uncomfortable. Guilt, regret ... it was difficult to put a name to it. All he knew was, seeing Lydia again had stirred up all kinds of complicated emotions and he wasn't sure he knew how to manage them. Maureen was sharp, too. The last thing he wanted was for her to discover the truth. But would it matter if she did? If she left him?

I'm a selfish bastard, he told himself. I had it all worked out. No one keeps house better than Maureen. She cooks as well as any chef. Wherever he looked, he saw a kind of beauty. The house was orderly, with not so much as a smudge on the wallpaper or a whisper of dust on the skirting-boards. She was a better gardener than any of that lot on TV. She was efficient. She kept track of his diary. She made sure his life ran like clockwork and that was something Graham needed. She knew he wrote poetry, but she left him well alone to do it, regarding it as a kind of indulgence, a silliness she forgave him. Maureen had, however, almost no claim on his heart. That had belonged to Lydia since the very first day he met her. Maureen didn't even realize that his love had mostly been given to someone else. They still fucked often enough. More often, he thought, than other couples in their fifties, but she had no notion that behind his eyes, he was conjuring up Lydia's pale face as it had been on that night, their one night together, when he'd actually considered how good it might be never to wake up and know what it was like not to be with her. His Lydia. The name he would always use, even though she was Jocelyn Gratrix. He went to the door. She'd be phoning him in half an hour. He had no idea what she'd say, but he had to see her. They needed to talk about this new situation. I'll walk round the golf course, he told himself, me and my trusty adulterer's phone. Maureen was at church. She wasn't a bit religious but had a firm belief in the desirability of being the kind of person who was seen in a pew on Sunday and, what's more, wearing better clothes than anyone else in the congregation.

'Such a shame!' said Edie Nordstrom, balancing a piece of *tarte aux pommes* on her fork before putting it into her mouth and munching it with her eyes closed to indicate pure pleasure, ' … that your guests never got a chance to taste this. Still, their loss is our gain. Your pastry's divine, Charlotte. As usual.'

Edie was a small woman with sharp eyes and short grey hair, cut in a style she liked to think made her look like Judi Dench. The pinkish shade of her spectacle frames, together with a taste for the pastel in matters of dress, led people to think of her as a sweet old lady. Nothing, Charlotte knew, could have been further from the truth. Edie was stubborn, intelligent, kind and rather cynical. She trusted no one except her children, Charlotte, and Val. Even Nadia with whom they played cards and took tea, she regarded as slightly unreliable (because she was foreign by birth) even though she conceded she was 'a good egg'. Charlotte had met her when she fell ill shortly after arriving in prison. Edie had been one of the youngest nurses in the sickbay, and did what she could to make the time her patients spent there both calm and pleasant. She thought of her charges not as criminals but as women who needed her help. Most of them were much older than she was, but even in those days she had a natural authority. She was, Charlotte thought, like Mary Kingsley, who in the nineteenth century had explored Africa and apparently used to subdue fierce animals with nothing more than a glance. She was also, in the modern phrase, n*on-judgemental.* It wasn't so much that she believed every single woman's assertion that she was innocent. Many, she knew, were as guilty as hell but in Edie's eyes that didn't affect their humanity or their needs. She would have been happier if there were a category called something like, *'Guilty but Justified,'* which described many of the women she had to deal with in prison. She'd done everything in her life with the minimum of fuss, marrying, having two sons and losing her husband in a slow, organized progress through the years. Nowadays, she spend much of her time fundraising for a local battered women's refuge and it was she who made sure that jumble sales and whist drives were put on regularly to benefit it. She'd helped to found it in the early seventies and still took an active part in running the place, sitting on the steering committee and frequently ringing up the newspapers to give them opinions on many issues relating to violence in the family, whether they'd asked for them or not. She even appeared on the radio from time to time, and when she did, she always spoke clearly and with a precision that came as a surprise to those who had written her off as a sweet old thing.

'Did you even get a chance to discuss things like the venue?' Val Handley asked. 'You have to start thinking about that months ahead, booking the church and so forth.'

She was sitting across the table from Edie and Charlotte, looking exactly like what she was: a middle-aged tomboy. At sixty-five, and because she was younger than her companions, Val refused to be categorized as 'old'. She wore corduroy trousers in what Charlotte privately considered an unfortunate shade of beige, a brown and orange hand-knitted Fair Isle cardigan, and her dark hair ('only about sixty per cent grey' she maintained) was tied back in a girlish ponytail.

On Sundays, Edie went to church, Val spent the morning in the garden and Charlotte cooked lunch. Today there was enough food left over from the engagement party to feed all three women. Val was a romantic and almost as excited at the prospect of a wedding as Isis, in spite of her own experience of matrimony. She'd been married at a ridiculously early age to a domestic monster and only Charlotte and Edie knew how little she regretted his death, for which she'd served six years in prison. He'd been an optician in a small market town and had taken in everyone with his façade of respectability. Behind closed doors, though, he'd made Val's life a constant torment. Everyone agreed on that, and she was very young, but the law was the law and this was in the days when desperately hitting out at an animal who repeatedly brutalized and beat you was not quite as sympathetically regarded. We've come a long way, Charlotte thought, looking at Val. She'd never have served a sentence like that nowadays. Mitigating circumstances. Today, someone like Val had people like Edie to help her and places like the refuge to run away to.

'I think Mrs Ashton has some ideas,' she said. 'She mentioned wanting somewhere 'suitable'. You can hire castles, she told me. She did strike me as the castle-hiring type. She'd want to make an impression.'

'But the young couple, what do they want?'

'Adrian will want what Zannah wants, unless his mother gets to him first. I don't know them well enough to judge how much influence she has on him. Quite a lot, I suspect.'

'I think,' said Val, standing up, 'that you ought to have a say, Charlotte. After all, you've been like a mother to Joss and a grandma to the girls. I know what I'd choose.'

'It's not your wedding, Val,' Edie said quietly.

'I know, I know. You should thank your lucky stars you didn't see mine! Cold sausage rolls left over from the previous evening in the local pub and a family who looked like gargoyles in fancy dress. I should have known, shouldn't I? That's why I think – well, never mind.'

'Oh go on, spit it out! You know you'll tell us in the end.'

'I think,' Val said 'that we could put on a damn good show right here. In this house. The garden would look lovely. We could have a marquee.'

Charlotte nodded. 'That's occurred to me too, but young people nowadays have their own ideas, don't they? I swore I'd never say that: *young people nowadays* but I do. All the time.'

*

'Don't hang up, Lydia, okay?' Gray said. He'd found a place where the reception was perfect and the silver phone had been pumping whatever ghastly radiation it possessed into his right ear for more than half an hour. Lydia, he knew, was on a landline, in the telephone kiosk she'd described to him in their emails. He also had a clear picture of her surroundings because she'd sent him photos of her kitchen, her study, her garden, the view from her windows. He'd offered to do the same but she'd refused. She wanted, she said, to think of him in an empty room in front of a blue screen. She wanted to know, to see, only his face so he sent her pictures of himself which she deleted from her computer after, as she put it, *learning them by heart*.

'Listen, just listen. I see why you're cross.' Wrong word. What could he call it? *Hurt, wounded, devastated*? 'But listen. All the time I've known you, the worst thing, the very worst thing has been the thought of you and Bob together. And you have been, haven't you? Go on. Tell me your married life hasn't gone on exactly as normal. You can't, can you?'

A silence hummed at the other end of the line. Gray continued, 'There you are then. Now get this: all that time, I've had to live with images of him smiling at you, touching you, sharing jokes with you, brushing his teeth while you're in the bath, eating breakfast with you, going to the movies with you, laughing with you, fighting with you and worst of all, in bed with you ... nothing but torture. Constant torture. How would you have liked imagining *me* doing all those things? Which I've done, Lydia, make no mistake. All of them. I wanted to save you that, can't you understand? I'm married to Maureen. We're connected in ways that have to do with time and children: things you know about because they connect you to Bob. I wanted to be a single person in your mind. I just wanted to have a universe I could go into that had nothing but you in it. No one else. And I did. Whenever I thought of you, I knew you were thinking of me all by myself, just working and writing.'

'I know.' Her voice was not much louder than a whisper. 'I realize you were protecting me, but now ... I can't bear the thought of you lying to me. Not trusting me to be grown-up enough to deal with the truth. Perhaps you're right too. Now that I've met your wife, it's hard to get certain pictures out of my mind. I know what you mean,

Gray. But I can't bear any of it any longer. All of it. And it's worse now, because of Zannah and Adrian. I had no idea Adrian Whittaker was anything to do with you. Zannah didn't mention that the surnames were different, though she did say his father was really a stepfather. I should have asked more questions, I suppose.'

'He's my stepson and I adopted him, but he chose his own father's surname when he was a teenager.'

'It doesn't matter. I've decided. We must stop everything. Now. At once.'

Gray nearly dropped the phone. 'What d'you mean?'

'Exactly what I'm saying. Nothing between us any longer. No emails, no letters, no poems. Nothing.'

'I can't do that, Lydia. I'd . . . I wouldn't be able to.'

'It won't be easy for me either, but I've promised. I told Bob that we'd only meet as Zannah and Adrian's parents in future. I'm not going to break my word.'

Gray closed his eyes. He spoke as reasonably as he could, although he was on the point of tears. He didn't cry often and when he did, he regarded it as a kind of failure. He said, 'And the promises you made to me? Don't they mean anything to you?'

The silence at the other end went on for so long that Gray checked the reception. It was fine. He said, 'Lydia, are you still there?'

'Please call me Joss. Lydia's just a pseudonym.'

'It's *not* just a fucking pseudonym!' He was shouting now. If he managed to hold back tears, this was what often happened: an explosion of frustration and rage. 'It's my name for you. You were Lydia when I met you and that's what you've been ever since. God, I don't know what's wrong with you. It's as if it all meant nothing. You're ready to give everything up. Everything we have . . .'

'What do we have, Gray, when you come down to it? Nothing. Words on a screen or on a page. Nothing real.'

'It is to me! It's real to me!' Even though he was shouting, the tears were now dangerously close. 'And it used to be real to you. Don't pretend it wasn't. What's your husband done to you? Has he threatened you? Tell me.'

'No, Gray. Nothing like that. But I can't leave him and I can't jeopardize my daughter's marriage to your son.'

'Stepson.'

'You know what I mean. I'm not going to say a word to the girls. I don't see that it's any of their business. I've got to return to normal and I can't do that if you're still part of my life. That's it, Gray. I've made up my mind.'

'Please, Lydia. Please meet me just once. I have to see you again. I won't be responsible for what I do if you refuse me . . .'

'Are you saying you'll tell Adrian about us? That's not worthy of you, Gray. I can't believe you'd do something like that.'

'I'm sorry. But please . . . don't you have to come to London for something? Please.'

'I do have to see my editor, that's true. I could arrange something.'

'Thank God. Next week, Lydia. I hate feeling like this. Next week?'

'Okay. Okay.' He could hear her sighing. 'I'll tell Bob I have to see Mal and that I want to chat to Zannah about arrangements. We did rather cut that short yesterday. Yesterday . . . God, it feels like a lifetime ago.'

'I don't care about anything, now you've agreed to see me. Walking on air. Email me, Lydia. Let me know which day. I've got to square it with work. I can't wait . . . I can't wait to see you.'

'I haven't changed my mind, Gray. I'm not getting back into what we used to do. It's over. You'll get one email from me telling you when I'll be in London and that'll be it. D'you understand?'

'I'll see you again. That's what I understand.'

'I'm going to ring off now. Goodbye.'

'Goodbye, my darling.'

Silence. More silence. Gray listened and heard nothing but the dialling tone. He turned to call history and deleted the call, which had used up most of the money on his phone. Never mind, only a few more days and then he'd see her. He'd be able to hold her. Kiss her. She'd relent when she saw him. She must. He could feel the blood moving more swiftly through his veins as he walked towards the car-park. Better get home before Maureen put lunch on the table.

'So how did it go, then, the family get-together?' Cal said.

'Don't ask. Really, don't ask. I can't go into it now.' Zannah looked round and saw that they were alone. Emily was still in the shower and Isis was getting ready to go to Wimbledon Common with her father.

'Bad as that, eh?'

Zannah did sometimes wonder at Cal's tolerance. He was perfectly happy for her, it seemed, to go out with Adrian, to fall in love with him and now even to marry him. How come he didn't loathe the very idea? How come he wasn't even the least bit jealous? She could still bring back feelings of searing pain just thinking about Cal and his Russian lover and she wondered how long she'd have to be with Adrian before the pain disappeared completely. And however hard she tried, she found it impossible to dislike her ex-husband. Her college friends, her friends from home weren't always available for confessions and discussions, so she relied on Claire and Louise, her fellow teachers. They'd become very close over the last couple of years. They sat in the staff room at school and one of the things they often talked about was amicable divorce. The others didn't believe in it, and maintained that the phrase was a contradiction in terms.

'Wanting to strangle your ex goes with the territory,' said Claire, who taught year four.

'That's my experience,' Louise said firmly, and when Zannah objected that Claire was happily married and Louise far too young and still single so how could she possibly know what she was talking about, they shook their heads, tucked into their sandwiches and declared that it was a matter of observation. You only had to look around you and it was obvious to anyone who had more than two brain cells to rub together: when love died, that was it. You hated the person who'd let you down, and if you were the one who'd done the letting down it didn't seem to make any difference.

'I don't hate Cal,' Zannah told them. 'Sorry. No one could hate Cal. Most people love him.'

They raised their eyebrows and muttered about 'denial'. They were wrong. Cal Ford was lovable, and that was that. For two pins, Zannah thought, I'd pour out my heart to him right now and tell him about Ma and what happened yesterday and even pick his brains about wedding venues. He looked just the same as he always had: like a large, rather friendly dog. His brown hair was shaggy without actually covering his eyes. They were brown too, and looked out at the world in a trusting way. He didn't care about grooming, and although he practically lived in the shower, his clothes were haphazard and he wore them to keep him warm and cover him up. Zannah never failed to be amazed that a journalist on a national newspaper could be so ignorant about matters of design and fashion. Cal claimed he never registered advertisements even when they were right there in front of him, and when Zannah had chided him for his ignorance, he would shrug and smile and say, 'Who gives a shit about the difference between Armani and Versani? Not me.'

'Versace,' Zannah had said, knowing it was useless.

'Whatever,' Cal would answer, waving his cigarette around and scattering ash all over the place. He was a smoker when they were first married and only gave up when Isis was born. Recently, she'd seen him smoking from time to time, although as far as possible never in front of Isis, who scolded him whenever she suspected he'd been at the fags.

'Daddy, I'm ready!' Isis rushed into the kitchen, her pink rucksack already on her back. 'Let's go. Now.'

'Hang on a mo, Icey, I'm having a word with your mum. We'll go in a minute, okay . . . oh, hi Em. You coming on a picnic with us, then? Go on. We're going to Wimbledon Common.'

Emily's smile, Zannah noticed, lit up her whole face. She couldn't hide it. She was thrilled to bits to be asked to join them. Zannah knew about Em's crush on Cal, even though she herself hadn't said a word. She hadn't needed to. Zannah had started going out with Cal when her sister was only sixteen and from the first time she'd laid eyes on him, it was obvious that she was besotted. She'd done quite a good job of hiding her feelings but they shone out of her eyes for anyone to see who was looking properly and Zannah was good not only at looking but at understanding what she was seeing. She'd been so in love with Cal back then, and he with her, that Emily's crush didn't worry them. She'd never been difficult or unpleasant about it. She didn't go into a decline. She didn't let Cal and Zannah's marriage cramp her style and their parents' house was always crowded with her admirers, boyfriends, hangers-on and cronies. Em's crush was exactly the same whether she was going out with someone or not. At the moment, she had a collection of boyfriends, but no one she could ever be committed to. Zannah wondered if it was worth asking Adrian whether he knew anyone eligible, and decided it probably wasn't. Her sister had very definite views.

When Zannah and Cal had divorced, Emily wasn't much more than twenty. When Zannah had suffered her kind-of breakdown, it was Em who had tried hard to persuade her to go back to him. She couldn't understand why one 'lapse', which was what she called it, should mean the end of a life together. Her face had been screwed up with pain.

'What about Isis, Zannah? She needs a dad. You can't do this to her,' Emily had said, and Zannah answered, 'I'd never stop him seeing his daughter. You know I wouldn't. But I can't trust him. I'll just keep thinking of him with that woman. I won't be able to relax. Images will come into my mind. You don't understand.'

'No, I don't. I think you ought to forgive him. He's asked you to, hasn't he?'

'I can't,' said Zannah. 'I just can't face him any more. He's not the same Cal.'

'But you still love him, don't you?' Emily asked.

Zannah didn't answer. She could see that her sister didn't understand how it might be possible for Cal's adultery to have killed off most of the love she used to feel. It hadn't stopped her hurting like hell, but the love ... that was something else. It had mutated; changed beyond recognition.

More recently, just before she met Adrian, she'd begun to wonder if Em might have been right and whether she hadn't been too hasty. Cal had been in Moscow when he'd slept with a fellow journalist. They'd been together for a couple of weeks. He broke up with her even before they arrived back in London. Zannah had only found out about it by accident, going into his email account to find an address she needed. He hadn't even had the cunning to hide or delete the woman's messages and when Zannah had confronted him, he'd told her all about it, vowed it was over and that it would never happen again. Too late. They were divorced a year later. Isis was only three. Zannah was in agony.

Divorcing Cal, living without him, was like being flayed. For a very long time, Zannah had felt as though she were missing a skin. She struggled at the whole business of being a single mother, too proud to stay in Altrincham with her parents and wanting more than anything to have her life back the way it was when she and Cal were everything to one another. Rage: a kind of blind, almost insane rage took hold of her at the most unexpected times, like when she was coming home from Isis's nursery in the twilight heavy with the knowledge that in spite of Em's company, in spite of the support of her family, she was alone. All the friends she and Cal had had in common seemed to melt away. For a while, there would be phone calls from one or another of them, but the invitations they offered seemed to Zannah half-hearted, as though part of them was still loyal to Cal. She didn't see any reason, on the face of it, why this should happen when a couple split up, but everyone agreed that it did: friends you made as a couple sided with one person or the other when the break occurred. She'd had to admit that Cal had a gift for friendship and many of their shared friends had been his in the first place.

When Cal came round to see Isis, which he did as often as he could, Zannah used the time to go shopping for food and see to all the things that were difficult to manage with a child in tow. Even more than taking advantage of his presence was the desire not to see him. Not to have to be near him, talk to him. It was hard for her to keep the conversation civilized.

I wouldn't have survived without Isis, Zannah thought. She saved me. Having to look after her, having to get her to nursery every day and fed and dressed took Zannah's mind off her unhappiness. Even on the occasions ... and there were plenty of them ... when she was irritated with her daughter, when she felt she couldn't go on any more because everything was just *too much* and she wanted to run away and never come back ... simply leave everything and disappear, even then she'd known that Isis was the one thing anchoring her to real life. To the possibility of something other than pure misery. Because that was what it was without her husband, pure misery, and there were a thousand occasions when she almost, almost picked up the phone to summon Cal and say: *I'm sorry. Come back. Let's be married again.* That mood never lasted long. Images would arrive unbidden in Zannah's head: of Cal repeating with some other woman all he had done with her. Kissing. Caressing. Sharing jokes, meals, baths. She couldn't go back to him, however lonely she sometimes felt.

When Isis turned four, Zannah took a job at St Botolph's. She'd taken her PGCE after studying part time for what seemed like ages and after she started work, everything got better. Not that Em didn't keep trying to reconcile her with Cal. Zannah was surprised to find how much she enjoyed teaching. Isis came to school with her, and loved the nursery class, which was very convenient, and as the months passed, the pain grew bearable. Then, a year and a half ago, she met Adrian and everything changed, almost overnight.

Zannah walked up the little staircase that led to the upper part of the flat, where Emily had her bedroom and she had what she called her studio, even though she knew it was a rather grand title for such a tiny room. It might not be big, Zannah thought, but it's got a huge window and good light. She opened the door and sighed with pleasure as she sat down in the well-upholstered office chair at the table that served as a desk. What Emily called her 'control freakery' was evident everywhere. Her schoolwork was neatly filed away in huge portfolios leaning against one wall. The table had piles of papers laid neatly all over it, with proper paperweights on each. Her laptop, with its mouse mat neatly beside it, was pushed to the back. She'd painted the walls herself: a pretty, buttery yellow (not a whisper of lime, and nowhere near orange, just a few shades yellower than cream) which lifted her spirits whenever she came into the room. She would never have been able to explain to anyone what keen pleasure it gave her to find precisely the right colour for something.

Her first wedding dress had been short, turquoise chiffon: much more cocktail-dressish than bridal. She'd been fantasizing about a proper wedding dress from the time she was Isis's age, but had considered it more seriously from the moment she'd agreed to marry Adrian. There was time enough to think about it carefully when they'd sorted out the venue, but she was already sure that it wouldn't be dazzling white. That was too virginal and besides, it made her look washed out. She'd told no one, not even Emily, about what was in the bottom drawer of her filing-cabinet in an unprepossessing orange folder from the school stationery cupboard. Folded among the deliberate camouflage of report forms and printouts of boring documents was a drawing she had made of her perfect dress. From time to time, when she knew she was alone, she took it out to see if it was still as lovely as ever. She had sketched in the lace she wanted. It would have to be lined, possibly with *crêpe de chine*. The waist, in true twenties style, was dropped and edged with scalloped lace, scattered with tiny pearls. The same lace bordered the square neck and the sleeves, which fell to just above the elbow. A scalloped edge to the skirt as well, and the length just above the ankle. This wasn't a style for those with thick legs but Zannah knew she could carry it off. High-heeled, satin strap shoes with a lace-trimmed 'v' just below the instep, in the same shade as the lace.

She'd drawn a back view of the dress too, showing the row of small pearl buttons done up with loops. Perhaps a bandeau with a tiny veil attached for her hair, which of course would be worn swept up, or would a tiara be better? She hadn't quite decided. There was time for that. She wondered how much she'd have to pay to have it made. She might find an off-the-peg equivalent, but doubted she'd be satisfied with that. I must, she thought, make enquiries about dressmakers. Really beautiful lace was expensive and there was also the bridesmaid's dress to consider. She was thinking of watermarked taffeta and it would have to be silk. The colours of the synthetic equivalents were nothing like as good. Would she be able to get away with a thousand pounds? The sum made her feel a little dizzy when she thought of it, but even that was probably optimistic. She'd been saving for a long time, putting a little money every month into what she thought of as her dress fund. She'd not even told Em about that. Not showing this drawing to anyone was a superstition, somehow bound up with the tradition of a groom not seeing his bride's dress until the wedding day. I'll show it to Em and Ma soon, she told herself, but meanwhile it can remain hidden for a few weeks longer.

Zannah glanced up at the enormous corkboard that occupied most of the wall facing the window. She'd found it in a shop in Camden Town and hauled it all the way home on the Underground, scowling at men who looked as though they were on the point of asking if they could help her. Ever since Adrian had asked her to marry him, she'd pinned up everything she thought might come in useful: cuttings from magazines, postcards, swatches of fabric from the shops she pretended she was just passing, news items, and a small collection of old wedding photos.

'What d'you think of my wedding board?' she'd asked Emily on the day she put it up. They'd been standing at the sink, doing the washing-up.

'Wedding *bored*. That's what I am.'

'Ha-ha, very witty.' Zannah threw a tea-towel at her sister. She wondered whether her desire to have the perfect wedding was a wish for the future: a fervent and almost superstitious hope that if she did things properly, her marriage would be strong and last for ever. She knew this was nonsense, but liked the feeling that this time she was following traditions that went back centuries. *Something old, something new, something borrowed, something blue*. She'd even made a note to herself so that those items weren't forgotten.

Now she sat down at the table, picked up a pencil and began to doodle on the sheet of paper lying in front of her as she remembered her first meeting with Adrian.

She'd been at a party. Ever since she'd started going out with Cal, she'd gone off parties. The only point of them was to meet a fanciable man, and if you were already hooked up with someone, the crush, the bad wine and the too-loud music were hard to endure after you were about twenty. She'd come to this particular bash because Louise insisted she went with her. Louise had had her eye on the brother of the young woman into whose tall, thin house they were currently being squeezed, along with a crowd of noisy people on the edge of drunkenness. Zannah had had enough and was making for the daunting pile of overcoats near the front door when someone said: 'Are you about to tunnel your way out?'

She'd turned and caught sight of Adrian, smiling at her as she flung various items of clothing about, searching for her jacket. He was so handsome that she actually stopped breathing for a second. He was also perfectly dressed, in a linen suit that managed to look fashionably rumpled and not slobbishly creased. His hair was dark and his eyes a pale, luminous blue that reminded her of icebergs. 'I've just decided that parties aren't my thing.'

'Nor mine. Mind if I escape with you? Adrian Whittaker. Friend of John Latimer's.'

That was the name of Louise's prey. Fleetingly, Zannah wondered if she should plead her case with this Adrian: say something like *my friend fancies your friend*. She decided against it and said instead, 'Okay. I'm going home, though.'

'I'll see you to your door.'

This struck her as so old-fashioned, so charming, that she burst out laughing.

'I'm not some young girl, you know! I'm a mother. I've got a seven-year-old daughter.'

'Are you here with your husband?'

'I'm divorced.'

'In that case, I think I ought to see you home.'

He took her gently by the arm and steered her out into the street. At her door, he asked for her phone number; asked for permission to call her. When she agreed, he took a notebook from an inside pocket of his jacket with a pen that Zannah recognized as a *Mont Blanc* even by the light of the street-lamp because she had wanted one for ages.

He rang her the very next day and asked her to meet him at Green Park station.

'Is four o'clock on Saturday all right? Don't wear jeans and trainers,' he said. She liked his voice on the phone. He sounded as if he knew what he wanted and was going to get it, without being at all harsh or loud.

'I never do,' she answered.

'I somehow knew you didn't. See you then.'

He'd taken her to tea at the Ritz. He'd obviously come straight from work and she smiled when she saw his briefcase, dark suit, collar and tie. They made him look like someone to be reckoned with, she thought, someone serious, probably earning serious money – which was only right if he worked on a Saturday. She'd always had a problem with what Cal wore to work. *Journalists can wear whatever they like*, he used to say, but she thought putting on the first thing he found when he woke up made him look like a student.

Adrian guided her to a table in a corner of the beautiful room and, with the tiered cakestand between them, and the cups and saucers like a still-life on a tablecloth as white as a ski-slope, she fell in love with him, all in one second, just like that. She bent her head over the Earl Grey. I wish I could tear his clothes off and kiss him all over, she thought and felt herself blush.

As the tea-things were taken away, Adrian leaned forward and said, 'Suzannah, I want to see you again. Actually, it's more than that. I want . . . well . . . I want us to be . . . Never mind. I'm sure it's too soon to say such things. But please come out to dinner tomorrow. Say you will.'

Zannah stopped drawing and looked out of the window. She was so high up here that all she could see was the sky. *Floating pictures from the cloud gallery*: where had she heard it called that? She'd been so restrained. She'd waited a whole week before going to bed with him. They saw one another four times; they spoke for hours on the phone every night, and then, on their fifth date, they'd ended up in Adrian's flat and spent the night together. A week later he'd taken her to the kind of jeweller's she'd never have dared to enter by herself to choose the beautiful ruby that was now on her left hand. They were going to be married. There was going to be a wedding and it was going to be the kind of wedding she'd been dreaming about, sometimes rather guiltily, for most of her life. Sometimes she worried about the expense of such an occasion. Emily had got to her with gibes about weddings costing more than most people's annual incomes, and Zannah knew that her family would be paying for most of it. Adrian, to whom she confided these doubts, kissed her when she'd finished speaking and said, 'Don't worry, my darling. There's plenty of money for everything. We'll sort it. No point being old-fashioned. I'll help, promise. My family isn't going to stand by and let your parents fork out for everything. It'll be fine.'

She believed him. One of the best things about Adrian was the fact that he wanted the perfect day as much as she did. That they agreed about what such a day should be like proved that they were made for one another. Her mother, Charlotte and even Em were a little startled by the speed with which she moved from just seeing Adrian to being engaged to him but she reassured them. 'I love him, Ma,' she'd told Joss on a visit home just after the announcement. 'It's going to be like coming home. Really. And you'll see. You'll love him, too. He's . . . he's *grown-up*. Cal was, well, you know what he's like. Just a kid in a way. It's not a rebound thing. Don't think that. I've been divorced for ages. And I've never before met anyone who's so . . . so *right*. He's right for me. He'll look after me.'

'What about Isis?' Joss had asked her.

'Adrian adores her,' she'd answered.

'Does she love him?'

'No, but she likes him well enough. And what she'll really love is being a bridesmaid.'

Her mother had smiled the enigmatic smile that meant *I'm going to let you get on with your life and not say a word*. But surely, now that she'd met Adrian, she'd have to admit how perfect he was. As soon as she's feeling better, Zannah decided, I'll ask her what she thinks of him. How could anyone not love him?

Some people had a gift for picnics. They managed to assemble food in fancy wicker baskets, and it wasn't just cheese-and-pickle sarnies but devilled chicken legs or perfect little meatballs, ciabatta rolls, dainty salads drizzled with the kind of oil you had to drizzle, olives straight from the slopes of a Greek mountain and fruit that looked as though each piece had been individually hand-picked. The wine was cold. There were proper knives and forks. Even the wasps that hovered politely near such feasts seemed posher than your average insect. No one in our family, Emily thought, has such a gift. Zannah had no imagination when it came to sandwich fillings and therefore there were no pleasant surprises or exotic combinations to be found when she had prepared the food. Emily was equally useless, getting into a panic and packing too much of one thing and not enough of another and forgetting to put in napkins or something to drink.

Cal, though, was a dab hand at the Supermarket Picnic. They'd just been through M&S like three whirlwinds, scooping up a combination of innovative sandwiches, small tubs of Mediterranean-type salads, packets of biscuits and crisps (*healthy eating?* said Cal. *Naaah, you can get that at home anytime)* and a selection of fruit juices and smoothies in magical flavours like mango and strawberry and banana.

Now they were on Wimbledon Common hunting for a good place to sit and eat what they'd bought. Isis had run a little ahead and Cal turned to Emily. 'What *did* go on yesterday, Em? Zannah was being a bit tight-lipped, or was I imagining it?'

'Nothing much, actually. Or I don't think it was anything. Ma went white and funny at one point and left in a bit of a hurry. She got Pa to drive her home. I don't know what was wrong with her. She said it was a migraine and so did Charlotte but I think it might have been something else. Maybe something to do with the menopause. D'you think it could have been that?'

'Menopause isn't one of my fields of expertise, I'm afraid. I can tell you all about the rigging of elections in Zimbabwe, but that's no help, is it?'

Emily laughed. Cal was so easy to talk to. Why couldn't Zannah see what she'd lost? She said nothing for a moment, wondering whether she would have been able to forgive his infidelity. She was pondering this when Cal spoke. 'What are his parents like?' he asked.

'You're very curious all of a sudden. Why's that? Not still pining after Zannah, are you?'

'As if!' He spoke with seeming sincerity and almost enthusiasm, but Emily was sure that some kind of hurt, some kind of resentment, was hidden away in him. It just wasn't like Cal to complain about a situation when there was nothing to be done about it. He went on, 'But there's Isis to consider. Those people are going to be her new family, aren't they? I want to know she's going to be okay. I feel bad enough as it is . . .'

'What d'you mean?'

Cal stopped next to a tree and patted it briefly with one hand. 'This'll do, won't it, for the picnic? Yes. I'll go and get Isis.'

'No, Cal, come on, you can't stop there. What d'you feel bad about?'

He shrugged. 'Not being around for Isis all the time. I wish I could be, really, but with the job and everything . . .'

'You're a fantastic dad! Isis sees you every week when you're here. She's fine, honestly. You'd be able to tell if she was unhappy, and she isn't, is she?'

'No, she's okay, I know that. And I also know I see a lot more of her than most divorced dads. Don't worry. I'm not going to be putting on a Batman suit or anything. And, Em . . .'

'Yes?'

'Will you keep an eye out for me? To make sure she's okay? I think maybe Zannah's a bit . . . well, taken up with her new man. She might not notice stuff.'

'She'd notice it if it had to do with Isis. You know that.'

Cal sighed. 'Yes, I suppose I do, but still. Not being there, you get to worrying. You hear awful things, don't you? About step-parents and so forth. Cruelty.'

'I'm sure Adrian's not cruel,' said Em, wondering how they'd got here, with her defending her sister's fiancé.

'I'm not suggesting he beats her or anything, just that ... Well, I don't know exactly, but I'll feel better if I know you're on the case.'

'I'm on the case, Guv!' said Em, saluting him. In the days just after he and Zannah had started going out together, Cal had started a running gag that continued to this day: they pretended they were in a TV police show. Possibly, shamingly, it had all started with *The Bill*, which she still watched sometimes. He called her Sarge and she called him Guv. Silly stuff.

'That's a weight off my mind, Sarge. I just miss her like mad when I'm not with her ... know what I mean?'

He started to run towards his daughter, who was standing some distance away and waving energetically. Emily stared after him. She had no intention of adding to Cal's worries by telling him that Isis missed him too, however *okay* she was. Let him think she was blissfully happy all the time.

Maureen Ashton admired Nigella Lawson, and thought of Delia Smith as very reliable but if she had a heroine, it was definitely Martha Stewart, the American lifestyle expert (*a lifestyle guru*, they called her these days) who had spent time in prison. Maureen had been deeply shocked to hear that her heroine had misbehaved so badly and wondered whether it would be possible ever to take her advice again. Prison was somehow so *low* and *drab*. It had to taint you in some indefinable way. Set you apart from decent society. For some time, she found herself condemning Martha, but after she had emerged into freedom again, Maureen decided to forgive her. In her heart of hearts, Maureen knew that if it had been anyone else at all, she'd have found it easier to shun them, but the fact was, she had missed Martha while she'd been out of action and longed to see what she would do when she returned to civilization.

It must have been strange for her fellow inmates to have such a person imprisoned alongside them. Maureen wouldn't have been a bit surprised to find that the cell Martha had inhabited ended up fit to be photographed for her lifestyle magazine. And now, according to her website, the empire continued as it always had. Maureen loved that word ... *empire* ... and in her more private moments daydreamed vaguely about magazines, websites, TV programmes, and more with her name on them. She knew it would never happen and, if she was honest, it didn't worry her. Her home was her empire, and she was proud of it.

The morning room, at the front of the house, was where Maureen went to do her thinking. She'd been at her desk since lunch, and her laptop computer was open in front of her, Martha Stewart's face beaming out of the screen. Graham had gone upstairs to his study. He must have a poem brewing, she thought. He'd been rather silent as he ate, and didn't seem to be in a mood to discuss the forthcoming wedding.

Never mind, Maureen thought. Plenty of time for that. She leaned forward and clicked on *wedding suggestions*. There were some rather good ideas here, she told herself. She'd pass them on to Zannah. Pausing for a moment to take a sip of coffee (ordered from Betty's in Yorkshire ... their special house blend which she enjoyed) she looked out of the window admiringly. Declan, her gardener, was good at keeping things trimmed and tidy, and her fuchsias and begonias were satisfyingly pretty: pinks and purples with touches of white here and there. The Clapham garden yesterday wasn't bad, but it was a little straight up and down for her taste. Just a long expanse of grass at the back, with borders on each side, when all was said and done. The dips and slopes of this lawn as it went down to the high fence that kept the road out of sight were more ... Maureen searched for the right word ... *landscaped*. Also, there was definitely something imposing about a detached house standing at the top of a longish drive that sloped up to the front door. The round gravelled space in front of the porch, with its flowerbed full of rosebushes in the centre of the circle, had been specially designed to ensure that even the largest car wouldn't have to reverse out of the gate.

Maureen liked looking at what she'd done to each room in the house and calculating how far she'd come. The girl she had been when she married Graham would have stood open-mouthed if she'd known that this was how she would end up. Still, she'd never had any intention of remaining in the rather genteel poverty of her childhood. Anyone who felt nostalgic for the fifties should have lived in Grandma Dora's poky little house, with the coal fires that had to be lit in grates, which needed clearing out every day. I was, Maureen thought, just like Cinderella. Everywhere was freezing cold in winter. If you moved six inches away from the hearthrug, that was it: you were in the Arctic. There was a tiny little two-bar electric fire in the bedroom, which meant that most mornings Maureen got dressed under the bedclothes. Her mother and grandmother did nothing but moan and complain all day long, and as soon as Maureen left school, she enrolled at a secretarial college, determined to get a qualification and a job as soon as possible.

Well, that nearly got scuppered, she recalled now, admiring the Colefax and Fowler fabric of the morning-room curtains, with their pattern of vaguely Japanesey flowers in warm, autumnal colours. She'd been stupid, no two ways about it. She'd fallen in love with Mickey Whittaker (who was a spiv and a layabout, but fanciable with it), and discovered that she had a bit of a gift for sex.

When she became pregnant with Adrian, Mickey said he'd marry her, but even while she was totting up how to afford the dress she coveted, he'd disappeared from their town and from her life as though he'd never existed. All attempts to trace him had failed until two years or so ago, when his sister, who'd been a skinny little slag of fourteen when Maureen knew her, suddenly got in touch (so she's kept her beady eye on me over the years, was what came into Maureen's mind, even before she'd taken in the contents of the letter) to announce that her brother Michael had been killed in a car accident in Australia. Maureen thought: typical of him to run away as far as he possibly could without falling off the edge of the world. Then she thought: Adrian mustn't find out. It probably hadn't been the most sensible thing in the world to tell her young son when he was about five, that his real father was dead, but it made life easier and she took a gamble on Mickey never coming anywhere near her. In his absence, she'd turned him into a kind of hero, telling Adrian tales of his wit, his looks, his charm and on and on. She hadn't realized, while she was building Mickey up, that the little boy was making comparisons with Graham that of course made his stepfather look bad by comparison. Anyone would have seemed inadequate. But it's not entirely my fault, Maureen consoled herself, that they don't get on well. Adrian was jealous of Graham and, as far as she was concerned, that was natural in a boy who was devoted to his mother. He'd always regarded Graham as a rival.

When Mickey vanished, just before his son was born in 1971, Maureen took stock. Without a husband to support her, she needed a job, and found one quickly in the local hospital, as a receptionist in the outpatients department. After Adrian was born, she left the baby with Grandma Dora because her mother was worse than useless and, anyway, at work herself, and continued to sit behind the desk at the hospital, smiling nicely and being good at filing. Babies, she admitted to herself, were not her thing, even though she worshipped her son. She resolved to be a perfect mother later on, but meanwhile it was important for Adrian that she find a father for him. As soon as she caught sight of the young Graham Ashton, she knew that he was exactly what she'd been looking for.

She wasn't disappointed. She'd been surprised by how quickly she had snaffled him. It was easy, she decided, to pull some wool over a man's eyes, particularly if you could make him feel as though he was rescuing you from some dire fate. She learned very early on that Graham became genuinely distressed when he had to deal with a woman crying. The only thing he knew how to do was put a comforting arm round her, so she made sure that her underwear was pretty and the top button undone on her blouse, then let nature take its course. She loved him, of course she did, but had to admit that that came later, once they were safely married. The only thing she could have found to complain about was that he was a little distant, unless they were actually in bed together.

He'd always been generous, which was fortunate. I couldn't have lived with someone mean, she thought. When they were younger, and he was less busy all the time, he used to come shopping for clothes with her. He'd sit for hours outside fitting rooms while she swanned in and out, showing off one article after another. Whenever she found it hard to choose, he'd wave a hand in the air and declare, 'Oh, for goodness sake, have both. Why not?' which was exactly what she wanted to hear.

He lived inside his head a lot and, given the choice, she'd have preferred a chattier spouse, but you couldn't have everything. He was good in bed, which was important. Mind you, she thought, that's down to me as well. He hadn't had much experience when she first met him. Missionary position. Five minutes from start to finish. The first time they went to bed together she thought: that's not how it's going to be. Not on your nelly. She'd taken charge and taught him, well, everything he was now so good at. To be fair, he was a quick learner. 'Five gold stars, sweetheart,' she'd murmured breathlessly in his ear within days of their first encounter. 'Top of the class.'

She'd developed a talent for sex with Mickey and was determined that it shouldn't go to waste. She was relieved to find that her marriage was going to be okay as far as that was concerned. Also, Graham was independently wealthy and that was even more crucial. He'd earn a good salary as a doctor of course, but it was reassuring to know that in the background there was the kind of money that meant she would never have to worry about (hideous word!) *economising*. And his parents had died when he was about eight, so she'd never had to deal with in-laws. That was a real blessing.

When Jonathan was born, two years after her marriage, things between her elder son and her husband went from bad to worse. Adrian had been such a sensitive little boy, Maureen recalled, and it must have been obvious to him that Graham really adored his own son and was, in some indefinable way, different towards Maureen's. The tantrums and arguments; the slamming doors and shouted swear-words that had become such a feature of Adrian's teenage years culminated in his adoption of Mickey's name. After years of being Adrian Ashton, he became Adrian Whittaker which hadn't exactly endeared him to Graham. Matters weren't helped by the fact that Jon seemed to go through life with no problems at all. He was a placid, kind, gentle child and managed to get on well even with his elder brother.

Of course, everything was more civilized now, at least on the surface, but a son can't hide the truth from his mother, and Maureen knew that Adrian wasn't Graham's biggest fan. She also realized that the feeling was mutual, although her husband had more sense than to say anything. Jonathan had become a doctor, which of course made his father love him even more. But I love Jon too, Maureen told herself. Of course I do. He's clever and sweet and doing wonderful work down there in South Africa, and I'm so proud of him. I adore both my sons, but facts are facts. Jon is Graham's favourite and Adrian is mine even though I'll go to my grave before I admit that to anyone. Adrian hadn't lived at home for years, which was a plus, but whenever he visited, all sorts of unspoken tensions filled the air and meals were forever on the verge of becoming a kind of battleground. She was grateful that he was getting married now. Zannah was a pretty woman and seemed pleasant enough and her presence would make family get-togethers much easier from now on.

Maureen took a last sip from her coffee cup (lovely, delicate, white bone china) and turned her attention to the letters she was about to write. First, a thank-you to Mrs Parrish then a note to Zannah. She wanted to invite her to lunch so that they might talk about the matter of the venue, just the two of them. It was to have been discussed yesterday, but then Mrs Gratrix ... Joss ... had thrown her wobbly, or whatever it was and that had been the end of that. Maureen wondered whether the little scene she'd witnessed was an indication of some kind of instability in the family. She'd have to ask Adrian tactfully if there was any history of such behaviour. You couldn't be too careful. Joss had been in a most peculiar state and Maureen thought the migraine story couldn't be entirely true. Maybe it was a cover for some sort of menopausal hideousness. She herself was fifty-four, only a year older than Joss, and so far everything in that department had been plain sailing, but the changes went on for years, and every woman was different, she'd read. If I ever start acting strangely, she told herself, I'll go on HRT at once.

Lunch with Zannah... there was a very good little restaurant she knew near Victoria that would be perfect. She opened her stationery drawer and took out a sheet of palest blue paper, engraved with her name and address, and began to write, pausing only to make a mental note that any wedding invitations that went out for her son's wedding would definitely have to be engraved and not printed. There were standards to maintain and she had no intention of settling for second best in any area of her life.

'I had a lovely time with Daddy,' Isis said. She was lying under her duvet in white pyjamas with butterflies printed all over them. Zannah, sitting on the end of her daughter's bed, wondered whether you could have too much of a good thing. She'd been the one to start Isis on her butterfly passion by painting a mural on one wall, a kind of collage of thousands of them in every colour she'd managed to get her hands on. Isis liked lots of other stuff, too, stars, rainbows, kittens and rabbits, for instance, but butterflies reigned supreme, possibly because they were quite easy to draw. All the books were kept on a shelf above the bed and there was a little desk under the window, but the room was tiny. I'll make sure she has a bigger one when Adrian and I are married, Zannah thought, and sighed. She'd been so absorbed in thinking about her wedding day that where they would live afterwards hadn't really crossed her mind in any serious way. I'll miss this flat wherever we end up, she thought. Never mind, there's plenty of time to worry about that when I've organized everything else. A small voice in Zannah's head whispered to her: *you'll miss this place because it's where you and Cal were together* but she brushed it aside. It was going to be wonderful going round with Adrian, choosing where they were going to live.

'We went to Wimbledon Common,' Isis went on.

'That's good,' Zannah said, turning her attention to her daughter again. 'Did you find any Wombles?'

'Don't be silly, Mummy,' Isis was scornful. 'Wombles are from TV, and there's books, but they're not real.'

'Well, you never know.'

'We walked for ages. And the picnic was fantastic. Dad's so great at choosing sandwiches. We're going to the Science Museum on Thursday. Mummy?'

'Yes?'

'Can I ask you something?'

'You're frowning. It's something serious, is it? Will I like it?'

'I don't know,' said Isis. 'You might not.'

'Go on, then.'

'You know Gemma?'

Gemma was Claire's daughter, and Isis's best friend. They'd been like twins ever since Zannah took up her job at the school.

'What about her?'

'Can she be a bridesmaid, too?'

Zannah was silent for a second. Then she let out a long breath as though she'd been holding it for the last few seconds. 'I don't know, sweetie. I'd not thought of having anyone but you. Two bridesmaids. I'll have to think about it.'

'I'd really, really love it if she could. She's going to get dead jealous if I'm one and she isn't and I won't be able to talk to her about it and then what'll happen? Also,' Isis was quick to continue, sensing Zannah's hesitation, 'it'll mean I've got someone to talk to and play with at the wedding. And at the rehearsals. And we can go to our fittings together. For our dresses.'

'I see you've got it all worked out.' Zannah got up. 'Well, I'll think about it, okay? You lie down now and go to sleep. We'll discuss it another time. I'll have to consult Adrian, of course.'

'Right. But don't think for too long,' said Isis and Zannah couldn't help noticing that a frown appeared on her daughter's face when Adrian was mentioned. It was natural, she supposed, to object in some way to another man in her mother's life and Isis had been very good most of the time. Just occasionally, though, Zannah got the impression that Adrian was not her daughter's favourite person. She'll come round when we're all living together, she told herself. She hardly knows him. Not properly.

'Night night, pet,' she said, and kissed Isis on the forehead. 'Sleep tight. Don't let the bugs bite.'

Zannah switched off the light as she left the room and the butterflies on the wall became a thousand black shapes against the pale background. Two bridesmaids! Would it work? Maybe it was a small price to pay for Isis to be happy.

Thursday

It hadn't been in the least difficult to get away. Joss sat alone in the café at the British Library and the delicious-looking carrot cake, which she'd ordered and started to eat because she was feeling faint, might as well have been made of cardboard. Her hand trembled as she took each forkful and the coffee she'd begun by enjoying had now turned cold and rather bitter. She'd chosen to meet Gray here. It was convenient for Euston, and one of her favourite places in the world. Where should a librarian meet people if not in a library? She liked the idea of being surrounded by books, and it also occurred to her after she'd suggested it in an email to Gray that in the whole of London this would be the one place Maureen would never think of visiting. She also doubted that it was much frequented by figures of the medical establishment who knew him.

Bob was in the middle of marking exam papers and had barely looked up when she'd announced, on Monday morning, that she had to go to London to see her editor. *All that stuff*, as he put it, by which he meant anything to do with the world of publishing, went straight past him. Joss could practically see her words flying through the air and out of the window. Her writing career up to this point had meant nothing to him. He was always happy when she had a poem appearing in a magazine and would turn the pages reverently and sometimes even read what she'd written, but then he'd hand it back to her and forget about it. Now that she was putting together her first collection, he'd no more take an interest in the day-to-day business of its publication than spend hours discussing the merits of a skirt she'd bought, or her latest shade of lipstick. *Very nice, darling* pretty well summed up his reaction to the daily traffic of her life. She'd felt a low-level resentment about this for years, though never enough to make a fuss about it. She wasn't quite sure whether Bob was a little suspicious about this trip, but if he did wonder about it, he made a good job of hiding his concern. Her emphasis on meeting her editor would most likely have persuaded him that this was a poetry outing and nothing to do with him.

One of the things she loved best about Gray was the way he took what she wrote seriously. He would point out particular things he liked in each poem; ask about anything he didn't understand, offer praise in words that no one else had ever used about her work: *I learned it by heart because I wanted it to be part of me, Lydia*, he'd written, after reading the latest. She hugged that sentence to her for days and now ... now there was a chance that she'd never again have someone who would speak to her on that level. Who would offer suggestions which were completely unmixed with envy, or flattery, or anything but love and intelligence and above all, a deep understanding of what she was trying to do, trying to say. She, for her part, wrote to him at length about his poems, which she loved, and not only because she loved him. Who would nag him into submitting them to magazines, if she didn't? Now that she'd met Maureen she wouldn't have been a bit surprised to learn that she'd never read one of her husband's poems in her life. Doing without this mutual support, the interchange which brought them so close to one another would be almost the worst of it. The deprivation. The loneliness.

She'd told Gray eleven o'clock. Her meeting with Mal in Bloomsbury was at two. She had arranged to spend the night with Zannah, Em and Isis, and when her emotions threatened to get the better of her, she envisaged the lovely time they'd have together. Em was going to cook a special meal and Joss longed to be with them all. Something to look forward to, she thought. Something not to lose sight of if things became difficult, as they were almost bound to.

She glanced at her watch. Gray was almost pathologically punctual and would be here in a minute. She only knew this because he'd told her. I know almost nothing about him from my own experience, she reflected. She'd deliberately arrived much earlier than the appointed time. She wanted to be sitting down, ready, her hair brushed and her lipstick on, looking what Em called, now that she was on so many fashion shoots for her firm, 'pulled together'. She'd spent most of Wednesday fretting about what to wear, like a teenager on her first date. Pathetic! She rejected anything that screamed *provincial librarian*, which ruled out suits, neat dresses and court shoes. But she didn't want to appear like a mad, middle-aged poet of the dirndl-skirt-and-peasant-blouse variety either. In the end, she settled for a pair of black trousers and a red silk shirt. She had a cashmere cardigan in her enormous red leather bag, which was what Americans called 'a tote' and quite big enough for an overnight stay.

She saw him approaching before he caught sight of her. She registered his height, his grace, his puzzled expression as he looked round the café. When he saw her, he lifted his hand in a gesture of delight and moved quickly to the table. The first few words, the *haveyoubeenwaitinglong* and the *I'lljustgetmyselfacupofcoffee* passed in a blur and Joss was relieved to have a few seconds to get her breath back and compose herself while he went to the counter. When he was sitting in front of her, not even two feet away and with his hand inches from hers, she took a deep breath. 'One of us has to say something, Gray. You look very well.'

'Lydia. I can't believe I'm here, sitting with you. I've imagined this so often . . . seeing you again. Talking to you.'

Joss looked down at the dregs of her coffee, then into his eyes. She could hear the beating of her own heart in her ears and was almost overcome with a longing to get up from her chair, fling her arms around Gray and hold him to her. She knew exactly how it would be, his warmth. The taste of him on her mouth. There was no coffee left, but she lifted the cup to her lips anyway, just for something to do. He'd been suffering, that was clear. There were purple bags under his eyes and he looked exhausted, drained. Or maybe it was just middle age and she looked just as bad. As though he was reading her thoughts, he said, 'You're beautiful, Lydia. Exactly as I remember you.'

'Gray, this is the last time I'm doing something like this. Meeting you, I mean. After Zannah and Adrian's engagement lunch, I wanted never to see you again. It's not just us now, it's them. I'm not going to spoil my daughter's wedding. Her life.'

Gray made a face as if he had been presented with something horrible to eat: a sort of disgusted twist of his mouth. It was gone almost before it appeared and someone less observant than Joss might have missed it. She wondered what it had meant. She said, 'Don't you approve of the marriage? Adrian seems very pleasant, and he's very successful at his job, isn't he?'

'I suppose so. I've had a problem with him from when he was a baby. It was natural that he'd be jealous, I suppose. I was a rival for his mother's love. Lydia, I don't want to talk about Adrian. Or Zannah. I want to talk about you. Me too, if you like, but mostly you. Please tell me you don't mean it. About not seeing me.'

'I do. I don't want to see you again, Gray. Never. I'm . . .' Joss felt the blood draining from her face. 'I'm going to put you and everything we've had together out of my mind. It's going to be difficult, but I am. I'm not going to answer your emails. I'm not going to open any letters. I'm going to throw the phone away. Really.'

'But why? How can you? How can you possibly?'

'Because now that I know the truth, I can't bear it. You were right. I hate to admit it, but you were. Ever since I realized what you'd done, after I'd got over it a bit: being hurt at the lies you'd been telling, I began to see that maybe you were right. It's been almost unbearable for the last few days, thinking about you and her. I've met her, Gray. I've spoken to her. I can't get some things out of my head. D'you understand?'

Gray didn't say anything for a moment. Then he reached forward and took Joss's hand across the table. 'Of course I do. It's been hell for more than two years. I calculated that it was worth suffering, just to be in touch with you somehow. Anyhow. I don't care *how* we're connected as long as we are. I can't bear the thought of life without you, Lydia.'

'Melodramatic, Gray. You're surely not going to throw yourself off the nearest bridge, are you?'

'No, I wouldn't do that. But my love for you will have nowhere to go and it'll eat me up from inside.'

'It's the same for me. You haven't got a monopoly on suffering, you know.'

'You've got your children. Your granddaughter. More grandchildren to come. You'll hardly miss me.'

'That's not fair, Gray. You know – or maybe you don't – that I will.

You've been at the centre of my thoughts, my imagination, my … everything really. Don't you understand?'

'Then let's go on. Please. Like before. We never hurt anyone, did we? It's been a private thing between us. Why shouldn't we go on?'

Joss lifted her eyes. 'We can't. I … I had to tell Bob something and I said that it had been one night. I made light of it, Gray. And I had to tell him it was over. I had to, because now … well, we're going to be related. There will be family occasions. The wedding. Birthday parties. Christmases. All sorts of days when we'd have to meet and be friendly. I can't do that. I couldn't survive such things myself and I certainly couldn't look Maureen in the face ever again if I was still seeing you. As things stand, I'm not going to be there on most of those family occasions. I'll make some excuse. There are plenty of families where the two sides never meet. Thousands of them. We hardly ever need to set eyes on one another again after the wedding.'

'What *about* the wedding though? Zannah wants all the stops pulled out, doesn't she? Everyone'll have to be there for that. We'll have to see one another then.'

'I'm already dreading the whole thing. I feel faint when I think of it. Isn't that a lovely thing to say about a day that means so much to Zannah? Oh, God, Gray, I hate myself. I hate … all this. I hate the fact that you're going back tonight to your house. Her house. Your house with her. I'd never, never have let it happen if I'd known you were married.'

'Are you saying you wouldn't have fallen in love with me?'

Joss considered. 'No, not that. What I mean is, I'd have fallen in love with you and kept quiet about it. I'd never have spent that night with you, and I'd never have written thousands and thousands of words to you. I wouldn't have sat up for hours talking on the phone in the middle of the night. I wouldn't have had the dreams I've been having since I met you. I'd have put you out of my mind and into a box labelled *Married man. Do not touch* and got on with other things.'

Gray smiled. 'So I was right after all, wasn't I, to lie to you? How do you think I've been feeling, imagining you with Bob? Not that I knew who he was, of course. You're very good at disguises. Jesus, Lydia, you didn't even tell me your real name but I don't mind. I like having my own name for you. All we have is a whole lot of emails.'

Joss thought of the way she felt when she opened her laptop every night and found his words waiting for her, like flowers growing and blooming, beautiful in the dark. His messages had given her nothing but pleasure, and now she was in danger of losing them.

'What if we wrote less often?' Gray was saying as she came to herself again.

'No, it's got to be a clean break. That's what I need, Gray. The only thing that's going to work.'

'You can do that?'

'I'm going to try. It'll hurt. I won't deny it. Of course it will. I'm used to you.' Before she could stop them, tears filled her eyes, and she stared down at her hands as she continued. 'I'm sorry. I promised myself I wouldn't do that. I wasn't going to cry.'

'Let's get out of here, Lydia and go for a walk.'

'I can't. I have to meet my editor soon. I told him I'd be there at . . .' She glanced at her watch. There was over an hour till she had to leave, but she didn't know how much longer she could bear to sit in front of Gray and not throw herself into his arms. She lied. 'At one. I'm sorry. I have to go now. All we're going to do if we sit here is go round and round in circles.'

'You could tell me what you've been doing.'

'You know exactly what I've been doing every day, Gray. There's nothing, nothing you don't know about me. Nothing I haven't told you. And I find I don't want to hear about *your* life any longer. D'you see? I don't want to hear what you've been doing with Maureen. I don't want to know what your house is like. I don't want to think of you in bed with her and I can't stop myself. She's beautiful, Gray, and I can't stand it. That's the truth. I want to go and never never see you again. It's . . . I can't . . .'

Joss stood up and grabbed the red bag. She started to walk out of the café and Gray followed her down the wide steps and out of the building. In the forecourt, he caught up with her. 'Lydia, please. Stop for a moment. Say goodbye at least.'

She paused, and before she knew what was happening, Gray's arms were around her. The tears came then. He held her close to him for a long time. She could feel the material of his jacket under her cheek. Every time she breathed, she could smell his fragrance and it made her want to howl with pain. She pulled herself away and said, tears still pouring down her cheeks, 'I'm sorry, Gray. I can't do this. You make me weep and then I look a fright. What's Mal going to think?' She could hear her voice wobbling as she tried to strike a more light-hearted note.

'Let me kiss you,' Gray said, very softly, and turned her face up to his.

Joss let him kiss her, and then her own mouth opened under his and she drank him in. I have to remember this, she was thinking. This is all I'm ever going to have of him. I must keep this for ever. She knew her hands on his back were clawing at him, wanting to pull him so close to her that he became part of her own body. This is what an electric shock is like, she told herself, as she felt herself shaking in his arms. We mustn't, she thought. We can't do this any more. She pulled herself away and said, 'Goodbye, Gray. I'm leaving.'

She walked away from him with her shoulders thrown back and her head held high. Let him not know how much I hurt, she thought. Let him think I'm okay. By the time she'd walked a few hundred yards up Euston Road, she could no long see for the tears, which seemed unstoppable. She went into a phone booth, one of the old kind you could step into and be private. She took a hankie from her bag, blew her nose and wiped her eyes. Then she dialled her editor's number.

'Mal? I've been delayed, I'm afraid. Can I come in at about four? Thanks.'

She left the phone booth and started to walk without knowing where she was going. Maybe by four o'clock she'd have recovered sufficiently to speak. Maybe the outward signs of her unhappiness would be under control. What would she do now? She felt like an amputee. Looking down, she let one foot follow the other. She stared at the pavement, at her shoes, without seeing anything. The silver mobile phone in her bag was making the noise that indicated a text message had been sent to it. I should have given it back to Gray, she thought. Like a ring. Like a love token. She wondered whether she ought to send it to him, but how could she do that? What if Maureen found it? Could she send it to the hospital? I'll throw it away, she decided. I'll throw it into a drain and it'll go down to the sewers. She scrabbled in her bag and brought it out to the light. I won't read his message, she thought. I won't.

The message said: *Know that I will always love you, Lydia* and she started crying all over again. She stood over a drain and nearly, very nearly, pushed the phone through the grating. I can't, she thought. I can't do it. She put the little silver rectangle back into her bag and went on walking.

July / August

Friday

Two days after Adrian had asked her to marry him, Zannah bought a notebook in the British Museum shop. Its shiny black cover printed with a pattern of roses and leaves; its very pale pink pages and the matching ribbon to mark a page were irresistible. It became her wedding notebook almost before she'd paid for it. She carried it with her always in a large handbag which fulfilled, according to Emily, much the same function as the shell of a snail: it was Zannah's home, in portable form. It was – Em's words again – beyond tidy. Zannah could always put her hand on anything she needed and there were no disgusting scraps of tissue or biscuit crumbs down there in the silky folds of the lining. Makeup lived in a pretty zip-up bag, made of silvery plastic. Pens and pencils rested in a little case, also silver. The novel she was reading was always in there too, with a proper bookmark to indicate where she'd got to. Cinema tickets, torn envelopes, empty crisp packets were nowhere to be seen. The wedding notebook lay beside whatever she happened to be reading, the two volumes propping one another up and keeping one another's covers unbent. The notebook was a treasure trove of ideas, cuttings neatly stuck in, lists, and doodles of flowers, dresses, decorations and anything else that Zannah felt she had to remember. Em was the only person who understood how she felt about notebooks: how every single one she'd ever bought made her feel dizzy with possibilities. This one, she'd confessed to her sister, had practically shouted at her from across the shop floor.

When Zannah had first announced her wedding plans to Em, she was taken aback by her sister's reaction. Emily knew her better than almost anyone, and yet even she didn't properly understand. Okay, she agreed that it was up to Zannah to decide what kind of ceremony she wanted, what kind of reception but, in her opinion, the whole thing was a waste of time, money and effort. Zannah found it embarrassing to explain, even to her sister, her reasons for wanting things to be done in this way.

She was behaving superstitiously. This wedding had to be as different as was humanly possible from her wedding with Cal. She wanted, even after several years, no reminders whatsoever of that day, when she'd thought she was embarking on a life of total happiness and love. The reasoning went: if I do everything differently when it comes to the wedding, then the outcome, the marriage, will be different too. She still remembered the immediate aftermath of her separation from Cal and how ill she'd been. That was what it had been: an illness.

On the morning after that night – the night she pushed out of her mind with something like a physical effort whenever it happened to float into it – she'd packed up Isis's things and a few clothes in a kind of daze and fled to her parents' house, like a wounded child. Isis was handed over to Ma and Pa and she lay in bed, weeping, sleeping, weeping again and feeling as though her misery was a stone she'd swallowed and couldn't expel from her body.

Ma used to bring Isis in to see her, and when that happened, Zannah sat up in bed and tried to cuddle her and talk to her, but she was so much like Cal that she always burst into tears again and buried herself in her pillows. I'm a useless mother too, she told herself. I can't look after my own child. I'm nothing.

Zannah realized now, after a few years had elapsed, that she'd had a breakdown. Not a major collapse, but still something that had taken some time to recover from. Gradually, slowly, she came back to herself. She and Isis stayed with Ma and Pa and Em for six weeks before she had felt strong enough to go back to the flat. Em came with her, which helped. It was lucky that she was about to start her job and needed a place to stay. But even with Em's company, the first few months were hard . . . harder than anything Zannah had ever done, but she had done it. Until a couple of years ago, she had still cried herself to sleep sometimes, especially after a day when Cal had come round to see Isis. Those were difficult to begin with. He'd occasionally ask her to forgive him and although in those days, when the parting was still raw and sore, she had sort of longed to agree, to get everything back to the way it had been, something inside her recoiled from the still-vivid images of her husband with another woman.

She was sitting in the staff room at St Botolph's, with the notebook open on her lap. Why on earth, she asked herself, am I harking back to those terrible days? It's all over now. I'm happy. I've found Adrian and I love him and he loves me and we're going to be together. And the manner of our getting together will be spectacular and quite different from what I had with Cal . . . what happened before.

The staff room was, according to Zannah and her friends, the ugliest room in the whole of London, with its porridge-coloured chairs, its sludge-beige walls and the mess of books, newspapers, leaflets, games equipment, lunch boxes, cardigans and spare pairs of shoes pushed into the corners. You grew used to it after the first few months and eventually stopped seeing what was around you. There wasn't time for contemplation in the whirlwind of school life, and even Zannah had stopped moaning about it. There was nothing to be done. Money was always needed somewhere else, which was fair enough.

'Problem?' said Louise. She was tall and skinny with round, John Lennon-type glasses and wore her long, fair hair twisted up and pinned to her head with a changing assortment of hair ornaments. She seemed unconscious of what she was wearing but always somehow managed to look both casual and elegant, in clothes that didn't shout at you but which you could be sure were expensive. You could lay bets that her black cardigan, slung over the back of a chair like a discarded rag, would be Agnès B or even Nicole Farhi. Her mother was French, which Zannah reckoned explained her particular style. Louise threw herself into the chair next to Zannah's and said, 'You're frowning on a Friday afternoon near the end of term. Surely some mistake.'

'She's busy, Lou,' said Claire, biting into a biscuit. She was Gemma's mother and Isis and Gemma were best friends. Zannah was grateful that her daughter had chosen to be buddies with someone whose mum she liked so much. She still hadn't made up her mind about the bridesmaids issue and in spite of Isis's constant nagging, she'd managed to fob off her daughter so far, declaring that such an important decision had to wait till other things were established, which wasn't quite true but seemed to satisfy Isis. She'd have to make up her mind eventually, but had persuaded Isis that it would be fun to discuss the matter at length over the summer holidays.

Claire was in a constant struggle with her weight which, in her words, 'the weight seems to be winning'. She was a good cook and quite unable to resist what came out of her oven. She often brought cakes and biscuits into the staffroom 'to undermine other people's ridiculous diets and bring them up to my size'. Her curly brown hair and light-up-the-room smile made her face almost beautiful, but she would never, she said, 'be any competition for Jennifer Aniston'. Now she said to Louise, 'Can't you see? She's in wedding mode. We're not going to get any sense out of her. Spit it out, Zannah. What's the problem? It's true. You don't look like a sunny bride-to-be.'

'Sunny's the last thing I am.' Zannah closed the notebook and put it back into her handbag. 'I'm having mother-in-law problems and I'm not even married.'

'Isn't she being very low-key and staying conveniently in Guildford?'

'She talks to me on the phone. She even emails me. Photos of floral arrangements, that sort of thing. I don't know ... I'll have to go and meet her one of these days and just tell her ...'

'Is this still about the venue? I thought you'd decided all that.'

'I've decided what I don't want. Well, almost. But Maureen has other ideas. She's keen on Kew. Can you believe it? Or a castle somewhere. You remember that ghastly lunch I told you about when she brought out these ideas and sat back waiting for me to say, "oh how lovely" and I didn't. I could see her becoming more and more frozen. And I tried. I kept telling her that it was up to me in the end, my wedding etcetera but that didn't go down too well. "Adrian is my son and it's his wedding as well" ... she sounded quite waspish. It doesn't take much to make her sound waspish, actually. She's been bombarding me ever since with ideas I hate. It's awful.'

'I've learned from experience,' said Claire, 'that mas-in-law are like kids. You have to start as you mean to go on. I laid down the law on the very first day. Things were going to be done my way or not at all. She could behave in my house or stay away. It was her choice.'

'You're unusual, Claire,' Louise pointed out. 'You get on well with your mother-in-law. Most people aren't so lucky. Think of all the jokes. There's got to be a reason for them.'

Zannah said, 'I got on well with my first mother-in-law. Cal's mum is a sweetie. Isis loves going down to visit her, so I'm still in touch.'

'And I get on well with mine,' said Claire 'because she knows I'd have nothing to do with her if she started any trouble. It's a fact that not only can you never change the man you're about to marry, you also aren't going to be able to alter his mum, or his relationship with her. I suppose I was in luck when I found Ian, and part of that luck was him having a nice mum. Lot nicer than mine, as a matter of fact.' Claire pulled a pile of exercise books out of her enormous holdall. Almost all of them had bent-over covers and spoke eloquently of the abysmal state in which Claire kept her possessions. 'Got to mark these before registration. Four B are eager to know what I think of their compositions about being a Victorian child. See you.' She went to sit at the table where the staff marked their work during school time.

Louise said, 'You don't have to listen to anyone, Zannah. If you don't want to have your reception in a castle, you don't have to. What about your mother? Can't you get her on your side?'

'Oh, she's on my side.' Zannah frowned. 'It's just that she lives so far away. And she seems ... I don't know. I'm a bit worried about her, actually. She isn't herself. She's fifty-two ... it could be the menopause, couldn't it? Does that make you not yourself?'

Louise nodded. 'My mum went completely bonkers. You ought to talk to yours about it, though. If she's having problems, wouldn't she want you to know?'

'I don't know if it's problems, exactly,' said Zannah. 'She was with us last night and she was just ... well, as though the stuffing had been knocked out of her. She'd been to see her editor and she's normally really excited and chatty after one of those visits but this time, she was staring into space for most of supper and could hardly even summon up the energy to read a story to Isis. That's very unusual. She's so good with her – they get on brilliantly. I asked her if Mal, her editor, had said anything, but she said no. Actually, she said, "No, it's not that at all," and when I asked her what it was, she clammed up.'

'Perhaps she and your dad have had a row? Could it be that?'

'I'm not sure, to be honest. I ought to ask her when we're alone, I suppose. She's very ... well, shy of talking about herself. Or maybe Em and I have always bent her ear so much with our problems that we're not used to asking her how she feels. I will, though. You're quite right. I have to speak to Ma and I have to point out to Maureen that it's my wedding. Sorry, make that *our* wedding. I will.'

'Invite her to lunch or something,' said Claire, turning round to face the others, unable to concentrate properly on her work. 'On your territory. Invite your mum and your great-aunt too. Then, with Emily, that'll make four against one. Good numbers. Dazzle her with your cooking. Fill her with comforting pasta and let her have it. And get Adrian on side beforehand. Lots of lovely sex usually persuades a man to agree to most things.'

Zannah laughed. 'I'll try it. Have to wait till the holidays now, but that's next week. I'm in the middle of making my guest-list and I haven't even sorted the church.' She sighed and opened her wedding notebook again, at the page headed: '*Churches.*'

This issue was causing Zannah some anxiety. She wasn't religious, but she had been christened and felt that a register office wedding, (like the ceremony she had gone through when she married Cal) wasn't quite a hundred per cent proper wedding. She knew this was complete nonsense, even without Em pointing out that if it was good enough for the Prince of Wales, it ought to be good enough for her. The theological ins and outs of a divorced person marrying in church didn't concern her. Because her first wedding had been a civil one, there was no problem. She wanted a nice vicar and a reasonable-looking building. Perhaps, Zannah thought, I'll ask Edie. She's a regular churchgoer. Zannah wrote the words *Ask Edie* under *Churches* in her elegant italic hand and felt better immediately. She let her mind stray to the matter of music. That was one of the best things about being married in church. You might have a real organist playing for you as you walked up to the altar and out of the church at the end. Under *Ask Edie* she wrote: *Not Mendelssohn's Wedding March.*

Six weeks. Gray thought of the days and days since he'd kissed Lydia . . . Joss . . . goodbye and that the people who put out all the crap about the healing power of time didn't know what they were talking about. He was lying in bed with a book propped open against his knees, pretending to read so that he did not have to engage fully with Maureen.

She was at the dressing-table, going through the ritual that she went through every night. It was taking, Gray registered, a hell of a long time. It probably always had done, but he'd never really noticed much till recently. For the last couple of years, this had been his best, his favourite time: a short period of privacy in which he wrote a good-night email to Lydia. He'd agreed with Maureen that it was convenient for him to deal with 'all that email nonsense' while she was going through what she called her 'routine'. He watched her, smoothing cream into her face, wiping it off with cotton wool, taking more cotton wool and wiping some clear liquid carefully over cheeks, chin, forehead and neck, then brushing her long hair for what seemed like many more strokes than the prescribed hundred and finally massaging a different cream from a different jar into her hands and arms. Gray felt a grudging admiration for the way she managed to do all that and still keep talking. Lately, some lines by Michael Drayton which Lydia had loved, and had once described as both economical and moving, had kept running through his head like a tune he couldn't stop humming:

Shake hands for ever, cancel all our vows
And when we meet at any time again
Be it not seen in either of our brows
That we one jot of former love retain.

Gray didn't know if he was capable of not showing any love when they met again. And they'd have to meet, at the wedding if not before. He sighed and tuned in to what Maureen was saying merely as a way of blocking out those lines, of escaping the yawning loss he still felt every night when work wasn't there to distract him from his feelings.

'I sometimes wonder, you know, if it's the money thing,' Maureen said. 'It costs about twelve thousand to have a reception at Kew and I'm not altogether sure of the Gratrixes' financial situation. Maybe we ought to offer to help, Graham. What d'you think? Would they be offended?'

'They might, I suppose,' he muttered. 'Though I don't expect they're rich, are they? Academics aren't usually.'

'But that house! Charlotte Parrish's house is quite grand, really. According to Adrian, it was an inheritance from her second husband.

There might not be any spare for grand receptions. I don't mind helping out, do you? It's surely too old-fashioned for words for the bride's family to do everything. And I get the impression ... now don't get me wrong, I think Zannah's a lovely young woman, but I do get the impression that she likes her own way.'

Maureen pronounced this last judgement as though she didn't devote every second of her time to making sure everyone danced to her tune. Gray had known since he married her that life would be much easier all round if he minimized the number of fights they had, and because Maureen had good judgement where domestic life was concerned, their marriage had been harmonious, for the most part. Now she'd turned to him and was asking his opinion.

'What do you think I ought to do?'

Gray was flummoxed for a moment. Then he recovered and said, 'Perhaps we could offer to pay for the catering, or something. That would be acceptable, wouldn't it? Worth trying, in any case.'

'You're so clever, Graham. Honestly, I do wish you didn't have to work so hard and could be more involved in this wedding. You've obviously got a talent for being diplomatic and that's so important. I'll suggest it to Zannah when I speak to her next. She wasn't as co-operative as she might have been last time we met. She's invited me to her flat, did I tell you? You, too, if you're free. Joss is coming, and so is Mrs Parrish. Like a summit conference. Next Saturday, a week tomorrow. We really do have to arrange the venue. Time is marching on.'

And it stops for no man, thought Gray. He said, 'No, you go on your own, Maureen. It'll be easier without men, I'm sure.'

'You're probably right.' She slipped into bed beside him and the fragrance of her liberally-applied body lotion (Oscar de la Renta, which he'd been buying her at Christmas for years) wafted over to him. Her nightdress was pale blue satin and her breasts, still full and creamy, showed above the lace trimming. Any other man, he reflected, would thank his lucky stars to have such a wife beside him. He knew that if he turned to her, took her in his arms, she would respond, but he couldn't muster the energy. In the past, thinking about Lydia was enough to give him an erection, but since they'd parted six weeks ago (*'Since there's no help, come let us kiss and part.'* That bloody poem again!) he was too unhappy even to feel desire.

Maureen leaned over and kissed him. She'd clearly been aiming for his mouth but hadn't quite made it, which didn't seem to worry her.

'Night, darling,' she said. 'I'll think about your idea. I like it, but I just hope Zannah won't object.'

She turned out the light on her side of the bed and lay back on the pillows. Canapés and table decorations would fill her dreams, Gray knew. As for me, he thought, as he turned off his own bedside light, I hope I'm exhausted enough to fall asleep at once. Lately, this had been hard work and there were often nights when what he saw as he closed his eyes was Lydia's face. Lydia's smile. Now he had to imagine her sitting at the same table as Maureen in a few days. How would she feel about that? He imagined her brow furrowing with anxiety, her beautiful mouth tightening with the tension. God, her mouth. He could taste it. He closed his eyes. He had never felt less sleepy in his life. How long, he wondered, is this torture going to go on?

Emily opened the door to the flat as quietly as she could. Zannah was with Adrian and wouldn't be back tonight and Cal had been babysitting for Isis, as he often did. Whenever he stayed over, he slept in the lounge on the sofa, which pulled out into a fairly reasonable bed. Emily fully expected to find the room in almost complete darkness, with only the landing light to guide her upstairs to her bedroom, but as soon as she put her head round the door, she saw that the sofa was still in sofa mode and Cal was stretched out on it, reading a novel with the kind of moody, blue, dramatically-lit cover that shouted 'non-cosy thriller' right across the room.

'Oh,' she said. 'I thought you'd be tucked up and asleep. What are you doing up so late?'

'It's not that late, is it? I was reading. Can't-put-it-down stuff, this.'

'Hmm.' Emily sniffed. 'Did you and Isis have fun?'

'Yup. We always do. She's great. We watched a DVD of *Singin' in the Rain*.'

'Your choice, right?'

'She loved it. It's my duty as a father to bring her up to appreciate proper movies. She can watch *Finding Nemo* and the *Princess* thingummies with other people.'

'I'm going to have a cup of tea,' Emily said. 'How about you?'

'God, I've been dying for one.'

Emily didn't bother asking why he hadn't made it for himself. He'd been waiting unconsciously for someone to come along and do it for him. Cal, unlike Adrian, knew his way round a kitchen and especially this one, which had, after all, been his once. But whether they were dab hands or totally useless, men's longing for a thing always seemed to grow amazingly when a woman was around to hand it to them. Cal followed her into the kitchen and sat down to wait for his tea. Emily opened the cupboard and took out the chocolate Hobnobs.

'Hobnobs! Great!' Cal took one out of the packet at once. He continued to speak through a mouthful of biscuit. 'I had a look in Zannah's studio after I'd put Isis to bed.'

'Are you allowed in there?'

'Why not? It's not private, is it? She is my ex-wife, you know.'

'Then I'd say it probably is private. The 'ex' counts for more than the 'wife.' If you see what I mean.'

Cal considered this. 'Okay. Sorry. No harm done, though, so don't let on to Zannah. No need to get her in a tizz over nothing.'

'Right.' Emily thought Cal looked very young. He was now on his second biscuit. She felt like putting out a hand and brushing his unruly hair away from his eyes. Should she tell him he really did need a haircut? No, it wasn't her business and she liked it anyway. One of the best things about Cal was that he didn't give a damn how he looked. She said, 'There's not much in there these days. Just a whole load of wedding stuff.'

Cal sighed. Biscuit number three was being eased out of the packet. He bit into it and said, 'Can you work out what's going on in her head, Em? I can't. I think she's completely crazy. I think you all are, actually.'

'Not me. Count me out. I've spent hours trying to talk her out of all that palaver. I've even suggested a flight to Las Vegas, a chapel with Elvis playing and attendants in white-fringed leather suits. She's not having it. She wants a proper wedding and she's not going to be dissuaded. They're all in it – Adrian, his mother, even Charlotte, for heaven's sake. They're itching to arrange and fix up and sort out and hire and decide and send out invitations, you name it. It's exhausting and we're still more than ten months away. I don't know how I'm going to survive it.'

'What about your parents, though? They've got more sense, surely. And they're the ones who're going to have to pay for most of it, too. Isn't it traditional for the bride's lot to foot the bill?'

'Ma, I'm sure, thinks the whole thing's mad, but she's not saying a word. She doesn't want to annoy Zannah. And although he keeps going on about how silly it is, Pa's secretly rather enjoying it, I reckon. You know how keen he is on tribal rituals etcetera. They'll chip in, I expect. Adrian's folks. He's loaded, you know.'

'Must be what Zannah sees in him. Can't be his looks. Or his scintillating conversation.'

Emily was surprised. It was the first time she'd heard him express any kind of opinion about Adrian. And that stuff about his looks. He could only have seen him in photographs Isis had shown him. Cal was jealous. He must be, or he wouldn't have sounded so bitter, so unlike his usual self.

'He's very handsome, Cal. Everyone says so. And what do you know about his conversation anyway? You've never met him.'

'Makes no difference. I know his sort. He's not nearly as charming, funny and altogether delightful as me, I bet. Is he? Be honest.' He helped himself to another biscuit and added, 'Put these away, Em. I can't stop myself.'

As Emily returned the Hobnobs to the cupboard, she thought about what Cal had said. It was true. No one was as charming, funny and delightful as he was, but she couldn't say so. She couldn't confess to anyone her most deeply-buried secret wish: that when he knew Zannah and Adrian were married, when he realized they were idyllically happy together, he'd move on. Start looking for someone else in a way he hadn't seemed able to while Zannah was still single. When that happened, Emily wanted be there. She'd be the first person he saw when the spell was broken and he'd suddenly grasp that it had been her, Emily, all along ... she was the one for him. It was this fantasy that had persuaded her to support Zannah in her wedding plans even more quickly than she otherwise would have done. What Emily truly wanted was to see her sister married as happily and speedily as possible to the man of her dreams, leaving the field clear for her. What a ridiculous idea it was! Dreams were rubbish and this one was a bigger load of crapola than most. She knew full well that there was more chance of

Cal falling over a precipice than falling for her. Never mind, she told herself. I'm not going to lie around languishing on a sofa, pining away. She squared her shoulders and began to hum 'I Will Survive' under her breath.

'I think,' she said, sitting down opposite Cal, 'that what Zannah and women like her really want is to be the star of their very own spectacular theatrical production. They want the drama. They want costumes, a set, props, music, lights ... the whole caboodle. Photographers. Makeup artists. Hairdressers. And Zannah's worse than most because she wants to design things as well. Not only her dress, Isis's dress and the decorations, but she's developing views on things like food. And flowers. And what kind of stationery they ought to have. She's got a list of hates too. That's fun. I'd like to add to it, but don't dare.'

'What's on the hate list?'

'Peach. Persil white rather than Chinese white.'

'What's that when it's at home?'

'Don't ask. It's a kind of white that doesn't dazzle and sparkle...sort of understated. Silver bells on anything. Cake icing like plaster. Bride and groom statues on the cake. Glitter on anything. Bare shoulders. Mendelssohn's *Wedding March*. Motorway hotels for the reception. Pink invitation cards. That sort of thing.'

'Bloody hell,' said Cal. 'It's a minefield, isn't it?' He frowned. 'Em, can I ask you something?'

'Go on.' Emily held her breath. What was he going to say?

'Is Adrian okay? I mean ... you know I asked you to look out for Isis ... what's been happening on that front?'

'He's okay. Really. You don't have to worry, Cal. Zannah would never get involved with someone who didn't get on with Isis.'

Cal took a sip of his tea. It was obvious that he was making a real effort to say nothing. She prompted him. 'Why're you being so quiet? It's quite worrying when you do that. You don't think I've neglected to do what you asked?'

'No, of course not. Just that I sense a kind of ... I dunno ... a reserve in Isis when I try to talk about him. She's probably doing it for my benefit. She's very keen to tell me every detail of the wedding arrangements but when I ask her about Adrian she just says, 'Oh he's okay' and changes the subject. She doesn't sound that enthusiastic.'

'Well, she wouldn't be to you, would she? It's obvious, Cal. She'd see it as disloyalty if she praised Adrian to the skies.'

'Really? At her age? Are children so subtle?'

'It's not subtle, Cal. She knows you'd be a bit jealous if she enthused too much. And you would. You'd hate it if all she did was talk about how wonderful Adrian is. She's a clever girl and understands an awful lot, you know.'

'Yes, you're quite right, Em.' He put out a hand and squeezed her arm. 'You're clever too. But you tell me ... he's not wonderful, is he? Adrian?'

'I don't think so,' Emily said. 'But, then, I'm not marrying him.'

'Zannah does think so is the implication.'

'It's quite normal, you know. It's what you're supposed to think about your fiancé.'

Cal sighed. 'Quite right. I'm off to bed now, Em. Ta for the tea and biccies.'

He stood up and blew a kiss in her direction, then disappeared into the lounge. Emily could hear the sofa being transformed into a bed. She took the cups to the sink and decided to leave them unwashed till morning. Why, she thought, as she made her way upstairs, do I suddenly feel a bit gloomy? She shook her head. No good reason. Things would seem better in the morning. She sat on the end of her bed, sighed and kicked her shoes off, then lay back on the pillows staring up at the ceiling, suddenly drained of every bit of energy. I must make a point of watching Isis more closely next time Adrian's around. Of course, it was natural for Cal to be concerned, but Emily was sure everything was okay, really. Zannah would be the first to notice if it wasn't.

'You're not listening, Adrian. How many times do I have to say it? You just keep going round and round in a bloody circle and saying the same things over and over again. I am not prepared to get married in a castle. Or in a public place of any significance. And I don't want a hundred and fifty people at our wedding. Seventy-five is the limit. Fifty would be better. Where were you when I explained this to you?'

Zannah understood perfectly at that moment why cartoons of married people often showed the wife wielding a rolling-pin and advancing on her husband. If she'd had such an implement to hand, Adrian would have been in trouble. They were, she realized with something of a shock to the heart, having their first row.

'It's not just your wedding,' said Adrian. 'It's mine as well, or had you forgotten that?'

'No, I hadn't. We've discussed it at length and you never uttered a squeak about castles and lakes and Kew Gardens. Never once. This is all your mother's idea. You're speaking for her, aren't you?'

'So what if I am? She's allowed a say, isn't she?'

'Maybe. I'm not sure she's allowed even that, if you really want to know, but what she isn't allowed is a decision. The numbers, for instance. You can't pretend we've got a hundred and fifty friends. We haven't.'

'You've got to take into account my family's friends. Doc's colleagues. My mother's friends. My colleagues. Your parents', too, come to that.'

'I'm not having a wedding filled with stuffed shirts from your bloody bank, or my pa's university, or your mother's tennis-club cronies, or the massed ranks of medical staff from Doc's hospital.' Zannah was shouting now. 'You've taken leave of your senses. I want you, our families, our friends and their children. And that's it. That is *it*! I haven't got seventy-five friends. I don't know if this wedding's going to happen at all, the way you're going on and on about it. You're talking about a completely different occasion.'

'It's a family occasion.' Adrian was evidently trying to keep a grip on his temper.

'It is, of course it is, but a family occasion doesn't mean what you think it means. It's about having your family around you when you celebrate getting married. It's not about impressing every single person you've ever come across in your life, most of whom you'll never see again.'

Zannah stopped herself saying: *And about whom I couldn't give a damn.*

'Well, I know it's not *about* impressing people, but what if you can impress people while you're getting married? What's so bad about that?' He was yelling at her now.

'What's bad about it is that it's ridiculous. This is supposed to be *our* day. Ours and the people we love. D'you love your colleagues? Do you even know who half of them are? It's pathetic!'

Adrian let out a long breath and threw his arms into the air. 'Fucking hell, Zannah, you don't half dish it out! Just calm down, okay? I'll talk to my mother. Better yet, you talk to her when she comes round to see you. I don't see why I should take the flak.'

'Do you admit it? D'you admit I'm right? About the wedding? It's our day, Adrian.' She was speaking quietly now, to calm both of them. It was a technique that sometimes worked with fractious children. Was she really going to have to treat her husband-to-be as though he were a bad-tempered kid? Apparently she was. What she wanted to say was: *Your bloody bossy mother wants it her way to impress the people she knows and not my friends. Not even our friends. I'm not having that.*

'I suppose so. I admit I don't want to spend the evening fighting with you. That's the main thing I admit. Come over here and let's make up.'

'This was a row, wasn't it? Our first row?' Zannah seized on his change of mood and went to sit next to him on the sofa where he'd flung himself. He'd made the admission. She had every intention of holding him to it.

'I suppose it was. Not bad, really. Only one row in six months.'

'But I'm right, aren't I?' She started to stroke his hand. 'You can't really want that sort of thing, a huge affair filled with faces you've never seen in your life?'

'Haven't given it much thought. All I've been thinking about is you. Come here.'

'You're a useless person to have a row with,' Zannah said, relaxing into his embrace. 'You never listen properly. You just get hold of a point and bring it out again and again. Sometimes you don't even change the words. You just repeat yourself.'

'What's the point of changing the words if it's the only thing you want to say?'

'Never mind,' said Zannah. 'I give up. We'll just have to steer clear of rows from now on.'

'Fine by me,' said Adrian. He started to kiss Zannah just under her ear, and she closed her eyes. 'Whatever you decide is okay. Really. Am I forgiven?'

Her answer might have been influenced by his hand, which had found its way under her skirt and begun stroking her thigh. She looked into his eyes, at his face. He was so handsome and so contrite that she could literally feel her heart jumping a little in her chest and there was that hand, moving over her skin. She said, 'Of course you're forgiven. But I'm not going to change my mind.'

'I don't care,' said Adrian. 'You can fight it out with my mum. You're what I want. Just you. Always. I love you, Zannah. D'you love me?'

'Yes,' said Zannah. 'You know I do.'

She closed her eyes as she spoke. She loved him, of course she did, but she had always had a problem with those three words. Saying them, because they were so weighed down with meaning, with a special importance, made her feel insincere and actressy even when she was loving most passionately. She and Cal had talked about it once and he'd agreed with her. He said that those three words had been used too often, that that particular currency was debased. Also, she remembered, he'd told her it didn't matter. There were ways of showing your love. There were even words that expressed the emotion without using what everyone else used. He'd had a few funny ones. *I want to be the person who finishes your chips* and *I'll never allow anyone else to scrub your back for you.* For a split second Zannah felt something like a sharp pain all over. How come thinking about Cal could still do that to her sometimes? It was as though her body was remembering a sorrow it was meant to have forgotten long ago. Pull yourself together, she thought. You're lucky to have Adrian. Lucky to be having a new start, a new marriage and a perfect wedding day.

Adrian was kissing her, and making moaning sounds in her ear, and soon they were naked together on the sofa and the quarrel was forgotten. Everything she'd been thinking was swept away by the smell of him, his mouth on hers, his hands touching her where she needed to be touched.

Much later, Zannah lay in bed suffering from Wedding Head. The 'head' was a Gratrix family tradition, started by Joss. When one of her daughters found it hard to fall asleep, she'd say: 'Oh, you've got Exam Head.' Or 'you've got Christmas Eve Head.' Or 'Boyfriend Head.' Anything that filled the space in your mind and prevented you relaxing was labelled in that way. It felt to Zannah like an endless loop of thoughts going round and round in her brain, repeating themselves over and over, which she couldn't stop. Since her engagement, Wedding

Head had been responsible for quite a few hours of lost slumber.

There was nothing to do for this condition but live through it. She tried to distract herself by thinking about Adrian's bedroom. No expense had been spared but it wasn't to her taste. In her opinion, it said 'debonair bachelor about town' far too loudly. There was an awful lot of maroon. Those curtains, for example, wouldn't have been out of place in the kind of corporate hotel she hated. She didn't altogether trust Maureen's taste, although you couldn't fault the quality of what she'd chosen. The most expensive wasn't necessarily the most beautiful. Zannah was sure, though they hadn't discussed it, that they wouldn't stay here after they were married. For one thing, there wasn't a bedroom for Isis. No, they'd have to find a house, and she was determined to oversee the decoration. She'd consult Adrian, of course, but he wasn't really interested in such things and, best of all, he wouldn't keep going on about how much things cost. Briefly, she wondered about their bedroom, its colours, then firmly put any such daydreams out of her head. One thing at a time, she told herself. I have to concentrate on the wedding.

She looked at the curve of Adrian's shoulder in the bed beside her and touched it gently. He wouldn't wake up, she knew. No Wedding Head for him. She remembered their lovemaking. The sex they had was always athletic, imaginative and thrilling. She sometimes found herself at odd times of day, even when she was in the middle of teaching, remembering something from the previous night then feeling herself blush. Her bloody redhead's skin could be a real pain sometimes.

Now Adrian was out for the count and she was awake with her mind racing. She turned on to her right side and wondered about Isis. What sort of an evening had they had together, she and Cal? And had Em met someone fantastic at the party she'd gone to? She deserved a really, really special boyfriend, Zannah thought, and slid at last into sleep.

Thursday

'If this is what we have to do now, imagine what it's going to be like in 2012 when we're actually celebrating the Olympics,' said Zannah, who was standing rather precariously on a desk in Louise's classroom, helping to take down the banners, streamers and balloons that the children had stuck up everywhere before the previous day's announcement of London's win. She'd agreed to help with the clearing-up over break, which Louise conceded was a sign of true friendship.

'Nearly finished,' Louise said. 'If we're quick, there'll be time for a coffee in the staff-room before the next lesson.'

Suddenly, the head came into the room. Mrs Greenford was the kind of woman who never ran, who was never flustered, yet she came bursting in without knocking and in what for her was a hurry.

'Zannah, there you are. I've been looking for you. There's a Mrs Parrish on the telephone. She says she's been trying to get you on your mobile, but they're all down at the moment. There's been ... well, it's an emergency. I've told the rest of the staff a moment ago, but of course you two are here ...'

Zannah climbed down and picked up her bag from the chair where she'd left it. 'What emergency?'

'They've closed the Underground. The police are speaking of bombs. No one has many details yet, but we've been told to stay with the children until their parents come to fetch them.'

Bombs on the Underground .... Zannah felt cold. Em ... Adrian! No, Adrian was in Edinburgh. He'd flown up last night. He was coming back tomorrow. Adrian was safe, from whatever it was. How odd ... Being frightened and no longer being frightened had happened to her at exactly the same moment. She hadn't known she was scared till the fear had left her.

In her head, a thousand questions immediately appeared. She didn't seem able to articulate them as words, but they were like a mist in her head, a confusion, a muddle. She was conscious of Mrs Greenford walking behind her down the long corridor to her office. My mobile ... Em might have tried to leave a message. And Cal. Where would he be? At work? Where were the bombs? What was happening?

In the office, she picked up the receiver.

'Charlotte? It's me ...'

Zannah closed her eyes and listened to Charlotte's voice, explaining, reassuring, setting out all the facts, one after another. 'And now that I've spoken to you, Zannah, I'll phone Joss again and tell her you and Isis are safe at school.'

'Thanks, Charlotte. And I've just remembered, Em was supposed to be going to a fashion shoot in Chelsea.'

'She got as far as Euston and was turned off the bus. She rang from a phone box. She's walked home, apparently. And she's rung your parents, so they know we're all safe.'

But Cal ... Where was he? She said, 'Thanks, Charlotte. I can't tell you how grateful I am to you for this. I'll phone Ma and Pa later. And Maureen and Doc. 'Bye.'

'Sit down, dear,' said Mrs Greenford, unexpectedly. 'Use this phone. There are all kinds of problems with mobiles. Come and tell me in the staff-room when you've finished.'

As soon as she was alone, Zannah scrabbled in her handbag for her mobile and found it nestled next to her book. She always turned it off during school hours. Now her fingers were almost out of control and she nearly dropped it in her haste to turn it on again. Five new messages. They must have got through before all mobiles were turned off, or scrambled or whatever had happened. Adrian: *'Darling, are you all right? Phone as soon as you get this.'* Ma: *'I've just spoken to Charlotte. Em's all right. Ring me.'* Tears in her mother's voice. Em: *'I'm at home. Phoned Ma and Pa. Ring when you get this.'* Maureen: *'Please ring us, Zannah. Hope you're all okay. Adrian is so worried about you.'* And Cal. *'Zannah? You and Isis okay? And Em? Please phone. I'm in Hampshire at Mum's but trying to get back to town soonest. Hope you're at school, Zannah. Please phone.'* A long silence on the line. *'Couldn't cope without you, you know.'*

Zannah used the school phone to dial Cal's mobile. No signal. She'd have to try again later. Or perhaps he was at the office. She dialled his work number and managed at last to get put through to his desk after speaking to three different people. He answered almost at once as though he'd been waiting with the phone in his hand for her to ring.

'Oh, Cal . . .'

'Zannah.' A long exhalation, as though he'd been holding his breath. 'You and Isis okay?'

'We're fine. At school. I thought you might be down there . . . in the City, near all this . . .'

Tears of relief came to Zannah's eyes. She wouldn't have to tell Isis her dad was hurt. Or dead. Some children would hear bad news tonight. How did the men who made the bombs and thought so carefully about their dispersal look their own children in the eye? Sleep? Live? She listened to Cal's voice telling her to take care. Then she rang off and dialled Adrian's number. *Couldn't cope without you* ... Cal had said. Why was she so pleased about that? Ridiculous, after all this time since the divorce. Before she rang Adrian, a thought flashed through her mind: I rang Cal first. I phoned him before I phoned Adrian. What does that mean? It means I was thinking of Isis, that's all. Her father. She took a deep breath and dialled the Edinburgh number he'd given her.

'Adrian? Darling, it's me. Yes, we're fine. At school. Yes . . . yes, we'll take care. You take care too.'

One phone call after another. Ma, Em, Maureen. At last Zannah stood up and made her way to the staff-room. Isis, all the other children, everyone who'd been so happy celebrating the Olympic win only yesterday. They'd have to be told something. They'd have to be shielded from the pictures. There were sure to be pictures everywhere. She rang Em as she walked along the corridor.

'Em? Take the fuse out of the TV plug or something before we get home. We can put it in later when Isis is in bed . . . . Yes, I know she's got to see something some time, but not tonight, okay? Not till I've tried to explain it. Reassure her a bit. Just for tonight, okay? We'll tell her the TV's broken. I don't care what kind of a fuss she makes. She won't, anyway. She'll be fine. Ta. See you soon.'

They'd all know soon enough, the children. There would be no school tomorrow, but Mrs Greenford would say something about it in assembly on Monday. Zannah had no idea how she would do that without terrifying the kids. And Isis will want to know everything, but tonight I'm going to lie to her if I have to, Zannah thought.

'But what if,' said Isis, sitting up in bed and looking serious, 'the bombs start a fire in the Tube and it just rushes down the tunnels to where we are? To our Tube station? Maybe there are tunnels under this house. It could come right up to the houses, couldn't it?'

'No, darling. That won't happen, I promise,' said Zannah, trying to sound braver than she felt. It sounded an altogether logical idea to her: fire whooshing out of control, fanned by the draughts ... there were always draughts down there ... licking through the darkness, leaping up and up to reach the houses, a conflagration, an inferno. She said, 'No, it's okay now, really. The police and the firemen have got everyone out and some people are in hospital, but no fires any longer. They've all been put out now. Really.'

'Are you sure? No more fires?'

'No,' said Zannah. 'No fires. You go to sleep.'

Isis lay down and stared up at the ceiling. 'Finn said some people died. Is that true?'

Isis admired Finn. Would it be wise for Zannah to contradict her daughter's friend? Should she lie? She'd been determined to do that, but in the end, it wasn't possible. On Monday morning, all kinds of details would be spoken about in the playground, so perhaps it was better that they came from Zannah than from someone else.

'Some people died, yes.'

'Is it anybody we know?'

'No,' said Zannah.

'It's still sad, though,' said Isis. 'I still feel sad, even though I don't know them.'

'Yes,' said Zannah. 'Of course you do. It's sad, and there's nothing to be done about that, but there won't be any fires now and no more bombs.'

'Promise?'

'Promise.'

There's a lie, thought Zannah, if ever there was one. But if it lets Isis sleep tonight, I don't care.

Wednesday

This is the sort of scene, Charlotte thought, that I used to conjure up when I was in prison, although I didn't know who'd be in it then. This is the sort of day that makes it hard to believe less than a week has gone by since the Underground trains and the bus were bombed. That bus, a red London bus, opened up like a tin can; a bus full of people. Since that Thursday, her head had been filled with the most unbearable pictures. It was hard not to conjure up what it must have been like down there in the tunnels when the media flooded your head with images that were impossible to erase: phone videos flickering and flickering. Everyone pixellated, glowing, walking silently, seemingly calmly, like shadows one after another down the tunnels. Bravery. Gallantry. Sorrow. Defiance. And London going back to work, down into the Tube, up into the big red buses, straight away. Val, who never went to central London if she could possibly help it, had made a special trip last Saturday. *Just to show the bastards that I can and I bloody well will*, she'd said. Charlotte read the newspapers obsessively for a couple of days, then stopped. It was too much. There was too much to take in. And she was certainly not going to spoil today by allowing herself to think about such things.

It's a sunny day, she told herself. My great-niece and her daughter are sitting on the grass under a tree in my garden. Edie, Val and I are at a table on the terrace, with the remains of a good chocolate cake on a flowered china plate. There's a pretty teapot standing among the cups and saucers. Silver spoons catch the sunlight. She closed her eyes. She scarcely ever, these days, thought of the time when the sky was what was visible from the small square of her cell window, when she couldn't walk out of her own front door and down the road. No one who hadn't been in prison understood properly what it was not to be able to do simple things: choose a pair of shoes, buy a ticket for the cinema, ride on the top deck of a bus. On the day she was released, Charlotte had vowed to enjoy the small things, the things that everyone took for granted, and she'd stuck to her resolve. This meant that she ignored nothing that gave her pleasure. An apple. A freshly ironed blouse. Clean surfaces in her kitchen. She realized that this was the secret of happiness. The real sadnesses: the cruelty of Nigel, her first husband, the death of Gus, her second husband, her childlessness, the injustice of her imprisonment – even those, though they never stopped being painful, were not as desperate as they might have been. Each had what some would have called a silver lining, though Charlotte never did. Augustus Parrish, for instance … darling Gus … had left her this house, and it was still haunted by him in the nicest possible way.

The greatest sorrow of Charlotte's life was the death of her younger sister in a car crash when Joss was ten years old. She herself had been only thirty. The horror of that – the car, ripped open, metal no more use than paper when it came to protecting the passengers – was made both better and worse by the fact that she had had to do everything. There were no parents to help her and no other siblings. Overnight, she'd become a mother to Joss. It fell to her to comfort the child and help her through the loss of both parents while she herself was still raw with pain. And, of course, to make things more difficult, Joss had come to live with her while she was still fighting for compensation for wrongful imprisonment.

When Charlotte was released, she had almost no money. In those days, Gus was no more than a person she'd glimpsed on visits to her own lawyer's office. He'd made a point of acquainting himself with the details of her case and one day, after a particularly gruelling session with a dry and rather unsympathetic elderly partner, he'd followed her out of the office and invited her to have tea with him. That had been the beginning of a relationship which had brought her nothing but good things.

Her flat in those days was not much more than a glorified bedsitter in a seedy part of Kensington. Charlotte had to work to provide for herself and Joss, whose parents had left a little money but not nearly enough. No one would consider giving an ex-con a job as an accountant, even though she'd been innocent. Every firm she approached had been sympathetic but adamant. She would be 'bad for business' in some indefinable way. Even after she married Gus, Charlotte had worked for years as a secretary in an advertising agency. Then Gus came into his grandfather's money, about twenty years ago, and they had moved into this house, where she'd lived ever since. When they first came here, Gus had asked her: 'Are you so devoted to your work that you can't bear to think of not doing it?' And she had told him, quite truthfully, that nothing would give her greater pleasure than to stay at home and work at making the house beautiful; their life together the very best it could be.

'Charlotte, wake up!' said Edie. 'You've dozed off again.'

'Nonsense,' said Charlotte. 'I just had my eyes closed.'

'Hmm,' said Edie. 'Have another slice of cake. Or a scone.'

'No, thank you. I'll have some more tea, though. Would you like some?'

Zannah had wandered up from the end of the garden and sat down beside Charlotte. 'I'll have some too, Edie. Thanks. It's such a gorgeous day, isn't it?'

Zannah, with her fair skin, had to be careful of the sun. She was wearing a very flattering wide-brimmed hat and a cotton dress in a shade of blue Charlotte always thought of as heliotrope ... a blue on its way to being mauve.

Zannah said, 'The garden's looking spectacular, Val. You must have been working overtime on it.'

'I do the brainwork, dear,' said Val, 'and the fiddly bits. I have some nice young men to do the heavy stuff.'

'How are the wedding preparations going, Zannah?' said Edie. She was knitting something shapeless in pale yellow wool on very fine needles. No one had ever seen a finished garment Edie had made. Charlotte had come to the conclusion long ago that knitting was just a kind of camouflage. There were stories of how Edie had managed to outwit not only violent spouses who threatened the women in the refuge she was involved with, but also their lawyers. 'Don't let the sweet manner fool you,' Charlotte told Joss once. 'She's about as sweet as a lioness and more obstinate than a beach full of donkeys.' Edie herself claimed that the knitting relaxed her and soothed her mind. It was, she said, as good as a tranquillizer.

Zannah sighed. 'Maureen, Adrian's mother, is nagging me about the venue. She wants something really grand and I just . . . I don't know. I don't seem to be able to convey to her the sort of wedding I'm after. I want something beautiful but not enormous. Intimate and pretty and not grand. I don't want more than seventy-five people.. She wants droves of them . . . oh, I don't want to bore you with this.'

'I find it fascinating,' said Edie. 'Other people's weddings always are. My own wasn't much fun – in the middle of winter and my dress was far too thin. I was blue by the time we went home for the reception. My mother and grandmother had made everything themselves, from the cake to the sandwiches. That'd never do these days.'

'Mum, look,' said Isis, running up the steps to the terrace. 'Look what I've done.'

She held up the sketchbook in which she'd been drawing.

Zannah laughed. 'Lovely, darling. It's beautiful.' Isis had produced a dozen new designs for her own bridesmaid's dress. Zannah turned to the others and said, 'My daughter is almost as obsessed as I am. Have a bit of cake, Isis.'

Isis put the sketchbook down and sat on the top step of the terrace with her plate on her lap.

'I think,' said Val, 'that I'd like to have my reception in a garden. Like this one. You could put up a marquee just there below the terrace and decorate the trees down by the fence and people could wander about on the grass. Lovely.'

For a few moments, no one said anything. Then Zannah said thoughtfully, gazing around her, 'I've considered gardens, of course. It'd be almost my best option, but . . .'

Charlotte smiled. 'I think,' she said, 'that I've been more than usually slow. Val's right. This garden is the perfect venue for the reception. Would you consider it, Zannah?'

'Are you sure? Really?' Zannah stood up. She walked down to the lawn and looked up at the terrace and the house. 'It's totally and absolutely perfect, Charlotte. Wonderful. Oh, it's the best idea ever. But won't it put you out? You'd have marquee people and caterers and florists swarming all over the place. Could you stand it? The disruption?'

'I'd be honoured,' said Charlotte. 'Truly. It'll be magnificent.'

Zannah sat down again, and picked up Isis's sketchbook. She began to draw. 'I'm thinking of something like this,' she said. 'What d'you reckon?'

In a few quick pencil strokes, Zannah had drawn a beautiful tent, with flaps pulled back, and the house behind it. In the foreground, she'd sketched in a few people with glasses in their hands. 'I just hope,' she said 'that Adrian likes it. Oh, how could he not? It's gorgeous.'

'Marquees these days,' said Val, 'can be terribly luxurious, can't they? And I'm sure you could decorate it yourself. Though I suppose there'd be people to consult if you needed to. Gosh, it's going to be fun. You must let us help. I can be very useful in the garden. I'll make it my business to see that everything's tickety-boo in that department.'

'Thanks, Val. I'm so grateful to all of you,' said Zannah.

'Mummy and I can do the decorations,' said Isis. 'For the marquee. We're good at decorating things.'

'I'm sure you are, dear,' said Charlotte. 'It'll look wonderful.' She turned to Zannah and added, 'I want this to be my present to you and Adrian. The house and garden. And I insist on paying for the hire of the marquee.'

Zannah went to kiss her. 'I'm speechless,' she said, wiping away a tear. 'Oh, God, I'm crying, Charlotte. You're so good to me.'

'It's my great pleasure.' Charlotte hugged her tight. 'I love you, Zannah. Your wedding day must be exactly as you want it to be. Be happy.'

'I am happy. I can't wait to tell Adrian. And Ma, on Saturday when she comes to dinner. And Maureen. I'm sure she'll love the idea once she hears about it.'

Charlotte wasn't convinced of that, but she said nothing. Let Zannah have a few days of pleasurable anticipation.

'Edie,' Zannah said, 'I meant to ask you before, but it went out of my head. What should I do about arranging a church? I'm useless when it comes to churches, I'm afraid. Would you help me?'

Edie put her knitting down on her lap and said, 'If you're not in a hurry, I can take you with me to midweek evensong round the corner at St James's. You must have passed it a thousand times on your way here. I often go midweek. It's a very nice service.'

Zannah blushed. 'I feel so guilty. I have noticed the church, you're right, but without seeing it, really. Can you introduce me to the vicar? Or whoever it is who agrees to marry people. Honestly, I am sorry for being so ignorant, Edie.'

'Never mind,' said Edie. 'Better late than never.' She glanced at her watch. 'I'll go upstairs and get ready. We'll leave in twenty minutes.'

'I'm very grateful,' Zannah said. 'I hope I'm properly dressed for church.'

'You look lovely,' Edie said. She picked up a flowered bag from the flagstones, thrust her knitting into it, stood up and made her way into the house.

Even though she only went into them at Christmas and Easter, Zannah had an idealised notion of churches and strong opinions about what she liked when it came to ecclesiastical architecture. She hadn't given proper attention to St James's, that was true, but she adored visiting cathedrals and abbeys as a tourist if not as a believer. She liked church decor – ornate altar screens, statuary, carved wooden pews and especially stained-glass windows. Colouring glass and using it to make pictures was, she reckoned, one of the best ideas any artist had ever had. She often wondered who'd first thought of doing such a brilliant thing. As she and Edie walked sedately along the pavement and round the corner (the church really was very close to Charlotte's house) she found herself wishing most fervently that it might be suitable. How convenient for the guests to be able to walk from the service to the reception!

St James's occupied a large corner plot, and the grounds were extensive. Zannah noticed the trees first: chestnuts and plane trees and a lot of lawn going up to the church porch. A traditional shape, vaguely Victorian Gothic, greyish brick, and best of all, a spire. There's something about a spire, Zannah thought, that's just that little bit more churchy and elegant than a squarish tower. This church even had a few rather undersized flying buttresses.

Inside, there was a vaulted roof, and glorious stained glass everywhere. The whole building was beautifully light and airy and the evening sun was shining in through the west window, making coloured patterns on the floor. The music coming from the organ loft filled the space and Zannah listened to it with growing elation. It would be marvellous. It would be splendid. She imagined the flowers that she'd make sure were banked there, and there, and perhaps she would copy the Prince of Wales and put a tree or two on either side of the big wooden doors. The vicar … Edie had said she'd introduce Zannah to him at the end of the service … had a pleasant voice and looked nice, too, like everyone's idea of an elderly uncle. She wished Adrian were there. He would love it. He was bound to. She could honestly tell him the church was exactly what she'd dreamed about.

She took out the embroidered kneeler and sank down with her head in her hands. Thank you, God, she said silently, feeling as though she'd been neglecting some distant and elderly relative. I'm so grateful to you for making this church absolutely perfect. When she met the vicar, she'd fix up an appointment for herself and Adrian to go and see him. They needed to talk about the date (surely ten months was enough to ensure this was still free?) and to find out what else needed to be arranged. The music? She was almost sure Pa would want a decent choir. Was there a local choral society who might perform for a small fee? And what about the form of service? Although she was not a believer, Zannah had strong views about the traditional marriage service. The old-fashioned language was so much more … What was the right word? Serious … elegant. So much more dignified. The words had substance and meaning. They had centuries of tradition behind them. They had weight.

Saturday

So far, so gut-twistingly ghastly. Joss was in the kitchen of Zannah's flat, getting the coffee ready to take in to the others who were still sitting round the table. She'd volunteered to do this, needing an escape from the unending awfulness that sitting opposite Maureen Ashton had turned out to be. She'd hoped that Isis might be there to distract her a little, but Zannah had arranged an outing for her with Cal, 'so that we can discuss everything we have to.'

She couldn't imagine why she was surprised by how painful this lunch had been. When Zannah rang up to ask her to come to London, she'd known two things. The first was that she couldn't get out of it. She'd made a quick trip down on the weekend after the bombings to check for herself that they were all right, but that had been a proper visit and this was almost like business. Joss hadn't had much to do with the wedding preparations until now and what excuse could she possibly give her beloved daughter for leaving herself out of them? There was none. She was going to be involved in everything and that was that.

The second thing was that playing a full part would be almost unbearably difficult. The fact that for the next ten months she would have to be in contact with Gray's wife was torment of the sort you found only in fairytales, where mermaids had to walk on knives and princesses were required to pass through fire and flames to prove their love. I have to do it, Joss told herself. It's lucky that I'm getting better at suffering. Maybe I'm even getting used to it.

She piled the chocolates she had made into small cut-glass dishes. They were her contribution to the lunch party. The girls had a modern approach to entertaining. Emily was a good cook, but her style was what Joss privately called Advanced Student. Meals in the flat were of the moussaka/pasta with a terrific sauce/frittata with a gorgeous salad variety. She hadn't thought that impressing Maureen was part of the plan, but it was clear from the menu today – smoked salmon, a very good lasagne, expensive wine and Charlotte's home-made raspberry Pavlova, carried in a gigantic Tupperware container on her lap in the taxi that had brought her to the flat – that some sort of statement was being made. Would her hand-made chocolates let the side down or earn Zannah a few extra Brownie points? Joss sighed. She'd have to go back to the table soon, and take part in the conversation. So far they hadn't touched on the matter of the venue, which was what they had come to discuss.

Joss looked out of the kitchen window as she waited for the water to boil. Over the past six weeks, she'd become, almost used to the daily misery that fell over her like a thick, grey cloak the moment she got out of bed in the morning. She could feel its weight as she went through the mundane actions of her daily life. Every night, as she lay back against her pillows, she mentally laid it aside, and sometimes she thought that she could even see it: a muffling, foggy dark shadow that hung in the corner of the bedroom she shared with a husband in whom she couldn't confide. At the beginning, in the days after her last meeting with Gray in the British Library, she'd had difficulty in falling asleep and the warmth of Bob's body in the bed, snoring away unheedingly beside her, was something of a comfort. It was like having a familiar pet, she thought, and then she was consumed with guilt. Bob, her husband for so many years, the father of her children, who'd never done her any harm and who, she was sure, loved her in his own way: surely he should be more to her than just a teddy-bear of a man to cuddle in bed when she felt unhappy? He ought to be, she'd concluded, staring into the darkness, but he isn't.

Gray has my heart now. *My true love hath my heart and I have his*. She loved the Elizabethan poets. Some of her favourite lines, lines to which she'd introduced Gray, came back to her. *Since there's no help/Come let us kiss and part*. How matter-of-fact Michael Drayton managed to be about it. He didn't say a word about the physical consequences of the parting, one of which was a longing so sharp that sometimes it felt to her like stomach-ache. The nights when Bob rolled towards her, indicating with unspoken but well-known signals that had grown up over years, that he wanted to make love, were few and far between now. For the most part, he came to bed so late that he was asleep before his head touched the pillow, but occasionally, she had to close her eyes and repeat the movements that had become like a dance she knew by heart. Sometimes she was able to float out of her body. She'd grown used to distancing herself from the entire process without Bob being aware of what was going on. Just occasionally, though, she surprised him with her passion and those were the nights when, usually after she'd had a glass or two of wine, she managed to conjure up such a powerful fantasy image of Gray that a tremulous orgasm gathered her up and rippled through her, leaving her shaken and ashamed at the same time. After what felt to her like earthquakes taking place in her body, she would go to the bathroom and sit on the edge of the bath, shaking. In the bedroom, Bob's snores were like a counterpoint to her own restlessness.

She'd gone through it all. At first she'd felt sick and hadn't been able to eat. Then she found it difficult to breathe. There was constant sleeplessness and occasionally, the sudden onset of tears. Even Bob, usually too involved in his own work to pick up on her moods, had noticed that something was wrong. He'd seemed slightly more aware – or wary – of her since the engagement lunch. At breakfast one day, he'd asked, 'You okay, darling? You look tired.'

'I'm fine,' Joss had answered hastily, smiling as brightly as she could. 'Just didn't get a very good night's sleep, that's all.'

'Why don't you phone in and tell them you're ill? They can manage in the library without you, can't they?'

'No, really, I'm okay.' She resolved to apply a little more *Touche Eclat* under her eyes, and helped herself to another piece of toast. The library might be able to manage without her, but she'd have lost her reason if there hadn't been work to run away to. Every morning, she couldn't wait to get into her car and drive away from the house, which seemed to be the place where her unhappiness had taken up residence.

How would she have survived without her poetry? Writing anchored her to the physical world. Even in her desperate state, she saw things that made her want to reach for a pen. Lines and phrases came into her mind. She was so accustomed to putting the words on to the paper, then transferring them on to her silver laptop, that even the loss of Gray couldn't stop her. Indeed, since they no longer communicated, her wildly fluctuating emotions, her desires, her sorrow, her jealousy and her anger went into the poems. She knew they were good, perhaps her best work, but she had no intention of publishing them. They were far too raw and personal and she was terrified of anyone seeing them. Except Gray. She longed to send him the whole lot at once. Part of her wanted him to know the damage he'd done. One of the things she missed most was Gray's careful attention to what she wrote. One poem of hers had gone backwards and forwards between them by email for about a month. He found things to say about almost every word. 'Why do you take such trouble with my work?' she'd asked him one night. They often conversed on email after midnight. His reply was: *Because it's so good. You can ignore what I say, you know.* She'd emailed back: *Would never do that. You're usually right.* His answering message arrived in her inbox at once: *Naturally. Sharp of you to spot that.*

Now, Mal, her editor was both kind and a fan of her work and he gave her wonderful feedback but it wasn't the same. How could it be? Fleetingly, she wondered whether Gray, too, was pouring his heart out on to paper. She found herself looking at the contents pages of poetry magazines with a greater interest than usual.

Her mobile phone was ringing. It was in her handbag on one of the kitchen chairs, and she took it out and looked to see who was calling.

'Mal? Hello ... I'm at my daughter's. It's a lunch party. Why are you ringing on a Saturday? Is anything wrong?'

She listened to what he was saying and felt a little faint. 'You're pulling my leg, Mal. I didn't even know you'd submitted it. Is it true?'

When the call was over, she put the phone back into her bag and took a deep breath. Her first poetry collection, *The Shipwreck Café*, which hadn't even been published yet, was on the Madrigal Poetry Prize shortlist. The prize was two thousand pounds and a great deal of glory. She leaned against the sink and felt a stab of true happiness, followed swiftly by the need to speak to Gray, to tell him. He'd be so pleased ... how wonderful it would have been to hear him telling her how clever she was, how well-deserved the prize would be if she won!

The kettle had boiled and Joss waited for a moment before pouring water into the cafetière.

'God, Ma, I thought you were growing the beans yourself!' Zannah said, as she went back to the others.

'I'm so sorry. I was taking a call from Mal. That's my editor,' she explained to Maureen. 'I've got some good news.'

'What is it?' Emily leaned forward.

'I'm on the shortlist for an award. Have you heard of the Madrigal Prize?'

The girls knew about it. Maureen did not. Joss explained, and everyone clapped and cheered.

'That's fantastic, Ma!' Emily said, and stood up to walk round the table and hug her mother. Zannah, who was sitting next to her, had already kissed her and flung her arms round her neck.

Joss felt a mixture of pleasure and embarrassment and tried to make light of it, even though she had tears in her eyes. 'I'm so sorry,' she said. 'I thought Gwyneth Paltrow was silly for crying at the Oscars but I sort of know how she must have felt and I haven't even won anything. My mascara will be all over my cheeks!'

'You look fine, Ma. Let's drink a toast to you in coffee,' Zannah said.

Joss wiped her eyes carefully with a hankie. She'd taken a great deal of trouble with her makeup today. It was a matter of pride. She'd chosen her clothes with care too: her best linen skirt and a shirt in the kind of pink that gave her skin a glow that could just about pass as youth in a good light. Maureen was wearing a trouser suit, clearly expensive but the colour, a kind of putty-beige, did nothing for her blonde hair, in Joss's opinion. Still, she thought, as she passed round the coffee cups, you can't deny the beauty of her jewellery. She glanced at the triple string of pearls and imagined Gray fastening them round Maureen's neck; imagined his breath on her face and felt quite ill. There was a movement in the region of her heart. How astonishing, she thought. My heart sank. It's literally true. I felt it sinking.

'Did you really make these chocolates, Joss?' Maureen was smiling at her. 'They're quite scrumptious! Imagine being able to write poetry and make lovely chocolates. You are clever! You must send me the recipe. You've got my email address, haven't you?'

Joss shook her head.

'I'll give it to you. We're going to have to communicate about so many things over the next few months, aren't we? I resisted computers for ages, but I'm a convert now. I do everything I can on the Internet. It's been a boon in the hunt for venues too. But perhaps . . .' She paused. 'Zannah, I don't mean to dominate the proceedings, but perhaps before we go on to talk about venues we ought to sort out what each of us is doing. Towards the wedding,' she explained, looking round the table.

'You're right, Maureen.' Zannah took out her wedding notebook, and Joss wondered whether a love of stationery got passed down in the genes. She, too, adored pretty paper, fancy pens and notebooks. 'I did mean to talk about that. Ma, could I ask you to do the stationery?'

'I was just thinking about it as a matter of fact,' Joss said. 'And, yes, I'll order the invitations. Will you leave me to work out the wording?'

'With consultation, of course,' Maureen put in. 'What sort of invitations were you thinking of, Zannah?'

'Engraved. Plain. Black on cream. Beautiful font. I'll leave it to my mother. She's good at things like that.'

'I'm very relieved you agree about engraving,' said Maureen. 'Some modern brides go in for all sorts of things – pink, decorated with spangles and roses and goodness knows what. Silver wedding bells!'

Skull and crossbones, thought Joss. Hammer and sickle. For a fleeting second she allowed herself to think of Maureen's reaction to those images on the invitations. Picked out in silver, of course. She suppressed a giggle. 'Dad's champing at the bit, waiting to be let loose on the music, Zannah. Is that okay? He's been making a tape, I think, of possible pieces.'

'Great. I trust him when it comes to music. He knows everything.'

Emily undertook to be in charge of the hen night. Zannah looked rather alarmed.

'I'm not going on a drunken pub-crawl round the West End,' she said.

'Relax,' said Emily. 'I've got it all sorted. You'll love it, I promise. I'm not saying a word about it though. It's strictly secret.'

'Surely you can tell me,' Maureen said, trying for a jolly, all-girls-together tone. 'Just to check that it's suitable.'

'It's eminently suitable, Zannah will love it and I'm not saying a word. That's it!' Emily took another chocolate and popped it into her mouth.

'I'm in charge of my dress and the bridesmaid's dress,' Zannah said. 'Or dresses, if Gemma's going to be a bridesmaid as well. And I'll sort the decorations and the flowers.'

'I suppose we ought to come back to the matter of the venue,' Maureen said, taking a file out of her handbag. 'I've taken the liberty of printing out a lot of stuff from the Internet. We can pass round what I've got and see what suits us. There really is no shortage of places. Some are nicer than others, naturally. Have a look.'

'Maureen,' said Zannah tentatively, and Joss could see that she was worried about what she was going to say. She recognized the look in her daughter's eyes. It had been there every time she'd had to perform in public when she was a child. It was a sort of panicked excitement, which made her skin flush pink and her cheeks burn. That was happening now. Zannah held her hands in a certain way when she had to make any kind of declaration or announcement and there it was: palms not quite pressed together, fingertips touching, almost but not quite in a prayer position.

'Yes, dear?' said Maureen.

Zannah plunged on, 'It's just that . . . Well. Adrian and I have talked it over and we've actually already decided on a venue. I didn't want to tell you over the phone. I hope very much you'll agree with us that it's a lovely idea.'

Maureen cocked her head to one side. 'Adrian's not said a word.'

'Well, we only made our minds up a couple of days ago.' She took a deep breath. 'It's Charlotte's garden. You've seen it, of course. We think it's absolutely perfect. A marquee on the terrace, with all the trees – you remember the trees down by the wall – the trees decorated too. And there's a really lovely church almost next door. I was there just the other day. What do you think?'

Joss watched Maureen adjust her face before answering. She was taking her time. Finally, she sucked in air through her nose like someone about to dive into a pool filled with icy water and said, 'I'm not at all sure I agree with this decision, Zannah. No offence to your beautiful garden, Charlotte, but from what I saw, I don't think a marquee capable of holding the number of guests I had in mind would fit on to your rather narrow terrace.' She smiled. 'Perhaps you and Adrian didn't take the numbers into account, Zannah.'

'Well, that's the other thing, Maureen. I don't want all that many people at the wedding. I thought seventy-five at most.'

'Seventy-five!' To hear Maureen, you'd have thought the mere mention of this number was one of the most shocking things she'd ever heard. She appealed to Joss. 'I despair!' she said, trying for a lightness of tone that would indicate she was still in some sort of good humour, though it was quite clear that she was, in a phrase beloved of Em, 'spitting cobs' behind the façade of her rapidly disappearing smile. 'Whatever do these young people think a big wedding is all about?' She turned to Zannah again and adopted the tone of an indulgent teacher. 'It's not just about you and Adrian, you know. Such a wedding is a family occasion. A statement to the world. It's an event to which you want to invite your colleagues, your friends, everyone. Graham has more than thirty colleagues at the hospital I'm sure he'd want to be there. To say nothing of your father's colleagues, and your mother's, and Emily's too. And of course, mine. It's a demonstration of who we all are. You agree with me, don't you, Joss? You tell her.'

'I'm sorry, Maureen,' said Joss. 'It's not up to me. It's Zannah's wedding, and Adrian's of course, and if they only want seventy-five people, then that's what they should have.'

Surely Gray couldn't want huge numbers of people at the wedding? But Joss wasn't sure of her own views about big weddings, let alone his. Mostly, she thought the whole enterprise a gigantic waste of time, and could think of a hundred other things the money could more usefully be spent on, but Zannah's single-mindedness and Isis's infectious enthusiasm had almost succeeded in changing her mind. Why shouldn't love be celebrated with a glorious, all-out, beautifully decorated party? Bob, surprisingly, was what he called 'on side' and what Em called 'up for it', which was a good thing, as their savings would be greatly reduced. She heard Maureen speak and turned to her. Joss could see that she was doing her best to keep her emotions under control, although she was clearly seething inwardly.

'I do think you might have given me a hint about this a little earlier,' she said. 'I've already spoken about this wedding to so many people.

What are they going to think?'

'I'm sure they won't mind.' Zannah spoke more firmly than Joss had expected. Perhaps that's the voice she uses at school, she thought, to keep the children in line. She felt like cheering. 'It's nearly a year before the wedding,' Zannah continued, 'so I'm sure you can't have told that many people. I want a small, beautiful wedding and Charlotte's kindly letting us use her garden. It's just right – and, what's more,' she smiled at Maureen, trying to dissipate the woman's anger, 'it'll be much cheaper than any hired public venue.'

'You keep saying "I", Zannah,' Maureen said, her voice a little lower and calmer now. ' I want ... I don't want. It's Adrian's wedding too, you know.'

'Yes, of course I know,' said Zannah. 'I do mean "our wedding" really. Adrian and I have talked about every single aspect of the day. I'm sorry I said "I" , Maureen. I didn't mean that.'

Maureen accepted the apology with a small dip of her head. She pressed her advantage and went on, 'I had no idea that financial considerations were uppermost in your minds. We're quite happy to help with expenses, you know. Adrian's my son and we'd be delighted to contribute. I'm sorry if I hadn't made that quite clear. It's a terrible burden for one family to carry on their own and I wouldn't dream of you, Joss, and your husband, taking care of everything.'

'I think,' said Joss, suppressing an urge to throw her coffee across the table at the velvety front of Maureen's beige jacket, 'that Zannah was saying something else. Not about money at all. It's about the sort of wedding they want. They don't want our friends to be there, or yours, or ... your husband's. It's kind of you to offer to contribute financially. I'm sure there'll be ways in which you can still do that. However, I would like to make it clear that we, as the bride's parents, are happy to pay for whatever we need to pay for.'

'Well,' said Maureen, gathering together her printed-out pages and pushing them into a soft, brown suede handbag, 'there were other things we ought to have talked about, but I suppose they can wait till another time. For instance, you say the church is perfect but I'd rather thought St Margaret's, Westminster, or Chelsea Old Church ... Never mind. I'll look into marquees and their hire on the Internet, and let you know what I find, Charlotte. There's nothing more to be said, if you've set your heart on it, Zannah. Though I have to admit, I've not quite given up, you know. I'll talk to Adrian. I just want to make sure you haven't pressured him, my dear.' She laughed without mirth, and pushed her chair back from the table. 'I really ought to go now,' she said. 'Graham's going to want supper when he comes back from the hospital, and we have covered most things, haven't we?'

She stood up. 'Thank you so much for a divine lunch, Zannah. And you, Emily. I believe you did the lion's share of the cooking. Perhaps Adrian ought to be marrying you!' She trilled out another laugh.

Emily said, 'Oh, you'd hate that, Maureen. I've set my heart on no wedding at all. I'm going to fly to America and get married there ... just me and my fiancé.' She grinned at the look of horror that crossed Maureen's face.

'Oh, dear, well ... maybe you're right. I'll just have to put up with Zannah!' Again, there was the silvery cascade of sound to tell the world she didn't really mean it.

Joss was so distressed by Maureen's casual mention of cooking supper for Gray that all thoughts of the wedding and where it was going to be and how many people were going to attend vanished out of her head. She managed to say a reasonably civil goodbye to Maureen and while Zannah and Emily accompanied her to the door, she sat at the table and helped herself to another of her chocolates.

Charlotte, directly opposite, was gazing at her searchingly. 'Is anything wrong, Joss darling? You looked so happy when you were telling us about the Madrigal Prize, but now you seem distraught.'

'I'm very happy about being shortlisted. Really. I'd not expected anything like that would ever happen to me.'

'That's the shortlisting. What about ... other matters? Are you unhappy about something else?'

'No, no ... really.'

'I don't know whether I believe you. You forget, I've known you all your life. You look ... well, as though there's some kind of shadow over you.'

'I've got a lot on my mind. The wedding. Managing everything. You know how it is.'

Charlotte nodded, and Joss knew she wouldn't pursue it. That was one of the best things about Charlotte. She made an effort to help. She wanted to understand, but if you sent out strong enough signals that said *Keep off,* then she wouldn't insist. Joss longed to tell her about Gray. What a relief it would be to have this lump of misery, this horrible anguish, out in the open.

Zannah and Emily came back into the room and sat down at the table.

'Fifteen-love to us,' said Emily. 'Terrific! What if Adrian takes her side?'

'He won't,' said Zannah. 'He wouldn't dare. He knows my feelings.'

'Little Mo might be able to persuade him.' Emily started to giggle. 'She has ways of making him obey her, I'm sure.'

'So have I!' said Zannah and, before long, she and Emily were helpless with laughter, almost lying across the table.

Emily reached for the wine bottle.

'Who wants to drink Ma's health? Congratulations, Ma dear. We're very proud of you. I think we ought to have some kind of party, don't you? Have you told Pa yet?'

'No, and I must. May I use the phone in your bedroom, Zannah?'

'Sure. I'll start the dishes.'

Joss went into her daughter's bedroom and lay on the bed. She held the handset against her shoulder and dialled. Bob would be pleased and proud and wouldn't properly understand how marvellous it was, how satisfying it was to have her work recognized. The shortlist would be published in the newspapers. Gray would see it. He always read the paper carefully. Oh, Gray, she thought as she waited for Bob to answer the phone. I wish I could phone you and tell you how I'm feeling. The answering-machine picked up her call and Joss heard her own voice asking her to leave a message after the tone. She said, 'Hello, Bob, it's me. I've had bit of nice news. Give me a ring at Zannah's and I'll tell you about it. I'm in all evening. Or I'll ring you. 'Bye.'

'What on earth's so urgent that it couldn't be done over the phone, Mum?'

Adrian's frown, in the dim shadows of this rather chi-chi little bar, made him look even more gorgeous than usual and it was all Maureen could do to stop herself reaching out to push his hair out of his eyes, as she used to do when he was a small boy. God, Zannah didn't appreciate what a treasure she was getting! She said, 'Honestly, Adrian. You can't say you weren't happy to get my call. Anyone would think you didn't want to meet me for a little drink. I need to speak to you, that's all. I'm in town – and it took some effort to convince myself that I was going to be safe, after the bombs and everything – it's nicer to chat to you face to face. I just didn't fancy trekking all the way to your flat. You can make a bit of an effort see your aged mother, can't you?'

'You look lovely, Mum,' Adrian smiled. 'You don't have to fish for compliments. It's just that I'm meeting Zannah later. But it's good to see you, of course it is. Everyone probably thinks you're my girlfriend.'

'Or that you're my gigolo!' She giggled. 'Forgive me, darling. We've been having a wedding-planning lunch at Zannah's flat. I expect she told you.'

Adrian nodded and Maureen realized she was hoping he'd say he knew nothing about the lunch. It would have made what she had to say next, that Zannah was doing all sorts of things without consulting him properly, more plausible. She went on, after another sip from her glass of white wine, 'She told me that you'd decided to hold the reception in Mrs Parrish's garden, and get married in basically the nearest available church, without looking into what other churches have to offer. Are you really in favour of that? Do you honestly want only seventy-five guests? What about everyone from the hospital and the bank? Zannah said she'd discussed it with you but I can't imagine you'd agree to that without a fight.'

'I don't care, to tell you the truth. Not that bothered, if you must know, about the people at the bank. I mean, my friends'll come, of course, but not everyone in the office. I bet Doc doesn't want the day full of everyone he sees at the hospital either. No, I'm with Zannah on this. And I reckon the garden'll be rather good. Not to mention more economical, right?'

Maureen sighed. 'It's your wedding as well, Adrian. Wouldn't you like the reception to be held somewhere ... well, somewhere a little grander?'

'Zannah has strong views. She thinks a family venue means more, and quite honestly, Mum, it's her day, really. Don't tell her this, and

I'm okay with a proper wedding, all the stops out, but it's mainly for her sake. I'd be quite happy with a register office and a flight to the Maldives. And, by the way, that's not where we're going on honeymoon. I'm keeping that secret.'

Maureen frowned. 'You aren't giving me the kind of support I expected, Adrian. I'm disappointed.'

'Darling Mummy,' Adrian said, taking Maureen's hand, and she relaxed a little at the affectionate use of a name she hadn't heard much since Adrian had grown up. He said, 'You know I'd never want to disappoint you, but I'm not upsetting Zannah. She's been planning her wedding since she was about six. It'll be terrific, you'll see. I'm sure Charlotte will welcome your input.'

'Hmm!' said Maureen. 'I don't know about that, but she's going to get it whether she does or not. I'm not going to be left out of everything. In fact, I'm going to offer to pay for the catering. I might use Veronica's firm, which is marvellous, but pricy . . . perhaps I'll look into some others first. What do you think of that?'

'Sounds good to me. Listen, Mum, I have to go. Really. There's still stuff to finish in the office. Don't look so horrified! I know what you're going to say – no one works on Saturday. Wish it were true, that's all. We lost a lot of time over the bombings. But it's good to see you. We'll come down to Guildford for the weekend one day soon, I promise.'

'Yes, I wish you would. I need to talk to Zannah about her dress. We did speak a little about the arrangements in general before the venue bombshell. The main thing is: we've got the division of labour sorted.'

'You make it sound like a Soviet five-year plan. What division of labour?'

'Poor innocent Adrian! You have no idea, darling.' Maureen took out a notebook covered with scarlet silk embroidered with gold dragons and opened it on the table in front of her. 'There is so much to do! Every single detail has to be ordered, checked up on, arranged, considered. It'd be a nightmare if you didn't share the work. So, Joss is in charge of printing the invitations and Bob's doing the music. Charlotte is the venue and the church – one of her friends is a proper churchgoer, apparently, which is a plus. I'm going to offer to do the catering, as I said. Emily's in charge of the hen night and Zannah wants control of the dress and the bridesmaid's dress for Isis . . . also the decorations and the flowers.'

'Isis never stops talking about being a bridesmaid. It's a bore, if I'm completely honest.'

'She seems a nice little girl,' said Maureen.

'You don't know her like I do. She can be a brat, believe me. No, she's okay. A bit talkative for my liking, but she'll be at school most of the time, right?'

Maureen wondered whether she ought to press Adrian on this. Could it be that he wasn't all that keen on Isis? Well, who would know better than she did how awkward the relationship could be between a child and a step-parent? Gray's troubles with Adrian started almost as soon as she married him. Perhaps men were genetically programmed to dislike other men's children. 'She likes you, doesn't she?'

'Oh, yes. A present here and a present there . . . it doesn't take much to win a child's heart.'

'I can't imagine anyone not loving you, sweetheart.'

'But you're my mother. You have to love me, don't you?'

'You make it easy for me. Give me a kiss before you go off to your boring old work. Though I shouldn't stop you, I suppose, as you're doing so well in this job. But one thing that did come out at lunch, while we were still doing small-talk over the smoked salmon, which I meant to tell you and nearly forgot is this: did you know that Mrs Parrish's first husband used to work for your bank years ago? Not in London, of course, but somewhere up north. She was an accountant, it seems, and that's how they met. Katchen was his name. Nigel Katchen. I wonder whether anyone still remembers him? It's not that long ago. I think that's quite a coincidence, don't you?'

'Absolutely. Small world too! Bye Mum. Must fly. Lovely to see you.'

Later, in the taxi on her way to Victoria, Maureen remembered the announcement Joss had made about that poetry prize. What was it called again? She'd forgotten. Graham would be interested, she was sure. He didn't make a fuss about his poems, but she knew he enjoyed writing them and she'd always considered it a harmless pastime. If Joss won the £2000 she'd be able to afford to pamper herself a bit. She could be quite attractive if she took more trouble. Perhaps it would be a good idea if Graham had a little tête-a-tête with Adrian. Nowadays, even though they weren't exactly bosom buddies, relations between the two of them were reasonably cordial. They could discuss things one to one, like, for example, the question of stepchildren. She'd speak to Graham tonight. She didn't want her son to think that every bit of attention was focused on the bride. He mustn't feel excluded, she told herself. As she paid the taxi-driver, the name of Joss's poetry thing came back to her. The Madrigal Poetry Prize, she thought, and felt pleased with herself for remembering.

Sunday

'Why's your book called *The Shipwreck Café*, Grandma? Is it about pirates?'

Isis was sitting up in bed, leaning against her pillows, legs stretched out on top of the duvet. It was a warm night. Joss was on the bed as well, with her back against the butterfly mural, and she wondered whether Zannah possessed such a thing as a summer-weight bed covering. That might be something she could put on a wedding list, if she and Adrian decided to have one.

'No, not pirates, I'm afraid. It's just a café I had tea in once. It was a strange place, because we had lovely china cups on crocheted tablecloths and everything was very ... well, very pretty. But on the walls – all over the walls – there were photographs of ships going down in the sea, or breaking up on the rocks, or lying on the shore in bits. It was most peculiar.'

'Were they real ships? Did they really break into bits? Did someone put bombs on them?'

'No, my darling, not bombs. But, yes, the weather broke them into bits. Storms. Terrible storms, I expect. Each photo had a date on it and the name of the ship as well.'

Isis slid down in the bed and began to pull the duvet over her. 'That sounds quite interesting. Can we go there?'

'It's far away, chicken. Down in Dorset. I was there a couple of years ago.'

'Hmm.' Isis's eyelids were drooping. 'Are you staying the night?'

'I've got to go and see my editor tomorrow. I think he's going to give me a copy of the book.'

'Will it be in the shops?' said Isis. 'Can we buy it?'

'Not quite yet,' Joss said. 'Not till the end of August. This is what they call 'an advance copy'. I'll send you and Mummy one long before it's in the shops.' She stood up and went to the head of the bed to kiss Isis goodnight.

'Are you going to read me a story?'

'Chancing your arm, aren't you? You're practically asleep.'

'I like hearing your voice,' said Isis, 'till I get properly asleep.'

'All right,' said Joss. She went to sit on the low nursing chair under the window and began to read. After a few minutes, Isis was breathing deeply, making a faint snuffling noise. Joss shut the book and stared at the butterflies Zannah had painted. If only, she thought, I could stay here. The love Joss felt for Isis was not something she'd examined or thought about very much. It resembled what she'd felt for her own girls when they were small, but Isis made her feel as though she were looking at the same time both at the past and at the future. Loving Isis, she realized, was uncomplicated. And of course, she'd spent so much time with her just after Zannah and Cal had split up that a specially strong bond had been forged between them.

That was the one good thing about Zannah's breakdown. Mostly Joss remembered that time with horror. While it was going on, every other feeling was pushed to one side and all she had room for in her head and in her heart was agony at the sight of her daughter's suffering and a determination that above all the baby, Isis, mustn't suffer. When Zannah came home, Joss did cheery, grannyish things like taking Isis to the park to feed the ducks, and to story sessions at the library. She'd loved the purely physical tasks like feeding Isis, and bathing her and holding her close. The smell of her hair . . . Johnson's baby shampoo made Joss feel weepy. But mixed up with those pleasures were the hours she'd spent sitting in Zannah's room, by the bed, reading to her, talking to her and getting no response. She'd manage to keep a strong voice and a cheerful tone while she was with her, but as soon as she left the room, the tears welled up. How could her beautiful Zannah be so cast down? What would make her better? Em sat with her. So did Bob. They told her stories and played music for her and nothing helped. Nothing worked. Joss used every ounce of her energy that wasn't devoted to Isis in thinking up strategies to bring Zannah back to herself and in the end it seemed that the passage of time made the difference. It was almost as though her unhappiness was a kind of fever she had to work through. Now, it was so good to see her happy again that Joss was determined to support her in having the kind of wedding she wanted.

Isis looked like Cal. Joss wondered whether it was grandmotherly blindness that made her think she was very pretty, but decided it wasn't. Everyone agreed that she was lovely. And what fun she was having over the wedding! Her enthusiasm for the project was another reason Joss fell in so readily with plans she would have thought were quite mad in other circumstances. But I must, she thought, ask Zannah about how Adrian is with someone else's daughter. It was at times like this that she wished she lived nearer London. It wasn't easy to keep an eye on things from a distance. She made a mental note to ask Em as well. Zannah was probably biased where Adrian was concerned, but Em would have her wits about her. It occurred to Joss that if anything were seriously wrong, she'd have known about it already. She relaxed a little. Isis seemed happy enough. She slept well, ate well, and as far as Joss could see, she wasn't displaying any signs of anxiety or stress.

She could hear her daughters talking in the kitchen. Their voices reached her here as a distant drone, punctuated from time to time with a dazzle of laughter. The wine at lunchtime, which was making her feel sleepy, had made them giggly. Outside, the summer evening was still bright with the last of the sunshine, but Zannah had done a good job of lining the curtains, and this room was beautifully dark. Isis, asking her about the Shipwreck Café, had brought that time back to her and she closed her eyes.

Gray had taken her there – only once, but it was enough. They went on the afternoon of the day that had ended with them spending the night together. The Day, she told herself. The capital-letters day. The best day. They'd walked down the path through what she recalled now as a tunnel of translucent green. They hadn't spoken much and he didn't even hold her hand, but Joss felt as though she were bound to him by invisible strings. She knew that at the end of this walk there would be a conversation: one she'd been dreading, in which she'd have to say something she longed not to say. She'd been aware of everything about him as they walked through the warmth of the afternoon: his shirt falling from his shoulders, his sleeves rolled halfway up his arms, which were smooth and brown. She was conscious of how near his hand was to her own. She glanced sideways and saw him leaning slightly forward, saw the left side of his face, half of the smile that touched his lips when she spoke to him. The café was Gray's discovery and he was the one who called it *The Shipwreck Café*. Its real name was the Fairford Tea Room.

He'd found them a table in the corner and ordered two cream teas without consulting her. She didn't mind. She'd been in such a stupor of lust and nervousness that she wouldn't have been able to decide anything. The waitress set everything in front of them: a pretty, rose-strewn white china tea-set, like something from a dolls' house; Earl Grey tea in the round pot; two scones each; butter, cream and jam in little dishes. Milk in a curved jug. She'd poured the tea, so as to have something to occupy her. Her hands were unsteady.

'Have a look round, Lydia. What do you see?'

She'd wanted to say: *You. I see you*. 'A tea room. It's lovely. And the scones are so fresh. Just out of the oven. Delicious.'

'Look at the pictures.'

She'd raised her eyes then, torn them from him, turned them to the walls of the tea room. Pink striped wallpaper. Photographs of ships. She stared at one after another. There were scores of them, covering the walls, with hardly any space between one frame and another. Not just ships, either, but ships in distress. Shipwrecks. Slabs of tormented ocean, cliff faces of water, broken vessels returning to the depths of the sea: the effect was overwhelming.

'Awful,' she said at last, feeling faintly sick. 'Such destruction.'

'I like the contrast,' said Gray, 'between them and the cream tea. It's ... well, it makes you appreciate the comfortable things in life.'

Joss had nodded. Gray went on, 'Have you thought about what I said?'

How could she tell him that she'd been thinking of little else? He had walked with her, after midnight on the previous night, to the room she was sharing with two other women. There had been no one else around. Everything was quiet. She'd been expecting it and there it was: his kiss. One swift, chaste kiss and then he left her at the door, saying, 'I love you, Lydia. And I want you. Please. Come away with me. I want us to be together. Just say. I'll drop everything – my work, everything.

You love me too. Admit it. I can see it. Please, Lydia, think about it.'

She said, 'I have thought about it, Gray, and I can't. I've decided. It's not fair ... to my husband. I don't seem to be the kind of person who can do things like that. It's not ... I mean, I want to. I do, but I'd never forgive myself for hurting him.'

'D'you love your husband?'

She hung her head miserably, wanting to shout: *but I love you too. It's different. I can't breathe when you're near me. It's not the same.*

'Then we shouldn't discuss it any further, Lydia. It's not fair on either of us. We'll just stay as we were, then. Friends?'

She was unable to think of anything to say, wondering why she felt so desperately unhappy when she had made the decision. He continued, 'If I thought you were going to stop writing to me, I don't know what I'd do. Promise me at least that you'll go on writing to me.'

'Every day. Every single day, I promise. And you must write to me, too'

'I will. And maybe we could meet from time to time ... we could have lunch? Tea?'

Joss had shaken her head. 'I don't think I could, Gray. It would be too hard to ... Well, I'd be so guilty. Churned up. I wouldn't be able to enjoy my time with you.'

'So that's it, right? Is that what you're saying?'

> *Shake hands forever, cancel all our vows*
> *And when we meet at any time again*
> *Be it not seen in either of our brows*
> *That we one jot of former love retain.*

'What's that?'

'Michael Drayton. A sonnet, that begins: *Since there's no help, come let us kiss and part.*'

Gray smiled. 'Is that what we're going to do? It hurts, Lydia. I have to tell you, I'm ... well, I'm sick about it.'

'So am I.'

'You're not eating those delicious scones.'

'I can't. I'm sorry.'

'Let's go, then.'

As they left the café, Joss had glanced back at one particular ship: its long body upended into a jagged black diagonal on the triangular pale mass of the rock on which it was impaled. She shivered and followed Gray into the sunshine. On the way up to the house, before they were in sight of it, just as they were passing under the low-hanging branches of a tree, he pulled her to him and she fell against his body in a storm of tears. 'Oh, Gray, what can I do? I want ... It's so ...' The words she was struggling to speak wouldn't come out.

'Tonight. Just tonight, Lydia. Please. If you spend the night with me, I'll never ask you for another thing ever again.'

She'd turned her face up to his and wound her arms round his neck. Yes, she said, over and over again and wondered whether he could hear her. Oh, yes ...

The door of Isis's room opened and there was Zannah, outlined against the light.

'You okay, Ma?' she whispered. 'We're ready to eat, if you are.'

'Fine,' Joss whispered back. 'Just fell asleep for a moment. I'll be down soon.'

The door closed and Joss sat open-eyed in the dark, pulling herself together. Her mobile was downstairs in the kitchen. She wanted to send Gray a text now, this minute, telling him about the shortlisting. She could imagine his reaction. Instead she would try Bob again, after they'd finished eating. He was bound to be home by then.

Monday / Tuesday

On the way home on the train, Joss looked and looked again at the image she and Mal had chosen for the jacket and wondered whether she could send one of her six gratis copies to Gray. No, that would be madness. She was so thrilled with the book that she even looked forward to showing it to Bob. Would he have anything celebratory waiting for her? Perhaps he'd booked a table for a meal. Maybe the house would be full of flowers. There might even be a bottle of champagne in the fridge. It would be too much to hope for all three, but she found herself excited at the prospect of a treat.

'Hello, darling! Where are you?' Joss said, as she let herself in.

'Here, love,' said Bob, coming downstairs from his study. 'Good journey?'

'Not bad. How's everything here?'

'Fine, fine . . . busy of course. When aren't I? Marking's a bugger as usual.'

Joss said, 'Fancy a cup of tea? I'm going to make one.'

'Good idea. You go and put your case away and I'll get the kettle on.'

Joss went upstairs and came down again. She made a pot of tea before she turned to him and, unable to bear the suspense any longer said, 'Well?'

'Well, what?'

'You're not saying anything, Bob. Why's that?'

'What on earth are you talking about?'

Sure enough, he looked quite bemused. His hair was sticking up. He'd been working and he always ran his hands through his hair when he was concentrating, focused on what he was doing.

'I'm talking about my shortlisting . . .'

'Oh, gosh, yes, that's terrific.' His puzzlement increased. Joss could tell by the deepening of his frown. 'I told you it was terrific on the phone yesterday, when I spoke to you at Zannah's?'

'So you did. I kind of expected . . . never mind. Anyway, this is it. The book.'

'Oh, God, I'm sorry . . . I should have said something again. I'm really sorry . . . I'm preoccupied, you see. This looks fantastic, darling and I really, really hope you win. Any chance of that?'

Joss answered quickly 'Not much,' then asked what was preoccupying him. She wanted time to think. To unpick everything that was wrong with what he'd just said. With how he'd behaved when he'd picked up the book for about thirty seconds and given it no more than a cursory glance, and hadn't even commented on the picture on the cover. Preoccupied, she thought. That means: to the exclusion of something he must know is important to me. He hopes I win, but isn't sure I will and winning's the important thing. The implication being, I'll pay proper attention if you're a winner. He is clearly not interested in the book, nor in what's in it. Now he was talking on and on about going away. Perhaps the shadow of the conversation they'd had about Gray was still there in the back of his mind.

'So I'll be away towards the end of September for two weeks. You'll be okay, won't you? I can't let this opportunity pass me by. Good connections for the future. Excellent prospects for more work.'

Joss nodded. He'd be in Egypt for two weeks, she'd grasped that much. External examiner to some university in Cairo.

'I'm tutoring a poetry course at Fairford for some of that,' she said. 'That's five days I won't be at home.'

'That's fine, then, isn't it? We'll both be busy at the same time. Right. Nice to have you back. Must go and do some more on my paper.'

He'd wandered out and left her on her own. I'm going to bed early, Joss told herself, and if I'm still awake when Bob comes to bed, I'll pretend I'm fast asleep. She knew he wouldn't wake her to make love. He'd never done that, in all the years they'd been married.

Next morning, after breakfast, Bob went straight to his study and Joss stood at her desk and read a few poems from *The Shipwreck Café*. Then she put the book down and stared at her laptop screen, wanting to write an email to Gray. She sent one instead to Maureen, assuring her that she had every intention of sorting out the stationery very soon. Joss imagined her opening her email, reading the message. Would she mention it to Gray? Oh, I had such a nice email from Joss . . . ? What would he think when he heard her say that?

The sun was out. Joss closed her laptop, and went to lie on the sunlounger in the shade of the laburnum tree in the back garden. Bob didn't even realize she was still sulking. That's the problem, she thought. It's not that he doesn't care, it's just that he's unaware of most of my feelings. And perhaps a fraction more withdrawn than usual since her confession about Gray. She looked round the garden. It was a small square of lawn edged by narrow borders containing nothing very remarkable: roses, honeysuckle growing against the high fence, and two mature camellia bushes, one white and one pink. In the spring, their flowers, thousands of them, filled her with pleasure, though it was always a shock to see how quickly the petals grew brown. Almost the very first poem she'd ever written was about that: *This is a flower to tuck into your belt/or wind into your hair with satin bands/before the fire of growing in the world/has scorched the edges of the petals brown.*

The trees that drooped their branches over her fence and made patches of welcome shade belonged to the house adjoining theirs, but Joss regarded them as part of her own garden. They'd been able to afford this big house early on in Bob's academic career because even for those days, it had been very cheap. A property of this nature, the estate agent had explained, usually had far more land at the back, not to mention a garage. They'd managed to build a garage about ten years ago, but the garden had remained tiny. When the girls were small, a climbing-frame took up most of the lawn. Bob wasn't a gardener and this never bothered him. As for Joss, she felt as though Charlotte's garden, which had been part of her childhood, part of her life, was still hers. That must be, she thought, why the idea of Zannah's wedding reception being held there gives me such a kick. Joss and Bob had not wanted a big wedding. They'd opted for a register office in Manchester, saving what little money they had for a few days in the Lake District. Charlotte had come up for the ceremony and a few friends were there too, but the occasion had been low-key. Now that Zannah was going in for the full works, Joss acknowledged that she was quite pleased to see Maureen's nose put out of joint about the venue. There was, though, something else: it would be as though Zannah was marrying from her mother's house, not the one she lived in today, but the one she used to live in, which could still make her feel nostalgic for a time when she was young, with nothing but possibilities before her.

Gray knew he would feel awkward talking to Adrian. He'd always had a problem with him, ever since he'd first met and married Maureen. Even when Adrian was very young indeed, he had known exactly how to make Gray feel like an unwanted intruder. He'd been a spoilt toddler who'd grown into a spoilt child, and even though the rows they'd had throughout Adrian's adolescence were over long ago, even though Gray had to admit he'd become a reasonably okay adult, it was always difficult even now, to know what to talk about, the kind of attitude to adopt, how to behave. He shuddered as he recalled a scene from Adrian's childhood that seemed to set a pattern for their relationship.

Maureen had gone out somewhere. Gray could no longer remember where. Jon was about five, which made Adrian seven. He'd worked out a plan for the day which involved taking the boys to the park for a kickabout with a football, followed by a session in the playground on the brightly-coloured equipment that always seemed to be swarming with kids.

'I don't need you to push me,' Adrian said on the swings, so Gray had turned to Jon. When they reached the roundabout, Adrian leaped on it and refused to move over so that his brother could sit next to him. 'Get off,' he'd screamed at Jon. 'No little kids on here.' As if to emphasize his point, he'd spread out his legs as wide as they would go. The girl sitting next to him moved up, clearly scared. Adrian could look very threatening for a small child. He glowered at Gray and stuck out his tongue.

Even now, he could remember how furious he'd felt and what hard work it had been to keep his voice even and pleasant. He said, 'I'm not asking you, Adrian. I'm telling you. Make room for your brother or you're off that roundabout and we're going home.'

'Get stuffed!' Adrian screamed. No one looking at them would have seen it like that, but he knew how nearly he'd lost it, how close he was to grabbing the boy by both legs and pulling him forcibly off the turning roundabout. He managed to control himself sufficiently to stop the bloody thing going round, then reached out and picked the boy up under his arm, as though he were no more than a baby. Adrian started to shriek. Gray shouted, 'SHUT UP! I've had quite enough of you for one day. We're going home.' He found he couldn't breathe properly. Jon was clinging to his legs, frightened by his brother's screams.

Adrian managed to keep screaming all the way home. Maureen came out to meet them, looking as though Gray had taken her beloved son and cut him up into small pieces.

'Mummy! Mummy! He hurt me. He wouldn't let me ... My arms hurt. He hurt me. He's horrible. I hate him. Send him away.'

Perhaps he had hurt the boy. Perhaps he hadn't been as gentle as he ought to have been. Later on, he'd explained everything to Maureen, but he could see that, in her heart of hearts, she believed her son's version of events. Nowadays, when they met, Maureen was like a kind of buffer between them, but one to one ... that was different. Gray was quite sure that the shadow of that tantrum and many others even worse fell over them every time they met.

Gray had no clear idea of why today's meeting was strictly necessary, but he'd been nagged into accompanying Maureen to town. She'd persuaded him to take one of the days off work that were owed to him and he wondered whether he'd agreed partly out of guilt. Perhaps he'd fallen in with her plans without much of a struggle because he knew that his heart and attention weren't with his wife, but with Lydia.

While Maureen was having her hair done, her son and her husband were supposed to air ... Gray wasn't quite sure what they were supposed to air, but he knew Maureen was concerned that Adrian shouldn't feel left out of the wedding preparations. Also, she'd mentioned Isis. Gray had been so shocked to see Lydia in Charlotte Parrish's house that he hadn't properly registered Zannah's daughter, but she'd seemed a nice enough child.

'Hello, Doc,' said Adrian. 'Been waiting long?'

'No, no, not long at all. Can I get you something?'

'Stella, please. God, it's hot, isn't it?'

'Stifling. You okay out here, or would you rather go inside?' Gray had taken a table under an awning in the pub's garden. It wasn't his kind of pub. Too trendily done up and full of braying young people, but the garden was pleasant and it was convenient for Adrian's work.

One thing about chichi pubs: they had waiters so you didn't have to go up to the bar.

'Bit like France, isn't it?' Adrian said, after Gray had ordered. 'One of the benefits of the EU. How are things at the hospital?'

'Oh, you know.' Gray smiled. He'd never known how to talk about his work. It absorbed him completely while he was doing it. The patient in front of him, draped in hospital green, almost a non-person away from the clothes and accessories of their life, became the only thing in the world he cared about. He always concentrated utterly on everything that was going on, aware of the others in the theatre: surgeons, theatre sisters, occasionally students. Everyone seemed to think that all an anaesthetist had to do was pop a mask over someone's face and that was it. Nothing could have been further from the truth. Gray got to know whom he was going to meet before the surgery. He followed their progress afterwards, sitting at their bedside to make sure they were recovering properly and enjoying (he admitted it, he was proud of it) the admiring – you might even call them *fond* – looks the nurses gave him. *Not many people would take the care you do,* one sister had told him a couple of years ago. But it was true. He loved his work and sometimes wondered if the reason he was so passionate about it was that it was the one place in the world where his private emotions fell away to nothing. It felt to him sometimes as though he left them with his clothes when he changed. After an operation, as he put his own garments on again, he became himself once more. Until then, he belonged to the patients. Also there was no ambiguity about who he was at work. The person he was when he was in the hospital was clear through and through: that was how it felt to him. Who he was in his non-working life seemed muddied and confused and sometimes downright unhappy: unfaithful to his wife and in love with a woman who was married to someone else. He'd always known she was married, but how much easier it was to put that knowledge out of one's mind when you hadn't met the poor bugger you'd cuckolded. Shit. That wasn't a word he liked and certainly not one he relished using in relation to himself, but it was a fact. One night only ... Did that make it any less of a cuckolding?

'Sorry, Adrian, I was miles away. Did you say something?'

'Just asked when Mum'd be joining us.'

'About two-thirty I reckon. Can't imagine what takes hairdressers so long.' He almost smiled. Adrian, he told himself, is as reluctant about this heart-to-heart as I am. Had Maureen said anything to him? Okay, nothing ventured. He took a sip of his beer. 'Your mother's quite immersed in all this wedding palaver. How about you, Adrian? Does Zannah nag you as much as Maureen nags me?'

'She has her moments. Told me the other night that she didn't want to be Whittaker. I wasn't having that.'

'So, what does she want to be called?'

Adrian looked a little puzzled. 'Ford, I suppose, but I'm not going to have that. We didn't really decide anything. But I'm determined. I reckon she'll be Mrs Whittaker in the end.'

'You finding Cal a bit of a problem?'

'Cal?' Adrian frowned. 'I'm not eaten up with jealousy, if that's what you mean. Never see him.'

'Zannah does, though, doesn't she?'

'Only when he comes to pick up Isis or bring her home. They have to be friendly for her sake, don't they?'

'Yes,' said Gray. 'Kids always have to come first.'

'Did you think of that when you met Mum? When you married her?'

'Well, it might not have looked like that to you, Adrian, but yes, we did think of you. And you weren't the most co-operative toddler in the world either.'

'It got worse, too, didn't it? I was the teenager from hell.' He sounded almost boastful.

Gray smiled to show there were no hard feelings. This was true, but even though Adrian's Conan the Barbarian days were long over, he'd always found it impossible to feel love for Maureen's son. He'd been quite pleased when Jon, his own son, had decided to go and work in South Africa. Much as he missed him, it made life easier to have him far away and not constantly existing as a contrast to Adrian. I love Jon, Gray thought, and although I get on with Adrian okay and don't mind him now, I don't love him. I never have. Now that he was no longer allowed to email Lydia, his messages to and from Jon were the one thing that made it worth switching on his laptop. Adrian was talking. Gray made an effort to tune in.

'Sorry, I didn't catch that ... say again.'

'Isis herself is more of a problem. I feel much more jealous of her than I do of Cal Ford and I can't admit it, which makes life difficult. I know Zannah loves me but she'd give me up in a minute if it came to a contest between me and her daughter.'

'It won't come to that, though, will it? You'll be a good stepfather.' Gray wondered as he spoke whether he believed this.

'Sure. Like you. I bet you thought you were the best, right?'

'I was. You can admit it now.' Gray smiled to show he was joking.

'But you weren't my dad, were you? And my mum loved you. I wasn't too keen on that idea.'

'While your dad was alive, he never came anywhere near you. You never knew him. You just made him into a hero because he wasn't me. Right?'

Adrian shrugged. 'S'pose so.'

Something occurred to Gray. 'Adrian, are you happy with this big wedding stuff? Did you and Zannah talk it over?'

'Course we did. As we're having a big wedding, I'm the one trying to persuade her to invite more people. She won't hear of it. She's got her own ideas about everything. She might look delicate but she's stubborn, you know.'

Like her mother, Gray wanted to say. Instead he asked: 'Do you love her?'

'Are you serious? What kind of question is that? She's fantastic. I said it at the engagement party. I'm the luckiest man in the world. I meant it.'

'Good.' Gray put his lager down. 'That's great.' He wondered privately what love meant to Adrian. Would he be faithful to Zannah? Did he dream about her? Run conversations with her through his head when they were apart? Perhaps Adrian lacked imagination. He blithely assumed that Cal Ford was out of his fiancée's life. And that's the difference between us. I torment myself by imagining Lydia and her husband in every sort of situation. I wish I were more like Adrian. It makes life much easier. He didn't seem too keen on Isis. Well, he probably likes her better than I liked him when he was a child, Gray thought, and I've managed to hide it for thirty years. In all the fights, in all the sulks, I've never let on that he wasn't as loved as Jon is . . . but he must have known. He probably picked up on my feelings. Children, even not very imaginative ones, are good at doing that.

'Another Stella?' he said, trying to catch the waiter's eye.

'Why not?' Adrian said, and leaned back so that his chair was balanced on two legs. It was the way he had sat when he was a boy at the kitchen table and in those days it had been a constant source of irritation. Things had moved on. I don't, thought Gray, give a damn how Adrian chooses to sit.

'And how, pray, is the future Mrs Whittaker?' Adrian slid into the chair opposite Zannah and added, 'I'm so sorry I'm late, darling. Frantic at the bank today. And I met Doc for a drink at lunchtime.'

'It's okay, don't worry. I haven't been here long.'

They were having dinner at one of Zannah's favourite restaurants, a French bistro called La Chaumière, whose garlic mushrooms were alone enough to justify a visit. It was a small, plainly decorated place which had the feel of a private house. You had the impression that you were dining *en famille* and Zannah loved that, but Adrian, she knew, thought it was rather like not going out to dinner at all. Nevertheless, he was indulging her tonight. Now, he was frowning slightly and probably wishing he were somewhere altogether flashier. She was surprised to find herself noticing things about him these days, physical things that she had obviously been blind to when they had first started going out together. His mouth was sometimes downright sulky when he wasn't getting his way. The blue eyes that had so enchanted her could freeze over and stare at her as though she were a stranger, but fortunately that had only happened on a couple of occasions. And anyway, she told herself, he's probably noticing things about me that he didn't take into account before, like the bags under my eyes, or the way I sometimes don't do my hair properly before coming out and just twist it up any old how as I did tonight. It was natural, she supposed, for the first glorious infatuation to wear off a bit, and as long as you still loved the person when it was gone, all was well. She loved Adrian, she was quite sure of it and this introspection came from the fact that she was letting organizational matters get away from her. *Control freak*, she heard

Em's voice say in her head. Relax. Everything's going to work out fine.

Zannah was feeling somewhat … She didn't know exactly what to call it. Originally, she'd intended them to have a quiet evening at home, discussing important things. For instance, she'd spoken to Edie and made an appointment for them to see the vicar at St James's next weekend and she was hoping Adrian wouldn't be difficult about that. They needed to discuss the order of service and the music. She'd already booked the date and the time: eleven-thirty. Also, she'd been wanting to discuss names again. She'd intended to leave it after their last discussion but now Adrian had raised it. She didn't say anything while they were ordering, but as soon as the garlic mushrooms arrived, she took a deep breath and plunged in: 'Adrian, you called me Mrs Whittaker just now. Remember?'

'By this time next year, it'll be your name.'

'Well, that's just it. I don't think it will be.'

'What d'you mean? It's my name …'

'But not mine.' Zannah took a sip of her wine. 'I have to have the same name as Isis. It's what she's used to.'

'She'll have to get unused to it then. Lots of kids do, don't they? Have a different name from their mother … Or she could become Whittaker too.'

Zannah looked at Adrian and wondered whether he was being deliberately stupid. It was hard to tell from his impassive face. She said carefully, 'I don't think Cal would be too pleased with that. She's his daughter. You wouldn't allow your child to carry someone else's name, would you?'

'Too right! Our kids will be Whittakers through and through.'

'Gratrixes, too, I hope. Maybe I should go back to being Suzannah Gratrix.'

'Over my dead body. I don't hold with that feminist nonsense. And,' he leaned forward and looked at her in a way that Zannah perceived as almost threatening, 'I notice you didn't have any objection to being Mrs Ford, did you? Well, by the same token, you'll be Mrs Whittaker from the day we get married.'

There was no answer to that. She'd agreed to be called by Cal's name, so now she didn't have a feminist leg to stand on. Still, the logistics were complicated. She'd be Whittaker and Isis would still be Ford. She'd have to explain the ramifications to her daughter. Thank heavens she was old enough now to understand, or at least Zannah hoped she would. Would she mind? She was more persuadable than Adrian, that was certain. A tiny unworthy thought – Isis would love me whatever happened – floated into Zannah's head and she pushed it away at once, but an echo remained and she felt she was being unfair to Adrian. Should she give in on this matter? Would 'Mrs Whittaker' be so dreadful? Perhaps it was a small price to pay for domestic harmony.

The garlic mushroom plates had been taken away. Adrian stroked her hand and said, 'I've got a suggestion to make, Zannah. Don't jump down my throat, just listen.'

'Okay,' said Zannah.

'Have you given any thought to Isis living with Cal? They're obviously devoted, aren't they?'

Zannah looked down at the salmon, lying pink and slathered in a yellowish sauce in front of her. She took a deep breath. 'I'm going to pretend you didn't say that, Adrian. You know Cal's always flying off on assignments. How d' you imagine he could look after her properly? To say nothing of the fact that she's settled in a school, with friends and familiar teachers ... and there's me, Adrian. Don't you know anything about me? Don't you know that Isis is the most important person in my life?'

'I thought I was,' Adrian sounded sulky.

'Oh, don't be childish, please!' Zannah was in severe danger of losing her temper. I mustn't, she thought. I can't make a scene here in front of everyone. 'You know what I mean. Isis is my child. You must understand, surely. It's different. It's not the same kind of love. Nothing like.'

'I see. Bottom line: she's more important to you than I am. If it came to a choice between us, you'd choose her. Am I right?'

'I don't have to choose between you! I thought I could have both of you. Why can't I? Other people have husbands and children. Why can't I?' Tears stood in her eyes and Zannah was uncertain what to do. If she wept, Adrian would be all sweetness and indulgence, she knew, at least for the time being. He hated tears. He behaved almost as though he was afraid of them.

'Stop being silly, Zannah,' Adrian said. 'Of course I'm not asking you to give up your daughter. I just thought Cal . . .'

'Well, don't. Don't think Cal. He does as much as anyone can who has joint custody and that's as much as I'm willing to ask him to do.'

'Okay, okay. We'll manage. Let's stop talking about this, agreed? Or our evening is going to go up in smoke and I won't enjoy the food.'

Zannah nodded miserably and wondered what they could possibly talk about now. She was starting to recognize something she'd either ignored or simply not considered before. Adrian would be perfectly happy for them to have a life alone together, a life without Isis in it, or with her transformed into an occasional visitor. Could that be true? She felt as though a tiny splinter of ice had entered her heart. I'll have to discuss it with him, she thought, but not tonight. He can't really mean it. He's fond of her. I'm sure he is.

'My mother told me the other day that Charlotte's first husband used to work at my bank,' Adrian was saying. 'Years and years ago, but it's still a bit of a coincidence.'

'He was a criminal. Did your mother tell you that?'

'She certainly didn't! You're not serious, are you? A criminal?' Adrian leaned forward, obviously fascinated.

'Oh, yes.' Zannah cut into her salmon and took a mouthful. When she'd swallowed it, she said, 'He was an embezzler or fraudster of some kind. I don't know all the details, but Charlotte served six months in prison. She was innocent, of course, but Nigel Katchen managed to implicate her and it took her ages to clear her name. She'd signed some papers, you see. She maintained he tricked her into it, but ignorance wasn't a defence.'

'What happened to him? To Nigel Katchen?'

'He killed himself before he could be brought to trial. That was seen as an admission of guilt. The jury didn't believe that Charlotte knew nothing of the scam. The fact that she used to be an accountant was proof, according to the prosecution, that she must have known what her own husband was up to.'

'Bloody hell, Zannah. You might have mentioned it.'

Zannah laughed. 'Why? It's not a big deal. I told you: Charlotte was innocent. It's been proved. There was an appeal and she was cleared of any wrongdoing. Nothing to make a fuss about. And it all happened ages ago anyway, in 1959.'

'What if she wasn't innocent, though? Are you a hundred per cent sure? And, anyway, aren't you even the least bit ashamed? I dunno. Something.'

'I *am* a hundred per cent sure. She was innocent. Charlotte isn't a criminal. God, Adrian, you've met her. Does she look like a criminal mastermind?'

Adrian leaned over, took Zannah's hand and squeezed it. 'Whatever. She's not a child murderer or anything, obviously. But you might have told me before.'

'I've told you now. I wasn't trying to keep it from you. We just take it for granted in the family.'

'I'll have to tell my mother,' said Adrian. He smiled. 'She'll have a fit, but she's got to know, right? And Doc, of course.'

'Okay, you tell them. I don't mind.'

'D'you want a pudding?' Adrian asked, relieved to change the subject.

'No, thanks,' said Zannah. 'Let's go home.'

As they left La Chaumière, she examined her mood. For almost the first time since they met, Zannah felt irritated by some of the things Adrian had said tonight. How many kisses and caresses would it take to banish that feeling? He'd be on his way to his own flat soon. They almost never spent the night together during the week because he had to get up very early for work. Did other brides feel like this? Bridal magazines spoke of stress and fallings-out over arrangements. Was that a kind of code for wanting to give your beloved a bloody good kick? Zannah squeezed Adrian's hand as they walked home, hoping to restore her own good humour. She was rewarded with a squeeze back and a tentative smile. Okay, she thought. That's a start.

Friday

'I don't know how you can be so calm, darling.' Maureen took a sip of her gin and tonic and sighed. 'London's becoming impossible. You cannot believe how long I spent on the phone yesterday, just making sure Adrian and Zannah were all right. Can you believe it? It's only two weeks since the last attack. What'll become of us, if we can't even go about normally on public transport? Honestly, Graham, you didn't see it all. It was like something out of one of those terrible movies where everyone's running around, but then you stopped and thought and it's London. I really feel so worried about Adrian living there now.'

'The police have been outstanding. You're not going to give comfort to those bastard terrorists, are you? Having Adrian run away to live somewhere else?'

'Well, put like that ... I suppose not. But still. It's very worrying.'

'That's true. Not the same world as it used to be.'

'I shouldn't think we can do much about it so we've just got to go on, I suppose. So I'm going to change the subject. I've been worrying about something else as well. Not as bad as terrorists obviously, but still, it's been on my mind. And you don't have to sigh like that. You can listen.'

Maureen leaned back against the blood-red velvet cushions of the enormously expensive sofa that was the main feature of the living room. 'I know you're going to say I'm mad, but I'm concerned about this Charlotte Parrish thing. What I think is: there's no smoke without fire. And what kind of a family has a jailbird in it? What if our friends find out? It's disgraceful.'

'Anyone would think,' said Graham, 'that she was Myra Hindley!'

'Don't be ridiculous. You know I'm not saying anything of the sort. Of course not. It's just strange, don't you think, that no one's mentioned it before? As though they knew it was a sort of disgrace.'

'It's not a disgrace. Adrian said Zannah didn't think it was important. They've forgotten all about it, so why don't you?'

'What if it should come out? What if some of our guests discover ...'

'Oh, for God's sake, Maureen, shut up about it, will you? I'm bored with the whole subject. Find something else to fret about, why don't you?'

He went back to reading his newspaper, in that special way he had which made sure you knew how angry he was. He was maddening sometimes, but she wasn't ready to give up quite yet. She said, 'You can hide behind your paper as much as you like but you have to admit, no one else we know has ever been within a mile of a jail and now suddenly, we're going to have a wedding in a house belonging to an ex-con. And frequented by others, too. She met both those friends of hers while she was inside apparently. I know that Edie was a nurse and the other one ... What's her name? Val ... Well, her husband was a complete bastard apparently, even though he was middle-class ...'

'There are middle-class wife-beaters, Maureen.'

'But what are people going to say?'

'I don't believe this! Listen to yourself! I've told you, no one else'll know unless you tell them. Now, just let me finish the paper.'

Maureen sniffed and turned her attention to the latest issue of *Bridal Bouquet*. She began to read a fascinating article about appropriate gifts for bridesmaids. Suddenly she was aware of Graham's newspaper being flung aside as he got up from his armchair. 'What's the matter, darling?'

'It's ... it's Joss Gratrix. She's on the shortlist for a poetry prize. Her book is, I mean.'

'Oh, God, I knew that! I forgot to tell you ... she found out when I was at Zannah's the other day. The Madrigal Prize. There! I've even remembered what it's called.'

'You forgot to tell me? You've known for all this time and not told me? That beggars belief.' He sat down again and glared at Maureen.

'Why are you making such a fuss about it? Did you even know she wrote poetry? Mind you, it figures. I do think there's something a bit, well, eccentric about her.'

Graham stalked out of the room, slamming the door behind him. Maureen sighed. What on earth was the matter with him? He was behaving most oddly. She picked up her magazine again and went back to reading about the competing claims of charm bracelets versus pendants as gifts from the bridegroom. Graham would get over it. He always did. He'd probably come in in a few minutes and apologize. Quite right too. Maureen felt she deserved an apology. She'd done nothing wrong and he'd flown off the handle.

Gray went to his study and turned on his computer. Bloody Maureen. How could she not have told him? Her stupid head was too filled up with guff about Charlotte having a criminal record to remember something she must have known he'd be interested in. She knew he wrote poetry. This was a demonstration, as if he needed one, of how much store she set by it. He knew Lydia's – Joss's – postal address now. Maureen had put it into the big address book that she kept in her desk and he'd copied it into his Palm Pilot. There were nights when he put a map of the area up on the screen and tried to imagine what her street looked like. Now, he stared at the bright rectangle in front of him and imagined how happy this news would have made Lydia: how happy it made him vicariously. He'd known her book was to be called *The Shipwreck Café*. He knew the poem of the same title by heart. *A sepia ocean washes into tea cups/moves in the curtains,/howls itself silent on the painted walls.*

Closing his eyes, he recalled how she'd looked that day, sitting against the background of those horrible, fascinating pictures. A white blouse embroidered with white silk flowers. Loose blue trousers. Flat black shoes. No jewellery, her hair falling over her collar in dark waves. He remembered how much he'd wanted to touch it. Her hand, lying on the tablecloth. He remembered her mouth, most of all. How she smiled. How she tasted, later on, when they'd kissed.

He shook his head to clear it, and found *The Shipwreck Café* on Amazon. There it was. An arty cover: a collage showing rose-patterned teacups and bits of wrecked ship. Maybe the publishers had got permission to use one of the actual photographs. Publication date 7 September. He pre-ordered the book, then moved to a florist's site, where he concentrated on the images of bouquets. Thank God for the Internet.

There was a bewildering array of choice. What should he send? In the end, he opted for two dozen hand-tied roses. Red? A symbol of love but a cliché. White? Too bridal. In the end, he settled for a kind of dark bronze: darker than peach, browner than red. In the picture, they looked amazing, on fire. He hoped the real flowers would be even half as lovely. He stared at the box marked 'Message'. He could send a few words and sign Maureen and Graham. That would be quite natural. Just politeness, really, between in-laws. No, he had a better idea. He left the message space blank. Lydia would know he was the only person who wouldn't say a word. Who wouldn't even give his name. Then he ordered a potted plant: a blue hydrangea, and wrote: *To Joss, with many congratulations on your shortlisting from Maureen and Graham Ashton.* He felt quite pleased with himself at this small trick: hydrangea as decoy.

Before he turned off the laptop, he put the words 'Fairford Hall' into Google. What had prompted him to do that? He had no idea. He clicked the link to *This year's programme* and scrolled down. He sat up straight and read again the words that had leaped out of the page at him: *18-23rd September. Poetry: Starting Out. Tutors: Lydia Quentin and Russell Blythe. Guest poet: Sheila Crawford.*

His heart, he noticed, was beating very fast, and he took a deep breath. He could go on the course. He could take a holiday. There was time to square it with the hospital. He could just turn up at Fairford. Lydia couldn't do anything about it. Once she'd realized he was there, as a paying student, it would be too late. She'd never leave and let down the other students, the other tutor, the Fairford Foundation. They'd have five whole days together. Four nights. He'd phone tomorrow and book a place. Should he say something in advance? Was it tricking her to do something like this? Perhaps it was, but she must, she *must* be happy to see him, if he was there. Best to say nothing in advance, though ... she might pull out if she knew he'd signed up.

When he appeared in the living room again, he was smiling.

'Well, I'm very glad you seem to be in a better mood. I don't know what got into you before,' said Maureen, who was surrounded by glossy magazines.

'I've just sent Joss' – oh, how easily and casually he said her name! – 'a potted hydrangea from us both.'

'Why on earth did you do that?'

'To congratulate her on her shortlisting. It's quite an achievement.'

Maureen said nothing for a moment. She shrugged her shoulders. 'A bit over the top, don't you think? She hasn't won anything yet.'

Gray couldn't think of a word to say that wasn't downright offensive so he picked up his newspaper again and hid behind it.

'God, you're sulky these days. I can't imagine what's got into you,' said Maureen. He ignored her and went on ignoring her till at last she left the room, sighing ostentatiously. The prospect of a visit to Fairford Hall glittered in the future, in the way that birthdays had when he was a boy.

Gray had grown up on his own in a adult world. He hardly ever thought about his early childhood in the way that was fashionable now, but when he did, he recalled his parents as kind and somewhat distant. He'd gone to boarding school at an early age, and various nannies were more vivid in his mind than what he remembered of his mother or father. That was another thing he and Lydia had in common: the early death of their parents. He'd been sent to live with his grandfather, taken out of one school and sent to another and he sometimes wondered what would have become of him if he hadn't been a child who liked school.

He'd been clever and reasonably good at sport. He'd made friends. He'd learned to hide his deepest feelings and hadn't even noticed that he'd been doing so till he met Maureen. It was thanks to her that he 'unwound' as she put it. She used to accuse him, in the early days, of being 'stiff' and 'too quiet by half'. It had been a bit of a shock to find, at medical school, that girls considered him attractive, and marrying Maureen had allowed him to form a better opinion of himself. After thirty years with her, he reckoned he could describe himself truthfully as confident, but the lonely and rather quiet child was still there somewhere. It was the part of him, he sometimes thought, that produced the poetry; an aspect of his character that neither his wife nor his colleagues knew about.

He would see Lydia at Fairford. He felt heroic and also reckless, having decided on this course of action. It made him feel as though he were properly alive. If Maureen wasn't around, he thought, I'd stand up and whoop and punch the air.

Saturday

'Delivery here for a Lydia Quentin and one for Mrs R. Gratrix ... same address. Is that right?'

Joss decided not to make the bewildered youth from the florist even more bewildered. She said, 'Yes, both here, thanks.'

'Lucky ladies,' said the young man. 'Lovely, these are.'

'If you could just put them on that table ... That's great.'

''Bye, then.'

He'd gone, and Joss stared at what he'd delivered. Lydia had an enormous, hand-tied bouquet of roses. No card. Obviously they were from Gray, who was the only person in the world who called her Lydia, and he must also have feared Bob seeing anything he wrote, however enigmatic. They had decided to break off all contact, hadn't they? He'd been surprisingly good about not getting in touch with her, and there were times when she longed for him to break his word, send her a text message...something. Now, here they were, these glorious bronze flowers ... two dozen of them. He still thinks of me, she told herself. He loves me. She didn't know whether she felt like weeping or hugging herself for joy. Did she have a vase that would do them justice? I wish they'd last for ever, she thought, and she resolved to keep a few as they faded. Sometimes, she liked roses even better when they were like papery ghosts of themselves. She turned to the potted plant addressed to Mrs Gratrix. It was hydrangea of a particularly attention-seeking blue, and Joss knew at once where it would look best: in the crescent-shaped flowerbed to the left of the front door. There was a card stuck among the blossoms: *To Joss, with many congratulations on your shortlisting from Maureen and Graham Ashton.* She smiled. She imagined Gray thinking how clever he'd been, covering his tracks, getting Maureen in on it too. Well, two could play at that game.

Joss put the hydrangea on a big saucer and placed it on the windowsill in the kitchen. She arranged the roses in her best and biggest vase, and decided to leave them on the hall table where they seemed to light up the space around them. She kept four to go in her study, putting them into a clear glass carafe that had once held wine but which she'd kept because she liked its shape.

Once she was upstairs in the study, she put it on her desk. She wanted the roses close to her, close enough to touch. Then she opened a drawer and took out her collection of postcards. She chose one of Fairford Hall, a pen-and-ink drawing of the house. She'd bought them two years ago, on the first day of the course, and kept them for very special occasions. Gray would understand what this image meant and why she had chosen it. She addressed the envelope to Dr and Mrs Graham Ashton. On the back of the card she wrote:

Many, many thanks to you both for the beautiful hydrangea. I've found the perfect place for it in the garden. Everyone's been so kind about the shortlisting. A glorious bunch of roses arrived today as well. I feel like a star. Thanks again. All the very best, Joss.

He would read that, and know that his flowers had reached her.

Friday

Isis looked into the dressing-table mirror, and wished she'd brought her face-painting kit on holiday. It was nearly a month since school had broken up but they'd only come here, to have their proper holiday, this week. This wasn't so much a hotel room as a kind of flat called a suite. There was a lounge, and a bedroom for Mum and Adrian and on the other side of the lounge, a much smaller bedroom for her. There was also a white and blue bathroom, with very sparkly tiles all over the walls and lots of little bottles of shampoo and body lotion in a basket near the washbasin.

It would have been cool to dress up as a princess but there wasn't that much to get dressed up in. Pyjamas weren't royal. Isis sighed. She shouldn't moan though, not when she was on holiday. This was a great hotel and she was lucky. Not many people had two holidays. Next week Dad was taking her to the Lake District. He'd promised they could go and visit Otto, her very own owl, who lived in a special bird sanctuary. Last year, when she turned seven, one of Dad's presents had been a certificate saying that she was now sponsoring a barn owl. There was a book about the sanctuary and a photo of Otto, who was beautiful. He had a notice on his cage now which said: *Otto is sponsored by Isis Ford* and she felt proud about that. She was longing to see him. Dad was going to take a photo of the two of them together.

Meanwhile, though, she was at the seaside with Mum and Adrian. There wouldn't be any bombs at the seaside, Isis was sure. Mum had said that even in London they were safe now and the police had caught a lot of the bad men, but there were times when she still felt worried and she tried not to go on the Underground too often. Adrian hadn't wanted to come on this holiday, Isis could tell. He'd grumbled all the way up to Scarborough in the car, and whenever she'd asked for anything, like a tissue or a fruit gum, he'd frowned. And he made a huge fuss when she wanted to play one of her story CDs.

'Won't music do, Isis?' he'd said and Mum had been on his side.

Isis sighed and said, 'I'm going to sleep. You two can play whatever you like.'

They'd put something on, opera. Mum liked that best. Adrian didn't, you could tell, but he couldn't say anything because he'd already made one fuss and asked for music. Isis hadn't really gone to sleep. She'd listened to them. It wasn't a proper row, what they were saying, but they sounded cross.

'I don't see why we couldn't go to the South of France or Spain or somewhere abroad,' Adrian said.

'Because we're going abroad for our honeymoon.' That was Mum.

'Not till next year, though. We could've taken a cheap flight. Isis could've gone to your mum's. We could have got in a bit of practice for our honeymoon.'

Mum had laughed at that. 'We need to economize, though, don't we? There's the wedding ...'

'Well, this is taking economy a bit far, don't you think? What on earth are we going to do in Scarborough in August? It's sure to rain. There'll be crowds of people everywhere. And Isis'll need entertaining, won't she?'

Isis, pretending to be asleep, thought, I don't need entertaining. I'm eight.

Mum said, 'Oh, stop grumbling, Adrian! We'll have a great time. It's a wonderful hotel.'

'Let's hope they have a good babysitting service. At least we can have our evenings to ourselves.'

Mum and Adrian were downstairs right now, having dinner in the room with the chandeliers. She'd had her supper earlier: a pizza from Room Service. Mum said she didn't need the babysitter, because they weren't going out and Isis could come and find them if she needed to, and it wasn't late, and when they'd finished eating they would come straight upstairs. They all had to get up early tomorrow morning to go home.

Adrian's cufflinks were on the dressing-table. They were really pretty. If I put them through the button-holes of my pyjama top, Isis thought, they'd look like jewels. Yes, that was good, but she needed something else. She looked round and caught sight of a silk scarf lying over the back of the chair. Adrian had given it to Mum last Christmas, and it was gorgeous: a lovely, dark red. She picked it up and wound it round her head like a turban, tying the ends in a knot at the nape of her neck, with the fringes hanging down. Cool! She paraded in front of the mirror for a while, did a bit of a dance and looked at the way the light from the lamp on the dressing-table made the cufflink-jewels glitter like stars.

'Isis? What are you doing?'

Adrian was standing in the doorway of the room, glaring at her.

'Nothing. I was just . . . I was dressing up.'

'Right. Well . . . I think it's probably time you were in bed, isn't it?'

Isis knew he was really, really cross, and trying not to show it. He'd gone white and he was smiling, but it wasn't a friendly smile. 'Are you cross because I'm dressing up?' she asked.

'No, no, that's okay,' he said, and he didn't mean it, you could tell. He frowned. 'But I think you should take all the dressing-up stuff off now and put it away, right? Make sure you put it back exactly where it was before, yes?'

Isis nodded. 'I've finished now. I will. I'll put everything back.'

'I'll wait, then. Till you've done it.'

Isis could feel him watching her as she put the cufflinks back on the dressing-table and laid the scarf over the chairback, looking just as it had before she'd picked it up. She heard him let out his breath as soon as everything was back to what it was before. 'There you are,' she said.

'That's fine. I'm going downstairs again now, then. I just came to see you were okay. You get into bed. We won't be long. Good night!'

He was trying to be jolly. Isis squeezed out a smile, even though she didn't feel smiley.

When he'd gone, she got into bed and looked at the ceiling. Sometimes she wished that Mum didn't love Adrian so much, and then she wouldn't want to marry him and then there'd be just the two of them, and Em, and Dad visiting. But if there was no wedding, she wouldn't be a bridesmaid, and she really, really wanted to wear a pretty dress and a headdress and carry a basket with flowers in it. And Mum had said that Gemma could be a bridesmaid, too, so she'd be upset as well if there was no wedding. Isis turned on to her side and stared at the wall. She wondered what would happen if she told Mum about Adrian being cross with her and not admitting it. He'd say he wasn't cross and she'd probably believe him. And maybe Mum would say she shouldn't have dressed up in Adrian's things without asking. Isis hid her face in the pillow. Adrian hadn't been very good at hiding his crossness. He doesn't really like me very much, she told herself. He keeps telling Mum he's fond of me, but it's not true. You could always tell if someone really, really liked you, and Isis knew that Adrian didn't. She could feel it.

Just before they came away to Scarborough, he'd found her reading one of her Malory Towers books. 'Not Harry Potter?' he asked her. 'Thought all kids liked nothing but Harry Potter.'

'I like lots of books,' Isis said. 'I like . . .'

'I'm sure you do,' he said, interrupting her. Isis turned away. Adrian kept on talking to her. 'That's a bit old-fashioned, isn't it? Enid Blyton. I read those when I was a boy. Some of them, anyway, but Malory Towers was too soppy.'

'This used to be Mum's book,' said Isis. It was rude of him, she thought, to call Malory Towers soppy. How did he know anyway, if he'd never read one? 'It's about a boarding school.'

'Would you like to go to boarding school, Isis?'

'People don't really go to boarding school,' she said. 'It's just in books.'

'Not at all,' Adrian said. 'Lots of people do go to boarding school. I did when I was a boy. So did my brother. How would you like to go to a school like that?.'

Isis thought about this for a moment, then shook her head. 'No, I like it here with Mum.'

Adrian had snorted and turned his attention to the newspaper. When Mum came in and asked how they were, he said, 'Fine. We were chatting about boarding schools.'

He hadn't told her that he'd asked Isis if she wanted to go.

I bet he'd like to send me away, she thought. But it's not up to him because Dad's the one who decides about stuff like that. And Mum. She wondered whether she should tell Mum what Adrian had said about boarding school and then thought she'd better not. Perhaps he was sort of joking. It was hard to tell with him sometimes. Maybe he'll like me better when they're married, when he gets to know me more. I'll be so good, he'll have to. It'll be okay.

Isis tried to think about something that didn't make her feel gloomy. Otto, she thought. I'll think about seeing Otto. I won't think about Adrian.

September/October

Thursday

'What the hell's the matter with you, Graham? It's only a bloody book when all's said and done. Anyone would think it's the Crown Jewels!'

'I ordered it!' He was shouting at her. He was red in the face with fury. 'My name's on the packet. Doesn't take a genius to know not to open it.'

'WHY NOT?' Maureen was screaming now. 'It's a book. Why shouldn't I open it? Since when do people order private stuff on Amazon, for God's sake? I've got a book on order too, and that's why I opened your stupid package. I wasn't looking at the name. Grow up! Anyway, now that I've seen what it is, the fuss you're making is even more ridiculous. It's Joss's book. I'm about to become related to the bloody woman. Why shouldn't I have a look at it? Not that I will again. It's totally boring and you're more than welcome to it.'

'Don't throw it!'

Too late. Maureen had taken the offending volume and hurled it at her husband. It caught him on the side of the head and he picked it up from the floor.

'I'm the one who orders from Amazon in this house. Not you,' he said.

'How dare you say that? Why not me? I've got just as much right to order books as you have. Can't imagine why you did order it, as a matter of fact.'

For a moment, Graham seemed confused. Maureen felt a rush of triumph. He hasn't got an answer, she thought.

'I'm interested in the Madrigal Prize. I write poetry, remember?' he said, sounding a little less furious. She hadn't seen him so put out for years. He muttered something about waiting for it for ages. And now, she could see he was about to make a fuss. Okay, the cover was bent back a bit, but that wasn't the end of the world, was it? She sighed. 'I'll let you open the next Amazon packet. All right? It'll be for me and you can open it.'

He didn't bother to answer and went up the stairs to his study. Maureen wished he was still within kicking distance. He was beginning to drive her mad. He was taking no interest whatsoever in the wedding. Whenever she brought up the subject, he either changed it or wandered off somewhere. He was doing very long hours at work and all she was good for, it seemed, was to put the meals on the table and provide sex when he needed it, which wasn't as often as she'd have liked. It was lucky she had other things on her mind. The dress. The food. She was in email contact with various catering firms and wrote to Zannah quite often with her thoughts on wedding-related matters. To be fair to her prospective daughter-in-law, her replies were always prompt but she didn't go in for long, chatty, enjoyable emails. She was always to the point: not a good communicator. Never mind, Maureen told herself. Some people just are like that when they're on the computer. They think they have to write in a kind of telegram-type style: as short as possible. Boring.

Maureen sometimes found herself wondering about Zannah. She was very attractive, if you liked the beanpole look, with not much in the way of a bosom, and hair that verged on ginger. Nice blue-green eyes. Tall, too, which would be useful when it came to wedding dresses. But there was a kind of reserve about her which she obviously got from her mother and that meant she wasn't the kind of prospective daughter-in-law Maureen would have preferred in an ideal world. She allowed herself to conjure up a plump blonde who'd have gone round the shops and wedding fairs with her endlessly, comparing samples of this and that and discussing the merits of fruit versus chocolate for the cake. Zannah was too much like Joss: another one who came over all tight-lipped in emails.

She wished that Adrian was in touch more often. There was the matter of Charlotte and the women she lived with to discuss and no one else would understand her feelings. She wasn't happy about that household. Since she had found out that Charlotte had been suspected of fraud and served six months, she'd also discovered that Edie – the sweet-looking dumpy one – was involved with one of those refuges full of women running away from abusive husbands and had once actually had an article in the *Daily Telegraph*. Maureen wondered how she'd cope if the media brought Edie to national attention while they were all involved with the wedding. The other woman, Val, was even worse. Apart from looking like an elderly and not very well-dressed scarecrow, she'd served six years for killing her husband with a kitchen knife. She'd never denied it, apparently. Maureen imagined a man's body slumped over a Formica table, the scarecrow cowering with bloodstained hands in the corner, shivering.

Charlotte had told her all this over lunch a few weeks ago. Maureen had practically invited herself to the house, telling the old lady that they had a great many arrangements to go over together. Actually, there wasn't anything that couldn't have been done on the phone, but Charlotte was not very forthcoming about the marquee, so she'd gone there to find out the details for herself. One thing had led to another and Maureen prided herself on being good at extracting any information she wanted from whoever it was she wanted it from.

When the story of Val's crime emerged, Charlotte had been careful to emphasise how cruel her husband had been. A brute. A rapist. Well, yes, Maureen thought privately, but still. Kitchen knives were not the answer and whenever that household came into her mind she felt a kind of sharp irritation bordering on distress. Imagine her son's wedding actually being held in that place! Her grandmother used to say: *What can't be cured must be endured,* but where was the sense in that? *What can't be cured must be changed as quickly and efficiently as possible.* That was Maureen's philosophy. But in this case, Zannah had set her heart on a marquee at her great-aunt's house and there was nothing to be done.

Where was that number for Dreamdress? Maureen picked up the phone and keyed it in. She'd managed to get Zannah to commit to a date for looking at wedding dresses and was about to confirm this with the shop: the Saturday after next. If it weren't for me, she thought, and to some extent Charlotte, this wedding wouldn't get off the ground. True, Joss had organized the invitations, which would be beautiful, she had to admit, but she was busy, apparently, next Saturday week. A reading in the local library. How could that possibly be more important than helping your daughter with one of the most important decisions of her life? Maureen had actually said something along those lines in one of her emails and Joss had written back to say that she trusted Zannah's taste. Not a word about my taste, Maureen reflected. Never mind, I'll be there when the dress is chosen, which is what counts. She could hardly wait to see what *Dreamdress* had to offer. The article in the *Daily Telegraph* had been full of praise for the individual care lavished on customers.

'Is that Dreamdress?' she purred into the phone. 'It's Mrs Ashton ... Thank you.'

As she waited to be put through to the lady in charge of appointments, she made a mental note to visit a few designer websites and begin thinking about her own outfit. Something in periwinkle blue, perhaps, but not too bright and vulgar. Or possibly pale coral.

Friday

'Okay. Update, please,' said Claire, taking another poppadom and breaking it into smaller and more conveniently sized pieces on her side plate. She, Louise and Zannah were sitting at the back of the Monsoon Nights restaurant round a table they regarded as their own. They came here about once a month, usually on a Friday evening, to do what Louise called 'putting the week behind us'. Zannah had thought about inviting Hazel, her best friend from art school, to one of these meals. Or perhaps Marie, who'd been at school with her, but Hazel had a toddler who didn't do babysitters, and Marie was a doctor whose leisure time had shrunk to two hours a month. Thank Heaven for email, she thought, and picked up the menu.

They'd been back at school a week and the first few days of term had been spent discussing every possible aspect of Hurricane Katrina and the terrible aftermath of the storm. The children had asked a thousand questions and some were easier to answer than others.

'First the bombs and now this,' said Louise. 'I don't know if I'm cut out for so much reassurance.'

'Isis wanted to know if her daddy was going to be sent there,' said Zannah, 'but thank goodness his paper decided to send someone else. And can you believe Cal was disappointed?'

'You must be so relieved. It's nightmarish even on TV. Imagine if you had someone you knew actually in New Orleans. Awful.'

'Let's talk about something else,' said Claire. Zannah took out her wedding notebook and laid it flat next to her plate. It fell open to a page in the middle headed 'Master List'. Louise peered across the table. She was, like most teachers, very good at reading upside down.

'I don't see anything there about transport. Flowers? Makeup? Hair? Photographs? Admit it, you haven't thought about those, have you?'

'I have, actually,' Zannah said quickly. 'No transport will be necessary. The church is near enough for us all to be able to walk from Charlotte's house. There and back. If Edie can do it, so can everyone else. It's literally round the corner.'

Claire and Louise were scandalized. 'No posh white cars with ribbons all over them? Whatever are you thinking of? And what about your dress, dragging through the dirt?'

'I've thought of that. I shan't be wearing a long dress and neither will Isis and Gemma. Calf-length, more likely. No long trains, either. And I like the idea of a procession, just like the olden days, in some village, with the bride leading the others to the wedding ...'

'And peasants no doubt lining the pavements and doffing their caps,' said Louise. 'I think you're crazy. What happens if it rains?'

'Not many peasants in Clapham,' Zannah replied. 'I suppose we might warn a taxi firm beforehand that we might need them. Anyway, it won't rain. It wouldn't dare.'

'Oh, that'll be really great.'

'Don't be such a pessimist! It'll be fine. I've already asked Charlotte. We're staying at her house overnight so the preparations, like hair and so forth, will be done there. I'll walk to the church and so will everyone else. Guests will come to Charlotte's first and leave their cars. Edie's son drives a big black Peugeot so, in an emergency, that'll have to do. He'll polish it beforehand, of course.'

'Okay,' said Louise. 'Let's leave the matter of transport. You've not even mentioned the most important thing of all. What about the dress?'

'I've got a day in town with Maureen next Saturday,' said Zannah. 'I'm dreading it. I wanted my mother to come down that weekend, but she's doing a reading in a local library and she also said that Maureen probably regards the occasion as a chance to bond with me ... God I hate that word. It makes me feel as though I'm being glued with epoxy resin, or something. Never mind, Em's coming with me for moral support, but can you picture it? Me trying on one hideous creation after another. In front of my future mother-in-law? I'd get Ma's view if I happen to like something, of course.'

‘What about a makeup artist?’ asked Louise. ‘You need one of those. And a hairdresser. Have you got one?’

‘Not really, but Em knows loads from her work. She’ll find someone. And she’s already volunteered to do the hen night. You two are invited, by the way. In fact, I think it’s just you two, me and Em. I can’t think of anyone else I’d want to ask.’

‘Great! Hope there are lots of naked men involved. Is there a date yet?’ Louise wanted to know.

‘No naked men, no pub crawls and the date isn’t fixed but it will be soon. Can we talk about something else now? I’m sick to death of weddings in general and mine in particular.’

Saturday

Joss leaned into the dressing-table mirror, making sure that her eyeliner was on smoothly, without the blotches and smudges she was inclined to make when she put on her makeup too quickly. No, that was okay. Em would be proud of me, she thought. She couldn't help feeling a thrill of excitement, and for a moment she imagined herself in one of those arty documentaries on BBC2. *Yes, I'm about to go and give a reading at the library ... only my friends and neighbours, I expect.* A modest glance down to the right. An enigmatic smile. A dress that made her look young and prettier than she was. Joss came back to reality. She was wearing French navy linen trousers with a pale jade-green linen blouse. She sighed. At this very moment Zannah would be going round that shop with Maureen. She hadn't been able to face it, which was the real reason why she'd decided not to go to London. Everyone, including Zannah, seemed to think a reading in a local library was something important and immovable. Of course, she could have changed the date in a second. It wasn't exactly the Festival Hall they were dealing with, but Joss had seized on the reading as an excuse. She simply didn't want to spend the afternoon with Maureen. Zannah was clear on the phone that she didn't intend to make any decisions about her dress and that Joss must enjoy herself being a famous poet, even if it was only in a suburban library.

The book was in her handbag. She'd dedicated it to her daughters and of course, a copy had gone to each of them, to Charlotte and several friends. She had no hesitation about not sending a copy to Gray and Maureen as a couple. She wanted more than anything to send Gray his own, signed copy, but couldn't. *Come, let us kiss and part* meant no contact, and she intended to stick to it even if he kept breaking their agreement.

Bob had taken her out to dinner the night before to celebrate publication. Charlotte, Zannah and Em had sent flowers, so had Mal, and Isis had made a special card, with a picture of pirates, a wrecked ship and lots of glitter sprinkled on the very blue sea curling round it. *Darling Grandma, lots of love from Isis.* It made Joss feel happy whenever she thought about it. She'd also printed out a lovely email Isis had written, all about her holiday with Cal. Joss kept it in her handbag, and took it out now to read again.

> *I went to see Otto in his sanctury. He's brown and has big white circly eyes he was asleep on his perch. That's because it was daytime. We went climing up a very green hill and I won. I got to the top first. Dad says it wasn't fair he was carying the food which slowed him up. I love Otto. We're going to see him again. I hope it's nightime and I can see his eyes. Dad says there orange. Here's a picture of an owl like Otto.*

'Joss!' Bob called her from downstairs. 'Package for you, love.'

'Coming!' She picked up her handbag and ran downstairs. The hall smelt wonderful. She was determined to take no notice of Bob's mutterings about turning the house into a funeral parlour with all these bouquets.

She opened the package, which had no return address on it. The name on the label was Lydia Quentin. Her heart began to beat more quickly. There were thousands of little polystyrene worms in the small box. No card. Nothing to say who it was from.

'What is it?' Bob asked. 'You're going to be late, aren't you?'

'No, I've got time still ... It's a cup and saucer.'

'Hmm,' said Bob. 'Funny thing to send, isn't it?' He wandered off before she had time to explain. Could he have guessed? No, she was sure he hadn't, but he *had* been perplexed. The cup and saucer were a present from Gray and they weren't a funny thing to send. They were just right. No one else would know that this was the pattern on the crockery at the Shipwreck Café. How on earth had he managed to find it? She could ask him. She could send him an email ... Surely just one email would be safe? To say thank you? No, she wouldn't. She'd stick to her resolve, not so much because she felt resolute but because she knew that if once she started, if once she allowed herself even one email message all the feelings she'd been bottling up for weeks would come rushing out, and carry her to places she yearned for; places that terrified her, too.

Bob came out into the hall again. 'Still mooning over that crockery?' he asked. 'Put it down now, Joss, for heaven's sake. We'll be late for the library.'

'Are you coming to the reading?'

'D'you want me to?' He looked genuinely astonished. 'I will if you like, only I thought I'd take the opportunity to have a dekko at the local history section. Is that okay?'

'Absolutely,' said Joss and she meant it. She had no desire for Bob to hear her reading her work aloud. As it was, she was nervous, and having him there would make things even worse. She got into the car, closed her eyes and leaned back against the seat as Bob drove off in the direction of the library. She thought of the cup and saucer sitting on the table in the hall: pretty, rose-patterned, almost translucent. A present from Gray.

Emily wondered if Zannah knew how much she'd sacrificed to come with her on her wedding-dress expedition. She could have gone to the movies with Cal and Isis. They were off to see *Charlie and the Chocolate Factory* and she'd have loved that. It would have been much more fun than spending any time at all with Maureen in full sail. Emily was longing for this afternoon to be over, because Cal was coming back with Isis to the flat for supper. If I were at the movies, she thought, I'd be eating popcorn and pretending that we were a family: a mum and a dad and their daughter out on a Saturday afternoon, having normal fun. How great would it be if Pa could suddenly materialize at her side, in the way he used to when she was a girl. They'd always had fun together.

'Psst ... wanna see a mummy?' This was on a Saturday afternoon when Zannah had gone off with some friends and she'd been feeling left out and grumpy.

'Egyptian kind of mummy?' Emily sat up, looking interested.

'Yup,' said Pa. 'A princess called Asru.'

They'd gone into Manchester in the car and had coffee in a funny little café just down the road from the university. When they'd got to Asru's display case, she was spookily and shiveringly and very satisfyingly dead and wrinkled and mummified. Pa had been the only person looking at her who knew anything about her, and Emily remembered being proud of him as he held forth in his rather too-loud voice. Which proves how young I was. It embarrassed me when I was a teenager. Wish I could be a kid again, she thought, and have some normal fun.

Normal fun was not what Maureen had in mind. She appeared from the depths of Green Park Underground decked in autumn colours, and it was clear even before she'd come up to them that she had dressed for this occasion as though it were some special kind of party. Not quite cocktail, but smart-smart. She looked, Emily thought, like someone from the days when a lady didn't leave her house without a nice clean pair of gloves. Okay, she wasn't actually wearing gloves, but you felt that they were there in her head, so to speak: part of her image of herself. Another part of the picture now, ever since the bombs on the Tube in July, was an almost visible air of Vera Lynnishness about her: a gallant smile, a devil-may-care stiff upper lip, a sort of squareness to the shoulders. She was probably imagining crowds of admiring people around her, commending her on her courage in undertaking this brave assault on Bond Street undeterred by the worst Al Qaeda could throw at her. One part of Emily chided herself for her unkindness, but still a voice in her head murmured: *I bet that's how she thinks of herself. I bet it is.*

Zannah kissed her politely on one cheek, and Emily smiled from the sidelines.

'Hello, Emily. I didn't know you were coming with us. How lovely!' Emily could see that Maureen would have been far happier to have Zannah to herself, and she noticed the barely perceptible hint of disapproval (slightly raised eyebrows) as she took in the black denim skirt and cream jacket that would evidently let the side down in whatever blisteringly chic emporium she'd marked out for them to visit.

'It's just down here,' Maureen said, striding briskly into the network of small streets behind Piccadilly. 'Not many people know about it – it's quite a trade secret – but it does have the most gorgeous selection of dresses from all sorts of designers. I've made an appointment for you, Zannah, and you can take your time trying everything on, with no pressure at all, of course. Just a little reconnaissance if you know what I mean.'

Dreamdress didn't look much from the outside. Zannah was dutifully talking to Maureen as they went in, so Emily had to keep her thoughts to herself. Discreet was the word that came to mind: a silver door, and that was it. You had to ring a bell and be let in, as though you were getting in to some members-only sex club. Members. Emily smiled to herself at the smutty joke and wished Maureen weren't there so that she could share it with Zannah.

Inside, a short flight of stairs led up to an enormous space, carpeted in a shade of pink so luscious you felt like sinking on to your knees and licking it. Doors all round the walls looked as though they led into other rooms, but turned out to be nothing but glorified cupboards. The saleslady was even smarter than Maureen, which was saying something. Her makeup was perfect; her nails likewise. She would have made most women – but not Zannah, who was seriously thin – feel positively chubby.

Emily found herself on a chair opposite Zannah and Maureen, who were sharing a sofa as though they were the best of friends. Only a sister would see that she's ready to make a run for it, Emily thought. Zannah kept biting her lip, always a giveaway. And her hands were literally twisted together in her lap as the dresses came out, one after another. Soon, there were about eight bridal confections hanging from hooks that hadn't been noticeable before because they were cunningly disguised to look like decorations on the doors/cupboards.

'Now take your time, dear,' said the supersmart saleslady. 'Try them on, one after another, and see how you feel about each one. Choosing a wedding dress isn't something one should do in a rush. And, of course, if there's a style or a look you fancy that you don't see here, just let me know. We have so, so much more to offer, if these don't appeal.'

'Thank you,' said Zannah, and stood up with the air of a Resistance heroine about to be interviewed by the Gestapo. She walked towards a dress that seemed made of a thousand layers of tulle and organdie.

Emily stood up as well, and went over to her. 'Shall I come too? To zip you up?'

'Thanks!' said Zannah, her relief obvious. She turned to Maureen. 'Won't be a moment.'

In the changing-room, Emily looked around and said, 'Get a load of this, Zan! They could let it out to a single mum and her kids, couldn't they? Or we could have the reception in here. Whaddaya say?'

'Oh, God, why did I agree to this, Em?'

'To please Adrian? To bond with Little Mo, in Ma's words? Perhaps even to choose a wedding dress ... Here, let me do that up for you. There you go. The cream-cake look!'

'It's awful. I hate it. I hate them all.' Zannah stood in front of the mirror, stricken.

'Nonsense. You look like a very pretty cream cake. Go out and show your ma-in-law.'

'Must I? Even though I know I'll never, ever wear anything like this. Not for love or money.'

'I'll tell them,' Emily said. 'I'll go and get another one and say you want something simpler. How's that?'

'Would you? Really? Please, Em ... go and get me something that at least looks wearable.'

Two hours later, Zannah, Emily and Maureen were recovering from the *Dreamdress* experience in Fortnum & Mason's.

'My treat,' said Zannah. This extravagance, Emily knew, was the result of guilt. Zannah was feeling bad about hating every single one of the wedding dresses she'd been shown. She would, Emily knew, try to put a positive slant on the afternoon over a soothing cup of tea and some cakes priced as though they were items of jewellery.

'Well,' said Maureen. She was making a bad job of keeping the bitterness of disappointment out of her voice. 'That was interesting, don't you think? I must say, Zannah, I'm not quite sure what it is you want. You seemed not to like anything we were shown. So many different styles ... so many fabrics. What was the matter with them?' Maureen was keeping her temper, but it was clearly an effort.

Zannah took a deep breath and launched into an explanation. 'I'm so sorry, Maureen. It's very kind of you to have come all this way and I'm terribly grateful, only the thing is ... well, I did tell you that I have a good idea of what I want. I've had the same idea for years, really. Since I was about twelve.'

'I was sure your childhood vision would be there somewhere. Are you quite certain there wasn't anything even remotely similar?'

'The main thing was, most of the dresses were strapless.'

'That's the fashion these days,' said Maureen. 'You've only got to look at a couple of magazines to see that.'

'Yes,' said Zannah. 'I've noticed. I'm not very keen on it.'

'Why on earth not?'

'That style doesn't suit me, I'm afraid. I'm too bony round the shoulders. I've got no bust to speak of. It's just . . . it's not a look I like, that's all. And besides . . .'

'Yes?' Maureen's teacup was halfway to her lips. The suspense was killing her.

'They don't look bridal, those dresses. Not my idea of bridal.'

'Anyone would think,' said Maureen, sweetly, 'that you were a virginal young girl walking innocently up the aisle. You're the mother of an eight-year-old child, though, and this is your second marriage.'

Emily was dying to make some really rude remark that would have put the kibosh on the whole afternoon, but restrained herself. She could see Zannah was hurt. She was doing that thing she always did when someone really upset her: biting her lip and looking down at her hands. Her voice was strained as she said, 'I'll think about it, Maureen, and get back to you. Perhaps I should look into having something made specially for me . . . to my specifications, I mean.'

'Anyone worth their salt as a designer-dressmaker would charge you a good deal more than a thousand pounds,' said Maureen, as though she'd already looked into it. She probably had, Emily reflected. You couldn't accuse her of not doing her wedding homework. Her laptop was doubtless steaming with the amount of Internet consultation that must have gone on. Now she was gathering her things together as though she was getting ready to go home, and not before time either. She was smiling at Zannah now, confident that she'd had the last word. 'You wouldn't want to spend that amount, surely?'

Which, being translated, meant: *you can't afford to spend that much*.

Zannah shook her head. 'No, of course not. Well, I'll just have to think, I expect. I'll let you know what I decide, Maureen, and it was kind of you to fix up the appointment for us. Really helpful.'

'A pleasure, dear,' said Maureen, standing up. 'You now know exactly what you don't want, which is half the battle, isn't it? Now I really must fly. Regards to your parents, of course. Such a shame your mother couldn't be here too.'

You had to be on Maureen's wavelength, Emily thought. What she's saying is: if Ma had been here, she might have talked some sense into her wayward daughter. And what sort of a mother isn't at her daughter's side when such earth-shaking decisions had to be made? A bad one, that's what Maureen evidently thought. Zannah just smiled, which was typical. If she'd said that to me, Emily reflected, I'd have found a suitably sharp response. Not to mention a suitably sharp knife to stick into the bosom which she doubtless thinks of as 'voluptuous' but which, Emily saw, was running the risk of becoming something more matronly altogether. She's making it seem as though Ma isn't interested, when the truth is much more likely to be that she didn't want to spend the afternoon with Maureen, and who could blame her?

Zannah stood at the sink, washing the plates and cutlery from the Chinese takeaway they'd just eaten. Adrian was out with the friends who were going to make up the guest list at his stag night. She thought of them privately as 'the lads' and while most of them were okay, she'd been quite relieved not to have to go out after the wearing afternoon she'd just spent with Maureen. Isis, exhausted from recounting the whole of the plot of the movie they'd seen that afternoon, had gone to bed without too much fuss. She'd even managed to eat most of her prawn chow mein while undertaking this marathon of storytelling, which was quite an achievement. She'd insisted on Cal tucking her in, but he was back in the kitchen now, and putting away the dishes as she washed and Emily dried them.

He knows where they go, she thought. I don't have to tell him. All evening, she'd felt relaxed and comfortable. She'd taken off the clothes she'd worn to go to Dreamdress the second they'd come back to the flat, and was now in black velvet trousers, an ancient sweatshirt and an even more ancient pair of sports socks. Her hair was up in a pony tail and it occurred to her that she wouldn't mind staying in this outfit for the entire weekend. Adrian would be shocked to know I think like that, she reflected. He likes me to be what he calls 'prettied up'. Cal never noticed what I wore and still doesn't. Once, years ago, she'd burst into tears because he'd said nothing when she'd gone to endless trouble to look gorgeous for some do or other, and then when she'd chided him, he simply hadn't known what she was talking about. *I see faces, Zannah*, he'd said. *I don't see clothes*. She could hardly believe it. She'd questioned him and it turned out to be literally true. A person could be wearing a binbag and Cal would only notice it if someone drew it to his attention. His lack of interest in clothes had irritated her when they were married, but now she found it refreshing. Did Cal remember what she'd worn at their wedding? Of course not. There were a few amateur snapshots of the party after the register-office ceremony (mostly taken in ghastly light in the pub) but none showed her outfit to any advantage.

It was a lovely dress, too. She still liked it and had recently taken to wearing it to parties and enjoyed the bluey-green swirly chiffon wafting round her knees as she walked. Cal had once, in an uncharacteristically lyrical turn of phrase, told her it turned her eyes the colour of aquamarines. Why had she suddenly remembered that now? Was she mad to keep it? No, not at all. Wedding dresses, she thought, lose any sentimental value they might once have had after you're divorced. It was just the fact that she looked good in it that stopped her from giving it to Oxfam.

Emily and Cal were giggling together.

'You should've seen her face, honestly,' Emily said. 'Disapproval written all over it. And Zannah stood her ground, which I wasn't expecting. I was sure she'd cave in before the combined forces of an intimidating saleslady and an even more determined Maureen.'

Zannah turned away from the sink to face them. 'I couldn't wear anything they showed me, Cal. Every single dress had something wrong with it.'

'Quite right,' said Cal, reaching up to the high cupboard to put away the glasses. 'Don't you let anyone bully you. Coffee?'

'Yes, please,' said Zannah and Cal took the kettle and leaned across her to fill it. His body was very close to hers, almost touching it, and he smelt exactly the same as she remembered. Suddenly, a rush of memories crowded into her head. She moved away from the sink to dispel them and distracted herself with finding the cafetière and the coffee. This is not, she told herself, a good time to get nostalgic about being married to Cal. Not a time to remember how he used to kiss me.

Think of Adrian. Think of your wedding dress. Think of walking up that lovely aisle in the church wearing it. Yes, she was okay now. An image of the dress had dislodged this totally unexpected parade of memories. Now she was back to worrying about it again.

'You just being difficult, Zan, or d'you actually know what you want?' Cal took over with the coffee. It was one of the things he was good at and always did when he came to the flat.

'I'm not being difficult. In fact, I've got it. My dress. I mean I've drawn it. I've just not shown anyone, that's all.'

'Doh!' said Emily. 'You're mad, you are. You should have brought it this afternoon, Zannah. Why haven't you shown it to anyone? Are you going to let us see it now?'

'Might as well. You pour the coffee, Em and I'll get my sketch. And the reason I didn't bring it today is because I didn't want to show it to Maureen. Certainly not before I'd seen what *Dreamdress* had to offer. Now I'm not sure I'd be able to afford it anyway. A good deal over a thousand pounds, didn't she say, to get a dress made . . .'

Zannah went upstairs to get her drawing. She'd still not told anyone about her secret fund. Now that she'd seen what was on offer, she was even more determined to have exactly what she wanted. Her parents, she knew, thought that the dress came into the part of the budget for which they were responsible, but Zannah wanted to be able to contribute a substantial sum. She'd saved nearly a thousand pounds. As she took out her sketch from its hiding-place, she said it to herself again: A *thousand pounds*, maybe more, for one dress. There was something grotesquely extravagant about that. Cal would be scandalized and mutter about justice and the world's poor and quite right too. Zannah decided she would avoid any hassle by never telling him how much her wedding dress cost, whatever the sum turned out to be. It was, after all, nothing to do with him.

Back in the living room Cal was stretched out on the sofa with his shoes off. Emily was telling him about Fortnum & Mason, and the cake extravaganza. She was sitting on a floor cushion, waving her hands about.

'Here you go,' said Zannah, putting a sheet of paper down on the coffee table. Cal swung his legs around and sat up and Emily crawled off the cushion to have a look.

'That,' she said 'is ... I don't have a word. Gorgeous. Beautiful. Perfect. You were right, Zannah. This is the only dress in the world for you. I feel like crying. I never cry about things like wedding dresses. I must be sickening for something.'

Zannah smiled. 'You're just being Emm-ish, Em. You'd have enthused whatever I'd drawn. It's how you are.'

'Bollocks! It is not! I do not enthuse about everything. Not at all. And certainly not when it comes to wedding dresses, which I can't bear usually. They're so ... so weddingy. I'm the anti-wedding one, remember? But this ... this is really amazing.'

'Well, thanks ... Cal? You're not saying a word. What's up?' Zannah looked at her ex-husband who was being uncharacteristically silent and pensive.

'It's smashing, Zan,' he said at last. 'And I've got an idea. D'you know who Verity Mason is?'

'Of course I do. I love her. She's one of the fashion people on your paper. You know her, I suppose?'

'Slightly. I never read her column, but people write to her with their problems when it comes to clothes. That's right, isn't it?'

'Yes, she's fantastic,' said Zannah. 'Seems to know the answer to everything.'

'And you think,' Emily butted in 'that Zannah should write and say: *I used to be married to Cal Ford, so will you help me with my wedding dress?*'

'No,' said Cal. 'I'll just get her to give you a ring. She might know someone who'd be good at that ...' He pointed at the sketch.

'What d'you mean, good at it? How good?' Zannah looked mystified.

'You'll want someone to make it, won't you?' Cal asked.

'It's very expensive, getting things made ...'

'I'll get Verity to call you tomorrow. Gotta go.'

'Right,' said Zannah. 'Thanks, Cal. That's terrific. D'you think Verity'll mind?'

'No, she's a good egg. Okay, you lot, I'm off.'

'Night, Cal,' said Zannah, and blew him a kiss.

It took him some time to locate his shoes but he found them in the end. Em showed him to the door. Zannah could hear them talking and laughing but she wasn't really listening. She couldn't stop staring at the thin black lines of her pen-and-ink sketch. Perhaps, perhaps, there was a possibility that it might become more than just a idea on paper. She might be able to make it real. Good old Cal. How unexpected he was.

Tuesday

Joss looked out of one of the upstairs windows at Fairford Hall and felt, for the first time in many weeks, a wave of pure happiness, untainted by any concern about the world out there, at the end of the long drive, where things were complicated and distressing. This was what she loved best about coming here: you were given five days away from your own life. Five days when you could be a person unattached to anyone else. Five days during which you didn't have to consider anything except your duties as a tutor. I might even, Joss thought, get down to some writing myself. It had been difficult, what with the wedding arrangements, getting Bob off to Egypt, sorting things out with the library so she could have this time off work, to say nothing of her own elation about the Madrigal shortlisting, to do any writing. Perhaps here she would be able to concentrate. She'd arrived early, wanting to be alone in the place before anyone else turned up. The first two times she'd been here, she and Gray had been hours ahead of anyone else and she remembered them sitting at the enormous oak table, smiling at one another.

The countryside round the house was like an advertisement for autumn. Leaves were turning and the mass of green was interwoven with scarlet, gold, bronze and brown. The sky curved pale blue above the trees. Just out of sight, the sea was waiting, in its sheltered bay, edged by high cliffs. Fairford Hall looked exactly like an oversized dolls' house, which was one reason why Joss loved it. It was pretty and welcoming, with dark panelling in the drawing room, and an Aga and a full set of copper-bottomed pots and pans in the kitchen. There were fifteen bedrooms. Groups of course members and the two tutors took it in turns to cook the evening meal. You helped yourself for breakfast and lunch from a fridge that was kept filled with goodies by the course directors, Agnes and Bill, who did all the administrative work and looked after the house.

When she'd been there before, Joss had shared a bedroom, but as a tutor you got a room on your own at the front of the house. It was like being upgraded to first class. She now had her own wardrobe with a pattern of tulips carved into the door, a view over the garden and down to the trees, and a table to work on. Her fellow tutor wouldn't be here for ages and neither would the course-members whom she thought of as students, even though some would probably be as old as she was or older. You never had any idea before you arrived of who would be coming on the course and that was part of the fun. She had plenty of time. She plugged in her laptop and turned on her modem to send an email.

Normally Joss wouldn't have thought about email while she was at Fairford, but she needed to send a message to Nora at the library about the copy for a leaflet that urgently needed to go to the printers tomorrow and which she'd forgotten to pass on to her. She clicked on '*Inbox*'. Not too many, she was glad to see, but she sighed when she saw Maureen's name at the top of the list. She wrote to Nora at the library first, because that was urgent, and then she read the messages from Isis and Bob. Isis had sent her a cartoon rabbit and a message that said, *I've found a picture of a rabbit. Hope your having a nice time in the country.* Isis loved rabbits, as well as owls and butterflies. Joss was always on the lookout for suitable postcards. She smiled and pressed the *'Reply'* button.

> *Hello, darling! This rabbit is sweet. I'll keep an eye out for rabbits while I'm here and if I see any postcards you'd like I'll send them. Here are lots of kisses till I see you.xxxxxxxxxxxxxxxxx*

Bob sent a message with his contact details in Egypt. Very curt and businesslike. He didn't believe in actual 'writing' on email, but used it as kind of shorthand way of conveying information, rather like texting but at slightly greater length and with all the letters included. She replied, in best war-movie mode:

Copy that. Over and out. Have a lovely time. Shan't be emailing in the next few days but will write in detail when I get home. See you soon. Love J.x

She wondered whether he would notice the kiss she'd added. Okay, she thought. That's that. There was a time when Bob had written long letters to her if he was abroad. When the girls were little, he used to add sketches of things like camels to amuse them. His signing off, which had always mildly irritated Joss, because she'd thought it a throwback to his schooldays, still said *Tons of love.* Perhaps he was short and cool in tone simply because the medium was electronic and not a handwritten letter. And perhaps not. She clicked on the next email, mentally bracing herself for one of Maureen's effusions.

She read the message through and when she'd finished, she found that she was grasping the edge of the table so hard that the tips of her fingers were white. It can't be, she thought. It's a mistake. He couldn't . . . She read the message again, more carefully.

Not much luck with wedding dresses, I'm afraid. Never mind, I've not quite given up yet! I'll get back to Zannah soon, for a chat. All on my ownie-oh for a few days, as Graham's gone off to Dorset on some poetry course or other. You'd know more about this kind of thing than me. I shall be putting my catering thinking-cap on while he's away!! Bye! Maureen.

Joss looked at her watch. Two-thirty. Course-members generally started to arrive at about four o'clock. She went over to the bed and lay down on it, staring up at the ceiling. There were no other poetry courses but this one in Dorset. He'd done it deliberately: booked himself in because he'd known she was a tutor. Perhaps he found out about it from a Friends of Fairford publicity mailing. What was she supposed to do? How was she supposed to feel? She felt rage washing through her. He'd deceived her again, not told her something she should have known. But if he had told me, she thought, I'd have said I was ill. I'd have cancelled. He knows I would never walk out on a course that's already begun.

She sat up. He was on his way here now. He might be there when she went downstairs. How should she behave? Pretend she'd never met him? Or tell people he was her daughter's future stepfather-in-law? What had come over him? Why had he done such a thing? Because he wants to see me, she thought. And because he knows that I'm longing to see him and won't allow myself even to think about the possibility. Now they were going to be together. Together. She imagined what the next five days might be like and the force of her vision made her feel breathless, as though she'd been picked up and swept along in a kind of emotional hurricane.

But no. They'd decided. They'd agreed. They had no future together. What Gray had done by enrolling on this course was unforgivable and she'd never, ever forgive him. She'd promised Bob that their relationship was in the past. Over. And it was. She'd been so strong-minded about keeping her word, even though there were times when the temptation to send Gray an email (just a written message, where was the harm in that?) was so overpowering that she had to close down her laptop. Promises ... She'd already broken the promises she'd made when she married. Perhaps people oughtn't to be allowed to promise things recklessly in case they couldn't keep them? There should be a mechanism for cancelling promises you made to someone you weren't married to that you found you couldn't keep. But Gray hadn't taken any such vow, and here he was, making it so hard for her to behave as she knew she was supposed to. She'd punish him for it. An idea was beginning to form in her mind. He didn't know she'd been forewarned. Maureen wouldn't have said anything ... Why should she? Okay, she'd behave as though she were made of ice where he was concerned. She'd treat him exactly like everyone else and not show by one single movement or word that she'd ever met him before or ever wanted to again. *Be it not seen in either of our brows/That we one jot of former love retain.* She took a deep breath and got off the bed.

In the en-suite bathroom (another perk for tutors), she stared at her face in the mirror. Was there time to do her makeup again? Someone was knocking at her door. Probably Agnes wanting to tell her something.

She went to open it, then stepped back.

'Lydia ...'

She stood in the doorway for a long time, saying nothing.

'Are you going to let me in? I want to explain ... Please?'

He looked anxious. Unsmiling. She had no control over her voice. Something like a squeak came out of her mouth. 'Yes,' she managed at last. 'Come in, Gray.'

He closed the door behind him and leaned against it. 'I'm sorry, Lydia. I couldn't help it. I wanted ... I just wanted ...'

'I don't forgive you, Gray,' she said at last. She was standing too near him, unable to put a distance between them, unable to move at all. 'You must have known how I'd feel. Didn't you know?'

'I suppose so. I suppose I did, but I wanted to see you. I hate not being able to write to you. This ... this seemed ... I don't know. We should be together.'

He put a hand out and touched her gently on the shoulder. She thought: No one'll know. No one will find out I've broken my promise to Bob. It's such a small parcel of time. No one'll be hurt. It's just us, just for now. Five days. Four nights. On Saturday we'll go back to what we were before, but now ... This is our place, away from everyone, away from our real lives. They're far away. We can forget everything. Oh, God, I love him so much. I love him.

He was waiting for her to decide, Joss could see that. She could end everything in a second. If she wanted him to, he'd go. He'll leave at once, she told herself, if I say he should. She opened her mouth to tell him to go and found she couldn't speak. She moved a step closer to him, put her arms up and round his neck and buried her face in his jacket.

'Stay.' She didn't know whether he could hear her or not and didn't care, but wanted only to breathe in the smell of him, feel the length of his body against hers. 'My darling,' she murmured. 'Stay with me.'

Zannah sat in Phyllis Hayward's living room and looked about her. It was the cleanest room she'd ever seen in her whole life. The skirting-boards were pristine and the carpet looked as though it had never had a speck of dust settle on it since the day it was put down. Miss Hayward's decor wasn't to Zannah's taste – cabbage roses on the overstuffed sofa and armchairs, china shepherdesses on the mantelpiece – but she herself was a gently-spoken, smily person with gold-rimmed specs and permed white hair. She was dressed in an immaculately tailored blue suit, and although she might have put on this outfit because she was expecting visitors, Zannah had a strong suspicion that this was what she wore every day.

'It's very kind of you to see me,' she said.

'A pleasure, my dear,' said Miss Hayward. ' I'm happy to help a friend of Verity. I knew her grandmother, years ago. I made her wedding dress, and one for Verity's mother too. Please help yourself to shortbread. It's the Prince of Wales's brand, you know, with lemon in it. Quite delicious, I think.'

A picture of Prince Charles in a flowered pinny, rolling out shortbread in the Highgrove kitchen, came into Zannah's head and she smiled. 'Thank you, it's lovely.'

'Now what's Verity told you about me?'

'That you were the best dressmaker in the country. She said you used to work for Norman Hartnell.'

'Dear Verity is exaggerating, but how kind of her. Hartnell's name isn't on everyone's lips, these days, but his standards were very high. Very high indeed. We made outfits for the Queen, you know. And the Queen Mother and Princess Margaret. I was there for twenty years. Then I started my own bridal dressmaking service, but of course I retired officially a few years ago.'

Miss Hayward put her cup on a highly-polished occasional table that stood beside her armchair. She said, 'Have you an idea of the sort of thing you want? I have albums you can look at with photographs of dresses I've made. I don't take on many commissions, because I find I get tired much more quickly these days. I'm nearly eighty, you know.'

'Goodness,' said Zannah. 'You seem much younger.' Zannah meant what she said. Miss Hayward was clearly someone who'd found her look a long time ago and stuck to it. But nearly eighty … Could she still manage what she used to? What about her eyesight? As though she were reading Zannah's mind, Miss Hayward said: 'My eyesight's as good as it ever was, and my hands are still steady. Have you set a date for the wedding?'

'May the twenty-seventh, next year.'

'That's good. Lots of time. You'd be amazed how many people think you can run up something in a day or two. Now, what have you been dreaming of when you think of your wedding dress?'

Zannah took the photocopy she'd made of her sketch out of her handbag. She'd had it folded in the pages of her wedding notebook for a couple of days, and now she opened it up and held it out to Miss Hayward, who took it and inspected it for a long time without a word. 'Most beautiful!' she said eventually and Zannah let out the breath she'd been holding. She used to do that as a child, waiting for a teacher's verdict on her work.

'Thank you,' she said. 'Will you ... Could you?'

'Make it? Oh, yes. It won't present too many problems, I don't think. You've chosen such a simple shape. *Crêpe-de-Chine* lining, I think, in the same colour as the lace. I've got a box full of bits we can search through for things like lace for the edges of the sleeves, the neckline and so forth. This is lovely. Very 1920s. The whole effect of a dress like this depends on the fabric. You're going to need the perfect lace and the exact shade of ... you've not said, but I think cream, écru or ivory, something like that, to go with your colouring. Not white, in any case.'

'No,' said Zannah. 'I had been thinking of it in cream ... thick, clotted cream. A touch of buttery yellow in it.' She was babbling about the colour because she didn't know how to broach the subject of money. What if Miss Hayward charged more than she could afford? She had to mention it before she committed herself. And she'd have to find out where one was supposed to buy 'perfect lace' to say nothing of *crêpe-de-Chine* for the underdress. She was about to speak, when Miss Hayward stood up. 'Come with me, dear. We'll go and have a look in my cupboard.'

Zannah followed her upstairs.

'This is my sewing room,' said Miss Hayward, leading the way into a bedroom at the back of the house. The window looked out on to a small and extremely tidy walled garden. A fearsomely modern sewing-machine stood on a table under the window and a fitted cupboard took up most of the longest wall. Miss Hayward opened it wide and said, 'There's sure to be something here that'll do.'

Astonished, Zannah gazed into the cupboard. She wasn't sure what she'd been expecting but it wasn't shelf upon shelf of neatly stacked rolls of material. They were lined up in order: palest colours on the left, darkest on the right.

'I try to have a bit of everything,' said Miss Hayward, 'but of course the paler shades are more popular with brides and bridesmaids. Are you having bridesmaids?'

'Two. My daughter and her friend. They're both eight.'

'How lovely!' Miss Hayward turned back to the cupboard. 'There's a bit of everything here, silk, satin, velvet, chiffon and even ...' she paused and walked along the massed ranks of fabric, like a general inspecting his troops. 'Lace,' she said with an air of triumph, pulling out a roll carefully. 'Most of this,' she added 'is what was left over when I retired. I won't use even a fraction of it in my lifetime, but I can't bear to part with it. And sometimes it comes in handy. Like now. What do you think of it? It's vintage, of course. I found it when a reputable wholesaler closed down ... oh, years and years ago. You won't find anything like it nowadays. I won't work with nylon lace. This is more expensive, of course, but well worth the extra money.'

Miss Hayward spread it out over the table. Zannah picked up a corner and it felt soft to the touch, not scratchy at all. The pattern was an intricate mesh of small flowers and ... Could it be? Yes! Tiny butterflies that appeared to have been caught up in the design. You wouldn't see them if you didn't look carefully. Zannah regarded butterflies as her emblem and finding them here, in this lace, was an omen.

Zannah noticed that her heart was beating fast, and that she was feeling most peculiar: moved and suddenly almost tearful. Em would say: *Cool it ... It's only a dress*, but her sister didn't understand. No one did. The dress, now that she could see the fabric in front of her, would be the embodiment of everything she hoped for from her marriage to Adrian. A strange feeling came over her, which she'd never articulated before: that the sheer contrast between this dress and the one she'd worn to marry Cal was a symbol of how differently the two marriages would turn out. She and Adrian would be happy. What she wore would underline that more than anything. The colour was precisely what she'd been dreaming of: a pale, creamy shade that reminded her of old parchment. She held the lace close to her cheek and glanced into the mirror that hung on the inside of one of the cupboard doors. She wondered whether perhaps it was the pleasure she was feeling that was making her skin glow, but no: it was definitely the colour. She'd known it would suit her as soon as she saw it. She said, 'It's exactly right. The perfect lace. I can't tell you how I feel ... It's beautiful. The colour is glorious. I love it.'

'I'm very pleased. It's always a relief to have the main decision taken care of. And we're in luck with the trimmings I think, too.' Miss Hayward was searching in a chest of drawers that stood against one wall. 'This is something I bought to make one of those enormously long veils that turn into a train ... Do you know what I mean? Never used it in the end. We can cut off the lace borders and put them round the neckline and sleeves. And here we are: I knew I had some scalloped lace somewhere. And in just the right colour. Perfect.'

I have to have it, Zannah thought. That lace. That colour. I don't care what it costs.

'Okay, let me get this right.' Adrian leaned forward and Zannah could see by the set of his mouth and by the way his forehead was furrowing that he was making an effort to keep his temper. 'You've just been to see an eighty-year-old woman in a small terraced house in Highgate. You've asked her to make your wedding dress. You've agreed to pay a thousand pounds.'

'That's a bargain,' said Zannah quickly. She wasn't telling him the whole truth. She'd agreed to pay fifteen hundred, but that included the bridesmaids' dresses. Surely, she reasoned, I'll be able to rustle up five hundred pounds from somewhere? Of course I will. She was so determined to have the dress made up that she would have agreed to almost anything. She added, 'There's a tremendous amount of work involved. Also lots of stuff that can only be done by hand. There are going to be tiny pearls scattered here and there. And she'll do the bridesmaids' dresses too, she said.' She could see that Adrian wasn't mollified by this information. She added: 'It's vintage lace, you know.'

'That's irrelevant.'

'It's not irrelevant. It's amazingly beautiful. And it doesn't come cheap. We're talking about my wedding dress. It's going to be our wedding, Adrian. You should be pleased. I was sure you would be.'

'Well, I'm not. My mother came all the way up to London to help you choose and you just set your face against her. You'd decided long ago, hadn't you? I think she deserves an apology, frankly.'

'She does not!' Zannah tried, but didn't manage, to keep the indignation out of her voice. 'I never asked her to come up to London. I didn't ask for her help. She ... offered it.' That had nearly come out as: *she pushed it down my throat*, but she managed to control herself just in time.

'You should've listened to her. Anyway, what does it matter? Honestly, I can't see what you're making such a song and dance about it for. It's only a dress ... and you'll look great whatever.'

'Mummy, you and Adrian mustn't fight!' Isis had come into the room from the kitchen. 'If you're getting married, you're not allowed to quarrel.'

'Shut up, Isis.' Adrian spoke curtly. 'Go and find something to do. We're talking.'

'We're not really fighting, Icepop,' Zannah said, pulling her daughter to her and kissing the side of her face. 'But we are having a discussion. We'll be finished in a minute but can you go and find something to do in your room for a bit?'

'Okay,' said Isis. She made her way to the staircase and Zannah could see from the way she walked that she was sad and confused. I'll talk to her at bedtime, she resolved and then turned to Adrian again.

'You shouldn't have shouted at Isis,' she said.

'I didn't shout. I told her to shut up. She'll have to get used to us having the odd fight.'

'Will she? Why? Are you planning to quarrel with me on a regular basis once we're married?'

'Oh, God, don't deliberately misunderstand me, Zannah. You know I don't mean that. Not at all. I just think it would make things easier if you let my mum handle all that. Save you trouble and money, probably. I just think you're barmy running off to some second-rate dressmaker when you have the pick of the London shops.'

'You're the one!' Zannah was shouting now. 'You're the one who's misunderstanding! I've got a picture of the dress I want and your mother's poncy shop didn't come anywhere near it, so I've found someone who'll make me something that's exactly what I want. For less money than anything at that ridiculous Dreamdress place.'

'It's not about the money,' Adrian said, also shouting now. 'I don't give a flying fuck about the money.'

Zannah was still furious and had no intention of stopping. 'And she's not second-rate, she's the best there is. She worked for Norman Hartnell, not that I'd expect you to know who he is, but your mother will. What part of that is barmy? Makes perfect sense to me, and in any case, it's none of your damned business. The wedding dress is my department. You stick to what you've been given to attend to – the rings, the honeymoon, and the stag night. Okay?'

Adrian said nothing. Zannah went on, 'I think you should apologize to Isis.'

'No way,' said Adrian. 'I'll try not to yell at her in future, but she's got to learn she's not the only person in the world. That's her problem. You've spoiled her.'

'Oh, go home, Adrian! I can't deal with this tonight. I've got a ton of work to do and I'm not spending the entire evening squabbling.'

'We were going to have a bite together.' He looked aggrieved. ' I've driven all the way up here from work, without changing or anything. What am I supposed to do about food?'

'Oh, for God's sake, Adrian, you're perfectly capable of finding yourself something to eat, aren't you? Phone a friend. Get a takeaway. Something. I don't feel like going out. Sorry.'

'If that's what you want,' Adrian stood up, 'there's no point in staying, I suppose. Goodbye.'

'Goodbye.'

He turned back at the front door to see if Zannah would weaken, she knew, but she made sure she seemed entirely absorbed in the headlines of the newspaper lying on the table. He left without another word. Zannah put her head in her hands and tried to calm down. Perhaps, she thought, I shouldn't have lost my temper with him – but he could be so annoying. She'd only just stopped herself throwing something at him. He'd phone her later, she thought. He was probably regretting their quarrel already.

'Mum? Are you okay?' Isis had crept downstairs, and put her arms round her mother without Zannah noticing.

'Icey! You're supposed to be in your room.'

'I didn't go. I stayed on the stairs to listen.'

'Naughty girl! That's eavesdropping.'

'But,' Isis said, 'I wanted to see if you made friends. You didn't, did you? Are you still getting married?'

Zannah laughed. 'Of course we are! People often get cross with one another, you know. It doesn't mean anything, really.'

Isis went to sit on the sofa, curling herself round one of the cushions. She didn't look entirely reassured, so Zannah said, 'Next time I go to see Miss Hayward, you must come with me. She's got lots of lovely ornaments and a cupboard full of gorgeous materials. When we've decided what sort of bridesmaid's dress you want, and Gemma, of course, you can help choose the fabric. That'll be fun, right?'

Isis nodded, glumly. 'Yes,' she said. 'I want it to be very pale pink.'

'We'll have to be careful with that, darling. It's got to go with my cream. Don't worry, though, we'll find something fantastic. Okay now? Ready for bed?'

'I'll go and get ready.'

'I'll be up in a minute.'

Isis turned as she reached the stairs. 'He doesn't like me very much, does he?'

'Adrian?' Zannah was shocked. Where had Isis got that idea? She made a note to tell Adrian in the strongest terms that he really mustn't shout at Isis ever again. 'Of course he likes you, darling. He's told me lots of times, really. Don't worry about him shouting at you. He honestly doesn't mean to be horrid. Would I ever think of marrying someone who didn't love you?'

Isis shook her head. 'No,' she said. 'S'pose not.'

'Go on, then. Get ready for bed and stop worrying.'

When Isis had gone, Zannah picked up the newspaper and folded it up to put away. She tried to recall the occasions when Adrian had mentioned liking Isis – actually said the words, rather than let the assumption stand on its own. She remembered him saying how talented Isis was, when he had been admiring her artwork, attached to the fridge. He'd said how pretty she was at their engagement party. He'd pronounced her clever when Zannah had shown him her school report, but had he ever said he liked her? In so many words? She couldn't bring a single instance to mind. But that doesn't mean anything, she told herself. I know he likes her. He wouldn't want to marry me if he didn't ... No one marries a mother unless they're sure they like her child. I'll ask him. I'll make sure, she thought, pushing this new worry to the back of her mind. She stood up and tried to think herself into bedtime-story mode.

She came downstairs just as Emily was letting herself in.

'Hi, Zan,' she said. 'Isis in bed?'

'Yes,' Zannah said. Emily threw herself on to the sofa and sighed. 'God,' she said, 'I'm finished. Just been to the opening of the most hilarious exhibition. Couldn't make it up. Camembert boxes turned into sculptures. *Cheese City*. I kid you not.'

'Could be good,' said Zannah. 'Depends how it was done.'

'Trust me, this guy wasn't a what's his name? Pizza-thingie?'

'Paolozzi. Em, can I ask you something?'

Emily sat up at once, frowning. 'What's up?'

'Maybe nothing. I've just had rather a ... well, a bit of strange conversation with Isis. She reckons Adrian doesn't really like her. That can't be, can it? Can it? I'd have noticed if ...'

'What did Isis say exactly?'

'Well, he shouted at her so she asked me if he liked her and I said of course ... you know. But she didn't seem all that reassured. He did say he was sorry for shouting at her. I tried to explain that sometimes you do just shout at people and it doesn't mean you don't like them. What am I going to do?'

'Have you asked him what he thinks of Isis?'

'Not directly. I've always assumed ... How could anyone not like her?'

'You're her mother. Of course you think that. So do I. We all do, in our family but...well, she's someone else's child, isn't she? Not his. That's the point. She's a reminder of Cal.'

Zannah ran her hands through her hair and closed her eyes. 'I don't need this. Really. I will ask him but I just cannot believe that this incredibly *primitive* stuff about whose child she is operates in the twenty-first century. It's ridiculous.'

'Men,' said Emily 'are primitive. Hadn't you noticed? Fred Flintstone, the whole bloody lot of them. Behind that investment banker's exterior, under the most spiffy and impeccable of Turnbull and Asser shirts there beats the heart of a wild creature. Me Tarzan you Zannah! Trust me.'

'I'm going to speak to him. And I'll watch him very carefully from now on, you can be sure of that.'

'What about Isis? What's she feel about him? Have you ever asked her?'

Zannah shook her head. 'I've always thought she likes him. She's very smily and pleasant around him ... I'll ask her, too.'

'D'you remember the coffin carving in Manchester Museum of Isis the goddess? Pa showed us when we were not much older than she is.'

Zannah remembered it exactly: the carving still touched with pink and green even after centuries; the Goddess holding out her wings, protecting Osiris. Perhaps it was seeing this at an early age that had put the name Isis into her mind when she was pregnant. That had made her love it so much. I'm the one, she thought. The one who has to do the protecting.

'Weddings,' said Val, 'are one thing. I love weddings. Marriage is quite another. Don't like that much. Mind you, I suppose I had a bad experience.'

Charlotte, Val and Edie were sitting round the kitchen table. They'd just washed up after a pleasant evening of bridge with Nadia and were having a glass of red wine together before bed.

'I'd have agreed with you if I hadn't met Gus,' Charlotte said. 'We didn't bother with a wedding and concentrated on our marriage. Probably the sensible option, when you come to think of it. No one came to our wedding except Joss. There's part of me that does still think the whole thing's a waste of money. But Zannah deserves to have what she wants this time. She was so ... so wounded when Cal ... when she divorced. She seems to want all this, the dress, the service, the reception, to make up for the pain she felt then. She said she wanted to do everything properly this time.'

'She's young,' said Edie. 'It's only when you've lived through a marriage that you know whether the ceremony was a wonderful prefiguring of your happiness or a really bad joke.' She took a sip of wine. 'They've been to see Geoffrey at the church. He thought they were a lovely couple and he's spoken to them at length about music and the order of service and so forth.'

Charlotte looked searchingly at Edie. Whenever she spoke of the vicar, a proprietorial and affectionate note crept into her voice. They used to call it 'soppy' when she was a girl . . . Was Edie getting soppy over the Rev. Geoff? He was a widower, and although he was a few years younger than Edie, a relationship wasn't out of the question. The trouble was, an unattached vicar who wasn't completely revolting attracted the attention of a great many women and this parish was particularly stuffed with widows and unmarried ladies of a certain age who, by Edie's own account, were falling over themselves in their eagerness to snaffle him. That the church was always so clean and well provided with flowers was witness to those ladies trying to outdo one another in their devotion. Well, Charlotte thought, this wedding'll bring Rev. Geoff and Edie closer together, but of course she isn't going to get involved with him. Edie had a dim view of relationships between men and women. The way she put it was: *my experience of the two sexes has shown me how incompatible we are.* She said, 'I've been in touch with the marquee people. It's all going to be quite straightforward. I have to give them final numbers soon, but Zannah told me the other day that they were in the process of finalizing the guest list.'

Val picked up Joss's book, which was lying on the dresser. 'You must be so proud, Charlotte! Isn't it wonderful? A poetry book . . . I love the picture on the cover. But why doesn't Joss use her own name? It's as if she's hiding, isn't it?'

'She told me she likes being someone else. Being able to say things she maybe couldn't say as Joss Gratrix. I can understand that.'

Val leafed through the pages. 'You don't mean . . . .?'

'No, don't worry.' Charlotte laughed 'Nothing she'd be ashamed of saying as herself, just . . . Well, she described it to me as a kind of dressing up. You pretend to be another person. There are love poems in there, but nothing too shocking.'

Charlotte wasn't telling the truth. She had been a little startled on reading some of the things Joss had written. Ever since her niece had brought Bob back to this house to meet her, all those years ago, Charlotte had been of the opinion that he was good and kind and pleasant and entirely unexciting. When Joss had told her she wanted to marry him, Charlotte concluded that she was looking for security. Ever since the death of her parents, and even with all the care that Charlotte and later Gus had devoted to her, Joss had been tentative. She'd gone through life giving too much attention to what might go wrong with it. She didn't dare to do things most young people wouldn't even have thought of as risky. Bob was safe. Bob had a good job for life, and if they'd never be rich, they'd never be poor either. He must have seemed a good prospect to Joss and she did love him, there was no doubt of that in Charlotte's mind. It was the quality of the love she sometimes wondered about, and reading some of the lines in this book, she simply couldn't imagine them applied to Joss's husband of so many years. These were words that went with a new passion. She could feel, when she read them, the force of an ungovernable longing, a lust that surely couldn't still exist after thirty years. Perhaps she was recollecting emotion in tranquillity and remembering how things were between her and Bob in the first few years of their marriage, but somehow that wasn't the impression Charlotte took from the verse. Of course, Joss and Bob must once have felt passionately about one another, even if she hadn't been able to see it. Joss had never displayed her emotions to the world, but she felt things deeply, and it was impossible to imagine her staying in a relationship that wasn't physically satisfying. Still, these poems didn't feel as though they were about Bob. Perhaps Joss was having an affair, but with whom? And when? As far as Charlotte knew, her life was spent either working in the library, or at home, or in London visiting her daughters and Isis ... Maybe she was simply projecting her fantasies into her work. That was more likely, Charlotte decided. In prison, she remembered, many women spent hours writing verse. Her cellmate, Wilma, had been a pallid, skinny, greasy-haired, middle-aged woman who looked like a wrung-out mop. She was in for theft and used to cover pages and pages with poems about stars and fields, seashores, puppies and kittens. *Why don't you write about your feelings?* Charlotte asked her once and Wilma looked at her pityingly. *What's the point of that? Shitty, that's what my feelings are. Poetry's not about shittiness, is it? You want to get away from yourself, doncha?*

Charlotte wondered whether Joss, too, was getting away from herself. Perhaps that was the way she kept her marriage going: by escaping into a fantasy world in her poems, where she could be Lydia Quentin who burned with desires Joss Gratrix couldn't admit into her own life. Well, if that was the case, nothing was wrong. She must have considered what Bob's reaction would be if he read some of them, Charlotte thought, and then something struck her. Bob would no sooner sit down and read a book of poems, even if they were by his wife, than spend his holidays in Disneyland. This made it safe for Joss to write exactly what she wanted, however erotically charged her work turned out to be. And if it was all a fantasy, no one would be hurt. She said to Edie and Val, 'This is the book I told you about. Did I tell you that the Madrigal Prize is worth two thousand pounds?'

Edie and Val were impressed and astonished. Clearly, they'd underestimated the book's worth.

'Well,' said Val, 'that's something to wish for, isn't it? It would be so lovely if she wins. Let's drink to that.'

Maureen would never have said so to anyone and felt a little guilty admitting it to herself, but when Graham was away, things in almost every part of her life became instantly easier and altogether more enjoyable. For a few moments, as she lay propped up against heaped pillows in the double bed with her lists, magazines, notebooks and other wedding paraphernalia taking up the space her husband would normally occupy, she considered what her life would be like if she were single. In many ways she thought, it would be much improved. Did that mean she didn't love Graham? Nonsense, she told herself. Of course I do. But I don't miss him when he's not here. Also, I've had a lovely day, doing exactly what I wanted to do when I wanted to do it, without stopping to think about a single other soul.

Unfortunately, she needed the money Graham provided to maintain the house and garden and her own wardrobe in a decent state, and she'd miss the sex. Still, she was sure – because there had been enough rather thrilling and unconfessed little kisses at various parties over the years and sometimes even a bit more, though never outright infidelity – that there were plenty of men out there who'd be willing, more than willing, to share her bed. She was, after all, only fifty-two. Just last week at the tennis club, the young and quite dishy coach had been positively flirtatious. She would only have needed to encourage him a teensy bit and he'd have been raring to go. She sighed, and scrabbled in the folds of the duvet for her pencil. The guest list needed doing, but she couldn't resist reading again the details of four houses she'd picked up that afternoon from the best estate agents in town.

She'd been to meet a firm of caterers who'd turned out to be useless, but on her way home she'd passed a house that had a big *for sale* sign outside. It wasn't very big, but it was pretty and on a tree-lined street where all the other properties had owners who cared. She'd looked at the hanging baskets, the shaved lawns and closely trimmed hedges, and thought, how lovely if Adrian could live here, close to me, in such a sweet little house. Away from London and all those ghastly security alerts. She'd vaguely thought about it before but now the idea seemed to her both so exciting and so somehow right that she'd parked the car and got out to have a closer look. She'd walked up to the front door and rung the bell, but there was no one at home.

While the cats are away ... Maureen said to herself, and walked all round the property, staring in through the windows. Parquet floor in the living room and dining room. Small garden at the back with lots of possibilities. Modern kitchen ... She'd felt quite breathless as she made her way back to her car. The house would be perfect for Adrian and Zannah. As she drove to the estate agent's to pick up the written details, enchanting fantasies unfolded in her head: Adrian and his children playing in that garden, the whole family coming over to tea on Sunday, Adrian transferred to the local branch of his bank, Zannah teaching at the local primary school ... The house was just round the corner from theirs. Maureen felt quite elated.

At the estate agent's she took the details of several other houses as well. You wouldn't want to rush into anything recklessly and it was better to consider all options before committing yourself. I'll email Adrian, she thought. I'll invite the two of them down for the weekend, maybe at the beginning of October. She didn't want to give the game away. Subtlety was important. This whole thing had to be done so that Adrian and Zannah didn't think she was interfering. The best thing would be if they could see the place and think they'd discovered it. She could arrange to drive past it. Maybe they'd fall in love with the house just as she had. The wedding wasn't until next year, true enough, but Adrian could apply for a transfer right away. He could move in down here before the wedding. Zannah and Isis could join him after the honeymoon.

Now, as she re-read the details, it seemed an even better idea. Zannah must have faced the fact that she'd need to move out of that grotty flat. It was big enough and in quite a reasonable location, but there was something terribly graduate-student about it and the decorative state they kept it in made her shudder. There was no way Adrian would put up with living there after the wedding and his place wasn't big enough for all three of them. This seemed the ideal solution. She had sent an email to Adrian inviting him and Zannah down for the weekend, and couldn't wait for his reply.

She got out of bed and went downstairs. In the kitchen, she assembled a little picnic on a tray: biscuits and Stilton, a nice ripe pear and a glass of red wine. She intended to eat in bed. No Graham there to wrinkle his nose and moan about crumbs. Utter bliss!

Thursday

Russell Blythe and Joss were having an after-lunch drink in the local pub with half a dozen of the course-members. Gray was one of them. The *Admiral* was only a short walk away and because the day was pleasantly warm, Russell had suggested that the workshop adjourned there. 'Otherwise,' he said, 'I don't know about all of you, but I'll fall asleep after that lunch.'

Joss had made a point of walking next to two women, and the talk was about children and husbands and, because Joss had mentioned Zannah, weddings. When they reached the *Admiral*, she took a seat as far away from Gray as possible because she wanted to indulge in something she'd learned was completely pleasurable: watching him without talking to him. Watching him talk to other people. She wouldn't have been able to explain it, but being separate from Gray and thinking of how they'd been last night, how they'd be again tonight, made her aware of every nerve ending in her body: almost painfully aroused. She watched in silence as, further down the table, his mouth moved in laughter and speech. Remembering how that mouth had felt on her skin, breathing words into her ear, opening under the pressure of her lips brought a flush to her cheeks that had nothing to do with the relative warmth of the sunshine.

Gray didn't usually say much in company. Bob was a jovial person and liked to be the centre of attention. He often did what Em called 'holding forth', but Gray usually sat quietly as the talk buzzed round him. Joss had noticed this during meals at Fairford. He knew how to listen. That must be one reason why he was so good at his job. She could imagine how soothed his patients must feel, how comforted to have him beside them, knowing he was attending to them *completely*.

Now Gray was discussing rhyming verse, which always got poets steamed up. He said, 'It's true, rhyme isn't *necessary* but I bet you've sometimes thought this or that poem was only a piece of prose cut up. Haven't you? Can you swear you've never thought that?'

Russell laughed. 'You're right, of course. Some poems are about as poetic as ... well, as some very unpoetic thing. But it's not rhyme that makes a poem, because then what's in a Hallmark card would be poetry and we know it's not.'

'Okay, that's true. But you have to have that extra ... I don't know. Not just description. And not just nonsense going under the banner of surrealism.'

'My skin tells me,' said one of the other course-members, a shy young woman called Maggie. 'If I get goosebumps, it's real poetry. And if I don't, it's not.'

'That can't be right,' said Blake, a dark-haired man who was just a fraction too old to be wearing the punkish clothes he favoured. 'Funny poems don't raise goosebumps, nor does political satire, but you're not saying that Dryden's not a poet, are you?'

'I agree with Maggie,' said Gray, smiling at her. Making her feel better. Protecting her from Blake's ill-disguised scorn. 'You have to be moved. And not necessarily in a sentimental way. You can be ... I don't know. Stirred. Thrilled.'

Blake sniffed. Came back with some remark about humour. Joss smiled to herself. She wasn't going to get involved in the general chat, then wondered if that would seem unfriendly or strange. She decided to speak and said, 'I read a novel once where the characters spent a few pages discussing what a poem was. The punchline was: that you know it's a poem if it has the name "*Ted Hughes*" at the end. Or any other poet would do, I suppose. T.S. Eliot. Yeats.'

Everyone laughed. Maggie said, 'I get goosebumps when I read all of those. Who said poetry was the right words in the right order?'

'Coleridge, I think,' Russell said. 'My round.'

The talk went on. Laughter rose into the air. Russell went inside to get more drinks. Joss was starting to count the hours until she could be alone with Gray, but she was sharply conscious of how happy she was now, this minute. I wish this afternoon would go on for ever, she thought. I want it never to stop: this delicious waiting for the day to end.

It must be nearly morning, Gray thought, and groped for his mobile on the bedside table. Just after five o'clock. I should go back to my room. Lydia – she'd asked him to call her Joss, but he couldn't think of her as anything but Lydia – was still asleep beside him. Everyone at Fairford always went to bed late, after wine and talk and laughter till the early hours, and then he'd had to wait until it was safe to slip along the dark corridors to her room. He smiled into the darkness as he recalled the hours that had elapsed since she'd opened the door to him. When they'd been together in public, he'd been careful not to give anything away. He'd been polite, smiling, signing up like all the other course-members for his time alone with her, when they would pretend to be talking about his poems, chatting to Russell – a chubby gay guy with a wicked sense of humour – about music and cricket and how wonderful it had been to see England getting the Ashes back after so long and who was sleeping with whom in the world of poetry, joining in with the writing exercises and volunteering himself for the first group in the kitchen and all the time dreaming about what would happen when they were alone. Today at the pub he'd felt her trying to not-watch him, which made him smile because he was also trying to not-watch her .

'Gray?'

'You're supposed to be asleep. It's only just after five-thirty.'

'I woke up,' Lydia said, and turned to him. He opened his arms to her and held her naked body close, close to his. She was warm and fragrant and he didn't want to leave her.

'I don't want to leave you,' he whispered.

'You must. There's always someone who's up before the others. It's not safe.'

'We've got to talk, Lydia.'

'Do we? Why do we?'

'Because . . . I want to ask Maureen for a divorce. I'm serious. I want us to be together.'

'How can you say that? You've been married so long. You must love her, Gray.'

'In a way I do. You can't live with someone for so long and not have ... Well, you know what I mean. Think of yourself and ... and Bob.' Gray shifted in the bed. He didn't like saying Lydia's husband's name, not even to himself, much less aloud.

'I can't leave him,' she murmured, and as she did, she pulled him to her and began to kiss his neck, just under his ear.

'Why not? Why can't you?'

'He wouldn't cope without me. He'd go to pieces.'

'He manages okay when you're not there. He's in Egypt now, not giving you a second thought, I bet. Maureen's having the time of her life in Guildford too, I expect. They're used to us, Lydia and that's it. It's not like this. Are we happy when we're together?'

He could feel her nodding, but she said, 'We made vows, Gray. We promised. That should mean something, surely.'

'It does mean something, of course it does, but there should be a way of cancelling them when we're not happy any longer. We deserve to be happy, don't we?'

'No one's completely happy all the time,' Lydia said. 'What if other people are hurt? I don't want to do that, Gray. I'm sorry. Imagine what would happen if no one kept any promises. If nothing were binding. It would be – life would be – impossible.'

'No one stays hurt for ever. What about Bob and Maureen living with us? We're unfaithful to them. Have you thought of that? And it's not just a casual affair, so it's an even worse betrayal. We've betrayed them. But we love one another, so how does that tot up, Lydia? Now, at this very moment. Are we being fair to them when we're like this?'

Lydia sat up in bed and rested her head on her clasped knees. 'I explained, Gray. As soon as I saw you, I explained. This ... These days are like time outside real life. Time out. We're not going to see one another alone again. I mean that.. This is it. I can't spoil Zannah's wedding. Adrian's wedding, too. It would ... Well, nothing would be the same again. You must see that.'

He began to stroke her back and felt her shiver under his hand. 'I don't think I can do not seeing you any more, Lydia. What if we're careful? We can be so ... discreet. No one need know.'

She shook her head. 'I'd be terrified. It's no good. I feel ... It's impossible. I can't ... I can't think about it.'

'Then don't. Don't think about it now. Let's discuss it. Seriously. When we have our session together tomorrow ... I mean today ... Not in bed, but face to face over a table. We can talk about the future. I want us to be together.'

She lay back and sighed. 'I want that as well. But it's difficult. Everything's so complicated. Let's just ... let's just have these days and ...'

'And what? Leave Fairford and forget everything? I can't. You can't either. Admit it. No emails. No phone calls. Nothing. Just think about it. What sort of a life is that? Not one I'm willing to live, Lydia.'

'Later. We'll talk properly, I promise. But it's getting late now, Gray. You should go.'

'In a minute. Come here ...'

'Oh, Gray, there's no ...'

He stopped her words with his mouth and she wrapped her arms round him. There was time. He felt her opening, softening under his hands, and closed his eyes.

Emily wished she'd taken advantage of her education while it was actually going on. She was out with Cal and Isis on a visit to the zoo, and whenever they were together, because Cal was so well informed, she became aware of how little she knew about almost everything. She'd gone down to London straight after uni to help Zannah after her breakdown and she'd never regretted that. She was eager to start working and had taken up her job in PR quite happily, but now she sometimes found herself thinking in ways most of her friends would consider most peculiar. For instance, she thought, I wish I could have gone with Dad to Egypt and had a good look at some mummies. She knew he was actually sitting in a university classroom, giving oral exams to poor foreign PhD students, but the image of herself accompanying him into the desert, with beige sand dunes all around and romantic-looking tents with lanterns hanging up in them seemed very attractive. I'm going to ask him one day, she thought, if I can go with him. And maybe I could do a doctorate or something. Later on. She shook her head to clear it of an image of herself in fetching khaki shirt and shorts. Cal and Isis had just come back from visiting the snakes. Emily drew the line at snakes (were there snakes in the desert?) and had waited for them on a convenient bench in the rather chilly sunlight.

Cal sat down next to her. Isis had gone off to get an ice-cream at the kiosk they could see from the bench.

'Makes her feel independent,' said Cal. 'She doesn't realize I don't take my eyes off her for a second.'

This was true. He was gazing fixedly at Isis's back and had half turned away from her. Emily fought an urge to put out a hand and stroke his hair. He was talking about the wedding dress. 'Icey's been telling me about the wonderful Miss Hayward. She wants a blush pink dress, apparently. What's blush pink?'

'Well, it's pale and very pretty. You know Zannah. It has to be the exact shade that goes with Zannah's lace, which is sort of like dead pale milky coffee . . . .It'll look marvellous, don't worry.'

'Worry? Doesn't matter a scrap to me. I'm sure they'll both look great, whatever. Hello, Mouse,' he said to Isis, who had come back from the kiosk to sit next to them. Emily closed her eyes and listened to them chatting. Every time she was with Cal, it became more and more obvious to her that he didn't think of her as anything other than Zannah's younger sister. She should give up daydreaming.

Since her early teens, she'd never been short of boyfriends. Now there were three young men who probably regarded themselves as . . . What could you call them? In her life, was all she was prepared to concede. They weren't boyfriends, and they had no intention of marrying her, so they weren't suitors, and Zannah called them 'your reserve squad'. The reserve squad dated from Emily's sixth-form days, when she'd had a boyfriend and always a notional list of others she was sort of interested in, even if only in her head. Nowadays, the reserve squad had moved off the bench, as it were, and into play. She went out to meals, movies, and parties with all three, though not at the same time, naturally. Grant was an advertising copywriter. He called himself 'a creative' which Emily thought was pretentious. She'd met him when he worked on one of her firm's accounts. He was the one who fancied himself a foodie and took her to fashionable restaurants and bar openings. Rory was the cultural one: theatres, concerts and movies. He was fun and flirtatious and Emily thought, because he'd never once made a real pass at her, that he was probably gay and not quite ready to come out. Matt was the one she went to bed with. He worked in her office, was handsome, uncomplicated, fun and had his own rather lovely flat in Notting Hill Gate. She couldn't say there was anything wrong with the sex, but that was all it seemed to be, and if Matt was a good lover, he wasn't in the least romantic and Emily reckoned that he regarded their lovemaking as a pleasant alternative to a workout at the gym. She sighed. Cal combined everything she liked about the three men. Or maybe not quite. She couldn't imagine him having the patience for some of Grant's restaurants and he'd faint if he saw some of the bills they ran up. He'd do the movies, if not the concerts, and he'd talk and talk, which was perhaps more important than anything else. He wouldn't change the subject when emotions or feelings came up in conversation. He wasn't afraid of relationships, because he'd married Zannah, hadn't he? As for sex, she tried not to think about the two of them together, because it made her feel too terrible. She already suffered awful pangs of guilt about her fantasies and had vowed to exclude any thoughts of Cal from her nights with Matt but it was harder than she'd expected.

'You okay, young Emmy?' Cal said now. 'You were miles away. I think we ought to be getting home. Come on.'

He stood up and gave her his hand to pull her to her feet. Perhaps when Zannah was married the penny would drop. Cal would see her in a completely different light and fall madly in love with her. And that aardvark in the enclosure over there would be asked to dance the lead role in *Giselle*. Grow up, Em, she told herself. Move on.

The room she was in reminded Joss of a monk's cell: plain, whitewashed walls, a pine table, two chairs, a high window. Those who came in here and sat at the table, close enough to touch the person opposite them, adopted a manner of something like reverence and modulated their voices to fit with the way the room made them feel: serious, scholarly and as though they were about to discover deeply buried truths about themselves. On the Fairford courses, each pupil was given an hour with each tutor, one to one. It was only in those circumstances, poring over single lines, discussing what they truly meant to say, that proper tutoring took place. The communal exercises were fun, but they often led to some course-members showing off, and others being almost entirely silenced.

Joss smiled. Gray would be here soon. He'd put himself last on the list, which revealed a sensitivity to her feelings, to what she might want, that few others in her life had ever shown. He knew their talk would disturb her, stir up emotions which she might find hard to cover up if she then had to go on and discuss their work with someone else. He also knew that if any session could overrun a little, it was the last one of the day. There was half an hour before supper. Neither of them was on kitchen duty.

While she was waiting for him, Joss closed her eyes and leaned back in the chair, trying to clear her mind. Other people's words were floating around in there, other people's personalities had left a sort of imprint on her, yet the thing she was most aware of was her own body. She couldn't stop herself. Her head had become a kind of kaleidoscope, and with every turn pictures of their lovemaking appeared and she was unable to prevent them filling her with the drunken dizziness of desire. She was just remembering how he'd left her this morning, how he'd clung to her as she opened the door, how he'd kicked it closed again just for a moment, just for one more kiss, just one . . . please.

'Okay to come in, Lydia?' He was, standing in the doorway, clutching his file, like everyone else who came into this room.

'Hello,' Joss said, blinking a little, trying to dispel what she'd been thinking a moment ago. 'Yes . . . come and sit down.'

Gray took the chair opposite her and put his file on the table in front of him. He smiled, but she could see that he was in a serious mood. 'I've not brought any poems,' he said. 'I want to talk to you about the future. I want you to leave Bob, Lydia. I know it's a lot to ask, but I've been thinking about nothing else for months.'

'Do we have to talk about this now? It's so . . . it makes it so . . . Oh, God, I'm scared, Gray.'

'What of?'

'Everything. If I left Bob, so many people would be hurt. There'd be problems. It'd be like an earthquake. How can we do that to people we love? And we do love them, don't we, Gray? You can't say we don't.'

'I don't. I don't say that. But let me ask you something. What would Bob really do if you left him? If you were to die, let's say, how would he manage?'

Joss said nothing. For the last five years at least Bob had been less interested in her than he was in many other things. She tried to reconstruct time they spent together and realized that this was just meals, often eaten quickly, with Bob's mind on something he was working on upstairs. He worked, they slept in the same bed and met in the kitchen. How many times had he made love to her in the last year? A dozen? She doubted it was as many as that. And if she wasn't there? If she was in London with Zannah and Isis and Emily, he appeared to manage perfectly well. And yet there was the weight of the years they'd been together. At the beginning, when they were first married, he could make her feel ... She could remember being swept away, perhaps not quite as she was being swept away now, but still, she could recall their love-making, that it used to be passionate and heartfelt and she'd been happy. She couldn't deny that shared history now, and it would be wrong to make light of it. Time had happened to them: time and habit. Surely that could happen to her and Gray as well? To any relationship? Was it right to break up two families just for a short period of intense gratification? She might feel exactly the same about Gray in a few years as she felt about Bob now. No, that wasn't possible. This was different, like no other love she'd ever known. Or had she thought that about Bob long ago? She no longer remembered properly. And there was something else, too. Now that she'd met Maureen, she could imagine only too well the kind of sex she must once have had with Gray ... maybe was still having. This thought made her feel faintly nauseous, but it was there, whenever she considered the whole situation rather than just her little corner of it. She answered Gray's question: 'He'd cope, I suppose, but I expect he'd miss me.'

'What would Zannah and Emily think?'

'They'd be shocked. I think they feel Bob and I are one person. I don't imagine they spend a lot of time worrying about us. If we're okay, then they're busy with their lives. That's as it should be. But if we parted...well, Zannah would probably be ... Well, it might upset her a great deal. She'd be more able to cope with it if she were happily married herself. She went through hell after she left Cal. What he'd confessed to was quite honestly no more than a fling in Moscow, but she was nearly broken by it. She divorced him, in spite of all my persuasion, and Bob's. If I told her about us now ... well, I don't know how she'd react but I can't take the risk of her going to pieces again. We can't, mustn't wreck the wedding. Zannah's thought of nothing else for months. And what about Maureen? She's also very involved with everything to do with the day. More than me, and I feel guilty about that, but she loves all the arrangements so much and is so good at them, and I'm not . . .' Joss's voice trailed away into silence and she pushed her hair off her forehead with both hands.

'Maureen,' Gray said, 'will be shocked and scream at me, but she'll survive. What you have to know about Maureen is that she's supremely selfish and she'll always see to it that she's okay. I'd let her keep the house. I'd provide for her – and I can – and I bet she's married again within two years. Men like her. She likes them. As long as the material circumstances of her life don't change, she'll come round.'

'D'you love her? Does she love you?' She wanted to ask: *what do you do in bed? How is it with her?*

Gray closed his eyes. 'I suppose I do. Just as you love Bob. I don't want anything bad to happen to her, but . . . we don't talk about anything, Lydia. The only thing we discuss is arrangements. When, where, who, how much. It's not like you and me. You . . . the way we talk about everything, the way we laugh about the same things . . . It's like being young again.'

'That's because we don't live together, Gray. If we did, we'd also fall into a routine. Everyone does. Everyone has to. You can't . . . I mean, things have to settle down, don't they? Perhaps it's because we've seen so little of one another, because we've not had time to get sick of one another that we're feeling . . . well, as we are. What if we got fed up, irritated with one another? Have you thought of that?'

'We might, I suppose. Though I don't think so. But Lydia, we're in our fifties. We could live for another thirty years. There was that couple in the newspaper . . . d'you remember? ... who'd been married for eighty years. It's entirely possible we could be together as long as we've been with Maureen and Bob.'

Joss smiled.

Gray continued, 'Tell me honestly. Can you face another thirty years with him? And remember that means without me, because you have this hang-up about not being unfaithful to him . . . if you knew he wouldn't fall to pieces, if you knew your children wouldn't stop talking to you, if you were sure that you'd be no worse off financially . . . in other words, if all practical matters were taken care of, how would you feel about spending the rest of your life with me? Marry me. Lydia, I'm asking you to marry me.'

Joss listened to what Gray was saying and suddenly she was in tears. She felt as though her whole life had been upended, tipped upside down.

'I'm sorry ... I can't ... Oh, yes, Gray, yes. Of course I want that too, but how ... When? I just don't know ...'

He took her hands and held them in his own. 'Listen, Lydia. Don't think about it now. Not in a practical way. There'll be plenty of time after the wedding. Once Adrian and Zannah have settled down, once Maureen's had her glorious party, then we can tell them. Honestly. Quietly. There won't be any need for scenes.'

'I'm not sure about that.' Joss imagined the conversation she and Bob might have. What would he do? Cry? Break down? She had no idea. What about the girls? Emily was more understanding than Zannah, but she was so much her father's daughter. .. what would she think of the mother who abandoned him? And Charlotte? Joss longed to confide in her and listen to her advice. Maybe she should. Maybe that would be a good way to help her decide ... show her what she really wanted. What nonsense. She knew that already. She took a deep breath.

'If I say yes, Gray, and if we wait till after the wedding, what does it mean? We can't meet. It would feel ... wrong. Deceitful. Underhand. I hate the very idea of hiding away, fearful of getting caught ... but how ...' How will I survive without you for nine months? How will I get through the days? It struck her suddenly that some people were better at adultery than others, and she was very bad at it. She'd watched many of her friends conduct casual affairs without any apparent guilt on the principle of 'what they don't know can't hurt them'. Was she a coward, fearful of discovery, or did she really inhabit a moral high ground? She suspected that the truth was much simpler. She had the kind of imagination that was always working overtime and she knew, from the way she felt when she had found out Gray was married, that her head was constantly full of pictures she couldn't erase and which tortured her. If she suddenly learned that Bob had been unfaithful to her over a long period of time, what would hurt would be that the whole of the life they'd lived up to this point would become a lie. Every memory she had of their marriage would be somehow falsified.

Gray broke into her thoughts. 'We're being deceitful now, my darling. Underhand. D'you regret the last two nights?'

She shook her head. Already, at half past five in the afternoon, she was wishing away the hours till tonight, and at the same time wanting it never to come. Tomorrow would be their last night together. After that, the future was like an empty desert of nothing but wanting him. Wanting to be with him. She said suddenly: 'I don't regret anything. And I will marry you.' As she spoke the words, she felt faint. This wasn't like adultery. This was commitment. 'But we must wait until the wedding's over. Then we'll be together. I promise. And until that time we can write. And we can phone sometimes, when we're sure it's safe. I won't lose you. I can't. It'll be okay. I have to believe it will be okay.'

He stood up then and leaned over the small table so that their faces were very close together. Without a word, he kissed her, and Joss allowed herself to dream, for just a second, of a time when they might go out of a room like this together. As it was, he went by himself, leaving her trembling. She had a sudden vision of tears, anguish, recriminations, fights, silences, reproaches and even though it cost her some effort of will, she pushed all of that, all those hideous things, out of her mind. I'm not going to think like that, she told herself. I don't have to deal with any of it for a long time. She packed her papers into her bag, and a feeling of lightness and elation washed over her. In a way, this was a return to being young and full of possibilities. There would be letters and emails and phone calls. Already, she could imagine the things they would write to one another and beyond that, she could see it clearly: a mirage at the far-distant edge of the very same desert she'd been picturing a moment ago. A house. Not her house, not Gray's house, but theirs. Their home.

'Zannah, have you read Ma's book?'

Emily was lying on the sofa. Zannah was sitting on the floor, drawing in the wedding notebook. Isis's designs for bridesmaids' dresses lay all over the coffee table and Zannah had promised to boil down her daughter's ideas into one sketch of a supremely pretty dress that would flatter both Isis and her friend Gemma, who was about the same height but a little stockier. Something simple was best, she was quite sure.

The dress she'd ended up with had sleeves puffed out and gathered up just above the elbow, where they'd be trimmed with dark pink ribbon and tiny satin rosebuds. The dropped waist and mid-calf length echoed her own dress. But pink was impossible. It just wouldn't look right. The girls would have to be talked into a dark, mossy, totally unyellow green … forest green, she thought it would be called … that would go well with her old-ivory lace. Watermarked silk taffeta. Once they saw what she had in mind, she was sure Isis and Gemma would love it. They could hold little round bouquets of bright pink or perhaps dark red, almost black roses and very dark green foliage. Maybe before she got carried away she'd better ring up the flower lady Louise had recommended, who might have other ideas for her to consider. The one thing she was firm about was no white lilies. No lilies at all because they were for funerals. She tuned in to what Emily was saying and found she hadn't heard it.

'Sorry, what was that?'

'I asked if you'd read Ma's book of poems.'

'I've had a look.. Read a couple, I suppose. Not sure that I know what I think about modern poetry, to tell the truth. Any good?'

'Yes,' said Emily, 'but they're very … Well, they're surprisingly sexy.'

'Really?'

'Yes. Quite a few are about love.'

'Lots of poems are about love, aren't they? Most, even,' said Zannah. 'Nothing strange about that.'

'No, but these are passionate. You'd think the poet was madly in love with someone.'

'I expect Ma does love Pa passionately,' Zannah said. Once she'd said the words out loud, she wondered if they were true. Perhaps her mother would be capable of having an affair without telling any of them. She was always wary of talking about her feelings.

'Oh, God, Zannah, you cannot be serious!'

'I am. Why shouldn't I be? They've been married for ever.'

Emily sat up and said, 'That's exactly my point. You clearly haven't been paying attention. They've been together so long that they hardly ever have a proper conversation. As for what happens in bed …'

'I don't fancy thinking about that, thanks very much.' Zannah wrinkled her nose. 'But they must love one another, even though we don't like to think about it.'

'Have a look, though. This book is full of stuff. Burning and melting and comparing herself to water and his hands touching her and all sorts of things. These poems are not written to Pa, I'm convinced of it.'

'She can't be having an affair, can she? I can't believe that. Ma? She wouldn't.'

Emily thought for a moment. 'Then is all this in her imagination? She's pretending?'

'She must be. We can ask her.'

'I'm going to,' said Emily lying down again and picking up *The Shipwreck Café*. 'Next time we see her.'

For a few minutes, there was silence in the room. Then Zannah said, 'Anyway, who on earth is there for Ma to have an affair with, even if she wanted to? She never meets anyone new, does she? All day at work and back home at night. I can't somehow see any of the regulars at the library melting her heart and turning her into this erotic creature you're describing. I'm sure she's, well, indulging in fantasies. I mean, it's out there in a book, where anyone can read it including Pa, so she's clearly not trying to hide it.'

'Can you imagine Pa reading poems? Even Ma's?' Emily laughed. 'Of course you can't because he wouldn't. He'd look as though he was but his mind wouldn't be on them. Not for a second. I love him to bits but he's not exactly a whiz when it comes to poetry, is he? Anyway, I'm going to try to forget what I've read. I liked it better when I didn't know what was going on in Ma's head.'

Friday

Only September, Joss thought, and already it's frosty at night. She drew the duvet up over her naked breasts and lay staring at the tulip patterns on the cupboard door, touched by the moonlight that was coming in through a gap in the curtains. Beside her, Gray was already fast asleep. His side, his thigh, his leg, the whole length of him was touching her. She could move away, turn over and go to sleep, but she chose not to. She chose instead to be awake, to taste each separate minute of this night, close to him, safe with him, happier than she'd ever been and also sadder, because this was the last night. The last time. *Don't say that. Don't say last time,* he'd told her earlier, murmuring the words into her hair and breathing them on to her skin, as his hands stroked her and touched her and opened her and his arms brought her so close that all she could feel was their hearts beating together and then she couldn't hear anything any more and she thought she must be dying, overcome with pleasure, and she cried out and she'd never cried out before, never been the sort of person who lost herself entirely in love-making and he'd covered her mouth with his hand, murmuring *Hush my darling hush*. She'd always kept something separate, watching, assessing, but this was more: this was taking her like a wave and a cry rose unstoppable in her throat and her body arched itself into a madness of sensation she couldn't contain and which came out of her mouth as a groan and a shuddering series of sighs and then it ebbed away, leaving her soft and slick with sweat, her breast heaving with sobs and then he was brushing away the tears and his mouth was on hers kissing her and kissing her and saying; *Don't cry my darling please don't cry* and her saying *I'm not I'm not crying I love you I can't I won't ....*

Earlier that day, they'd gone to the Shipwreck Café again. The visit was supposed to bring back happy memories for them, but it didn't. Joss tried to be as joyous as she had been for the last four days and couldn't. Could you be nostalgic about something that wasn't even over? She thought of the last few afternoons when it had been enough just to sit on a bench together outside the house. She'd managed to go through the motions during workshops, during meals, and reckoned that no one could tell she was in a kind of fever. Every night, by the time the knock came at her door, and she ran to open it, she was in such a frenzy of desire she could scarcely speak.

They'd walked back to the house almost silently. Everything had been said. There was nothing to add. They would phone one another on the silver phones whose numbers were known only to the two of them. It wasn't much, but it was, as Gray said, something. And he spoke again about the divorce, about leaving Maureen, about how in the end it was the right, the moral thing to do. He'd almost convinced her, too, but she knew that once Bob was back from Egypt, there in the house with her, everything would be harder. She'd feel guilty because she wasn't very good at breaking rules, at misbehaving, and his presence might shake her resolve. Today, in the café, Gray asked if she could ever get away on her own.

'We could meet from time to time,' he said. 'In a hotel.'

'I love hotels,' said Joss, 'but what reason could I give for going to one by myself? When I'm in London, I stay with Zannah and Em.'

'What about the prize-giving? For the Madrigal Prize?'

'Bob won't want to come to that with me, I'm sure, but it's in London, so both girls will be there. Isis, too, if it's early enough in the evening.'

'Can't you make something up? Tell Zannah and Em that your publisher's paying for a posh hotel and you don't want to miss out on the treat. They'd understand, wouldn't they?'

'He's offered. My publisher, I mean. Mal knows I've got family in London, but I suppose I could say that the spare room was already taken . . .'

'There you are, then,' said Gray, looking properly happy for the first time since they'd sat down. He picked up the teapot and refilled his cup. 'Something to look forward to. November the twenty-eighth. I'll make sure to fix things at the hospital. I wish I could come to the ceremony, but I'll meet you later at the hotel. Can't wait.' He squeezed her hand.

'How d'you know the date? I'm sure I didn't tell you.'

'I looked it up on the Madrigal website.'

Two months to go, almost exactly, Joss thought now, staring at the curve of Gray's back under the duvet. She turned on her side and slid an arm round his waist, pressing herself to him. He stirred and murmured and she clung to him.

'What's the matter?' He was suddenly awake, speaking in an almost normal voice. 'What's wrong?'

'Nothing. Go back to sleep.'

Too late. He'd seen that she was wide awake and unhappy. He whispered. 'Come here,' and she came to him, burying her face in his chest.

'I don't want this night to end ever. Ever,' she said. 'What'll I do? How will I get through the time, Gray?'

'We'll think of one another,' he whispered. 'We'll write and phone, and soon it'll be November. And then May and after the wedding, however hard it might seem, in the end, it'll be you and me.'

He started to kiss her.

'We can't,' Joss whispered. 'It's nearly morning. There's no time, Gray . . .'

'Don't speak.'

She closed her eyes, and as he touched her she had a vision of herself as nothing more than the separate strands of her desires and needs: wound up, urgent, tangled into a knot that he was unravelling, smoothing out. Her darling. Her darling Gray. Hers.

Monday

'I'm not very good at this, Gray,' Lydia said. However hard he tried, he couldn't call her Joss, couldn't think of her as that because the name went with Gratrix. 'Some people must have a talent for adultery and I haven't. I feel . . . I feel terrified. I thought we wouldn't be seeing one another till November. I'd have had time to get used to it. As it is . . .'

'I know. We said goodbye, didn't we? And now, here we are, barely forty-eight hours later. Amazing stroke of luck.'

'I'm so on edge, Gray. What if someone I know sees us?'

They were in the dining room of the Malmaison Hotel in Manchester. Lydia had phoned him as soon as she got home on Saturday night with the news that Bob had been held up and would be in Egypt for an extra two weeks. He'd lied to Maureen and told her he had an important meeting at Wythenshawe Hospital on Monday and of course there'd be a dinner afterwards. He'd persuaded Lydia to meet him at the hotel for dinner. It had taken a great deal of effort. His room was upstairs, empty. There was no one waiting for her at home. He hadn't said a word about wanting her to spend the night with him, but he could hardly eat with wondering what the end would be to this meal.

'If anyone sees us,' he said 'anyone you know, there's nothing wrong in having dinner with your daughter's future father-in-law, is there?'

'I suppose not.' She smiled at him. 'I can't pretend it's not exciting. It's just . . . I'm not used to it. I feel as though I'm acting. Being someone else.'

'I'm glad you're not anyone else. I don't want anyone else.'

'That's my phone, Gray. I have to take it, in case it's . . .'

'I didn't hear anything.'

'It vibrates. I felt it. Excuse me a second.'

He watched her walk out of the restaurant and begin to talk as soon as she was outside. He could see, even from here, that she was blushing. Talking and smiling too, so the chances were it wasn't Bob calling from Egypt, nor any emergency. When she came back, she said, 'That was Em, wanting to know if she could come for the first weekend in October. She says Zannah's visiting you with Adrian and Isis is going to Cal.'

'That's right. It'll be good to see them. I like Zannah very much. Actually, I think she's far too good for Adrian but, as you know, I'm not the person to talk to about him.'

'I must invite them up here as well. I feel I hardly know him and I also feel . . . this is a terrible thing to confess and I can't think why I'm telling you, except that I want to pour out every single thought I've ever had . . . well, I miss Cal. I liked him so much and now I never see him, and that's a loss. When Zannah divorced, it really was like losing a son. And I couldn't say a word to Zannah who was . . . She was so desperately unhappy, Gray.'

He knew what her next thought was bound to be and spoke before she had a chance to express it: 'I know what you're going to say, Lydia. Divorce is painful and how can we inflict it on Maureen and Bob? Yes?'

She nodded. 'Perhaps I said some things at Fairford that I shouldn't have said. We ought to think again.'

His heart suddenly seemed to be taking up an enormous amount of space in his chest. 'D'you mean that?'

Just then the waiter arrived at their table, and while their desserts were put in front of them, the time between his question and her answer seemed to go on and on. At last the man disappeared and still Lydia hadn't answered. In the end, he said, 'You don't mean it, do you?'

She shook her head. 'No, I don't. I want to be with you more than I've ever wanted anything, but it won't be easy. I told you, I'm not good at this. Part of me wants to run away. To get up and find my car and drive home and never leave my study ever again.'

He took her hand across the table. 'You won't, though, Lydia. Will you? Please stay. Stay with me tonight.'

She nodded, smiling at him and squeezing his fingers. He had to make a real effort to stop himself leaning across the table and kissing her. A whole night. Breakfast together. He ran his fingers up her sleeve. 'Hurry up and finish your pudding,' he said.

Saturday

October already, Zannah thought. Where did the weeks go? Ma had been back from her Fairford Hall course for a month and she still hadn't been to London to visit them. Pa was back from Egypt now, though he'd stayed two weeks longer than expected. Surprisingly, Ma hadn't seemed to mind too much and though Zannah had volunteered to go up there for the weekend, she'd been adamant that she was fine, happy on her own and actually quite busy. Em was going up this weekend, and that made Zannah feel a bit better. It occurred to her to wonder what on earth her mother had to be busy with, but she pushed this thought to the back of her mind and forgot about it. Now they were in Adrian's car, on their way to Guildford to stay with the Ashtons for a couple of nights.

Isis was with Cal. She'd packed and unpacked her suitcase a hundred times, changing her mind every day about what she needed to take, but always making room for the scrap of her bridesmaid's dress material, the exact shade of heavenly forest-green taffeta she'd dreamed of, to be made up into a style that would look summery in spite of the dark colour, and the sketch copied on the school photocopier so that she could show her father exactly what her dress would be like. Isis had given up the idea of her beloved pink after just one glance at her mother's picture, carefully coloured in. She'd agreed that a headband with little pink roses on it, and pink bits on her sleeves would be *sooo* fantastic and that forest green was now her second favourite colour. Especially when the material was the kind that *'changes when the light shines on it and the colours sort of swim about'*. Gemma, Isis assured her, loved it too, and she was going to come with them to see Miss Hayward in a couple of weeks, when they would have their first fittings.

Zannah had only visited the Ashtons once before, quite soon after she'd met Adrian. Then she'd been anxious for them to like her and she'd made a point of being more than usually helpful and friendly, and had given every appearance of being entranced by what she saw, exclaiming with delight at everything Maureen showed her.

Her future mother-in-law, to give her credit, did things in style. The house and garden were spectacular, and Zannah felt, that first time, as though she were being allowed to spend the weekend in a particularly gorgeous show home. The parquet floors, the rugs, the curtains – custom-made without a doubt and from fabrics that she could see were fiendishly expensive – the light-fittings, the tableware: everything looked as though it had only just been unpacked. In her parents' house, most things looked as though they'd been used for years and years, which, of course, they had.

There weren't all that many books in this show home, except for the ones in Graham Ashton's study. Zannah had seen them as she passed the door a couple of times, crowding the shelves that lined one wide wall from floor to ceiling. Maureen's taste, though, had spread even to this room, and the desk was state-of-the-art glass and steel, a far cry from her father's scratched old brown wooden one, which, he always boasted, cost him only three pounds in an auction at Alderley Edge. And that's just what it looks like, Dad, Emily used to say, smiling fondly at him.

'D'you think I'm going to be bullied, darling?' she said to Adrian, who was driving. He put out a hand and caressed her thigh briefly.

'Nonsense. Mum just said it was ages since we'd been down. That's true, isn't it? And isn't it super to be on our own for a whole weekend?'

'Lovely,' said Zannah. It was true: last night had been wonderful. They'd had dinner in a restaurant Adrian had discovered that did authentic Lebanese food, and then, full of red wine and baklava, they'd gone back to his flat and he'd made love to her passionately, tenderly. Then this morning, he'd got up early and brought her a croissant and a cup of coffee on a tray and they'd been late starting out for Guildford because one thing had led to another and then they'd had to clear the crumbs out of the bed and after that they both had to shower and now she felt as though she'd been in an especially energetic game of tennis: pleasantly relaxed in all her limbs and half asleep from the motion of the car. Suddenly, love for Adrian flooded her and she squeezed his thigh. It wasn't going to be an ordeal at all, this weekend. Now that they were on their way, she was quite looking forward to it.

'Where did you go on your walk, you two?' said Maureen, topping up Zannah's glass with a little more whisky.

'Just round and about, you know,' Adrian answered. 'Nowhere special.'

'The trees are so lovely, aren't they? Did you go down Marlborough Drive?'

He nodded. 'Think we did, as a matter of fact. Didn't meet anyone you know, Mum.'

It's no good, Maureen told herself. They'd been here for more than a day and would be going back up to town later this evening and she'd missed her chance. So much for letting them decide for themselves. They were obviously so much in love (and it was sweet to see Adrian like that, though she thought Zannah was a bit less keen...maybe just her mother's antennae being over-sensitive) that they'd walked right past the house she'd earmarked for them without noticing it. She took a deep breath. She was going to have to broach the subject herself. She said, 'Did you notice a rather pretty little house, about halfway up Marlborough Drive?'

'No,' said Adrian. ''Fraid not.'

'We weren't really looking at the houses. More at the leaves and trees,' Zannah added.

'I was just wondering ... Have you two given any thought to where you're going to live after you're married?'

'I was thinking about that just the other day,' Adrian said. 'I suppose we really ought to start looking for somewhere suitable. My flat's too small.'

Zannah, Maureen noticed, said nothing but had begun to pick at one of the fringes on the silk shawl that she was wearing round her shoulders.

'Wouldn't it,' Maureen said, speaking gently 'be a good idea if you found somewhere down here? You'd be able to get a transfer from the bank, I'm sure, Adrian, and Zannah, there's never any problem about finding a job if you're a teacher, is there? Think how lovely it will be for us to have you so close. I was quite sure you'd see that marvellous little house and fall madly in love with it . . .'

'Now Mum,' said Adrian, 'how many times have I explained to you that it's not that kind of bank? Not the kind of place that would have a branch in Guildford. It's an investment bank, for heaven's sake! Don't you know what that is?'

'No, I don't,' said Maureen. 'And I don't care to. I'm just proud of you being so successful and I suppose I did know that your bank didn't have a branch in Guildford, if I'd stopped to think. Still, it had slipped my mind. I would so love it if you could live a little closer to us, that's all.'

Graham said, 'Don't nag them, Maureen, about where they're going to live and so on. They're not even married yet . . .'

'And there's the question of my job as well,' said Zannah. 'I'm sorry, but I couldn't possibly leave London . . .'

'Why ever not?' said Maureen. ' It'd be much better for your little girl. Cleaner air. Better schools. That sort of thing. And I don't believe you're so committed to your present school that you wouldn't think of changing. And, besides, think how much safer it'd be . . . No danger of any policemen taking pot-shots at you here, like they did at that poor Brazilian man, and I'm sure bin Laden has no interest in bombing Guildford.' She laughed to show that this last point was light-hearted. 'Still, it's all beside the point, as Adrian can't leave his bank. Though lots of people commute, you know.'

'It would be so awful . . . all that travelling every day! In any case, I wouldn't take Isis away from her father. She sees little enough of him already,' Zannah said. She looked more normal by now and spoke, Maureen noticed, calmly and pleasantly. 'And I'm afraid I'm very happy at the school I'm at. I really wouldn't want to uproot myself and go somewhere else. So sorry, Maureen, if it's a big disappointment to you, but we'll be staying in London.'

'Right, well,' Graham got up and made for the stairs, 'must just write a couple of emails, I'm afraid. What time are you two setting off?'

'About seven,' said Adrian.

'I'll go and fix a little snack for you to have before you go,' said Maureen, getting up and moving towards the kitchen. 'You stay here and relax. Have another drink, Zannah. We'll say no more about my little plan.'

Maureen knew, and had always known, about Adrian's investment bank but things might change. There was nothing to say that a person had to stay in the same job for ever, was there? She'd planted the thought in Adrian's head and now it must be left to grow there, like a seedling. If he could be persuaded, he might manage to change his fiancée's mind in the fullness of time. All was a very long way from being lost.

'Zannah? May I have a word?'

Zannah stepped into Graham Ashton's study. He'd been waiting to speak to her, evidently, and had caught her going downstairs just after she'd finished packing.

'We'll be leaving in a minute, Graham,' she said.

'Come and sit down. I just wanted to say something before you go ...'

Adrian had persuaded her that quarrelling within earshot of his parents wasn't a good idea. They could talk, he said, in the car. Zannah wasn't looking forward to it. She looked round the study and admired a couple of watercolours on one wall. A silver laptop lay open on the desk and next to it ... Was it? Could it be? Yes, it was. *The Shipwreck Café*. How surprising people were, she thought. She said, 'I see you've got my mother's book. I didn't know you liked poetry.'

'I love it,' he said and, most astonishingly, blushed scarlet. He had fair skin and darkish brown hair, and Zannah was surprised to see him so flustered. Perhaps he thought liking poetry was something to be ashamed of. Lots of men did. He collected himself and said, 'I do like it. I even write a little, though I don't often talk about it. Not as well as your mother of course. She's very ... very accomplished.'

He sat at his desk and smiled at her. Maureen was lucky, Zannah thought. He was a lovely-looking man for someone of his age and she felt sure that any patient who saw him in the operating theatre would immediately feel better. She smiled back. What on earth did he want? He said, 'I just thought I should say, don't worry about Maureen. She gets these ideas. I could see you weren't a bit happy about the moving to Guildford thing and you mustn't let yourself be bullied. That's it, really. I hope you don't think I'm interfering, but I just think you should … well, you have to see to it that you're happy, even though it might seem selfish. It's important that you two are unanimous about decisions like this. Maureen has … well, she has quite an influence on her son and people can decide to change jobs. Don't let yourself do something you'll regret, that's all I'm saying.'

'I hope Maureen doesn't think I'm against her ideas on principle? And it's really nice to talk to you about it.'

'I'll have a word with her when you've gone, and she'll move on to something else in no time. She's good at that.'

As he spoke, Graham's right hand stroked the cover of her mother's book from time to time, as though it were a small pet. She caught his eye and he blushed again, 'It's such a beautiful cover, isn't it? I hope it wins the Madrigal Prize. The shortlisting must be a great feather in your mother's cap, I should think.'

'Yes, she's thrilled about it,' said Zannah, and stood up. 'We should get on our way now, I think. I'll go and find Adrian.'

'I'll come too. Wave you off.' He stood up and followed her out of the room.

All that blushing … Perhaps he was a secret fan of Ma's without telling her. I'll phone her tomorrow and let her know she has a secret admirer, Zannah thought. She'll be so pleased.

'Okay, okay,' said Adrian. 'I give up. I'm not going to pursue it, right? I promise. I'll phone my mum tomorrow and let her know, though God knows, Zannah, why you've taken against the idea in this completely demented way.'

'Demented? Me?' Zannah could scarcely believed what she was hearing. From the moment they'd left the Ashtons, they'd done nothing but yell at one another. At one point, Zannah had made him stop the car in a lay-by because she couldn't trust herself not to become hysterical and she knew that would make Adrian careless as he drove. 'It's you. You've come to your senses. I thought you'd taken final leave of them. Guildford, honestly.'

'What's so terrible about Guildford? As far as I can see the only disadvantage would be the commuting because, of course, I can't leave the bank and wouldn't want to, but from all other points of view, I reckon it wouldn't be a bad move.'

'Your job, my job, the whole thing's senseless. It's just one of your mum's hare-brained schemes.'

As soon as the words were out, Zannah regretted them. You could think whatever you wanted about someone's mother, but you never told them. Even when they weren't that keen on their mums, blokes hated other women slagging them off and Adrian, far from not thinking much of Maureen, reckoned she was the model to whom other women should aspire. She added, quickly, 'I don't mean that. She has very good ideas usually, Adrian, but this giving up of my job and moving to some dinky little establishment down there ... I'd hate it.'

'What's so special about St Botolph's? I thought you might give up work altogether after a bit. Certainly after we start having children.'

Zannah turned to look at Adrian's profile, and was relieved to discover that at least he was still as handsome as he'd always been, because he was suddenly saying things that he'd never even hinted at in the months that they'd been together. She took a deep breath and struggled to sound loving and reasonable. 'Darling, of course I'm not giving up my work when we have children. There's a very good crêche attached to St Botolph's, which is one reason I like the school so much. Plus it's convenient for the flat.'

'Ah, but we won't be living there, will we? You know that. In fact, now that you've put the kibosh on Guildford, we ought to get ourselves sorted as far as houses are concerned. I'll make a few enquiries. No reason we can't view places now, is there?'

Zannah shook her head. There was no reason at all and any other bride would be eager, thrilled to look for a house to share with her new husband. And I am, I am, Zannah thought. It'll be great. I can decorate it from scratch and make it just the way I want it. Why was it, then, that thinking of the flat, her little studio up that flight of stairs, the views out of the kitchen window, she already felt something like sadness at the prospect of leaving it? It wasn't even as though she'd lose the place altogether. Em would still need somewhere to live and she could get friends in to share. I could still visit, Zannah thought. It wouldn't be the same, but maybe it would be better. I'm just suffering from wedding nerves. Wedding nerves are real. Everyone says so. She leaned back against the seat and fell into a light sleep as Adrian drove through the darkness towards London.

Isis asked, 'Will Mummy be here when I get up in the morning?'

Emily had come home early so that she could be in the flat when Cal arrived to drop Isis off and now she was sitting at the end of her niece's bed. They'd just finished a takeaway pizza which Emily had hoped Cal might stay and share, but he'd had to hurry off, almost before he'd got there. There was something about Sunday evenings that was almost tangible: a sort of dread and heaviness left over from the days when you didn't want to get up on Monday morning for school. She said, 'Yes, they're driving back now. She'll be here in a couple of hours. She's sure to come in and give you a kiss. She always does.'

'I'll be asleep,' Isis said. 'But tell her she has to anyway.'

'Okay. And I have to give you a kiss from Grandma and one from Grandpa. They really loved the pictures you sent them.'

She kissed Isis three times, tucked the duvet round her shoulders and left the room. Down in the kitchen, she threw away the pizza box and washed up the glasses they'd used. Ma had been in a funny mood over the weekend, Emily thought, and wondered if Zannah would be up to discussing it when she came back. Probably not. She'd be full of Maureen stories and if Emily was honest with herself, she was quite keen to know how the weekend *chez* Ashton had been. What, in any case, could she tell her sister that would convey the impression she'd had of their mother's state of mind? She seemed to be ... well, not quite in the same world as the rest of them. There'd been a couple of occasions when Emily had had to say something two or three times before getting her attention, as though her mother's mind had been on something completely different. During meals, while Pa had told amusing stories of his time in Egypt, Ma sat there smiling, not hearing a word, Emily was quite sure. Once or twice, she'd wandered into the study while Ma had been sitting in front of her open laptop and she'd had the distinct impression that some file or other was very quickly shut down. Once she even joked about it. *Bet you're playing Patience, Ma,* she'd said. *We've got people in my office like you.* Ma had blushed and mumbled something about work. Could be true, but still, Emily had left her parents' house feeling that all was not quite as it had been through her childhood. For one thing, Pa never really talked about anything of real interest to Ma any longer. Had it always been like this, with her and Zannah just not noticing? I'll ask Zannah what she thinks, Emily resolved and settled down to watch *24* on Sky One.

November/ December/January

Friday

There wasn't, Maureen reflected, all that much time left till the Day, which was what she called the wedding. This year, though, she didn't have Christmas to think about, which in one way was a blessing but in another was rather a shame. It would have been so lovely to have Adrian, Zannah and Isis, too, down to Guildford to celebrate with them but Graham had arranged the trip to South Africa to see Jonathan ages ago and at the time, Maureen had been thrilled to bits. Even now, when part of her longed to have the pleasure of the preparations, she was feeling quite excited about getting together a whole lot of super new outfits and shoes for a warm climate. There was something extra pleasant about doing this when the weather was cold. And of course, they'd be with darling Jonathan, whom she loved with a passion. It was ages since they'd seen him.

Maureen had never told anyone that Adrian was her favourite but she'd have bet her bottom dollar that many mothers were in exactly the same position. For instance, she was sure Zannah was her mother's favourite. Emily was a daddy's girl if ever she'd seen one and it didn't take a genius to see that Graham loved his own son a great deal more than he loved Adrian. Actually, she didn't think he loved Adrian at all. He used to tell her he did, in the old days, at the beginning of their relationship, but that was to keep her happy, she was convinced of it. She was pretty sure that love had never been a part of what Graham felt for her son and Adrian made no secret of not having much time for his stepfather. It's to my credit, Maureen thought, that they've arrived at some kind of truce that enables us to rub along together well enough.

Next year, she told herself, I'll make sure they all come here and it will be so good to have a child in the house. She'd already made a note to email Zannah and find out what Isis wanted for Christmas. A gift from her and Graham, most beautifully wrapped, would have to be sent with the other presents to the Gratrix house, where the whole family was gathering. How on earth would Joss manage? No one would call her one of the world's natural hostesses. Maureen made a note to herself on a nearby pad to research presents for Isis. She was quite out of touch with what was *de rigueur* for eight-year-olds, and as she was going to be Isis's honorary granny, it was time she got her act together.

A granny ... She sat up straighter and looked down at her hands, still mercifully unspotted, apart from a small outcrop of brown marks that were, frankly, more like freckles than what they rather chillingly called grave spots, just near the thumb. Was she ready to be a granny? Even an honorary one? Well, there was nothing to be done about it. Isis would be, to all intents and purposes, Adrian's daughter, so she'd just have to get used to it. Perhaps it was not too much to wish for that by the time they came to her next year, Zannah would be carrying her son's baby ... How divine that would be!

She looked at the file on her computer labelled *South Africa: Christmas* and moved the cursor down rather regretfully to *Wedding*. On Monday, which would be the twenty-seventh, there would be exactly six months to go to the Day. She had to concede that things were going quite smoothly, even though she mentally crossed her fingers as she thought this. Zannah had been stubborn when it came to the dress, and not as grateful as she might have been for Maureen's help and input, but still, someone who'd worked for Norman Hartnell wasn't to be sniffed at. Zannah's sketch, she could see, was quite a different concept from the one she'd had about what one might wear at one's wedding. It was a beautiful drawing, there was no doubt about it, but one word came into Maureen's mind whenever she thought about it and that was 'old-fashioned'. It looked, if she was completely honest, like the sort of thing her own mother might have worn at a wedding some time in the 1930s ... perhaps 'vintage' or 'period' was a politer way of putting it. She'd mentioned this tentatively to Zannah, and was astonished when her future daughter-in-law, instead of frowning or sulking or losing her temper, smiled at her with genuine pleasure and said, 'Exactly, Maureen. Vintage ... That's just right. I'm so pleased you understand. That's what I'm after, the 1930s look.'

So on that front, there was nothing to be done. The bride has the last word when it comes to the dress, Maureen reflected, and you have to make the best of it, and she had to admit that the bridesmaids' outfits, also designed by Zannah, were too sweet for words. At first, Maureen had blinked a little at the idea of dark green, but the samples of taffeta Zannah had shown her were lovely and would look gorgeous trimmed with pink velvet ribbon. Isis and her little friend were going to carry small round bouquets studded with pink roses and the foliage, Zannah assured her, would match the green of their dresses as nearly as it was possible to match anything. Also, there was no getting away from the fact that the ancient dressmaker in charge of all three dresses had a certain cachet and it was the Norman Hartnell connection that Maureen had been busy emphasizing to her friends.

Joss, to give credit where it was due, had come up with beautiful invitations: stiff, cream card engraved with black letters in a really elegant font, called Garamond. *Robert and Jocelyn Gratrix invite you to celebrate the marriage of their elder daughter Suzannah to Adrian Whittaker, elder son of Graham and Maureen Ashton* ... She wasn't quite sure about the wording, but it was too late now. The cards had been printed and would be sent out straight after Christmas. She herself would have favoured Professor and Mrs Robert Gratrix ... and then there was the small matter of Adrian not being Graham's son. Surely there was a way of indicating this tactfully, maybe by putting Maureen's name first. Never mind. No one else would even think twice about it. I'm just fussier than most people, she thought, and remembered a time straight after their wedding when Graham used to tease her about it, calling her the Princess, after the Hans Andersen story, 'The Princess and the Pea'. She'd never seen anything strange about that young lady's behaviour. I'd probably have felt that pea through all the mattresses too, she thought, and why not?

Zannah had been to see a florist and they were working on variations on cream roses, woven with glossy foliage, and very dark red roses dotted here and there with just a hint of pale pink. She hadn't seen the actual sketches for the bouquets, but Zannah had forwarded several photos of arrangements for the tables and the marquee and Maureen couldn't find fault with them. You had to be careful with flowers for a marquee because of the masses of space between the tables and the roof but hanging baskets seemed a good way to get over that problem.

Charlotte had the marquee under control. It would be white, and the lining was going to be cream, striped with palest gold. Charlotte had sent her the bumf from the company and there had been nothing she could object to. The question of buffet versus tables had been hotly debated by email and it was a good thing that the whole matter had been dealt with electronically. In a normal conversation, someone would have lost their temper, but somehow they'd arrived at what Maureen considered the right decision. Tables had won the day, thank Heaven. There was nothing worse than being stuck with a plate to balance, when your best handbag was either clutched in your other hand or slung over your shoulder and slipping maddeningly down to the crook of your elbow. Infuriating and unnecessary. The list had gone down from seventy-five to about sixty, apparently, and they'd all fit comfortably into Charlotte's marquee. The best thing about tables was the opportunity they gave for glorious centrepieces and the ones that Zannah had emailed her looked lovely: square, crystal vases filled with the same red/cream/pink roses and foliage as the bouquets. The hanging baskets, Zannah had decided, and Maureen had to admit that she had a good eye for such things, would be mostly foliage, with perhaps some lisianthus but hidden among the leaves, ivy and trailing green plants would be little gold and silver butterflies, and very nice they looked too.

As far as food was concerned, there would be both a buffet *and* tables, so that everyone could help themselves and still sit comfortably to eat. The menus she'd been sent by Genevieve, who was so helpful when she'd been to see her last week, had been bewildering in their variety but she'd narrowed it down to four main dishes (seared duck breast salad with raspberry, balsamic vinegar and shallot dressing; wild mushroom and mozzarella tart; summer-fresh mint and honey marinated lamb fillet salad on tabbouleh and whole poached salmon with fresh herb sauce) and a few side salads. She still had to choose these, but there was plenty of time for that. And there was time for deciding on the desserts. Just reading the names of what was on offer made her feel hungry: pistachio nut and raspberry cream roulade; dark chocolate and fresh ginger ganache tart; mango and amaretti cheesecake; cinnamon pavlova with strawberries and cream … even thinking about them was a treat. None of this, of course, would come cheaply. Thirty pounds per head with drinks and staff on top of that. Not for the first time Maureen blessed Graham's parents for dying so young and leaving him well off. It was comforting not to have to worry about money and Maureen couldn't think of anything she'd rather splash out on than her son's wedding. She was helping the Gratrixes as well, which gave her some satisfaction, but that mainly came – Maureen didn't admit this to anyone but she wasn't in the habit of kidding herself – from being able to choose and control. She liked being the one who was in touch with the caterer, the one who was constantly consulted.

The cake had been ordered from a local baker called Ronald Sprackley and she was immensely proud of it. Not only had she practically designed it herself, but she was supporting a small local firm and helping a talented young baker acquire a reputation. She'd opted for three square layers, not divided by columns, iced in white, with a waterfall of dark red rosebuds and tiny ivy leaves tumbling down one side and curling round to embrace three sides of the square. It would look heavenly, Ronald assured her, and she believed him. All she had to do now was discuss what the cake itself was to be. Wedding cake meant rich fruit cake to Maureen, but Zannah might have other ideas. She opened the email and typed in Zannah's address.

The phone, which was on her desk within easy reach, rang just as she was getting started on her message.

'Maureen Ashton.'

'Mrs Ashton, it's Genevieve. From the caterers …'

'Oh, Genevieve. I was just thinking about you. I've practically made up my mind … Still a few things left to decide but we can do that later, can't we?'

'Yes, of course. No rush at all. But I'd like to come in and talk about your plans if that's all right?'

'That'd be lovely. Are you free tomorrow?'

'Yes, tomorrow's fine. About eleven?'

'Marvellous! Thanks so much. You know how to get here?'

'Oh, yes. I've often passed your house. I'm looking forward to seeing you.'

'Till tomorrow, then.'

Maureen put the phone down. Genevieve knowing her house and talking about it in those admiring tones was gratifying. She came very highly recommended by everyone at the tennis club. She'd catered the last New Year's Eve ball there and the food had been heavenly. It would be good to meet her in person.

'Darling?'

'Yes?' Joss turned to Bob. Something in his voice alerted her to the fact that he had something important to say. He usually left the room immediately after they'd watched the news on TV and disappeared to his study for an hour or so before bed. Tonight, he was sitting up and smiling at her in a most unusual way. He looked almost impish.

'Monday's the day, then, isn't it? Madrigal Prize day.'

'I'm surprised you remembered. Yes, I'm excited. Can't wait to see the girls, of course, but a night in a lovely hotel ... you know how much I love them!'

'I do and I feel ... well, not to put too fine a point on it, Joss, I think I've been neglecting you, what with Egypt and all the work I've been caught up in recently. So I've been thinking. And not just thinking either, but acting! I've got a surprise for you.'

Joss looked at him. He was smiling so broadly, so sure that he'd done something tremendous, that she smiled in response. What on earth had he been up to?

'I'm coming with you. To London. To the prizegiving. I'm going to stay with you at the hotel. And that's not all. I'm taking you out to dinner after the ceremony – whether it's for a celebration or a commiseration, doesn't matter, really, and, what's more, I've invited everyone – Charlotte, the girls, Isis, even the Ashtons.'

The Ashtons. Joss felt as though her heart was shrinking in her chest. How could this be happening? Bob? Coming to a poetry event? Inviting everyone to dinner? Why suddenly? Could he suspect something? She started to speak, then didn't know what to say and closed her mouth.

'I see I've silenced you, Jossie. I did hesitate about the Ashtons, as a matter of fact, in view of ... well, in view of your ... Never mind. I decided that it was childish to let that get in the way of what should be a proper celebration for all the family. What d'you think?'

Play for time, she told herself. Ask him something. She said, 'How did you get in touch with the Ashtons? Did you speak to Maureen?'

He nodded. 'An hour ago. Em gave me her phone number. Maureen seems very keen. Strikes me she's the sort of person who's always happy to dress up and go out. Likes a bit of an outing, that's the impression I got.'

But what about Gray? she wanted to ask, but couldn't. What would he think? Their night together, the night they'd waited and planned for ever since they'd met at the Malmaison, had disappeared. Part of her was so disappointed that she wanted to cry, like a child deprived of a treat. Another part was relieved. She'd been having nightmares, full of dreadful things that were a mixture of anxiety, guilt, fear of discovery, mixed up with left-over memories and flashbacks of the July bombs. Bob's initiative got her off the hook. Did she want to be off that particular hook? She feared what Gray would say. Might he wonder if she'd been the one to chicken out? Perhaps he'd think it was her idea to instigate the invitation as a way of avoiding him. I must speak to him, she thought. I must reassure him. Maybe I can persuade him not to come to the dinner. How will I sit at the same table with him and Bob and Maureen? That would be like a particularly ghastly kind of torment.

'That's lovely,' she managed at last. 'A lovely thought on your part, Bob. I'm touched. Really.'

'There's more,' Bob went on. 'I'm taking you to Paris for a couple of nights afterwards. We'll get the Eurostar on Tuesday morning.'

'Bob! Paris!' Joss could hardly believe what she was hearing. It was as though he was doing it deliberately: tearing her apart. He was making such an effort to show her that he still cared, still remembered how happy they'd been on their honeymoon, and all the while she didn't want to go. She wanted to stay here and be with Gray and not have to travel with her husband to a past she'd thought he'd left behind long ago, as she had. What kind of horrible, ungrateful person had she become? This unwonted demonstration of Bob's love was exactly what she didn't need. Not now. She couldn't refuse to go. She wished this conversation had never happened. She wished she didn't have to face Gray, who would by now have left a message on her phone. What would he say to her? What would she tell him?

'Are you happy, sweetheart?' Bob came and sat down on the sofa next to her, put one arm round her shoulders, pulled her to him and kissed her full on the mouth. She must have seemed taken aback, because he said, 'Don't look so shocked, Joss. I do love you, you know. And we'll be able to relive our youth a bit in Paris, won't we?'

'Yes,' said Joss, weakly.

Bob stood up and said, 'I'm off to do a bit of work before bed, if that's okay. Don't wait, if you feel sleepy.'

'I'm going to write a couple of emails before bed, I think. And thank you, darling,' said Joss. 'This whole thing ... it's a lovely thought. It's ... well, it's very kind of you.'

Kind. Alone in the room, she covered her face with her hands. What an inadequate word *kind* was! The Madrigal prizegiving, the dinner, the trip to Paris ... She didn't know what she thought about any of it and went upstairs dreading the message she knew she would find on her phone.

The snores coming from their bedroom were reassuring. Bob was fast asleep, so it was all right to talk on her mobile, but still Joss closed the door of her study and turned to face the window in the hope that the drawn curtains would muffle the sound of her voice. She'd sent Gray a text on her hidden phone when she'd taken it out before bed, ready to send the last message of the day. They'd fallen into a habit of exchanging texts late at night, wishing one another good night with silly xs like the ones Isis always used at the end of her messages. Tonight, his text read: *Phone me, however late. Urgent.xxx* and Joss was trembling as she keyed in his number. He answered at once. He must have been waiting for her to ring.

'Lydia, darling ...'

'Gray ... Maureen must have told you. Bob's... I don't know what to do. I can't not go. I can't refuse to take part. I can't get out of it.'

'I know. I know you can't. It doesn't matter, Lydia. We'll arrange something else. This hasn't ... I mean, you still ... ?'

Joss knew what he was asking. Do you still love me? Will you leave Bob? Are we where we were? How to answer him? How could she convey the complete powerlessness to decide what was right that she frequently felt these days?

'Lydia? Are you there? Did you hear me?'

'Yes, Gray. I heard you. Of course I haven't changed my mind. Don't think that. It's just that … it's hard, that's all. Bob's taking me to Paris for a couple of days. Did Maureen tell you that?'

'Yes … I wish, well, never mind what I wish. I'll take you somewhere else, very soon.'

'But what'll it be like, with everyone else there? I won't know where to look. I don't know if I can do it, Gray.'

'I could have an emergency at the hospital and not come. How about that? I'll do it if you want me to.'

For a second, Joss thought of saying, 'Yes, do that. Don't come. Don't let's put ourselves through this,' but she wanted to see him. Wanted at least to look at him and listen to him speak. There would be no chance to see him alone, of course, but that couldn't be helped. If she won, she wanted him to be there. If she lost, she wanted him to be there. Sadly, she came to the conclusion that she wanted him to be there all the time. She said, 'No, I want you to be there, if you can stand it.'

'I will. I'll come. It'll be hard …'

Joss had an image of herself and Bob in the hotel, then of Maureen and Gray driving together back to Guildford. Unbearable, but she would have to bear it. 'It's six months, you know,' she said, 'till the wedding.'

'I know, I'm counting the days. We'll be together very soon. You must hang on to that.'

'I do. I think of it all the time. Good night, my darling. Sleep well.'

She cut the connection, and found herself almost out of breath. What she didn't tell Gray, what she'd never told him, was the turmoil she felt every time she considered the future carefully. Part of her was terrified of turning everything she'd taken to be her life completely upside-down. She found herself staring at Bob as they sat together in the kitchen and thinking, Do I love him? I must do. I do. Does he love me? He must … mustn't he? As the time passed, as the days and nights since she'd seen Gray face to face went by, the doubts came and wouldn't go away. She asked herself constantly, How can I do it? How can I leave him? He's what I know. He's what I'm used to. He's my husband. It means something. It counts for something. He'll be hurt. Can I hurt him?

Then there were the moments when she found him annoying, when he didn't seem to take any account of her presence in the house, when he lost himself in his work, when he went into his study and rarely came out and worst of all, when he didn't speak to her about anything that was of importance to her. Oh, they chatted about the girls, and about Isis and his work and his colleagues and that was that. *The Shipwreck Café* hadn't had many reviews, but when they did appear and she showed them to him, he'd smile and say: *Jolly good, darling. That's great,* and move on almost at once to something more urgent. He glanced at them, and never read one twice. Nor did he ever discuss their content, even though it had been favourable. With the first review, Joss decided never to show him any bad ones.

But, she told herself, if I do love Bob, then why do I think about nothing but Gray? Dream about him? Long for every message on email, on the phone, by text? Treasure every word he sends me? Is it about sex? Is it simply that Gray is a better lover? Makes me feel things Bob has never, ever made me feel? Is that all it is? She knew it wasn't. She just couldn't face the thought of years and years of not looking at Gray's face, not saying the silly things, the mad and ridiculous things that people who loved one another said when they were together. She and Bob had always been good friends, but the excitement of their first years together hadn't ever been like this. Their lovemaking in those days had been energetic, and loving and enthusiastic, but they'd never been … .Joss struggled with herself to know how to describe it … They'd never been mad, crazy, unbridled, even in the early days. Bob didn't do unbridled. He was too rational, perhaps, for unrestrained passion. That was the truth about him, and until she'd met Gray, Joss had assumed she was not particularly passionate either, but now she'd found that she was, and it was addictive. She wanted so much more now than she'd ever dared want before. She wanted everything: every sensation, and every taste and every adventure. She wanted to fuck in hotels with crisp linen sheets, on the grass in a wood, on a beach. For the very first time in her life, that word, one she'd never used, appeared in her innermost thoughts and Joss recognized the thrill that comes with breaking the rules. Most people, she reflected, get over this sort of thing when they're sixteen. I'm too old. I'm scared. I'm elated. I can't sleep. I want to sleep and dream and hold Gray in my arms in my dreams and taste his mouth on mine all day long, every day. If I close my eyes, I can always bring back the taste of him. The touch of him on my skin.

She stood up, left the study and went to lie next to her husband, who had stopped snoring and was now simply hogging most of the duvet, as he always did. Joss pulled some over to cover her shoulders and closed her eyes. I'll see Gray on Monday, she thought. Whatever else happens, I'll see him.

Monday

'What do you think?' Charlotte stood in the hall and peered into the mirror. 'Is this formal enough?'

'You look lovely as usual, dear. Don't worry.'

'Yes, Charlotte, have a good time,' said Edie. 'And give dear Joss our best. How wonderful if she wins!'

Charlotte was pleased with her reflection. She was wearing a blue woollen two-piece and had a smart black coat to go over the top. Joss and Bob were coming down on the train and meeting everyone at the venue. Zannah, Emily and Isis were going with Adrian in his car and the Ashtons were driving up from Guildford and picking her up en route to the restaurant. She'd have been quite happy to get a taxi, but it had been a kind thought, and however much she didn't want to discuss wedding arrangements with Maureen, Charlotte felt that the subject was bound to come up. Never mind, she thought. It's not too long a ride. She'd have been happy to attend the poetry award itself, but tickets were limited to five for every poet and, of course, Bob, Zannah, Emily and Isis had a prior claim on them, and Adrian could hardly be asked to wait outside like a chauffeur, so he had to be there too. Actually, Charlotte would have bet good money that neither Adrian nor Bob was particularly exercised about whether or not they attended the ceremony, but she couldn't say so of course. Never mind. The girls would give her a good account of the occasion, and besides, Charlotte wouldn't have enjoyed the tension before the announcement. It wouldn't have been good for her blood pressure.

'They're here!' Edie had stationed herself at the hall window and was now waving frantically. Charlotte stepped out into the porch and found that Graham Ashton was already holding the back door of his car open for her.

'Hello, Mrs Parrish,' he said. What a lovely smile he has, Charlotte thought.

'Charlotte, please.' She smiled back and said hello, and settled herself on the back seat, not forgetting to wave at Edie and Val, who could be seen, as the car rolled away, framed in the window.

'Well,' said Maureen, 'I'm getting quite excited. Imagine if we had a prize-winning poet in the family! Though of course, she might not win. Mustn't forget that.'

As she talked – and when Maureen talked, there was little that could stop her – Charlotte had a good view of Graham's profile. His mouth was clamped shut and he looked as though he was driving to some sort of trial or ordeal instead of a convivial dinner in an Italian restaurant. Who had told her that he wrote poems too? Joss, she thought, or maybe Zannah. She couldn't remember.

'You write poems yourself, don't you, Dr Ashton?'

He glanced back at her, smiling again. 'You must call me Graham, please, if you're to be Charlotte. Yes, I do. I write a bit. Nothing like the success ... er ... Joss is having. That's wonderful. I hope she wins, I really do.'

He meant it. And he was blushing. Why was that? Charlotte would never have been able to tell anyone exactly why, but she had the distinct impression that Joss's failure or success meant something to him. She wondered about it. As far as she knew, they'd not spoken or met since the day when Joss had run away from the engagement party. And he called her 'Joss'. Maybe, she reflected, that was simply because Maureen never stopped mentioning her name. Still, when you also considered the tone of the poems in *The Shipwreck Café* perhaps there was more here than met the eye. Could her niece be somehow involved with Graham Ashton? How could that be? Surely Joss would have mentioned knowing him if she'd ever met him before the engagement party. A mystery. She made up her mind to reserve judgement and be alert this evening.

For a few moments, Emily couldn't think what the poets, standing in a line on the stage, with the Madrigal organizers already in full flow at the lectern, reminded her of. Then it occurred to her that it was the TV coverage she'd seen of the declarations from town halls all over the country at the time of the general election. All four looked nervous. Ma was white. One of these days, Emily thought, I'll have to have a serious talk to her about blusher. Still, if this was a beauty contest, she'd have won, hands down. The other shortlistees were all most unprepossessing. One was clearly fond of the bottle. His nose was like an enormous strawberry. Another was stick-thin and almost as pale as Ma, but not as well dressed. In fact, he looked as though someone had pulled him out of bed five minutes before bringing him here. The other woman might have been quite striking once, but had retained, almost unaltered, her hippy attire: cheesecloth and sandals in November, not a good look, particularly when worn with shoulder-length hair that was crying out for the attentions of a talented hairdresser. Ma, on the other hand, if you didn't count the pallor, had made a real effort. She was wearing a dark red dress which was just the right length, the right fabric, the right style for this sort of occasion and at this time. Who'd helped her to choose it? Emily wondered. Could she have been looking at magazines? And her hair, fortunately, was so thick and glossy that it didn't really matter that the style hadn't changed for years and years.

The chap at the lectern was still droning on and on. Mal, Ma's editor, was staring at the floor, biting his lip. Emily wished Zannah, Isis and Adrian were standing near her so that at least they could have exchanged a look or a shrug. Isis was being very good, considering how boring the event was. Her hair was held back with butterfly slides and she kept smoothing the skirts of her party dress, knowing, Emily was sure, how pretty she was. Zannah, as usual, looked fabulous. Emily had long ago realized that it was pointless to envy her sister's effortless beauty. Tonight she was wearing a long dress in pleated kingfisher-blue silk. I look, Emily thought, like a magpie in black and white. She's like a heron.

'And the Madrigal Prize,' said the man at the lectern, interrupting Emily's thoughts, 'for 2005 has been awarded to Lydia Quentin for *The Shipwreck Café* which, in the unanimous opinion of the judges, is one of the most accomplished and elegant first collections we've read in a long time. Many congratulations!'

It took Emily a second to grasp that Lydia Quentin was her mother, and when she did, she leaped into the air, shrieking as though she were at a football match. Zannah and Isis, she could see, were also jumping up and down and Pa, who'd been standing at the foot of the stage, punched the air. Mal looked as though he'd won the prize himself, which, in a way, Emily supposed, he had. Ma was now no longer pale, but scarlet. She was being led to the lectern to say a few words, and Emily could see that she was wishing she didn't have to do that. At last, a hush fell on the crowd.

'Thank you,' Joss said, her voice quiet in spite of the amplification. Flashbulbs were going off in her face and she was trying, Emily could see, not to blink or look disconcerted. A couple of the photographers had come up on to the stage and positioned themselves near the lectern as she began to talk. 'I haven't prepared a speech because I didn't think I'd be winning today, but I would like to thank the judges. Thank you very much to them, and to my family. Thank you.'

Well, Emily thought, she's no Churchill, but on the other hand she's not Gwyneth Paltrow, for which we must all give thanks. A skeletal bloke in a suit that looked as though it had recently been excavated from one of Pa's Egyptian burial chambers tottered up to her and handed her a cheque. Joss stepped away from the mike holding the piece of paper in one hand and not knowing what to do with it. Mal came to her rescue and tucked it into the breast pocket of his jacket. Emily smiled. Ma's going to forget all about it, she thought, but I'll remind her. Then the besuited skeleton took her elbow. Together they made their way down the stairs at the side of the stage. Pa, Zannah, Isis and Adrian gathered round her and Emily pushed through to join them. By the time she reached Joss, everyone else had kissed her, and hugged her and congratulated her.

'Clever old Ma!' Emily said, throwing her arms round her mother. 'I knew you'd win.'

'No, you didn't, silly,' Joss said, hugging her younger daughter, 'but it's lovely of you to say so. Em, will you text Charlotte for me? She's driving to the restaurant with Maureen and— with the Ashtons. She'll be anxious. Tell her the good news, d'you mind? You're the fastest texter in the family.'

'No problem.' Emily fished in her handbag for her mobile, turned it on and sent a message to Charlotte. She could see her father coming towards her, purposefully. 'Faster than the speed of light, me! Hiya, Pa!'

'Hello, my darling. How are things with you? Hungry? I'm starving. I thought that organizer bloke was never going to shut up.'

Zannah took a spoonful of zabaglione and looked round the table. The talking hadn't stopped since they'd sat down. Toasts had been drunk to Ma, to the Madrigal Prize, to poetry, and everyone was very merry indeed. Isis was next to Pa, and the two were having what seemed a high old time, giggling away together. It had taken Isis a while to get used to it all, and she'd been overawed at first by her surroundings, which she pronounced 'easily the poshest restaurant I've ever been in'. She soon relaxed, however, and having established that she could indeed order what she still called *'forgetti Bolognese'* ('Don't be silly, Mummy. I know that's not its proper name'), she settled down to eat and drink and exchange jokes with Pa.

Zannah wished that things had been arranged so that she hadn't had to sit with one Ashton on either side of her. The table was round and, in theory, everyone could have chatted to everybody else, but in practice, you were stuck with your immediate neighbours and that was it, really. So, because Charlotte and Emily were in conversation with Graham, Maureen was the person she'd spoken to for most of the evening. They'd discussed flowers, and her future mother-in-law had talked at length about how wonderful Genevieve's food for the wedding would be. Now, thankfully, she'd turned her attention to Adrian, who was sitting between her and Joss and was being charming and attentive to both of them. He was at his best on occasions like this, and even more handsome than usual. He made it seem as though the conversation was exactly what he wanted to hear. For a moment, Zannah tried to imagine Cal in his place and smiled to herself. He'd have been totally out of his element. He regarded long meals in restaurants as a bit of a waste of time and wasn't good at the kind of inconsequential chat ... not exactly small-talk but not deep discussion either ... that was happening round this table. Emily was laughing at something Isis had just said, which Bob was relaying to everyone. Zannah was quite enjoying not talking to anyone for a bit and used the time to study her mother. They'd not had much chance to say anything to one another before sitting down but Ma looked ... How did she look? Not as happy as someone who had just won a prestigious prize ought to look. Feverish. Smiling, but nervously. Whatever was the matter with her?

'Excuse me,' Ma said, and pushed back her chair. 'I'll be back in a moment.'

'I'll come with you,' said Zannah, rising to her feet. She smiled at Adrian and bent to kiss the top of his head as she passed his chair. 'Won't be long.'

She followed her mother into the ladies'. As they were standing at the washbasin staring together into the mirror, Zannah said lightly, 'In *Cagney and Lacey* the two of them always used to go into the loo to have revealing conversations, didn't they? D'you remember?'

'Nothing to reveal,' Joss answered, speaking cheerfully enough but, Zannah thought, with a shifty air. She said, 'You're looking shifty, Ma. Are you quite sure nothing's the matter? You would tell me, wouldn't you, if anything was wrong? If anything was bothering you?'

'You've got enough on your plate with the wedding, darling.'

'Is that a yes, then? There is something worrying you?'

'No, no, really. Not a bit of it ... Honestly, Zannah. It's wonderful ... this prize. A great surprise. I suppose I'm wondering a bit if my life will change now because of it. I don't think it'll make much difference, but you can't help feeling a little nervous.'

She was still washing her hands. At last, she straightened up and said, 'I don't know why they put such ghastly lighting in these loos. I look like a ghost. And so do you, which is more surprising. Isn't Isis enjoying herself? Let's go back, if you're ready.'

'Are you looking forward to the hotel? Paris?'

'Oh yes ... You know I love hotels. And Paris ... yes, I'm longing for that. It's years since I was there. Always lovely to be in France.'

She sounded sincere but still, Zannah was uncertain of her mother's state of mind. It was almost as though she was under strain. But what on earth could possibly be stringing her out and stressing her at such a convivial party? A mystery.

Their table was on the far side of the restaurant and Zannah followed her mother towards it. Her gaze fell on Graham Ashton ... She'd been looking in Em's direction, wanting to catch her sister's eye, wanting to convey something of her unease about their mother and she happened to intercept . . . . What was it? What had she seen? Had she really seen it, even? She sat down, without a word to anyone, and tried to relive the last few seconds in slow motion. Graham had been gazing at her mother as they approached the table, Zannah was sure of it. She saw . . . she'd thought she saw a slightly raised eyebrow, perhaps a hint of a smile, she wasn't quite sure. What she was a hundred per cent certain of was the force of his gaze and the emotion behind it. You didn't send such a glance to a near-stranger. The love she thought she'd seen . . . but how could it be? It was impossible . . . shining out of his eyes for a few seconds was evidence of some kind of relationship, and Zannah was pretty sure that Ma hadn't even seen Graham Ashton since May.

I've had too much to drink, she thought. They hardly know one another. I'm imagining it. She addressed a remark to Graham, and he answered in his usual voice, completely normal again. He hadn't seemed in the least normal a few moments ago. He had been . . . What was the right word? Transfigured. That was it. Different. She'd forgotten to look at her mother. Had Joss seen Graham staring at her like that? Had she caught the smile, the raised eyebrow? Had anyone else noticed anything? Now Ma was talking to Pa, but there were two spots of colour on her pale cheeks that hadn't been there before she came out of the loo. How Zannah wished the evening was over! What she most wanted to do now was get home and discuss everything with Em.

Isis was nearly asleep in the back of Adrian's car. It was the latest she'd ever been up in her whole life. The street lights, traffic lights and neon signs, in lots of different colours, were streaking past the car windows very fast, looking like fireworks. Mummy was sitting next to Adrian in the front and she and Em were in the back. Isis leaned on her aunt's shoulder and said, 'I'm not really sleepy, just resting.'

'You go ahead,' said Emily, and she tucked her soft woolly scarf round Isis's neck. It smelled lovely, just like her. Adrian was talking about how well the evening had gone and the murmur of his voice and her mother's voice soothed Isis and her eyelids grew heavier and heavier. Adrian couldn't help it, she decided. He was nice really, but sometimes he just had to be bossy, even when he didn't need to be. I wasn't being naughty, she reflected. I was just laughing a bit loudly, that's all. He didn't have to say what he did. The others thought it was a good joke. He'd leaned across the table and smiled straight at her.

'Don't you know the old saying, Isis?'

She'd shaken her head instead of answering. She had no idea what he was talking about.

'Little children should be seen and not heard.'

He'd laughed then, and some of others round the table laughed too. Isis blushed and couldn't think what to say. Mum would be cross if she was rude, and Granny's evening would be spoilt if she burst into tears. In the end, it was Grandpa who came to her rescue. He said, 'Isis isn't a little child. She's wise beyond her years as befits a goddess. Aren't you, my dear?'

Everyone thought that was quite funny and then the waiter came and gave them some food and that stopped the others looking at her. She bent her head and didn't say another word till the meal was over. She just listened to the grown-ups. It wasn't very interesting and she was quite glad when they finished and got into the car to go home. Adrian was giving them a lift. Mum isn't speaking to him now, Isis noticed briefly before her eyes closed altogether. Maybe she's cross with him for being so horrid to me. Maybe she'll tell him off. The lights travelling past the window grew blurred and fuzzy and she fell asleep, still dimly aware of the movement of the car.

'Just going to have a quick bath, Bob,' Joss said. 'I'll be with you very soon.'

'Righty-ho,' Bob called. 'I'm perfectly happy, darling, soaking up all this unaccustomed luxury. Exploring the mini bar, actually. Take your time.'

Joss sank into the scented water and leaned back with her eyes closed. She felt, still, as though she were being slowly torn in two. All day long, she'd both wanted the day never to end, and longed for it to be over. Winning the Madrigal ... She'd been so worried about the dinner, seeing Gray, coming here with Bob and then going to Paris with him for two whole days, that the poetry prize and whether she might win it or not had receded to the back of her mind. When she won, a great wave of joy and elation took hold of her and she almost stopped fretting about what would happen when she was sitting with Gray in the restaurant.

The round table meant that they were all quite close to one another. She was actually opposite Gray and it took some effort not to catch his eye. Maureen was sitting on the other side of Adrian, but still, Joss heard 'Graham and I' and 'my husband' far too often for comfort. If someone burst into the bathroom now and asked her what she'd had to eat, she would have had to make an effort to remember. She'd spent most of the meal in a sort of daze. She'd drunk more and more wine, to give herself the courage simply to keep on sitting there. She made a point of watching Isis, to be sure that she was all right and enjoying the evening. Adrian was being charming to everyone, from what she could see. It was difficult not to like him, Joss reflected, and he was certainly handsome, but she didn't feel she knew him very well yet. Zannah and he hadn't visited Altrincham together. She must try to arrange something. From time to time, she lifted her eyes to see who Gray was talking to: Em, Zannah ... that was all right.

Then she'd gone to the loo, and Zannah came with her. She'd guessed that something was up, of course, but Joss was reasonably certain that she'd reassured her. Then on the way back to the table, she'd caught Gray's eye and seen ... She'd seen everything in his gaze that she hadn't even realized she'd been waiting for: love and admiration, passion and dismay. A tiny smile, a raised eyebrow: an acknowledgement that the feeling between them was there, like an invisible rope binding them together. She smiled back at him. She couldn't help it. It had been such a relief to her that he knew. That he understood how she must be feeling. That he was experiencing, as she was, anguish and desire and a love he had no way of expressing.

There had been the usual press of people around the cloakroom, as everyone was handed coats and scarves and Adrian his briefcase. They had milled around the door of the restaurant and walked together to where their cars were parked. Joss frowned as she reconstructed the choreography of their farewells. The Ashtons were taking Charlotte home again. Adrian was giving Zannah, Emily and Isis a lift. Kisses were exchanged. Maureen kissed Zannah and Emily. Then she kissed Isis. Zannah, Emily and Isis got into the car. Maureen kissed Adrian. He got into the driver's seat. Then Maureen kissed Joss and Bob and got into the passenger seat of Gray's car. Then Charlotte kissed Joss, murmured 'Bon voyage' and got into the back seat of the Ashtons' car. Then ... Bob had shaken Gray's hand and moved away. She and Gray were alone together on the passenger side of the Ashtons' car. He leaned towards her, and kissed her cheek, politely, suitably, but his hand found hers and squeezed it so hard she almost cried out and she couldn't stop herself: she brought his hand up a little and pulled it into her waist, as though she was reluctant to let him go. Their hands were still clasped together tight, so tight, and then he leaned forward suddenly and whispered in her ear. 'Text me. Please...'

She'd nodded. She couldn't speak. There wasn't time and the words were on her lips and she moved them silently. *I love you* ... Had he seen? Did he know she'd said it? She'd held on to his hand as long as she could, but the whole exchange couldn't have taken longer than a few seconds. Adrian's car was already moving as Gray was kissing her goodbye. No one in Gray's car could see them, Joss was quite sure. They'd been shielded by the bulk of the taxi that Bob had ordered to take them back to their hotel. Bob himself was settling down in the back seat, waiting for her to get in. Both Maureen and Charlotte waved gaily out of the window as they drove off. Gray's eyes had been fixed on the steering wheel. They were safe. No one knew what had passed between them.

She sighed and got out of the bath. I have to enjoy this, she told herself. I wish I was anywhere but here. I wish I was at home. I must put Gray entirely out of my mind for the next few days, or I shall go mad. Bob's waiting. My husband. Father of my children. The man I've loved for more than thirty years. He loves me. He's arranged this treat for me. She fastened the towelling robe provided by the hotel around her waist and tried to pull together all the love that was there, somewhere, she knew it. It was a love she'd relied on for years and years, a love that had nothing to do with Gray and what she felt for him. This was a different emotion altogether and Joss set herself to find it, to remember it and to show Bob that she was still a good wife. It must still be there, somewhere.

It was touch and go. Either Maureen was saving his life with her incessant chatter or she was slowly killing him. The irritation he felt every time he tuned into what she was saying was certainly raising his blood pressure, but the good thing about Maureen was that you didn't have to listen to much. As long as you put in a non-committal remark from time to time, she was exactly like one of those toys that you wound up: she would buzz around in ever-decreasing circles and only come to a full stop at bedtime.

'... not a bad place, really. Lasagne maybe not quite up to scratch, but of course they haven't got enormous amounts of money and it was rather a romantic gesture from Bob Gratrix, wasn't it? To take his wife off to a hotel for the night and then to Paris. I wish you'd do something like that, Graham.' She sighed theatrically. Gray was just about to say something that would, the way he was feeling, have come out sounding even crosser than he felt, but no, she was off again. About the clothes, this time. Here he really tuned out and almost immediately wished he hadn't because what was in his head was such torture that he'd almost have preferred to listen to Maureen.

He could imagine everything. The room, the bed ... Would they be in it already? Had he torn off her clothes the minute the door was closed? No, speaking to Bob, looking at him carefully, as he'd done tonight, the man didn't strike him as the tearing-off-clothes type. For long minutes across the table, he'd watched him. He couldn't see anything about Lydia's husband that was in the least remarkable. He seemed pleasant enough, not good-looking, but okay. It was now, because he'd heard him speak, watched him chatting to his wife, very much easier to see the two of them as they must be at the moment, or very soon would be. Unthinkable that Bob wouldn't want to make love to her on the night of such a triumph. Gray shivered. Stop thinking about it. He tried to turn his mind to other things which led him to Paris. He made a huge effort and tried instead to picture himself, there in Paris with her. A café on the Left Bank, holding hands across a marble-topped table. Walking along the streets together. His imagination wasn't up to much except fantasies of the two of them making love then making love again. Waking up together. Sleeping together. Together. The thought of it made him grind his teeth in frustration and he concentrated on changing gear.

Maureen had moved on from discussion of this evening's party to the wedding. She was talking about flowers. He glanced at her.

‘Mmm,’ he said, as a kind of encouragement. For a mad second, he thought of interrupting her. *Maureen darling, I’m in love with someone else and I want a divorce.* What a relief it would be, to have everything out in the open! He stopped himself. He’d promised Lydia that they’d wait till after the wedding. How would Maureen take the news? Would she cry? Hit him? Yell at him? And what would she feel, really feel? After she’d got over the pain that hearing such words would cause her, Gray comforted himself that she’d be okay in the end. She was a survivor. She always had an eye to the main chance. She was a good-looking woman still. It was hard to believe that she wouldn’t find someone else, if she wanted to. Gray indulged himself in a short fantasy of Maureen swanning off on a Caribbean cruise, surrounded by hordes of admiring suitors, beating off requests for a dance, a kiss, a marriage. Who was he trying to kid? He was using these daydreams to comfort himself. She’d be devastated, of course, but perhaps he would cushion the blow a little by leaving her the house, just moving out. He would also, as he had told Lydia, have to provide for her generously.

‘I’m going to make a cup of tea, darling,’ Maureen said, as they turned into their drive.

‘Right,’ said Gray. ‘I’ll put my stuff away in the study and I’ll be down in a moment.’ He raced upstairs and took out the phone he used only for his conversations with Lydia. There was a text message waiting for him.

I’m thinking only of you. Love you.

He sat down and punched in a reply:

Me too. Will wait for you.

He couldn’t say what he wanted to say, which was: I’m trying not to think about you because I can’t bear it. What are you doing now? Are you in his arms? Kissing him?

He walked downstairs to the kitchen, wishing it was tomorrow. As soon as he woke up, he’d be able to work all hours in the hospital and not think about a single thing to do with Lydia, but there was the rest of the night to get through first.

‘I’ve already told you what I saw,’ Emily said. ‘Ma kind of pulled his hand towards her and kept on holding it for longer than she needed to. I wouldn't have thought twice about it, but after what you've just said . . .'

Zannah sighed. 'I think she's having an affair with Graham Ashton. It's the only explanation. But how? And when? They hardly know one another . . .'

'You've forgotten what happened at your engagement party. Remember how she rushed out like that and made Pa drive her home? That was a bit strange.'

'But Em, they'd never met before then, had they? I don't know what I think.'

'We've gone over and over this. My head feels like scrambled eggs, Zannah. Can't we leave it?'

'But what if it's true?'

'I don't see how it can be.'

'But what if it is? Ma having an affair. What'd happen? What about Pa?'

Emily picked up a cushion and punched it. Then she put it behind her head and leaned back. 'I reckon,' she said, 'that we should talk to her. Ask her straight out.'

'And what if she says she is? What then?'

'I don't know. It's late, eh? Let's go to bed. We'll talk about this later. Ma and Pa are in Paris now . . . They'll be living it up. We're stymied till they get back . . .'

'So we might as well forget about it? Are you saying that?'

'No, not at all,' said Emily. 'But we can't do anything now.'

'I know. I know. You're right. And there'll probably be a completely innocent explanation. Let's go to bed.'

'I'm off,' said Emily. ''Night, Zannah.'

Zannah stared after her sister, who, it seemed to her, was escaping with unseemly haste from a conversation she found uncomfortable. And I'm being a control freak as usual. What if Ma is having an affair? Is it anyone's business but Ma and Pa's? Yes, it is, she told herself. It'll affect us all. Not just me and Em but Isis . . .

She stood up and turned out the light. Then she went upstairs to her bedroom and sat on the bed. Emily must be right. It was completely unlikely and all the evidence . . . Well, what evidence was there? A half-smile intercepted. But that look in his eyes . . . what about that? A raising of an eyebrow. An extra squeeze by her mother of Graham Ashton's hand. Oh, and the way she had left the engagement party. They had to remember that as well, but they'd never met at that time so it couldn't count. So it was nothing, really. They hardly knew one another, so it was impossible. They'd met once, so briefly that the meeting couldn't be called a proper meeting at all. The whole thing was one great big zero. She undressed, washed, got into bed and stared at the ceiling. Then something she'd forgotten floated into her mind. Zannah sat up in bed, feeling faintly nauseous. She pulled back the covers, got out of bed and walked along the corridor to Emily's room.

There was a line of light showing under the door. Zannah knocked and opened it at almost the same time. 'You're not asleep, are you?'

'No, but ...'

'I know, I know, it's late and we've got to get up for work, but I have to tell you this.' As she spoke, Zannah flung back the bedclothes near Emily's feet and settled herself at the bottom of the bed, facing her sister across an expanse of duvet. 'We used to do this all the time, remember? When we were kids. I'm sorry, Em, but I've got to ask you what you think.'

Emily leaned back against her piled-up pillows. 'This is about Ma again, right? Her so-called affair with Graham Ashton.'

'Yes ... But the thing is, when Adrian and I were staying at the Ashtons', I went into Graham's study and *The Shipwreck Café* was lying on the desk. I actually saw him stroking it.'

'So?' Emily sounded bored. 'It's on sale, isn't it? And Graham writes poetry. You told me that. Or Ma did.'

'The book on its own isn't the point. Don't you see? It's the combination of all sorts of things.' Zannah ticked them off on her fingers. 'The love of poetry, the kind of poems they are. Have you forgotten, well, how sexy they are? Plus there's the fact that he had Ma's book on his desk, and this is the clincher. Where was Ma while Pa was in Egypt?'

'Doing a poetry course at Fairford Hall.'

'Exactly!' Zannah sounded triumphant. 'That was where they met. Properly, I mean. I've worked it out. It's logical, isn't it? He likes writing poetry, she's teaching a course, she's going to be related to him ... What could be nicer than booking a place on her course? Opportunity, motive, method ... everything.'

'It's not a murder, Zannah. You sound like a detective.'

'Tomorrow, I'm going to find out. I'm going to phone Fairford and ask.'

'They'll never tell you who was on the course.'

'I'll pretend to be Maureen ... make it something financial. Don't worry ... I'm good at stuff like that. I bet it was there that they got closer to one another. You know what Ma's told us. They're a hotbed of lust, those courses.'

'You've not taken account of one thing, though.'

Zannah smiled. 'Go on, then, clever-clogs. What's that?'

'Ma. Her character. She wouldn't ... well, you know. She wouldn't be unfaithful to Pa. It's just not like her. She hates rocking the boat. She's quiet. She's not ... well, I don't know ... but would you honestly say she was tempestuous? Passionate? Impulsive? In spite of the evidence of the poems, which can't be all that recent, so they sort of don't fit in to your solution, do they? The Fairford course was only a couple of weeks ago.'

Zannah buried her face in the duvet and thought that she would never have chosen such a pattern. Very minimalist: white, with small black gatherings of squares dotted here and there. She said, 'Well, you're right in one way, of course. I wouldn't have said Ma was passionate, really, but then I read the poems and they're quite different. I mean, what I get when I read them is someone not a bit like Ma.'

Emily frowned. 'Well, yes, but if she wrote them before she met Graham Ashton, which she must have done, then they're just a kind of pretending, aren't they?'

'I thought so, till tonight. Anyway, we've got to ask her. In confidence. D'you think she'd stay over with us on their way home? They're back on Thursday night and I know Pa has to be up north by Friday, but maybe Ma would stay and we could ask her ...' Zannah's voice faded away.

'I don't fancy that much, do you? I mean, what are we going to say?'

'We'll just ask her straight out. Are you having an affair with Graham Ashton?'

'Brilliant! What if she doesn't tell us?' Emily said. 'She could take offence and storm out.'

'Ma's not a stormer-out.'

'You thought she was someone who'd never have an affair, too, and now you're changing your mind about that.'

Zannah said, 'What happens if she denies it? Will we believe her?'

'We have to, don't we? We can't start assuming she's a liar as well as an adulteress.'

'Don't call her that . . . .it's horrible.'

Emily leaned forward and took Zannah's hand. 'It's not horrible, Zannah. People do it all the time. Lots of them. That doesn't make them bad people. Look at Cal, for instance.'

Tears came to Zannah's eyes. 'It's because of Cal that I'm so . . . well, so upset about this. I felt . . . well, you know how I felt when all that happened. I can still make myself miserable if I think about it too much, even now.'

'And you're worried that if Ma's having an affair, it'll hurt Pa?'

Zannah was silent for a long time. Of course it was mainly Pa she was concerned about, but she realized that her own security would be shaken if anything was wrong between her parents. She said, 'I've never really thought about Ma and Pa's relationship. I suppose it would be Pa who'd be most affected if they split up but there's also us, and Isis and . . .'

'God, Zannah, you're letting your imagination run away with you! We don't even know there's anything going on yet. And as for Ma and Pa's relationship, well, quite honestly, I never think about it. They're just there, in Altrincham, leading their life like they've always lived it. That's all.'

'That's not all. Maybe they have . . . I mean, what d'you think their sex life is like, after all these years?'

'No, Zannah, I'm absolutely NOT going there! Ugh! I've never wanted to picture such a thing and I refuse to start now. And as for Ma with Graham Ashton . . . that's just as bad. I'd rather not imagine Ma having sex at all. Nor Pa, either.'

Zannah nodded. She didn't relish the notion any more than Emily, but nevertheless, she couldn't help wondering. She said, 'They're sort of settled in their relationship, aren't they? D'you reckon they ever row? I've never heard them. Pa goes off in a sulk if he's cross and then he calms down and sort of wanders in again expecting everything to be all right. And Ma . . . well, she presses her lips together and gets on with it. Have you ever heard her shout?'

'What's that got to do with anything?'

'Maybe settled and calm is boring. Maybe Graham Ashton is a more . . . I don't know. A more lively person.'

'A better lover than Pa, d'you mean?'

'I never said that,' Zannah murmured, but Emily had set her mind on a path that it seemed to be following whether she wanted it to or not. She had a sudden vision of her mother and Graham Ashton in the throes of passion . . . she closed her eyes against this image and tried hard to think about something else.

'We're not going to get any further with this, Zan,' said Emily. 'And my eyes are closing. You go on and do the detective work. Your whole theory falls down if Graham Ashton wasn't at Fairford Hall.'

'Right,' said Zannah. 'I'm going. Ta for listening.'

'No problem. 'Night.'

''Night.'

Zannah went back to bed and lay staring at the ceiling. She thought of her mother possibly having an affair and didn't know exactly what she felt. Was it a possibility? They'd find out soon enough, but she thought that if it *were* true, then the discovery would upset Em more than it would her. She'd be worried about Pa. Well, so would I, Zannah told herself, but not to the same extent. She'd often wondered in the last couple of years whether her mother was truly happy, and now she felt guilty for not having spoken properly to her for so long. These days, she reflected, I mainly talk to Em but it's been years and years since we did that: sat in the same bed discussing things. For a moment, she felt nostalgic for her childhood, when she and Em used to spend hours tucked up at either end of one of their beds. Would Isis ever have a sister to share that with? Zannah thought of Adrian and wished he was here with her. She wouldn't have dreamed of talking to him about her mother, and wondered why that was. Surely if she was going to share her life with him, she should be able to tell him everything. She was almost certain that she would have been able to confide in Cal about something like this, but in Adrian's case, not only was he close to his mother, he was not nearly as friendly with Ma as Cal had been. Zannah didn't feel she could take the risk of any of this speculation getting back to Maureen. Also, he wasn't too keen on his stepfather and she had no wish to make things difficult between them. No, she was determined to keep her thoughts to herself, but how comforting it would be to have his body next to hers, his arms round her. At last, she drifted into sleep.

Wednesday

'Dad!' said Isis, catching sight of Cal standing by the school gate. 'Mum said you'd be here to collect me. Cool! Here's the key. She said to give it you. Can we go to the movies?'

'Not on a school night, Icicle. I'm going to take you back to the flat for a bit and once Em's home from work, we'll all go for supper at Luigi's. That okay? Your mum's having dinner at Adrian's.'

'I know.' Isis took her father's hand and they set off. She knew her dad wouldn't make her put her hood up even though it was cold and her breath was like smoke coming out of her mouth. Mum sometimes made her cover her head, but Dad never took any notice of the weather. She said, 'They're going to discuss lists.'

'What sort of lists?'

'You know . . . lists in shops telling people what you want them to buy as a present.'

'That's ridiculous. Why would anyone want to do that?'

'So they can get nice things they like.'

'Oh, right, so they don't trust their friends to know what they'd like?'

'Don't be silly, Dad. It's supposed to help you get what you really want. Anyway, lists are boring. I went to try my dress on last week. Did Mum tell you? I thought it would be nearly ready but it wasn't. There was a sort of white cotton dress I had to put on instead. Mum tried hers on as well. Miss Hayward says she makes a cotton one first and if that fits, she cuts out the silk one and sews it up. Miss Hayward's like a granny in a book. Her hair's white.'

At the flat, Cal opened the door. 'Right, let's get the tea made then.'

Isis sighed. 'Adrian doesn't know where anything is. Mum always has to tell him and then he says: *I don't do tea*.'

'Yeah, well, he's not Superdad, is he? I'm good at things like tea.' He sounded cheerful and Isis wondered if he liked it when she told him about things Adrian couldn't do.

'He's not nearly as nice as you, though,' she added, pleased that he was happy.

'Very few people are,' said Cal, reaching up for the teapot and nearly dropping it. He was just pouring in the boiling water when Isis said, 'I don't want tea, though. I'll have juice. It's in the fridge and I can get it myself.'

'You should have said earlier, then I'd have used a teabag. Never mind, I'll drink two cups.'

'Have you seen Mum's pictures for the florist?'

'No, I haven't.'

'They're in that book over there by the TV. She's done loads. She met her last week. Have a look . . .'

Isis ran to pick up the sketch book which was still lying on the table where Zannah had left it the previous evening. She watched as Cal turned the pages. He wasn't saying anything. 'Don't you like the pictures, Dad?'

'No, they're wonderful . . . I just . . . I don't know. Where's she going to put all these flowers? Anyway, I thought the whole idea of hiring a florist was so that they could tell you what flowers to have. But your mum's done it the other way round and told them what she wants . . . Oh, hi there, Em! You're back nice and early.'

Emily and Cal hugged one another. They always did that. Sometimes Isis thought Em liked Dad better than Mum did. Did Dad like Em better than he liked Mum? Isis didn't think so, but she couldn't ask anyone. Emily said, 'Hello Iceypop. We're off to a restaurant for our tea . . . how posh is that? Give us a kiss. I've had a hard day at work.'

Isis ran to kiss her aunt. 'I'm showing Dad Mum's flower drawings.' Then, she turned her attention to Cal again and said, 'I'm having a round bouquet. With pink and dark red roses. And leaves the same colour as my dress. It'll be soooo fantastic.'

'Exactly. You took the words right out of my mouth,' Cal said and he and Em laughed together. Isis wasn't quite sure what was so funny.

Taking words out of people's mouths sounded horrible to her. If you could really do it, they'd come out covered in slimy spit. Double yuck! 'I'm going to change,' she said. 'I'll be back in a minute.'

Emily had been looking forward to tonight. She'd just been through an extremely tedious photo session. People who in an ideal world should have had better things to do were moving tubs of butter-substitute around a table, adding this or that prop, changing the colour of the background, adjusting the light and generally jumping at the promptings of a director who clearly thought he was making something only marginally less significant than the next Tarantino movie.

'I'm exhausted,' she said, sinking down on to the sofa, 'but it'll be great to go and have a meal at Luigi's. Nice treat for us.'

'And for me.' Cal flung himself into the armchair next to the TV. 'Isis seems very excited about all this wedding stuff.'

'Well, she's eight.'

Cal caught her eye and they both burst out laughing at the same time. At last, Emily thought. Someone who also thinks the wedding nonsense has a seriously juvenile side to it. Why weren't the men she went out with on her wavelength in the way that Cal seemed to be? There wasn't one who'd have understood what she meant without her having to explain. She said, 'Actually, there are times when Zannah isn't as thrilled about everything as you'd expect.'

'Has she said? Some particular thing?'

'Lists at the moment. Poor old Adrian. He thinks they're going to have a nice romantic evening.'

'Isis was telling me about lists. Sounds mad to me.' Cal was still looking at the flower drawings in Zannah's sketchbook. 'She's good, isn't she? I never thought I'd find flower pictures beautiful, but these are, aren't they?'

'Yup,' said Em, feeling unworthily jealous. Why shouldn't Cal praise her sister's drawings which were, indeed, exquisite? You want him to say something nice about you, she chided herself. That's what it is. You want him to think about something . . . someone . . . other than Zannah and he doesn't seem able to. She said, 'Cal, are you going out with anyone?'

Bloody hell, where had that come from? How had she found the nerve to say it? Emily knew she was blushing scarlet and would Cal wonder why? Perhaps he wouldn't notice. She added quickly, 'God, sorry, it's really none of my business. Don't answer if you don't want to.'

'I don't mind. No one at the moment.'

'But you've had ... I mean, since you and Zannah split up ... relationships with other people?'

'Well, yeah, but nothing serious ... you know. How about you? Mr Right come along yet?'

'No, but I live in hope.'

Cal beamed. 'The wedding! That's where you'll meet him. It's one of the main wedding clichés! Who's Adrian's best man? He'll be the one. Wait and see.'

'Not if I've got anything to do with it. All his pals are either bankers or stockbrokers or else people he plays squash with or was at school with. Too much money and not enough chin. Not my scene. No way.'

'You don't know. Cupid lets his arrow fly in the most extraordinary places. All the romantic novels I've ever read say so.'

'How many have you read?'

'None.'

They started giggling again. Just then, Isis came back in jeans, pink trainers and a matching pink jacket. She said, 'What's funny? Tell me.'

'It'd take too long to explain,' Cal said. 'Let's go and eat.'

'As far as I can see,' said Adrian, pulling up the duvet and settling down against the pillows, 'we have to choose between John Lewis and Harrods. Or possibly Peter Jones.'

Zannah propped herself on her elbow and began to trace circles on his chest. He bent over and started kissing her. She pulled away and said, 'Concentrate, Adrian. I really need to talk to you about this and you're distracting me. We can't get carried away. I'm hungry for one thing.'

'I know, I know ... but it's been ages, hasn't it? You can't believe how I'm longing to be married to you. Bloody sick of counting the days till I see you.'

'Me too. But Adrian, we've got to talk about lists.'

'Fire away, then. I've laid out the parameters of the discussion. Up to you now.'

'Parameters ... Well, I don't know about that. We have to go back to basics.'

'Really? What're the basics?'

'I'm pretty sure I don't want a list at all.'

It was Adrian's turn to sit up in bed. 'What? Why on earth not? Everyone has lists. How else d'you get the presents you want? I'm going to assume you've taken leave of your senses temporarily and you'll soon be back to normal.'

'No, I'm quite serious. Look, we've got all the crockery and cutlery we need. We can't ask people to buy the sort of thing they'd choose for a couple setting out to furnish their first house, can we? And besides, if you do the presents that way, it's so much less ... personal. How can you remember whether this person bought that cruet set or that person came across with a toaster?' Zannah paused for breath but Adrian didn't look as though he was about to speak so she plunged on. 'Also, even if you could remember, I don't think it's right to be able to check exactly what this or that friend forked out for you. I'd never use a list to buy a wedding present, so I think it ought to work both ways. I reckon our friends should use their imagination.'

Adrian made a sound that was almost 'Pah' but not quite. It sounded crosser than that and Zannah was quick to insert herself into the curve of his arm and snuggle close as she said, 'Don't be angry. Humour me. Everyone'll manage perfectly well and we won't have to stand around in John Lewis for hours deciding on things we want. Yes?'

'Oh, God, I suppose so. I can't win when you dig your heels in, Zannah. You know that.'

'Am I so bossy?'

'Yup. But so's my ma and I'm going to have to break the news to her.'

'She won't mind, will she?'

'Probably. But I'll blame you. How's that?'

'Okay ...'

He was kissing her again. Zannah closed her eyes and allowed herself to be carried along in a stream of desire. It was only after they'd got up and dressed and started looking for something to cook for supper that Zannah remembered about tomorrow night and the conversation she and Emily were going to have with their mother. God, it would be difficult. She sighed and Adrian said, 'Something wrong?'

'No, darling,' she answered. 'Nothing, really. I love you.'

'Me too,' he said, and slid his hands round her waist.

'Go away, please,' Zannah said. 'Or this food will never be ready.'

'I don't care. Do you?'

'Yes, I do. I'm hungry.'

'Okay, okay. I'll wait till after supper.'

Zannah smiled. 'I've got to go home after supper.'

'Not at once.'

'No, not quite at once. God, you're greedy.'

'You're greedy too. Admit it.'

Zannah grinned. 'I suppose I am.'

Thursday

'This is lovely, isn't it? It's so long since it's been just the three of us together. Years, really.'

Joss took a sip of wine and smiled across the table at her daughters, happiness rising in her, flooding her with an almost physical love for them both. Zannah had bought lots of delicious food ('All M&S, though. Can't do cooking on a school night. Not proper cooking.') and during the meal they'd laughed and she'd described the lengths to which their father had gone to avoid accompanying her to the places she'd wanted to visit.

'Mostly shops, I suppose, but also the Palais de Cluny to see the Lady and the Unicorn tapestries. They're my favourite things in the whole of Paris and he only came with a moan and a sigh, muttering about 'that unicorn novel you ladies were all so keen on'. I did point out to him that there's more to the past than Egyptian mummies, but he wasn't happy. You could tell. His attention span, for a scholar, is dreadful if he's not actually studying the thing that's in front of him. Never mind . . . .It was lovely, really. A wonderful break.'

Zannah and Em said nothing, which surprised her. Surely they couldn't tell, from that anecdote, how difficult some parts of the last couple of days had been? True, there had been good times: pleasant meals when she and Bob had started to speak to one another in a way that Joss had almost forgotten was possible: as though they were single people without jobs or children. Bob talked about Egypt. She tried to talk about her poems, but it was hard to articulate how she felt about them and it was clear that he wasn't interested, even though he made an effort to pretend to be. After about a quarter of an hour, though, Joss noticed that they always went back to discussing the girls (their name, still, for Zannah and Emily) and Isis and Bob's work. The wedding. A long debate about the music for the service took up the whole of one lunch and that was the nearest Joss came to forgetting about everything else. The rest of the time, she felt as though she were carrying a burden and couldn't identify what it was, but only knew she couldn't put it down.

Each night, Bob had made love to her, in the same way he had made love to her for over thirty years: gently, pleasantly, kindly. Joss grew to dread bedtime, but she couldn't refuse him and, in a way, she didn't want to. She was used to him. It was soothing to be held and kissed, even absent-mindedly. She closed her eyes and went through every kind of mental contortion to stop herself thinking about Gray. She did what men were always advised to do, to defer their orgasms: she made lists. Lists of flowers she would have in the bouquets, if it were left to her. Things to do when she got home. People to whom she had to send postcards. Anything to distract her mind and body from the weight that had taken up residence in her being: her love for another man. The heaviness, she knew, came from uncertainty and doubt about the wisdom of leaving Bob and everything she'd known for so long to live with Gray. When she thought of the two families being broken up, it was a visual image of ruined buildings and smashed wooden beams that came to her mind, just like the pictures that followed a bombing. It wasn't like the ships on the walls of the Shipwreck Café. Those were going down, broken into pieces, but they were alone and separate. She was going to help explode two entire families ... Was she capable of doing that?

'Ma?' Zannah had sat up in her chair and adopted a pose that Joss recognized from her daughter's earliest childhood: a sort of alertness, a neatness, the hands clasped together in front of her on the table. It was the way she always looked when she wanted to broach a difficult subject. Joss glanced at Emily. She was staring down at her plate, and to anyone other than her mother, the tension in her wouldn't have been apparent.

'Yes?'

'We ... I mean, there's something we've got to ask you and I don't want you to be cross. D'you promise?'

'That's a bit much, isn't it? I don't know what you could possibly ask me that would make me cross, but I don't know if I can promise.'

'Okay, then, but be calm. Right?'

'Now you're worrying me. What is it, Zannah?'

Zannah and Emily looked at one another and Zannah took a deep breath. Then she said, 'Ma, are you having some kind of relationship with Graham Ashton?'

Here it is, Joss thought. Okay. She took a deep breath. Her heart was thumping so loudly that she heard its beat in her ears. Blood rushed to her face and she knew it must be scarlet. Part of her was detached from what was happening, as though she were floating above herself, but she was aware of something like an explosion taking place where only she could feel it, deep within her. There was a sudden, agonizing pain in her stomach, which she recognized as fear. Was her love for Gray capable of standing up to this sudden exposure? She knew, with a certainty that surprised her, that she wasn't up to it. Couldn't cope with the girls knowing. And, it occurred to her, if they knew, others might also have found out. I can't do it. I must give him up. I'm not brave enough to leave Bob. But I can't ... I can't live without Gray. Can I deny everything? She took a deep breath. How many seconds had passed since Zannah had asked her question? Don't panic, she told herself. Must be calm. Mustn't say anything I'll regret. Play for time. Stall. Think. When she spoke she was conscious of picking her way from one word to the next, as though they were unsteady stones in a stream: wobbly footholds that might collapse beneath her and plunge her into disaster. At last, she said, 'Well, we know one another, of course. I mean, not only because of the wedding ... because of you and Adrian. He ... I mean, he writes poetry and he came on my course. The Fairford course.'

'But you know what I'm asking, Ma. I don't just mean that. I saw the way he looked at you in the restaurant. And Em saw you saying goodbye to him. It didn't look ... I mean ...'

'Yes,' said Joss. Perhaps she ought to tell them everything? But if she spoke now, what about Zannah's wedding? She was determined not to jeopardize that. And she couldn't, she didn't have the strength to face the breakdown of her family, and Gray's family, without any kind of mental preparation. Perhaps she never would. For one blind moment, she was ready to renounce Gray and never see him again just to have a bit of space in which to think. In the few seconds before she spoke again, she'd arrived at a compromise. Would it be enough for the girls? Keep them from worrying? Put them off the scent? For the first time in their lives, she was going to lie to her daughters, or at least not tell them the whole truth.

'Well, if you must know ... this is a bit embarrassing. He ... he's rather keen on me.'

'How keen? What does that mean, Ma?' Zannah asked.

'He says he's in love with me.'

'And you?' Em sounded tentative. 'What about you? Are you in love with him?'

'No, no,' Joss said. 'He's just ... well, he's an attractive man and of course it's flattering but ... no, of course I'm not.' Oh, Gray, forgive me. I can't say the words. I can't tell them how much I love you. They're Bob's daughters.

'Have you slept with him?'

The split second before she answered seemed, to Joss, to go on for hours. She said, 'No. No, of course I haven't.' (How firm was her voice? Had she sounded convincing?)

And there it was, out in the open: a second lie. Now that she'd spoken it, said it aloud, Joss wondered what its effect would be. Would it stop the questions? Would they be satisfied?

'And you won't?' Emily wanted to know. 'You wouldn't, Ma, would you?'

'No, I wouldn't.'

Lie number three. How easy it was, once you'd started. She was even going to elaborate, to embroider, just in order to make her daughters feel better. She said, 'You've got to understand, you know. Much as I love your Pa, there are huge ... huge parts of my life that he's just not interested in and when I met ... Graham Ashton, well, he knew how I felt about so many things that Bob just ... isn't ... that aren't part of my life with him. We were drawn to one another. We're ... friends. Good friends, that's all.'

'But it's not all, Ma. You've just said he's in love with you.'

Make light of it, Joss thought. Downgrade it as much as you can.

'Well, people sometimes say things they don't quite mean. And he's devoted to Maureen.'

'Really?' Zannah smiled for the first time since they'd started this conversation. 'Can't think why.'

'You're biased, darling,' Joss said, seizing gratefully on the lighter tone. 'She's a wonderful homemaker and a terrific cook and these things are important, you know. She's the mother of his son and they've been together for years.'

'Like you and Pa,' Emily added.

'Yes, like me and Pa. And, girls …'

'Yes?' Zannah spoke for both of them.

'I want to ask you a favour.'

'Go on,' said Em.

'Promise me not to say a word – not a word, to anyone – and especially not to Pa. Promise?'

'God, Ma, you sound like a teenager.' Zannah was cross and impatient, Joss could see. 'We won't say anything, but you've got to promise us something as well. Okay?'

'It depends. What d'you want me to promise?'

'That you won't see Graham Ashton again. Alone, I mean.'

No, Joss thought. Not that. If I promise that, what'll happen? What'll I tell him? I can't break my word to Zannah and Em. Tears pricked at her eyelids and Joss looked down at her lap to hide her anguish, to blink them away.

'I promise,' she said. In her head, she was frantically calculating what she'd say to Gray, because she meant to keep her promise. It wouldn't be so bad. Perhaps if she broke off entirely with him, never saw him, never spoke to him, simply severed every tie, she really could learn to love Bob properly again. Paris had been okay. She'd had fun. The lovemaking wasn't spectacular but it was comforting and good and what she'd been used to for years. Surely she could go back to where she'd been two and a half years ago. But did Zannah, did anyone, have a right to tell her what to feel? Joss knew that they didn't. She said, rather tentatively, 'You seem quite upset, both of you, but you don't have to worry, really. Nothing's going to change.'

Zannah said, 'You know how I felt about Cal, Ma. I hate anything like this; it … Well, it upsets me. I don't think adultery is something you can get over, just like that. I don't want you to be unhappy. And you would be. I know you would. How could you live with yourself if you . . . ? Well, you know what I mean.'

Joss said mildly, 'It's not true, though, is it? You can get over adultery. Look at you and Adrian. You're in love with him now, and going to marry him, and presumably you've forgiven Cal. People do get over such things, you know.'

Zannah had the grace to blush. 'Yes, I know . . . I was lucky to meet Adrian, and of course I have sort of forgiven Cal but . . . I can still get quite upset if I start thinking about that time. I was so unhappy. I really did think I'd never get over it.'

'What about you, Em? How d'you feel about all this?'

'I don't want you to hurt Pa and I can't imagine you doing it. It's not going to be too hard, is it? Not seeing Dr Ashton unless it's for a family thing? And you and Pa are happy together, aren't you? He's never said anything about . . . well, about anything like that, really.'

'Well, no, but he wouldn't, would he? Not to you,' Joss said. 'You're his daughter.'

'I'd know if he wasn't happy. And I'm certainly not going to tell him about this conversation, because I don't want to make him miserable.'

Joss said nothing. Neither of her daughters had ever been able to guess at her own state of mind. She'd made a decision early on not to include her children in any quarrels she might have had with their father, and it had worked almost too well. Now Emily thought they were idyllically happy. Not for the first time, Joss wished she were a different kind of woman. There seemed to be thousands of her sex who managed to carry on two relationships at the same time, who could be casual about extra-marital sex, who could sleep with another man without falling in love utterly, completely, painfully. What was the matter with her? She wondered whether Em believed her denial. Had she sounded convincing? As she was wondering about this, Em added, 'Pa would be devastated if you left him, you know.'

The unfairness of this remark made Joss catch her breath. What about me? she screamed, inwardly. I might live to be ninety. Is it fair to me to be denied real love, real passion, and be asked to spend the rest of my days with someone who very rarely reads a word I write and doesn't understand it when he does? Why am I the one who has to make sacrifices? God, if I had any gumption at all, I'd just tell them, 'I'm leaving and the rest of you can get stuffed.' I wish I were that kind of person. I'm not. I can't. I can't do it to Zannah now and I don't even know whether I can do it after the wedding. 'Don't worry about it, either of you. I'll make sure your father's not hurt.'

'Ma?' Zannah took her hand across the table. 'You don't think we're bullying you, do you? I don't want you to be hurt. Nor Pa. Nor Isis.'

'Isis? What's she got to do with this?' Too much, Joss thought. Much too much, to use darling Isis in this argument.

'She loves visiting you both. Your house. She loves Grandma and Grandpa as a kind of unit. You're the solid people, the unchanging people in her life.'

'Well, I'm delighted she's happy with us, but you didn't stop to think of the effect you'd have on her when you left Cal. You simply did what you needed to do.'

Zannah's eyes filled with tears. 'That's not fair, Ma. She was much, much younger. And it's not the same. You've said that this is all on his side and you haven't slept with him. You're not committed. Nothing's happened. It's easier for you to ... well, to step away.'

Nothing to say to that, Joss thought. All she wanted now was to talk to Gray. It would have to be on the phone. She made rapid calculations. She didn't have to leave at any particular time tomorrow. Would he be able to come up to London at such short notice? Probably not, but at least they could discuss things on a landline. She could phone him from Euston. Her mind was racing. 'I think I'm off to bed, girls,' she said, standing up. 'Don't worry about this, please. And remember, not a word to anyone. D'you promise? Both of you?'

Zannah and Emily both nodded. Joss walked round the table to kiss them goodnight. She went slowly up the stairs, trying to seem collected and composed but inside every bit of her was frantic to get to her mobile and text Gray about tomorrow.

Friday

'Tell me again,' Gray said. They were walking in Green Park. Lydia was wrapped up in scarf, gloves and hat, and all he could see of her was her face. When she'd texted last night, he'd just sent her a message proposing a meeting in London today. As soon as he'd learned when she and Bob were coming back from Paris, he'd arranged to take a day off from the hospital. All the time the two of them had been in France, he hadn't been able to stop himself imagining what they were doing and the one thing that had kept him going was the possibility that maybe, if he was lucky, she'd manage to ditch Bob on the way home, get him on to an earlier train or something, which would allow her to spend a couple of hours with him. They'd go to a hotel room. What they'd do there played over and over in his mind like a movie on a repeating loop: clear in every detail. Thinking about this had kept him more or less on an even keel while she was in Paris.

Then, last night, she'd texted him. He thought it was in answer to his own text but it was obvious she'd not seen that when she sent hers. She would have discovered his message as she began to write her own. *Can you meet me tomorrow? It's terribly urgent.* He'd texted back to say yes, he had the day off, and would meet her at Victoria station at half past nine.

He started to run towards her as soon as he spotted her at the barrier. For minutes, they clung together without speaking, and he felt her pressing herself against him, burying herself in his coat. He'd turned her face up to his, wanting to kiss her, wanting to breathe her in ... How long had it been since they were together? Weeks. But he stepped back when he saw tears pouring down her cheeks and said, 'Lydia? What is it? What's happened?'

'They know. Zannah and Em. About us. They know ...'

'Don't say a word. Not till we're sitting down. Let's go and find a place.'

'No, not a café. I couldn't ... I want to be outside.'

'But it's freezing ...'

'I don't care. I don't want anyone – anyone at all – to see us. Or hear what we say.'

'I'm not going to say anything. Except it's great to see you.'

They had come to Green Park because it was the nearest open space. The branches of the trees made a lacy, black pattern against a sky that was almost white. Their footsteps made a crunching noise on the path. The park was deserted.

'Tell me,' he said at last, when they'd been walking for some minutes.

'Zannah and Emily saw us in the restaurant. Zannah caught you looking at me. Emily noticed me squeezing your hand when we ... when we said goodbye. They asked me if we were having ... having a relationship.'

'What did you say?'

Lydia didn't answer. Gray prompted her. 'Tell me what you said.'

She came to a standstill in the middle of the path and turned to face him. 'I told them you loved me. And I said that of course we hadn't slept together.'

'Did you say you loved me?'

Lydia shook her head.

'You didn't tell them?'

'I couldn't.'

Because she was obviously distraught, because he felt as though his heart was breaking (and part of him, the detached part, was thinking, it really does feel like that. A pain. Sharp. Localized. There, in the centre of my chest.) he said nothing, but a mixture of fury and dread filled him. He said, 'Why not? I know we said we'd wait till after the wedding, but if they know already, then maybe it's best to bring everything out in the open now. The wedding's months away still.'

'But we can't. You must see that. Think of the embarrassment.

It's impossible, Gray. I couldn't. And besides, I promised them both ...'

'What? What did you promise them?'

'That ... that I wouldn't see you again. Except, of course, for family things ... the wedding and so forth.'

A bench. There's a bench, Gray thought, and stumbled towards it. He sat down, feeling as though some heavy blow had felled him. Lydia came to sit beside him and murmured, 'I'm sorry,' under her breath.

'Fuck being sorry. That's not good enough, Lydia. You promised me something, too. Or don't you remember? Maybe Paris with your husband was so idyllic that you want to put everything we ... everything ... behind you. D' you want out, Lydia? Is that it? Is it? Tell me now, if you do.'

Lydia burst into tears again. Gray waited till the first paroxysm was over, deliberately not putting his arms round her, keeping his distance. Rage surged within him like a liquid that he could feel burning his throat, his face, every bit of him. He wanted to smash something, hit out blindly, but stopped himself. He sighed and said, 'I'm sorry, Lydia. I don't know what you want. What you want to do. About us. About me.'

'I think ...' she said, 'that we should ... I didn't promise not to email you or write to you. I just said I wouldn't see you. That's all.'

'That's all? Are you mad? That's ... it's ridiculous. How could you promise such a thing?'

'I thought ... I mean, it's only five months till the wedding and I thought ... .' Her voice faded away to such a soft whisper that he could hardly hear her.

'What did you think?'

'I thought we could wait. That's all. I thought we'd get through it.'

For a few moments, Gray sat in silence. Then he said, 'And during those few months till the wedding, you would, naturally, not sleep with Bob?'

'I can't say that, Gray. You know I can't. You and Maureen ...'

'Maureen and I have nothing to do with this!' He was furious now, shouting at her. 'If you asked me, if you said so, I'd not even go back there tonight. I'd leave my wife, my job, everything. D'you get it? Every single thing. For you, now this minute. Just ask me to and I will. But you … you're happy with not seeing me at all. Not for months.'

'I promised the girls …'

'And they're more important than I am?'

'Yes!' Lydia was on her feet now. 'They are. They're the most important thing in the world. More than you. More than Bob. More than anything. I can't hurt them.'

'But you can hurt me? Right?'

'Not right, Gray. You know that's not right. I don't want to hurt you. I love you. You must know I do.'

Silence. He couldn't think how to answer. All the words he wanted to say stuck in his mouth and he couldn't speak. At last, he said, 'Okay. Let me get this straight. You love me, but you're not prepared to leave Bob yet. You're willing to wait till after the wedding, but while you're waiting you're not going to see me because you've promised your daughters.' His voice grew harsh and he glared at her. 'What's the matter with them anyway? They're grown women, for God's sake, not little kids. What d'you think's going to happen to them if you leave Bob? Will they fall to pieces? Bollocks.'

'Zannah was terribly hurt when she left Cal. I don't want to … unbalance her and make her unhappy before her wedding. Is that wrong of me? If it is, I'm sorry, but I've got to think about her more than anyone till May. And Em … Well, she's worried about her father. How he'll feel. She doesn't like the thought of him being hurt. You must see that, Gray.'

'Well, I don't. I've got to make do with emails and texts and the odd phone call. Is that right? Have I left anything out? Oh, yes, of course! Stupid of me. You're still going to have sex with your husband. Is that a fair representation of what's going on?'

Lydia nodded miserably. 'I suppose so … but, Gray …'

'I don't want to hear justifications. Okay? I don't want to hear them. This is what's happening. I'm going to cut this off now. Right here. Don't get in touch with me. Don't write to me, don't text me, don't email me. I won't answer. I promise you I won't. D'you understand? This is it, Lydia. It's not going to work. It'll never work while you're … while you're still … I'd rather have nothing to do with you at all than this. I can't deal with what you're suggesting.'

'You can't … Oh, Gray, please. Listen, please, listen. I don't want …'

'So break your promise to your daughters.'

'I can't do that.'

'Yes you can. Tell them you've made a promise you can't keep and you want the right to act as you feel you must when it comes to your relationship with me.'

'I couldn't do that.'

'Oh, God, we're back to that again. I've heard it. Zannah will be in pieces. It'll wreck the wedding. Em will be upset at her father being hurt. I know. Fine. You're not moving and neither am I. Frankly, I don't see what's going to change after the wedding. How come you're going to be so firm then and you can't face it now?'

'It'll be easier, that's all. Maybe I want the extra time to make up my mind. What's wrong with that?'

'Nothing, nothing. Maybe it'll be okay. Maybe you'll decide it's not worth breaking up two households that have functioned perfectly well for thirty years and more, just on a whim?'

'It's not a whim, and you know it.' Lydia was angry now. 'You're being unreasonable. Cutting off your nose to spite your face. Making sure we have nothing instead of simply less of one another. Anyone'd think you're only in it for the sex.'

This struck Gray as so monstrously unfair that he stood up, and said only, 'Right, I'm not discussing this any more. Goodbye, Lydia. Don't contact me, please.' He strode away towards Piccadilly. When had it started to drizzle? She would certainly run after him. She would come down the path shouting: *Stop, Gray, don't go. Come back* ... Nothing. Silence. She wasn't coming after him. He was alone. This was the end of something. He could feel it. He allowed himself a glance over his shoulder and saw her, sitting on the bench with her head buried in her hands, not even looking at him. Not the end of something, the end of everything. That was what it felt like. The drizzle blowing against his cheek mingled with his tears. When was the last time he'd cried? He couldn't remember. He was finding it difficult to remember anything except Lydia's voice. Her face.

Monday

Charlotte and Edie were sitting at the kitchen table. Charlotte was wrapping Christmas presents, and Edie was busy totting up the cash from that afternoon's Christmas sale at the women's refuge and putting the piles of coins into small plastic bags from the bank. There was more than a week to go before she had to leave for Altrincham but it was impossible to break the habit of a lifetime, and Charlotte had always liked to have everything prepared well in advance. Besides, there were the gifts for everyone she was leaving behind here in Clapham and their relatives. She was in the habit of giving small but luxurious presents and she enjoyed choosing them throughout the year. They went into a deep drawer and came out at the end of the second week in December. The routine had been laid down over years.

'What's Val up to?' said Edie, skilfully cutting some invisible Sellotape with silver scissors. Not for her, thought Charlotte, the undignified chewing of the tape with her teeth. Or for me. Edie had just stuck a rosette of silver ribbon to the parcel and held it up to be admired. 'Jo Malone for Joss,' she said. 'The new one she said she liked so much ... *Pomegranate Noir.*'

'Lovely!' said Charlotte. 'She'll love it. Mind you ...'

To give credit where it was due, no one was quicker than Edie when it came to picking up hints. Charlotte could see her friend's eyes open a little wider and it wasn't more than a second or two before she asked, 'Is anything wrong?'

'No, not really.'

'That means yes,' said Edie, 'doesn't it?'

Charlotte sighed. She wasn't sure whether it had been intentional on her part, but now that it had happened she was quite grateful for the opportunity to discuss Joss with Edie. She said, 'Joss isn't as happy as she ought to be. That's it.'

Edie picked up some pretty, holly-sprinkled paper and began wrapping the flat box of Caran d'Ache crayons she'd chosen for Isis. She said, 'How happy ought she to be?'

'Happier than she seems now. She's won that prize, and she's had a trip to Paris. She should be looking forward to having her whole family around her at Christmas, yet when I speak to her, she seems . . . It's as though there's a shadow behind her. In her voice. Somewhere. Oh, take no notice of me. It's probably nothing.'

'What's probably nothing?' Val came into the room bearing armfuls of holly and ivy. 'I've been in search of stuff for decorations. And I'm dying for a drink. Whisky, anyone?'

'Yes, please,' said Charlotte. 'We're talking about Joss. She doesn't seem very happy.'

Val had her back to them as she reached for the glasses on the top shelf of the dresser. 'Could be the menopause, couldn't it? It's hard for some women, I know.'

'I don't think it's that. Or let's say if it were that, she'd have told me.'

'You could,' said Edie, 'ask her what's wrong. She'd tell you, wouldn't she?'

Charlotte nodded. 'I might. If the chance presents itself.'

Val spoke soothingly as she poured drinks for all of them. 'Don't worry about it, anyway. Joss is very sensible. I'm sure it's nothing too terrible.'

Charlotte wondered whether she'd have shared the details of her anxiety with Edie if Val hadn't happened to come in when she did. Somehow she'd felt that if she told more than one person, her worries might acquire some sort of substance; some truth. As long as it was just Edie who knew what she thought, Charlotte could delude herself that maybe she was imagining things.

It was a careful reading of *The Shipwreck Café* that had first aroused her suspicions. After going through all the poems more than once, Charlotte had come to the conclusion that Joss was in love. Before the Madrigal Prize ceremony, she'd thought it might just be a terrific imaginative feat but after that dinner in the restaurant, there couldn't be any doubt about it. It seemed to her that Graham Ashton was besotted with Joss. He hadn't taken his eyes off her for more than a second. And Joss, for her part, had been flushed and agitated. As far as Charlotte knew, they'd never met, apart from once, briefly, in this house last May. And at that time, she'd had a migraine and hadn't exchanged a word with him. Could they have struck up a friendship somewhere else? It was a mystery, and she meant to get to the bottom of it. She'd nearly asked on the phone, but something in her niece's voice held her back. They'd been discussing who was going to be in Altrincham this year. Adrian, Zannah and Isis ... It was then, at that point, that Charlotte had mentioned the Ashtons, and Joss had waited a long time before answering. At last she said, 'They're going to South Africa to see Jonathan, Adrian's brother.'

Perhaps there was something on the line, but Charlotte heard a hint of anguish in that disembodied voice. She'd said, 'Joss, darling, are you okay?'

She waited for the 'fine' but it didn't come. Instead, Joss had answered enigmatically, 'I'll be all right.'

'What d'you mean?'

'Nothing. Really. It's just ... Never mind. I'll be fine.'

Charlotte hadn't pressed her but now, thinking back, she made up her mind. There would be a chance to speak alone with Joss over the Christmas weekend, and she wasn't going to be fobbed off. Joss was like a daughter to her and she knew she wasn't simply being nosy. She pulled her thoughts away from this problem and tuned in again to what Edie and Val were discussing.

'Something old, something new, et cetera,' said Val. 'Is Zannah going to be doing that? I've got such a pretty blue handkerchief. I must show her next time she's here. It's lace-trimmed. From Bruges.'

'And I,' said Edie, 'have got something old that I think she might like. A very beautiful handbag that once belonged to my mother. Small, a lovely shape embroidered with a pattern of butterflies with tiny pearls dotted all over it. I've only ever used it a couple of times, not being the butterflies-and-pearls type, but I think it would make a wonderful present. Mother must have bought it in the twenties, and I'm sure it would be perfect with the kind of dress Zannah's thinking of.'

'That's enormously kind of you, Edie,' said Charlotte. 'Zannah'll be thrilled. But what about your daughter-in-law?'

Edie smiled. 'I love her dearly, but she's even less butterflies-and-pearls than I am, if you can imagine such a thing. She'd think it was dreadfully old-fashioned. Zannah would appreciate it properly and therefore ought to have it. I'll show it to her next time she's here.'

'That's lovely,' said Val, and turned to Charlotte. 'Don't you worry, though. Everything will work out.'

Outside, dusk had fallen. The winter solstice was nearly upon them: the longest night of the year. On the table, the whisky glasses stood among the scraps of wrapping paper and curling ribbons of scarlet and silver and gold. Val, in spite of her experience of neglect during her childhood and violence in her marriage, in spite of years in prison, always thought things would work out for the best. Charlotte tried to relax and be more optimistic. She would make a point of talking to Joss as soon as she could.

Friday

Tomorrow was Christmas Eve. Charlotte and Emily had arrived in Zannah's car just after lunch and Adrian was driving up with Zannah and Isis. They'd be here very soon. Charlotte was at the kitchen table, helping Joss to make garlands of holly, ivy and assorted foliage, bound up with scarlet satin ribbons. The scones Joss had made that morning were set out ready for tea. Bob was up in the attic, getting the enormous decorations box, full of ancient treasures, ready for him and Isis to search about in after she had arrived. Emily had gone to the local shops to buy the last-minute bits and bobs that year after year she somehow managed not to get round to in London.

'Sometimes,' Joss said, 'I wish I'd learned about flowers. Done a course or something. I love this. I'd happily spend every day putting garlands together. I like chatting to Zannah about her wedding flowers, but there's a lot to be said for winter stuff, isn't there? I love holly. Always looks dangerous ...'

'Can we talk, Joss darling? This seems like a good time ...'

Joss pretended to be absorbed in a particularly difficult tying of one end of a ribbon to another. What was this about? Charlotte was so serious. In the last few days, Joss had been struggling with her feelings and had just about got them under control. She'd come back from London three weeks ago in a daze of sorrow, almost as though she were in mourning. Which, she reflected now, I was. I am. My love for Gray is supposed to be dead and I'm meant to have buried it. It's not ... it will never be ... a part of my life any longer.

During the day, she'd taken to running herself into the ground with Christmas preparations. She'd cooked and frozen what felt like a thousand mince pies, she'd iced the Christmas cake, she'd gone on endless shopping expeditions as far from home as she could to use up the hours, fill them with stuff. The idea was to stop herself thinking. She wished she could write, but that seemed to be impossible and there were times when she wondered how she'd ever written anything. She was making an attempt to wipe her mind of everything except the item in front of her at any given time. She was doing quite well as far as the days went, but the nights were awful and she dreaded them. Often, she'd find something extra to do in the kitchen so that she could put off the moment when she was lying in the dark, with Bob asleep and oblivious next to her. In bed, she was completely alone with her misery, which was so real that she imagined it had a physical shape. It was a black fur coat, lying like some almost living thing on top of her, stifling her, weighing her down, burying her. She lay there, unable to move, and the tears kept coming into her eyes. There was now a hankie permanently under her pillow which she used to wipe them away.

Sleep arrived after what seemed like hours and when it did, it was even worse than being awake, staring into the darkness. She sometimes dreamed of Gray. When she woke, the dream evaporated and she couldn't recall more than fragments of it, which surfaced from time to time as she was working and working at the physical things that wore out her body and were supposed to stop her dwelling on the past too much, but were pretty useless at doing that. She was starting to forget what he looked like. What he sounded like. Why had they never exchanged photographs? They could have sent one another photos by email, like the ones she'd sent him of her house and study, but somehow they'd never done so and now it was too late. How easy it was to leave things to another day when you thought you had all the time in the world. Now, she would have given anything, any money, just to gaze at a picture of his face. She'd tried to escape into words on the screen and found that none came to mind. She was incapable of expressing how she felt. When she opened her laptop, she stared at the image of Isis as a baby that was still her screensaver and fell into a kind of stupor. One night, she had written to Gray. A long letter, spelling out everything in tedious detail. Vowing endless love. Justifying her behaviour. Trying to explain. When she read it over, it seemed to her so feeble and stupid that she deleted it at once.

'Joss, darling,' Charlotte spoke again. 'I want to tell you something. Look at me.' Charlotte was smiling. She leaned across the table and took Joss's hand. 'I've looked after you since you were a child. You're like my own daughter. You know that, don't you?'

'Of course I do. You've been my mother for years and years.'

'Then I want you to know that you can trust me. Completely.'

'What d'you mean? Of course I trust you ...'

'I mean ... whatever you say to me when I ask you what I'm going to ask you will stay private between the two of us. I'd never tell anyone ... anyone at all ... what we say to one another.'

'I ... I don't know what you mean, Charlotte.'

'I think you do. Graham Ashton. I want to know about you and Graham Ashton.'

Joss sucked her finger. She'd pricked it on a holly leaf as his name was mentioned and she was grateful for the sharp pain. What could she say? She stared at Charlotte.

'What about him?'

'I've read your poems carefully, Joss. They're written by someone who's in love. I think ... forgive me if I'm wrong about this, but I've been worried about you ... I think you're in love with Graham Ashton. I'm almost certain he's in love with you.'

Joss put aside the garland and said, 'I don't know what to do, Charlotte. I'm in agony.'

'Tell me about it.'

'I don't know if I can ... I haven't – I mean, no one knows. The girls suspected something. They asked me about it and I fobbed them off. But it's true, Charlotte and I don't know what to do. It's ... I've never ...'

'I'm going to make some tea,' said Charlotte, getting to her feet. 'Start at the very beginning. Don't cover up, don't lie. Don't make light of things that are serious. Tell me everything.'

It was astonishing to Joss that it took such a short time to explain and unravel the enormous mass of feelings, doubts, lies, everything that she carried inside her. The complications of the relationship, of all the relationships, and especially the love: what it felt like to be swept away by the force of the passion were all laid out in a few minutes. She spoke and as the words left her lips she was filled with such relief that by the time she'd come to the end of her account she was weeping. Charlotte took a clean handkerchief from the pocket of her cardigan and handed it to her. 'There. Good girl.'

Charlotte makes me feel like a child again, Joss reflected. As though I've handed over my troubles to a grown-up. She said. 'No one else knows about this, Charlotte. Not the whole truth. The girls don't know that we're lovers. And no one knows he's left me now. He's never going to come back, Charlotte. What am I going to do?'

Charlotte sat for a long moment saying nothing. Then, 'We don't know what'll happen in the next few months, Joss. Things change. What I care about is that you, Bob and the girls should get through this in a way that hurts everyone least.'

'So I'm never to see Gray again? I just accept ... this ... my life as it's been so far. Is that what you're saying?'

'Breaking up a marriage that's lasted more than thirty years isn't going to be easy, Joss. You've got to recognize that. I'm not saying it mustn't in any circumstances be broken up, and if you and Graham Ashton genuinely love one another ... well, I wouldn't stand in your way. I'd help however I could, but the truth is: you're my main concern. You're my child. I have to acknowledge what's best for you, for your happiness, even though it might strike everyone else as ... well, as though you're discarding poor Bob in favour of someone else. People can't understand these things from the outside. It's hard for them.'

'It's academic at the moment. Gray's on his way to South Africa. I think Adrian was going to take them to the airport before he drove everyone up here. Gray's the one who's broken it off. He won't accept that I can't break my word to Zannah.'

'But you might change your mind ...'

'You don't think I should, Charlotte, do you? I promised the girls I wouldn't.'

'Well ... a promise is a promise. You've made promises to Bob too ... Those are less difficult, aren't they? But time will pass. The wedding ... after that's over, things'll be different. With Zannah happy and settled, you won't feel as though you're unbalancing her, or reminding her too much of how she felt when she left Cal.'

'But what about Em?'

'She's so much Bob's daughter, isn't she? She's sure to be upset on his behalf. You have to expect it, Joss. You have to accept that you can't do this without hurting them. Don't think you can.'

'But I don't want to hurt them . . . Oh, God, Charlotte, why's everything so hard?'

'You've got to be tough. One thing I learned in prison was this: unless it's going to destroy something you love and need, you've got to do whatever you have to, for yourself. Such a cliché, I know, but a lifetime is so short. So short. Some people would choose everyone else's good opinion of them over their own happiness. Don't be like that, Joss.'

Joss picked up the teacup from the saucer in front of her. 'This is cold now. I'll make some more. And I think we could treat ourselves to a scone.'

For the first time in many days, she told herself, as she filled the kettle, I feel a little like myself. Like how I used to feel.

The plane was making a comfortable droning sound as it flew south. They'd been in the air for about six hours and now Gray was sleeping. Or he's pretending to be asleep so as not to have to talk to me, Maureen reflected. Well, sod him. He'd been behaving most oddly for a few weeks now and she'd said nothing. That, she'd found, was the way to deal with his moods. Very occasionally, he did go into a silent phase and walk around like a zombie. After a bit, the mood (or whatever it was) always lifted and he was fine again. South Africa would do that, Maureen was sure. It would cheer him up. Perhaps he'd been working too hard. Jon couldn't put two of them up in his little flat and it was with some glee that she'd chosen the fabulous-looking hotel they were going to stay in. She'd found it on the Internet, and over the last few days she'd visited the site more and more often, staring at the turquoise water in the pool and drifting into daydreams of the two of them, stretched out on white sunloungers. She'd quite got over her regret at not doing Christmas in Guildford. This was going to be perfect from beginning to end.

She thought of her best Christmas present, which she'd packed carefully in her luggage. Darling Adrian! How clever of him to think of such a thing! Matching camera phones. She'd give him one; he'd give her one. 'This way, we can take pix of our respective Christmas dinners and send them to one another. It'll be great. And you can email all your friends with photos of that swimming-pool and make them really, really jealous.' Maureen smiled to herself. Her son knew her so well. But what a good idea it had been! She'd had special permission to open her present in advance, so that Adrian could teach her how to operate it. I can't wait to take some pictures, she thought. I should have packed the phone in my hand luggage.

Never mind, she thought. She reached into her bag and felt a pang of guilt at the extravagance that had made her splash out on a Mulberry. She'd hovered over the new *Bethany*, but decided in the end that *Bayswater*, in a delicious shade of pistachio green, was a better shape for her needs. It was years and years since she'd had such a holiday and some sort of celebration was called for. She stroked the leather – what a thing of beauty this handbag was! – and took out a printout of the wedding menus that Genevieve had sent her. She'd managed to pin down Zannah and Adrian to choosing desserts, and they'd been sensible and agreed with her, so there was no problem there. It would all, she knew, be amazing. She'd decided right from the beginning that you had to stay away from pork, because so many religions forbade it. Chicken was too much of a cliché and brought to mind things like 'the rubber-chicken circuit' even though that was political dinners, so duck was a good substitute. Salmon would be popular and you had to consider how many people were veggies, these days. Perhaps they ought to have another main course for them.

Maureen looked out of the window at the lumpy white clouds below the plane. Adrian would be in Altrincham by now with Zannah and the others. She tried to imagine what Christmas there would be like. Well, perhaps she'd see when Adrian sent her his photographs on the phone. It seemed to Maureen that the modern world was packed with things that worked by what she regarded as a kind of magic. I wonder, she thought, whether he'll have the sense to take a picture of their Christmas table. She was curious to see what it was like. She turned to Gray but his eyes were firmly closed. A little strange, at this hour of the morning . . . He was probably sleep-deprived. There had been an article about that in the *Daily Telegraph* only last week.

Sunday

Since their conversation with Joss a couple of weeks before, Emily and Zannah had discussed what might or might not have been going on in their mother's life a few times and then, as though by common consent that there was no longer anything useful either of them could say, they'd stopped. Zannah had so much on her mind with the wedding arrangements that she seemed to have stopped worrying about their mother altogether. And now, buying presents, wrapping them, talking about who was going to be in Altrincham and when they were arriving and how long they'd be staying had pushed most other subjects out of the way. Even the wedding had taken a back seat, and Emily was grateful for small mercies. She'd begun to make some preliminary arrangements for the hen night, but nothing that took too much of her time.

Now they were in the thick of Christmas and although she'd been a little nervous about confronting her mother again, she had to admit that Ma seemed absolutely normal. No *angst* discernible anywhere, and Emily had had her eyes peeled at all times and her antennae out for signs of a broken heart. Everyone seemed to be behaving well. There could have been rows about many things. Magazines often spoke of the festive season being a minefield for all concerned, but the Gratrixes seemed to be having a great time.

Even the decoration of the Christmas tree the night before had gone without a hitch. Pa and Isis had undertaken to do it with no help from anyone else and they'd made a good job of it, although Emily could see that it took an almost physical effort on Zannah's part to keep from interfering. True, she'd probably have made it somewhat more artistic.

Isis was obviously mad keen on hanging glass baubles in lurid colours and masses of tinsel on every available branch and Pa had generously decided to give her a free hand. There was a star at the top of the tree, and a fairy doll as well. Why not? Emily couldn't think of a better time than Christmas to over-egg every available pudding. That was part of the fun.

Now they were in the living room and the opening of presents was going quite well. The Gratrix family tradition, begun when she and Zannah were very small, was to gather straight after breakfast with a pile of everyone's gifts on the carpet at their feet. Then they took turns, youngest first, then round the room in order of age, to pick a parcel out of the heap, with everyone chiming in to admire what others had received. The process took ages, but no one minded. Mince pies were eaten, sherry was drunk and if anyone happened to receive a box of chocolates, the custom was to open it at once and pass it round. Every so often Ma left the room and went into the kitchen to put this or that bit of the dinner into the oven. Over many years, Joss had perfected her routine. Every component – turkey, stuffing, potatoes, sprouts, pudding – had been prepared the night before and needed only to be cooked. Various attempts to change the menu, do something different, be creative, had been resolutely vetoed by Emily and Zannah. Change was all very well for other things but Christmas dinners had to stay the same, always and for ever.

They'd nearly finished doing the Pile, as it was called. Drifts of gift-wrap lay all over the floor. Presents were carefully arranged by each person's chair. They'd exclaimed over everything and – this happened every year – the gifts were pronounced the best ever. Adrian had just opened a present from Maureen. He held it up for everyone to see. 'Well, I knew I was getting this but have a look everyone . . . I've promised to use it to send some shots of our Christmas to my mother in South Africa.'

A camera phone shone silver in his hand. Could it be that Adrian hadn't owned one until now? No, apparently he had, but this one was clearly the latest model.

'Take a picture of me, Adrian. I want to see it. Please, please.' Isis was excited and pushed herself closer .

'Hang on a mo, Isis,' said Adrian, sounding cross and clutching his present to his chest in what seemed to Emily a rather childish reflex. 'I'll take your picture in a minute. Sit down for a sec. I want to get a shot of the whole scene.'

He sprang up and went to stand at the window. Everyone froze, transfixed by the sight of a camera. 'Right ... Don't move. There you go!'

He walked around after taking the picture, showing everyone the result of his labours. To give him his due, Emily thought, it wasn't bad. He'd got everyone in except Ma. Zannah, Isis, Pa and Charlotte were smiling. She herself didn't look as dreadful as she sometimes did in photos. The tree was as sparkly and garish as it was in real life.

'You're not in the shot, Joss,' Adrian said.

'I don't mind, really,' said Ma, turning her face away from the camera, which Adrian was now pointing in her face. 'I hate being photographed. And especially not now ... I look ... I'm not ready, honestly.'

'Nonsense,' said Adrian and clicked. 'There you go! Lovely shot.'

Ma was flustered. Adrian showed the picture to Pa, who announced that it was terrific and that Ma looked 'a treat'.

'Now me, Adrian. Please. You promised.' Isis was jumping up and down.

'Okay, okay! Anything to stop you nagging!'

Adrian didn't sound as light-hearted as he should have done and Emily glanced across at Zannah to see whether she had spotted this exchange. Of course she had. Her sister would notice the smallest detail right across a room. She was frowning. Emily didn't fancy Adrian's chances of getting through the day without a row.

'There you go, Isis. How d'you like that?'

He sounded more friendly. Isis said, 'Can you print it out for me? Later, on the computer.'

'No problem,' said Adrian. 'Now, watch out, everyone. I'm going to see if it works. I'm going to send these shots to my mother in South Africa.'

He did a bit of fiddling with buttons on the silver face, then said proudly: 'There they go. And, what's more, I'm expecting some back from her any minute. We gave one another matching presents.' He smiled at Zannah.

Ma stood up and said, 'I've got to check the turkey.'

She left the room rather quickly. Emily thought she'd caught panic on her mother's face and followed her. No one else was bothered. They were all too busy with their presents.

'Ma? Are you okay? Is anything wrong?'

'No, not really. I'm a bit annoyed, though, to have my photo beamed to South Africa so that Maureen can gloat about how awful I look in comparison to her. You wait, she'll be dressed up to the nines in the one she sends back.'

'You look fine to me, Ma.'

'I suppose so,' she said, sounding unconvinced. 'It's just that I'm not even properly dressed yet. I don't really relish being photographed in this state.'

'Don't worry about it, honestly. No one takes that kind of photo seriously. They just delete them and move on to the next thing. And maybe Maureen'll have pulled a horrible face. She's just the sort of person who mugs in front of the camera.'

Ma bent to open the oven door. She basted the turkey with its own juices and replaced it before she answered. 'I'm sure you're right, Em. Silly, really, to be so vain at my age. I'm going to put on some makeup now. Can't believe Adrian won't be taking photos as we're tucking in to Christmas dinner.'

'That's the spirit,' Emily said. It was only after her mother had gone upstairs that she realized what was behind her mother's unwonted vanity. It was about Graham Ashton, she was quite sure. He'd be seeing those photos too. Even though Ma had promised she was never going to see him alone again, it must still be flattering at her age to have a man declaring his love, and she'd be less than human if she didn't want to look her best.

'Have a look at this, Graham!'

Maureen's voice sounded too loud in his ear but it was Christmas Day so he smiled and said, 'Adrian's sent you a pic already, has he?'

'It's the Gratrixes' lounge. It's rather a mess but it's hard to judge properly. They've obviously been opening presents. Still, that tree's a bit of a disaster. I'm surprised. Zannah should have been allowed to do it herself. That's probably Joss trying hard and not getting it right. I'm not at all sure her talents lie in an artistic direction.'

Gray stared at the small screen. There they were, smiling, happy, and Lydia wasn't in the picture. Perhaps she'd stepped out of the way. It was perfectly possible that she wouldn't want to have her photo beamed across the world to him.

'Here's a picture of Joss herself . . . and this one's the dining room before they sit down to eat. Good old Adrian! I did ask him specially to take one of the table. It looks all right, doesn't it? Old-fashioned, of course, but very nice and traditional. I like the centrepiece. There was something not unlike it in Martha Stewart's Christmas book. Joss is pale, isn't she?'

Maureen had passed him the phone and he gazed at Lydia's picture. She *was* pale. There was a hunted, anxious look about her, and no wonder, with Adrian pointing the camera at her when it must have been the last thing she was expecting. Still, it was a photograph of her and the only other image he had was the jacket photo from *The Shipwreck Café*. They'd been mad not to send one another photographs over the Internet. He wondered how he would be able to transfer this, his first sight of her for a long time, to his own email. He said, 'Nice pictures, aren't they? Send them to my email and I'll get them printed out for you if you like when we get home.'

'Will you? How lovely! Thanks, darling.'

She fiddled with her phone for a while and Gray leaned back against the cushions of the sunlounger beside the pool. He was having a much better time than he'd expected. Mostly this had to do with seeing Jon again. He'd forgotten how well they got on; how restful it was to be with a son who loved him sincerely and wasn't constantly judging him. Ever since he and Maureen had married, Gray had been aware of Adrian contrasting him with an ideal, never-seen father and finding him wanting. This evening, they'd be having Christmas dinner here in the hotel with Jon and his girlfriend, Lynne, and Gray knew Maureen would take pictures of the occasion to send to Adrian's phone. It couldn't be helped and a part of him wanted Lydia to see him. Let her think he was having the finest time in the world and getting over her nicely. He smiled to himself at how often the camera lied. It was true that here, at this distance, it was easier to forget about Lydia for hours at a stretch, but then something would remind him of how much he loved her. Whenever they lay beside the hotel pool, Gray closed his eyes against the dazzle of the sun on the turquoise waters and imagined that she was next to him.

Maureen wasn't waiting for Christmas dinner. She was taking a photo of him now, as he lay there. He opened his eyes and smiled straight at the camera. He said, 'I hope you've got the pool in. The umbrellas, the table and so forth.'

'Absolutely. You look fine. Now it's your turn. Take a couple of me and we'll send them straight away. I don't want Adrian to have to wait till tonight to see how lovely it is here. What a good time we're having.'

Dutifully Gray took a couple of shots of Maureen, who was looking particularly sleek and happy. When he'd finished, she called over his shoulder to someone walking behind them. 'Hello? Excuse me, I wonder if you'd mind? I'd love a photo of me and my husband to send to my son. Would you mind taking it?'

The hapless hotel guest who'd been landed with the task did it with rather too much enthusiasm for Gray's liking. 'Ach, that's lovely ... Cuddle up now! Put an arm round her, man! That's right. Terrific. I think I'll take another. Turn to look at her ... Yah, that's great. Fabulous. Have a look!'

He held out the phone so that Maureen could check the shots. 'They're marvellous!' she said. 'Thanks so much. It's very kind of you.'

'My pleasure.' The man wandered off and Gray closed his eyes again.

'I've just sent them to Adrian,' Maureen announced.

'Fine,' he answered. Would Adrian show the photos to everyone? He and Maureen had appeared radiantly happy and together. Would that cause Lydia pain? Part of him hoped it would but mostly he flinched at the thought of how she might feel. He wished he could phone her this minute and say: *It's not true. None of it. It's just a show. I wish I could be with you.*

'Best Christmas dinner ever, darling,' said Bob.

'You say that every year.' Joss took a sip of wine.

'It's true every year,' said Charlotte.

'I don't want any of my sprouts,' said Isis. 'Can I leave them? Can I get down?'

'Not yet, sweetheart. There's pudding still to come,' Zannah said.

'I don't like pudding. Can I get down?'

'Go on, then, if you must. It's better than having you grumbling away down there at your end.' She wasn't exactly irritated, but Joss could tell that Isis was getting excited and that would only lead to Zannah being cross with her later.

'Who wants more roast potatoes?' said Bob. 'I know I do.'

Emily stood up. 'I want to drink to Ma,' she said, 'and say thanks. Not just for a lovely Christmas dinner but also for a really amazing Christmas present, which you might not all know about.'

'Em, please,' said Joss. 'That's between me and you girls.'

'No, I think everyone should know. Ma is sharing some of her Madrigal money with me and Zannah, which is more than nice of her. Thanks, Ma.'

'It's a pleasure,' Joss said.

'I tried to talk her out of it,' said Bob. 'I said she ought to keep the whole lot, but she wouldn't hear of it.'

'Can we change the subject, please?' Joss said. She'd decided to give her daughters five hundred pounds each almost as soon as she'd received the cheque. Zannah, she knew, from the relief and delight on her face as she'd opened the envelope, would probably use it for something specific, her wedding dress perhaps. She'd told Joss that it wouldn't cost more than a thousand pounds. She'd explained about her savings and her special fund, but since she was a teenager, Zannah had been so clever about fudging, concealing and downright lying about the cost of things that Joss didn't believe her. With the bridesmaids' dresses, fifteen hundred could be considered a bargain. What Emily would spend her share on, she didn't know.

'Look, everyone!' Adrian said, as Joss was cutting the Christmas pudding. 'My mother's sent some photos from South Africa.'

'Fantastic,' said Zannah.

'Let's have a look,' said Bob. The silver rectangle was passed round the table and finally reached him. 'God, what amazing definition. Must see about getting one of these, Jossie. I could send home photos of the desert when I'm away. Here, have a look, darling.'

He held out the phone so that she could see it and helpfully scrolled through the pictures for her. A couple of Maureen in a swimsuit, irritatingly glamorous. Good figure. Good skin. She seemed to be shining. Suntan oil, Joss thought, but she took in the gold chains round the neck, the manicured hands and the smile, lipstick carefully on, even though Maureen was by a pool, for Heaven's sake. She was meant to be swimming, not at a cocktail party. There was a shot of Gray, looking slightly away, almost in profile. Then one of him staring straight at the camera. Joss's heart thudded in her chest and seemed to be growing, expanding to take up all the air so that every breath she took was difficult. She closed her eyes. Gray. At that precise second, she would have given anything, anything, to transfer those two images to her laptop. To make them hers. She wanted to skip the jolly games they'd be playing after lunch, run to her study, stare at the screen and kiss his picture, like a soppy sixteen-year-old. She had to clench her hands under the tablecloth and smile inanely to deflect the sharp glance she could feel Charlotte giving her across the table. I'm not cured, she thought. I'm as bad as I ever was. I want him. I want to be with him. At that point, she was almost ready to stand up and announce to the lot of them that she was leaving, going to be with Gray however it might affect other people's happiness

Then Bob clicked through to the next shot, and everything changed. There was Gray again with his arm round Maureen and they looked . . . they looked happy. They looked like lovers. They looked together. Joss felt nauseous. She couldn't bear to think of them like that. They couldn't – Gray couldn't – put on such a show of marital bliss unless it was at least partly true. Maybe he still thought of her sometimes. Maybe in the dark hours of the night he regretted the way he'd walked out on her, but here was the proof that he was perfectly composed. He was unmarked by the experience. He didn't seem to be suffering in the very least. He appeared carefree.

South Africa was only a couple of hours ahead of Britain. What were they doing now? Would they make love tonight, all cosy and comfortable and happy after Christmas dinner with the wine flowing? I must stop, she told herself. I must stop thinking about it. She wished she could do what Isis had done and ask to get down from the table. As it was, she had to go on sitting there, eating Christmas pudding which might have been baked cotton wool for all the pleasure it was giving her.

*

Technically, Boxing Day was already here. It was three o'clock in the morning and Joss was wide awake. The whole house was full of people: Bob in their bed, Zannah and Adrian in Zannah's old bedroom, Em in hers, Charlotte in the real spare room and Isis on the divan in Joss's study. She'd gone downstairs at about two, after lying staring at the ceiling for hours, using all the relaxation techniques she could remember, and trying to block out the sound of Bob's rather snuffly light snores. Nothing helped. Her head was full of rags. That was what it felt like: someone in there stirring up everything and leaving it in chaos.

She went downstairs to sit in the dark living room. The fairy lights on the tree had been turned off and Joss wondered whether she should turn them on, but decided against it. The light from the street was quite bright enough to see by and if she turned anything else on, her wakefulness would be official. As it was, she hoped she might just float into sleep by stealth, curled up on her favourite chair.

Christmas was over. Joss had always felt it ended at midnight on the actual day. Boxing Day was like an even more Sundayish Sunday as far as she was concerned, not part of the holiday at all. While the girls were living at home, they'd insisted that decorations stayed up till Twelfth Night, but to Joss they looked used and over almost by the time the turkey was eaten. If she'd had her way, everything Christmassy would be cleared away by lunchtime tomorrow. Today, she corrected herself. It's today already.

So far, also, there had been no quarrels, though Joss was rather dreading Cal coming to fetch Isis. Would he and Adrian have to speak to one another at any length? There had been a few moments when she could see that Isis was being irritating. Zannah had got annoyed with her once or twice and Adrian, though he tried not to show it, had been a little fed up with her exuberance. What would it be like after he and Zannah were married? Sometimes it seemed that her daughter would have two competing children to deal with. Step-parenting was difficult, whoever you were, and Adrian didn't appear cut out to be indulgent to another man's child. But perhaps, she thought, I'm being unnecessarily alarmist. Cal was very easy-going. It'd most likely be fine and she made up her mind to be there when the two men met, to take the edge off any tension that might arise.

Every other year since the divorce, Cal had come up to Altrincham on the day after Boxing Day to pick up Isis and drive her to Hampshire to visit his mother. When he didn't come to them, Zannah drove down to the Ford house. They took it in turns to make the long journey. They always exchanged gifts. Bob and Joss – but really only me, Joss told herself: the Fords had long ago passed out of Bob's sphere of interest – sent down a present for his mother. This year, Joss had baked two batches of lemon biscuits and wrapped them in tissue, then put them into a beautiful hand-painted cardboard box she'd found in the craft shop at the Exchange Theatre in Manchester. Cal would arrive bearing clotted cream, flowers and home-made jam. The contact pleased Joss. One of these days, she thought, I could go down there and visit her. In the spring, perhaps. She tried to conjure up the pretty garden in Hampshire; the rowan tree by the front gate. Surely there must be a way of superimposing good, pleasant thoughts over the images that had invaded her head and prevented her sleeping. I must go back to bed, she thought. There's still time. If I go on like this, my eyes'll be red when everyone wakes up. Will I be able to get through the day if I haven't slept at all?

She knew she had to pull herself together, but she sat on in the armchair, conscious that every single part of her was hurting. She hid her face in her knees, willing herself not to cry. Gray had forgotten about her, and she would learn to forget about him. It might take a long time, but she was determined to do it.

Tuesday

The whole picking up and taking Isis to Hampshire thing, Emily thought, should have been arranged differently. Ever since Zannah and Cal had divorced, they'd taken it in turns to do what the family called the Transfer. There didn't seem to be any other way of achieving this while Isis was still young. Everyone had got into the routine. Transfer Day was the day after Boxing Day and Isis stayed with Cal and his mother till just after New Year. This year Cal was driving up north and there was no way he could just turn round and go back without so much as a cup of tea.

In the weeks before Christmas, Emily and Zannah had discussed it for hours. Various desperate and silly suggestions had been made, like taking Isis to a motorway service station and doing the swap there, but in the end sense had prevailed. Cal would come to the Gratrixes' house like a civilized person. Adrian would be there. He'd meet Cal. Cal would meet him. They'd have to speak. What would happen?

'Nothing'll happen. They're not kids,' said Zannah. 'Each of them's going to have to come to terms with the fact that the other exists.'

'That's in theory,' said Emily. 'In practice, they'll hate one another. They're bound to. And it might just be … I don't know … a bit awkward. Can't you do the driving this year?'

'No, I can't. I've promised Adrian we'd go back to London first thing tomorrow. Some bigwig from the US branch of his bank is here for a day or so and he's keen for us all to have dinner together. Can't get out of it.'

'Okay, but then you've got to be prepared for a few "More tea, Vicar," moments. I know they're not going to hit one another.'

In the event, there were so many people in the hall when Cal arrived that everything went quite well, at least on the surface. Perhaps Ma had been a little too fulsome in her greeting, but Adrian wouldn't be jealous of that, would he? Emily hadn't noticed any signs of a real relationship between her mother and Zannah's fiancé. One of these days, she thought, I'll have to ask Ma what she really thinks of him. Or maybe I'd better not.

'Darling Cal,' Joss said, kissing his cheek. She was looking properly happy for a change. Emily had noticed that their mother was a little subdued this Christmas whatever she'd said and wondered whether it might have anything to do with the Graham Ashton thing. Surely not. She'd been quite upbeat that day and denied that there was anything for them to worry about. She'd promised them. No, perhaps it was just the strain of having a full house at Christmas. She was talking to Cal still. 'Have you had a good drive? Come in, sit down, let me take your coat.'

'Hello, Joss,' said Cal. Isis was clinging to his arm. She'd gone out into the drive and flung herself round her father's neck as he stepped out of the car. 'Hi, Bob,' he added, stepping up to shake Pa's hand. 'And Charlotte, how lovely to see you. Hiya, Em!'

He gave her a big hug, and she hugged him back, blushing. When was she going to be able to be cool around him? 'Hi, Cal,' she said, aware that Zannah was standing right behind her in the crowded hall. She could feel him looking at her sister over her shoulder and she stepped out of his arms to let him greet her.

'Hello, Zannah.' Formal, not kissing or touching her because, next to her, even more of an alpha male than usual, was Adrian.

Zannah, Emily could see, was a little agitated. She was pink in the face and she stumbled over the introduction. 'Adrian, this is Cal,' she said.

'Hi,' said Cal.

'Hello,' said Adrian, stepping forward and putting out his hand. You had to hand it to the public schools, Emily thought, they certainly taught you how to be smooth in difficult social situations. Adrian was smiling, but Emily could see how stiffly he was holding his whole body. The physical difference between the two men was striking. Cal was in jeans, with an ancient grey Aran sweater over a red shirt. Adrian was in dark moleskin trousers and his shirt, discreetly checked, a beige and brown pattern, was as smoothly ironed and smart as his work shirts always were. Adrian didn't really do casual. He looked like a model in a Boden catalogue: dressed up even for his time off.

They moved into the living room, where Charlotte and Ma brought in tea and Christmas cake and the talk was of Pa's next trip. Good old Pa. He was clever at steering his way through choppy conversational seas as though there were no subtexts.

'I'm off straight after the wedding,' he declared to Cal. 'Very convenient timing, I call it. Fascinating excavation near Luxor. I expect I'll need the rest after all the excitement ...' He chuckled. Was he aware that he was talking to Zannah's ex-husband about her impending marriage to someone else? Cal, to do him credit, didn't bat an eyelid but started asking intelligent questions about Egypt, what the politics were like these days, security concerns, guiding Pa skilfully away from anything to do with weddings.

'Daddy,' said Isis, 'I want to show you my presents.'

'Not now, Icepop,' said Cal, smiling at her. 'Plenty of time to do that at Granny Ford's. She's longing to see you. And I've got a basket in the car, Joss, for all of you. You know my mum. Jam, clotted cream, a cake or something. She doesn't believe in supermarkets.'

'Lovely, Cal. Thanks so much. I've got a parcel for her, too. Isis, did you pack the presents for Granny Ford?'

Isis nodded. Zannah was restless, pleating the fabric of her skirt and fiddling with the collar of her blouse. Emily could see that she was counting the minutes till this would all be over. Cal, perhaps becoming aware that Adrian was sitting around not saying much, started talking to him about boring bank-type stuff. It always surprised her how well informed Cal was about all sorts of things. He was making an effort for Zannah's sake and Emily loved him for it. He must be able to see how uncomfortable she was feeling. Before too long, Adrian had relaxed a bit, and was answering him as though he were any old person in the world and nothing to do with Zannah. Good old Cal. There was also the fact that men were like that ... they were always able, it seemed, to rise above the emotional content of any situation and concentrate on other stuff: sport, geography, hill-walking, whatever. And Adrian, to give him credit, was even asking Cal the odd question back. Charlotte was throwing in the occasional remark, Joss was giving everyone more cake, and even Zannah was almost normal. The Transfer was going better than Emily had expected.

Adrian was quite tactful when Cal and Isis left. He disappeared halfway through all the farewell hugs and kisses. Emily smiled at Zannah and winked. She smiled back but, oddly, she was starting to look anxious again. Why was that? Have I missed something, Emily asked herself. From the hall window, she watched Cal's car disappearing down the drive. Isis was in the back, with her cassette tapes, ready to play, in the pretty bag Emily had given her for Christmas. She wished she could be in the car with her and Cal, driving down to Hampshire. At least she didn't have to go back to the flat just yet . . . no work till January.

The hall was empty. She could hear Ma and Charlotte in the kitchen, getting supper ready. Pa must be in his study. Where were Zannah and Adrian? Up in Zannah's room, probably, having a bit of a snog. Nothing more, she was sure. There must be something very offputting about sharing a bed in what used to be your childhood bedroom. I couldn't do it, she thought. Just the idea makes me feel about as sexy as a frozen fish. She was almost sure Zannah would agree with her.

'I saw you, you know. You thought I'd gone back into the living room but I saw you.'

Adrian was stretched out on the bed. Zannah was sitting at the dressing-table which she remembered wanting almost more than anything else in the world when she was about twelve. She'd been given it for Christmas after waging a six-month campaign of hints and nagging. She still remembered how happy she'd been that day. She'd gazed at the lace-trimmed skirts that hung down from the shiny glass surface; the bevelled triple mirror; the drawers with their little gold-tipped knobs, and the brush and comb set that Charlotte had given her at the same time, and felt nothing but the purest joy. She could even remember Emily coming in and announcing, in her bumptious, eight-year-old way, that it was 'silly'. She'd been quite right, Zannah now saw. Silly was exactly what it was, and off the twee scale altogether. She'd never choose a pink like this nowadays. She said, 'I don't know what you're talking about. What did you see?'

'I saw you kissing him goodbye.'

'Cal, you mean.' She turned to face Adrian. 'I cannot believe you're saying that. Are you telling me you're jealous? Honestly?'

Nothing from Adrian. He simply lay on the bed, frowning. Zannah sighed. What a waste of time this was! Now she'd have to persuade him there was nothing to be jealous about. She got up and went to sit next to him. 'You're going to have to get used to him, you know. He's Isis's dad. He'll be coming to pick her up and bring her home. I was just about to congratulate you on how well you behaved. How well you seemed to get on, the two of you.'

'Glad you noticed. He's not as bad as I feared, actually. Can't think what you ever saw in him, though. Not exactly an oil painting, is he? A bit scruffy.'

'If that's the case,' said Zannah, 'there's nothing for you to be steamed up about.'

'I'm not really steamed up. I just . . . I didn't like to see you kissing him. That's all.'

'It was hardly a snog, was it? Just a kiss on both cheeks. If you were really looking, you'd have seen that.'

'He put his arms round you.'

'Doh!' Zannah said, and as she said it, she remembered that yes, Cal's arms had gone round her briefly and she also remembered how good it had felt, how grateful she was for his affection. 'You can't really hold your hands at your sides when you're kissing someone goodbye.' She stood up suddenly. 'I can't believe we're having this conversation, Adrian. Really. Just grow up.'

'Come here, then. Come here and give me a proper kiss.' He sat forward on the bed, took her hand and pulled her down to where he was. Zannah closed her eyes as he began to nibble at her lips, touch her breasts. 'It's going to be so great,' he murmured, 'being on our own for a bit. I can't wait to have you to myself. No family to bother us. No children to interrupt all the time.'

Zannah wanted to pull away and defend her daughter. No way did Isis interrupt them all the time. She got on his nerves sometimes but she wasn't always under their feet. What could Adrian mean? I'll ask him later, she thought, and kissed him back. She, too, would be happy to be away from this house now that Christmas was over. They'd twice made love in her childhood bed and it felt very odd. Between having to be quiet, because of everyone else so close by, and the strangeness of doing anything so grown up in this room, she'd felt inhibited and slightly foolish both times. Never mind, they'd be alone soon. She closed her eyes and tried to concentrate on Adrian, his lips, his hands, but found that part of her was thinking of Isis and Cal in the car, driving down to the Fords. What were they talking about? Was Isis missing her? Whenever she was away from her daughter, the initial euphoria of not having to take her needs into consideration, of being free to please herself entirely and selfishly, gave way after a while to missing her. I love her more than anyone, Zannah reflected. That's the truth. She's the one I can't live without.

'House is jolly quiet without young Isis, isn't it?' Bob said. 'We'll soon change that. Listen to what I've got here. Zannah's approved all this, of course. I played it to her yesterday, but I want to know what you think.' He pressed a button on the CD player and organ music, a gloriously sonorous, dense and textured sound, filled the small study. Emily loved this room. She'd always been allowed in here on condition that she didn't touch any of the small bits and pieces – pottery, pieces of ancient metal, beads, fragments of paper and what looked like grass or straw – that were strewn on the desk, in boxes on the floor, on shelves attached to the wall: everywhere.

'It's gorgeous,' Emily said. 'Will the organist in Clapham be up to it, though?'

'A bit of Purcell? Lovely, isn't it? ... I should think most church organists worth their salt would manage it, but I'll ask Charlotte. And we can have the local choral society to beef up the singing, apparently. Courtesy of Edie. "Love Divine All Loves Excelling", sung to the Stainer tune. Very good choice, I think.'

'It's going to be terrific, Pa. You've really worked on it, haven't you? Zannah loves it, I know. She told me she wished we could have fewer words and more music.'

'You do need the words, though. They're full of poetry in the traditional form. I'm so relieved Zannah's gone for that and not one of the modern versions. "With this ring I thee wed, with my body I thee worship and with all my wordly goods I thee endow." Spot on, that. Beautiful!'

'I didn't know you were such a softie, Pa.' Emily smiled.

'Nothing soft about it. I enjoy ritual, the older the better. In fact, speaking of old things reminds me: I'm glad I've got you on your own. I've mentioned this to your mother, naturally, but not given her the details. It's about my next trip to Egypt. Just after the wedding, actually. May the thirtieth. Absolutely essential that I'm there, so it's a bit of relief that the dates don't clash with the big day. I'd have been in a real fix then.'

'That's good,' said Emily. 'Wish I could fly off to Egypt.'

'Why can't you? I'd love to have you. It could easily be arranged. You could be my assistant, if you're willing to fetch and carry a bit. It'll be bloody hot in May, though. Sure you're up to it?'

'I am if you are. But what about my work?'

'Holiday? Aren't you due some?'

Emily thought for a moment. If she took the whole of her summer holiday in May, she'd be wanting another by the end of August. On the other hand, she'd always wanted to go on an expedition. The timing, too, was perfect. She wouldn't have to be alone in the flat straight away, with Zannah on her honeymoon, and Isis staying with Cal and his mother in Hampshire.

'Yes,' she said. 'I might look into it. Thanks, Pa.'

He pressed pause, and leaned over the machine looking serious. 'Will you be all right in the flat with Zannah gone? I presume she and Adrian will find a house, won't they?'

'Oh, yes. They're starting to look straight after Christmas. I've already spotted a few of those sheets from estate agents lying about. I'll find some friends to share with me. Don't worry, it'll be fine.'

She didn't mention that she wasn't looking forward one bit to Zannah moving out. She was used to having her around. And she would really miss Isis. What were the chances of Adrian and Zannah buying a house in the same area? Very slender, knowing Adrian, Emily thought. He'd be keen to move somewhere like Chelsea or Kew. Very nice too, and bully for Zannah, snaffling a bloke who could even think about those prices, but much too far away for daily visits.

'What you need,' said Bob, 'is to find yourself a young man, you know.'

'Oh God, don't you start,' Emily said. 'I can sense Charlotte and her cronies eyeing me in a desperate way every time I go there. They switch on their engagement-ring alert the second I walk through the door. I thought you and Ma were cool about stuff like that.'

'Good heavens, we're totally "cool". Just want you to be happy, that's all.'

'Perhaps I'll meet a handsome archaeologist while I'm in Egypt next May.'

'I suspect,' said Bob, laughing, 'that I'm the last of the breed, but you never know.'

'You're certainly very conceited,' said Emily.

'Enough of this frivolity,' said Bob. 'There's still lots of music I want to play you.'

As Emily prepared to listen, a thought crossed her mind. If Pa was going to Egypt after the wedding, why didn't he ask Ma to go with him? As far as Emily knew, he never had. Why was that? Maybe she'd already told him she didn't want to go. I'll find out later, she thought.

'Will I see Mister and Hamish?' Isis was sitting in the back seat of her father's car, and they were going to be driving for ages. It was miles and miles from Grandma and Grandpa's house to where Granny lived in Hampshire.

'Of course you will,' said Cal. 'They can't wait to see you, I bet.'

Mister and Hamish were Granny's cats and Isis thought it was funny that they were even older than she was because they'd stayed exactly the same all the time she'd known them. There were photos of her when she was really, really tiny and the cats had been huge even then. They were both ginger-and-white all over. Granny said she'd chosen Mister and Hamish when they were kittens because they matched the two ginger-and-white china cats that sat on her mantelpiece at either side of the clock.

Dad didn't normally speak much when he was driving. They listened to music. Dad liked White Stripes, Radiohead and the Kaiser Chiefs and Isis knew lots of the songs. Her best song for singing in the car was called 'I Predict A Riot'. When the CD finished, Dad said, 'Why don't you have a nap, Icey? I can drive without music.'

'I'm not tired.' This wasn't quite true, but she loved being by herself with Dad and she didn't want to waste any of that time by sleeping.

'Fine,' Dad said. Then he didn't say anything for a bit. Isis was just wondering what was the matter, and whether he was going to put on another CD, when he said, 'Are you getting excited? About the wedding, I mean.'

'I'm dead excited. So's Gemma. We're going to have a fitting after New Year. I can't wait to see my dress. Try it on, I mean. I've seen what it's going to look like.'

'Great. You'll have to get Em to take a photo to show me.'

'You'll see it at the wedding.'

'Sweetie, I'm not coming to the wedding. Didn't you know that?'

Isis thought about it. Dad was right. Adrian wouldn't like it if he was there. She said, 'I suppose I did know really. I wasn't thinking.'

'That's okay. I'm sure it'll be smashing and you can tell me about it afterwards, right?' Then he added, 'How're you getting on with Adrian?'

'He's okay.'

'How'll it be, living with him and Mum? Will you like that?'

Isis thought about this. 'I expect so. I'll be at school mostly.'

The car drove along in the dark for a while and then Dad said, 'Well, there's still evenings and holidays.'

'It'll be okay. He's nice to me.'

'That's fine, chicken, if you say so.'

Isis felt ashamed of herself for only telling her dad the good part of the truth. Adrian was nice to her most of the time, but he got cross if things became too messy or noisy; he called it 'chaotic'. Mum got cross sometimes and so did Dad, but it was different somehow. She knew they'd always make friends with her afterwards. She didn't want to upset her father and she knew it would cause trouble if she told him about Adrian and the boarding school. Her mum, too, would've gone mad if she'd heard what Adrian had said to her.

A few days ago, just before Christmas, she'd been alone with Adrian while Mum was upstairs getting ready to go out with him, and he'd started telling her again how happy he'd been at boarding school, how happy the daughters of a few of his friends were at this amazing boarding school in the country which had a heated swimming-pool and everything. He said it was really brill, and if she felt like going he could speak to Mum about it. Isis hadn't known what to say. She didn't know what she thought about going away to boarding school. It might be great, like in the Malory Towers books, but it would be awful to be away from Mum and Em. She knew she'd miss them. She even missed Mum a bit when she was staying with Dad. And what about Gemma and all her other friends?

'I wouldn't mention it to her now,' Adrian had said. 'She's so busy with all the arrangements. We'd better wait till later, okay? After the wedding.'

Isis hadn't said a word to anyone. Maybe she should've, but maybe not. Mum is busy, she told herself, and if I told Dad, he'd just worry about me. She wasn't quite sure why, but she thought that if Mum and Adrian quarrelled, then there was a chance she wouldn't want to be married to him and if she didn't want to be married to him, then there'd be no dress and no party and no flowers. She decided to do what Adrian told her to do and not say anything till the wedding was over.

The sound of 'Planet Telex' by Radiohead filled the inside of the car. Isis looked at the back of her father's head. She closed her eyes. Maybe if she went to sleep now, she wouldn't have to think about it. And when she woke up, they'd be at Granny's house and the cats would be there, waiting for her.

Sunday

'How come,' Cal said, 'you're not dancing the night away like Zannah? There must be at least three parties you could be at right now.'

'I don't do New Year,' said Emily, who was stretched out on the sofa sipping brandy. Cal was slumped in the chair opposite her, looking as unfestive as she was feeling. She went on, 'All that enforced jollity and not knowing the person you've just kissed and not really wanting to. Ghastly "Auld Lang Syne" and in Zannah's case, Hooray Henries from Adrian's bank and their girlfriends. Not my thing. And you're a fine one to talk. Where's your party?'

'Didn't fancy it, to be honest. Much rather be with Isis. And you, of course,' he added gallantly.

She didn't say *And I like being alone with you*. Lately, Emily hadn't seen much of Cal, but since she'd officially given up hope long ago of him falling in love with her, she was trying hard not to care too much about whether she saw him or not. But Cal was right: she'd turned down four different invitations, and she was glad she had. They'd had a good time here in the flat. Two movies on DVD – one with Isis, one after she'd gone to bed – and lots of wine before the brandy meant that Emily felt pleasantly woozy. Not drunk but not sober either: the perfect way to greet the next twelve months.

'You could have gone to your parents' or Charlotte.'

Emily thought of what went on in Altrincham at New Year and said, 'Ma and Pa have a dinner party with some old friends and that's it. Not worth going all the way up there for. And Charlotte and her pals are probably fast asleep. They've seen too many New Years to be impressed by another. Or maybe they're knocking back the Glenmorangie, just the three of them, all nice and cosy. And I dread to think what Maureen's idea of a New Year's Eve party is like. Multiple balloons and full evening dress. And champagne, of course.'

'I bet,' Cal said, 'it's after midnight. What's your watch say?'

'Hmm.' Emily sat up. 'Quarter to one. How come we missed it? What were we doing at midnight?'

'Watching Tom Cruise triumphing in *Collateral*. Never mind.' Cal got to his feet. 'We'll say "Happy New Year" right now. Get off the sofa and give us a kiss.'

Emily jumped up and Cal hugged her, then kissed her, first on one cheek then the other and once on her forehead. She thought, he's not quite drunk enough to forget himself and give me a proper snog. The kissing came to an end, and Cal sat back on his chair and Emily returned to the sofa. She said, 'You don't look terribly happy, Cal. What sort of year's it going to be if you've got a long face on New Year's Eve?'

'Sorry, Em. I'm okay. I'm just . . . Well, there's stuff I'm not looking forward to, that's all.'

'Like what?'

Cal poured himself another glass of wine. 'I don't think I should tell you. You tell Zannah everything.'

'No, I don't,' said Emily, reflecting that she'd managed to keep her feelings for Cal completely to herself. 'There are some things we don't tell one another.' She leaned forward and whispered 'Your secret is safe with me,' in an accent that was supposed to be mystical and gypsy-like and came out sounding completely ridiculous.

'Not worth mentioning, really.'

'Go on, Cal. You can't not tell me now. Shan't breathe a word.'

'It's nothing you don't know. I'm not . . . Well, I wish Zannah wasn't marrying that wally.'

'Adrian's not a wally.' She thought, he's not Cal, but no one could call him a 'wally'.

'I was being polite. That was a mild version of what I think of him, actually.'

'He's okay, Cal. And anyway, Zannah loves him. I sort of see what you mean, but he's not bad, honestly. He's very . . . well, very attentive to her. Does what she says, I suppose, is what I mean.'

'And I didn't?'

'I'm not saying that. You know I wish she'd stayed with you. Really. But now that, well, Zannah's moved on . . .'

'I should as well. I know, but you asked. I'm not doing anything about it. I'm not telling a single other person. Sometimes I don't even admit it to myself. It's only when I get a bit pissed that I feel like this. And that's probably why I'm blabbing to you. Sorry, Em. Don't mean to burden you with my troubles.'

'You should find someone else. It's no good mooning over Zannah.'

'Don't think I haven't tried. There's been the odd person, but no one who . . . well, no one I'd like to be married to.'

'Apart from Zannah?'

There was a long silence. For a moment, Emily thought Cal might have fallen asleep. Then he said, 'Right. Zannah. I'd marry her tomorrow if she'd have me.'

Emily looked carefully at Cal in the dimmed light that shone from the one lamp they'd turned on. Were his eyes filling with tears? Cal? For as long as she'd known him, he'd laughed his way out of any emotional impasse, but now he was almost in tears and there was a suspicious crack in his voice as he said, 'I rely on you, Em, to keep this entirely to yourself, okay?'

'I've promised, haven't I?' Emily thought she should dispel the heavy mood. She said, lightly, jokily, 'Besides, she wouldn't have you. She's completely obsessed with this wedding.'

'And Adrian too, I presume, so there's nothing more to say. Keep mum, Em, and let's have another drink.'

New Year's Eve. Drinking more wine was about the only thing worth doing.

'Right. I've had some brandy though. Will it make me throw up if I mix them?'

'It shouldn't, but we'll soon find out,' said Cal, pouring wine into a clean glass and holding it out to her. 'Cheers.'

Wednesday

'Is it too late to wish you all a happy New Year?' Miss Hayward smiled at what seemed, in her small living room, to be a crowd of people. Joss had come down at Zannah's request to see the dress, which was having its first proper fitting today. Isis was there too, to try on the bridesmaid's outfit, and visibly excited at the prospect. Joss suspected that part of the reason she'd been invited was to keep an eye on her granddaughter in case boredom set in during the afternoon. Emily had taken time off work to accompany them, refusing to be left out of such a fantastically important occasion.

'You need us both, don't you, Zannah?' she'd said while they were on their way to Highgate. 'You need our opinion on this very important matter, right?'

Zannah had agreed, of course. If she could have had Charlotte there as well, she'd have been even more delighted, but it was quite fortunate she hadn't joined the party. Miss Hayward's living room would've struggled to cope with even one more body. As it was, Isis was sitting on the floor at Joss's feet.

'No, not late at all,' Zannah said. 'January the eleventh is still very much New Year, I think.'

'Well, everything's ready for you to try on, my dear,' said Miss Hayward. 'If you come upstairs with me, I'll get you into the dress and then we can call the others up to see how it looks. Is that all right?'

'That's lovely. Thank you.' Zannah sprang up, smiling. She followed Miss Hayward out of the room.

'Mum'll call us soon, won't she, Granny?' Isis had got to her feet and was examining the china figurines on the mantelpiece. 'Isn't this lady pretty? I like her hat!'

She was looking at one of the shepherdesses who was dressed in foaming pale pink lacy skirts and a wide-brimmed hat trailing green ribbons. Real agriculture was obviously the last thing on her mind.

'Yoo-hoo! You can come up now!' That was Miss Hayward.

'Did she really say yoo-hoo? I thought that was only in books.' Em took Isis's hand and they went quickly up the stairs. Joss followed. Miss Hayward was waiting on the landing, holding open the door to one of the bedrooms.

Zannah was standing next to the window. Joss blinked, and couldn't think of a word to say. Her daughter was beautiful: ethereal and delicate in a dress that draped her body and fell elegantly to mid-calf. She saw lace, edged with more lace; flowers and butterflies hidden in the pattern; tiny pearls scattered around the square neckline, around the hem, and the edges of the sleeve. The dress was still pinned in places; one of the sleeves hadn't yet been set in but Joss could see how it would be. It was the perfect dress for Zannah. Joss said, 'It's ... it's completely amazing. D'you like it? Are you happy? Is it what you imagined?'

'Better. Miss Hayward has made it even better than I'd hoped it would be. Isn't it fabulous? And look ... here's the headdress – a 'fascinator' – it'll be done up with my hair ... kind of wrapped round it. Em, what d'you think? Icey?'

'You're dead pretty, Mum!' Isis said. She'd been standing quite still by the door, her mouth open in astonishment, but when Zannah spoke, she ran to touch the dress, to look at it more closely.

Em was smiling. She said, 'I dunno. Are you sure you wouldn't rather have had a Maureen Meringue? I'm kidding, you idiot,' she added, seeing the look of horror on Zannah's face. 'You couldn't possibly have a better dress. Fantastic. Honestly. I love it. You'll be ... You are ... Well, there's nothing to say except: WOW!'

'What about me, Mrs Hayward?' Isis said, bouncing up and down with excitement. 'Can I try my dress on too?'

'Of course. Here it is. Just take off what you're wearing and we'll see what you look like.'

She held up a hanger with one of the bridesmaid's dresses on it. The green of the fabric was the exact colour of dark moss. 'The other little girl ... Gemma? Is she going to come for a fitting soon?'

'Yes,' said Zannah. 'I'll bring both girls in next week. But I'm afraid Isis couldn't wait ...'

'Perfectly understandable,' said Miss Hayward. 'Now, slip this on, dear. Remember that it's not trimmed. You can help me choose the right decorations next time you come. I've got a whole drawer full of pretty things you can look at.' She was pinning the dress together at the back as she spoke. 'Of course, on the day, you'll have little buttons here, and not pins.'

Isis went to gaze into the full-length mirror. Her eyes widened as she took in the full glory of the taffeta, the rustle of it, the sheen, the way the sleeves puffed out. She let out a breath and sighed with pleasure. 'It's ... it's like soooo cool! I can't wait to show Gemma. Is there going to be a ribbon here?' She pointed to the high waist of the dress.

'Yes,' said Miss Hayward. 'And also on the sleeves, I think. Perhaps with some tiny satin roses. What do you think?'

'Roses! Yes, please. Oh, I wish it was the wedding tomorrow.'

'But if it was tomorrow,' said Miss Hayward, 'the dresses wouldn't be ready. Now stand very still and I'll put pins in to show me where the hem should be.'

While Isis was having her skirt pinned up, Joss moved to where Zannah was standing near the window. She leaned forward to whisper in her ear. 'You look so beautiful, Zannah. And so does Isis. It's going to be a lovely wedding.'

She and Em went downstairs to wait for Zannah and Isis to change and join them.

'We'll have to start thinking,' Joss said 'about what we're going to wear.'

'You should consult with Zannah,' said Emily. ' She's often said she'd like to dress you up.'

'Really? She's never told me that.' Joss wondered what Zannah would advise. She was willing to allow her a reasonably free hand, but they'd have to find out first what Maureen was intending to wear. As though she'd been reading her thoughts, Em said, laughing, 'We'll have to find out about Maureen first, though, won't we? I wouldn't put it past her to go for something like brocade. She'll look like a very smart sofa.'

'Now now, she's not fat, you know,' Joss smiled.

'No, she's not, but she's well-upholstered. Like I said: a sofa.'

Joss smiled but she didn't want to think about Maureen. She knew exactly where such thoughts always led, and she wasn't going to allow herself to grieve for what she had lost. Not on a day like this, at a time like this. Pretend he doesn't exist, she thought, not even letting his name come into her head. Think of Zannah. Think how happy Isis is with her outfit. Concentrate on the good things. The dress. The lovely, lovely dress.

Friday

'I've spoken to Charlie,' said Edie, 'and he's happy to have me and Val stay overnight on the Friday. And he'll drive us to the church in good time for the wedding.'

'I'm sorry,' said Charlotte. 'I don't like turning you out of your rooms, but if Zannah's in the big spare bedroom, Em in the small one, then Joss and Bob can go in your room, Edie, and Gemma and Isis in yours, Val.'

'Of course,' Val said. 'You can't have them coming from North London on Saturday morning. Too much could go wrong. Very kind of your Charlie, Edie, I must say.'

They were sitting at the kitchen table after lunch. Outside, a thin, late January sun was struggling through the clouds and the back lawn was dotted with the first purple and yellow crocuses. Charlotte said, 'There's going to be a Wedding Summit at the beginning of March. Maureen calls it that. She's sent me all the catering details. She is an extremely efficient and organized woman. If a little tiring.'

'The whole thing,' said Val, 'is running well up to now.'

'Throw salt over your shoulder or something, Val,' said Edie. 'That's tempting Fate.'

Charlotte nodded. 'I'm pleased there's been no panic so far, I must admit. They came over yesterday to look at the garden and apparently there's plenty of room for our portable loos. They will, I'm promised, be "of the highest possible standard".'

'Not then, *bog* standard . . . such a relief,' said Val, and laughed at her double pun. 'By the way,' she added, 'I've been in touch with Maya, the flower lady, and she and Zannah have discussed the colour of the bouquet roses. And the foliage. She wants dark leaves to match the green of the bridesmaids' dresses. Maya's coming to the church on the Friday afternoon to oversee the flowers in there, and she's promised to be here in plenty of time on the Saturday morning, with the bouquets, buttonholes and table arrangements. She wants them to be as fresh as possible but it'll mean an early start, I'm afraid. Six o'clock. I've said I'll be up to help her. No need for anyone else to be disturbed.'

'I'm sure Zannah'll be wide awake,' Charlotte said. 'Em too, probably, with all the excitement. And the hairdresser's arriving at nine. Everyone can help themselves to breakfast in here. The caterers bring everything they need, Maureen says, and won't bother us in the kitchen..'

'Where are the Ashtons staying? And Adrian?' Edie asked.

'At the Savoy,' Charlotte said. 'Adrian's stag night'll be the weekend before the wedding, I believe. He and some friends are off to the Highlands for a party, Zannah says.'

'What about Zannah? Is she having a hen night?' Edie smiled.

'Emily's taking her and two friends to a spa in the country. A very luxurious one, apparently. They're going to have beauty treatments and different sorts of bath and end the day with a lovely dinner.'

'How many kinds of bath can there possibly be?' Val looked bemused.

'You'd be amazed,' said Charlotte. 'Em showed me the brochure. Hammam tubs,which are a kind of oriental bath, I believe. Jacuzzis. Spring water. Plus things like hot stones, saunas, steam rooms and facials. And there's a swimming-pool, of course.'

'And who,' said Val, ' is paying for that?'

'They all pay their own way. That's how it's done, I'm told. I suspect Bob's helping Em, but I didn't enquire too closely.'

Edie stood up. 'I must go,' she said. 'Choir practice. I have to check with the organist about the music.' She tapped her handbag. 'I'm going to give him the list Bob sent.'

'And I'm off to the garden. Things to be done there.' Val followed Edie out and Charlotte was left alone. The wedding arrangements were under control, but she was less certain about Joss's state of mind. She hadn't seen her since the beginning of January, when she'd visited to report on how beautiful the dress was. She hadn't stayed long. It seemed to Charlotte that she'd lost weight and she could ill afford to. She looked drawn. Older. They hadn't been able to talk properly, but Joss did the dishes after lunch and Charlotte volunteered to dry. Edie and Val disappeared in a suspiciously prearranged way and when they were alone, Charlotte had asked her, 'Are you bearing up, darling?'

Joss had paused before she answered. 'Bearing up describes it, I think. I try to keep busy. I do a lot of late nights at the library.'

'Are you writing?'

'A little. Not as much as I'd like. Not the sort of thing I'd like to be writing either. I'm all right, Charlotte.'

'You're very thin, dear. Are you sure you're not neglecting yourself?'

'No, really. I just . . .'

She stood with her hands plunged in the soapy water. Charlotte longed to put an arm round her shoulders. At Christmas, she'd told her that the pain would ease. That things would get better. Now, she was almost sure they were worse. She'd hesitated before asking, 'Have you heard from Graham?'

Joss shook her head and turned away quickly, so that Charlotte couldn't see her face. Were those tears in her eyes?

They'd changed the subject and since then, all the phone calls and emails had been, Charlotte thought, deliberately cheerful and upbeat. Joss was doing her best to give the impression that everything was fine, but she didn't fool her aunt for a second.

February / March

Saturday

'Can't paint sunsets any more,' said Zannah. 'Can't write poems about them either. Or about the moon.'

'Why not?' Adrian, she could tell from the way he asked the question, was paying more attention to following the path down the gentle slope towards their hotel than to what she was saying. He probably wasn't even expecting a proper answer, but Zannah said, 'They've become clichés. It would take a real genius to tackle a subject like that. I think so, anyway.'

Adrian smiled over his shoulder at her. 'Never mind. Just enjoy the view. And in a few minutes you'll be gazing at a very beautiful gin and tonic.'

They walked along together without speaking. Dusk was falling and the Cotswolds were already shrouded in mist. The sky was darkening to mauve and the first stars were out. Even though it was February and spring was supposed to be just round the corner, it was cold and their breath curled into white mist in front of their faces. Zannah sighed.

'Is anything wrong? You sound . . . well, a bit down, darling.'

She laughed. 'No, I'm fine. I was just feeling . . . I was missing Isis, actually.'

'Not seriously?' Adrian laughed. 'I'd have thought if anything, you'd be getting ready to miss me. I'm the one who's off to the States for a fortnight on Monday morning.'

'Of course I'll miss you too, but it's not the same thing. Isis is . . . much younger, for one thing. And besides, for the last eight years I've spent practically my whole waking life with her. For most of that time,

I was on my own. When she was little, she drove me mad some of the time, but I'm used to being with her.'

'But she's not little any longer, is she? She's getting on for nine. And I should think you'd be glad not to have to worry about her for a bit.' He added magnanimously, 'I expect her other granny's enjoying having her to stay for half-term. And her dad. And you, my darling, deserve a combined birthday and pre-Valentine's Day treat.'

'That's lovely of you. She does get on my nerves sometimes and I know I get cross with her, but I'm always glad to see her when I pick her up.'

They were nearly there. The windows of the hotel shone a yellow light into the gathering darkness at the end of the tree-lined drive. The gravel crunched under their feet. Then Adrian stopped and reached for her hand. He said, 'Darling, it's probably not a good time to raise this, but it's been on my mind for a bit and as we're on the subject ...'

'What subject?'

'Isis. I want to talk about Isis. Well, you and Isis, really.'

Zannah felt faint. She thought, maybe I should have brought some Kendal Mint Cake out with me. I expect it's hunger that's making me weak. She said, 'Isis and I are fine, Adrian. I just said I'd be glad to see her again. That's all.'

'I think you're a bit ... I think she's too dependent on you and you're too dependent on her. Not good for either of you.'

'What are you saying?'

'I think Isis should be learning to ... separate herself from you a little.'

'Separate?'

'Well, obviously not separate in that sense. Of course not. I don't mean that. It's very important for children to have close ties with their parents, I know, but still, I reckon it'd do her a world of good to go to boarding school. Jon and I both went and we loved it, as you know. I think it she'd love it, too.'

There was a bench under one of the trees along the drive. Zannah walked towards it and sat down. Adrian came after her and sat beside her. He said, 'Zannah, don't be angry for God's sake. I'm thinking of Isis's welfare. Truly. And our lives together. Just give it a bit of thought, that's all I'm asking. Nothing more at this stage. You probably think boarding schools are for older children, but there're plenty of junior ones as well. Paul Claythorpe's kid goes to one near Haslemere and she loves it. Made fabulous friends. Goes on amazing trips. It's incredible. Really. Isis'd have a great time. And our sprogs, too, when they're old enough.'

Zannah knew that if she spoke at once, she would regret it. She sat and stared at her knees. One of Em's presents for Isis at Christmas had been a bag full of plastic strings to weave into bracelets. She'd had good fun with them, but the last time Zannah saw them, they were all tangled up in the bottom of a carrier bag in her cupboard, a mess of fluorescent colours like thousands of thin worms twisted up together. That's what my head's like, she thought. I don't know what I think any more. Does Adrian understand the meaning of what he's just said?

'Adrian,' she said at last, 'I'm going to ask you something. Please answer me honestly. Okay?'

He nodded.

'Is this about getting Isis out of the way? This boarding school stuff? Tell me I'm wrong. Please tell me I've got it entirely wrong.'

'You have and you haven't. Didn't I just say that I'd like our kids to go too? You can't say I'm wanting a boarding-school education for Isis because she's not mine. But you've asked me to be honest, so I'm going to be. And please, Zannah, don't bite my head off, right?' He rubbed his hands together.

We ought to have worn gloves, Zannah thought. It's so cold. I'm cold all over.

'Right. Okay. I can't pretend I'm a hundred per cent happy about living with another man's child. Much as I like Isis...that's got nothing to do with it. Only, I feel that ... well, I reckon we need a balance between time we have with Isis and time we have on our own. There's nothing wrong with that, surely?'

'You're saying you'd rather she lived somewhere other than with us, is that right?'

'Well, not lived, perhaps. Just maybe spent a bit more time with her dad. Or, as I said, at boarding school. I know Cal's often out of the country.'

'I don't want to hear "boarding school" again, Adrian. I mean it. I'm not sending my daughter away and that's that. I'm also not sending away any children we have. D'you understand? Promise me you won't say another word on the subject.'

'God, Zannah, don't get so shirty. There's no harm in discussing it, surely?'

She stood up and shouted, 'There is harm! I suppose you think you're talking about education but you're not. You want to be rid of Isis. I don't know how I didn't see that before. You wish she wasn't around. You've been so happy these last couple of days, much happier than you ever are in London and I thought it was me, but it wasn't. It was Isis not being here. That's what makes you happy. Deny it – go on! Say I'm wrong. Say it!'

'I do like being alone with you! And I don't deny it – why should I? I love you and I like being together without having to worry about the needs of a child, who, let's face it, has been spoilt rotten. She's had nothing but total love and attention from you since the day she was born.'

'That's what she's meant to have!' Zannah yelled. 'She's my daughter. What else am I supposed to give her if not unconditional and total love and care always? And I do not spoil her. How can you say that? She is not spoilt. She's normal, and I should know – I'm a teacher, for God's sake. D'you want to know what your problem is? Because I'll tell you. *YOU'RE* the child. *You* have to be the centre of attention. *You* have to get any unconditional love that's around. It's because your mother's made you believe you're king of the world. I haven't noticed you objecting to her total obsession with you. You just can't bear the competition.'

She walked away from him very quickly, seeing nothing, stumbling in the darkness. Tears sprang into her eyes. Could they ever recover from this? How would they make it up after what they'd said to one another? How was she going to marry him now? Live with him for the rest of her life. And would he still want to marry her? She wasn't going to compromise where Isis was concerned. Adrian would have to take back every single word. Would she be able to believe his apologies? She knew he would come after her full of remorse, regret and blandishments. But even if I said I forgave him, could I really? One thing was certain: she'd never forget what he'd said. Another man's child. That was the bottom line. That was what he thought in his deepest heart. If we have a child together, he'll favour that child over Isis. There was no way in the world that wouldn't happen. Adrian wouldn't even bother to pretend that both children were equally loved. He'd told her often about how badly he and Doc, as he called him, had got on during his own childhood. Why did I think my lovely Isis would be one of the exceptions? One of the few children to be truly, truly loved by a step-parent? Because I love her so much, that's why. But I'm a fool, Zannah told herself, as she went upstairs to their bedroom. Naïve and stupid.

She went into the bathroom and locked the door. He couldn't follow her in here. She sat on the edge of the bath, and the cold she'd felt outside was still with her, even in this heated room. Get a grip, she told herself. Pull yourself together. She closed her eyes. I'm not going to do it again. I'm not going to let myself disintegrate. No way. Suddenly, a longing to be out of there, away from Adrian, seized her. Thank heavens they'd driven here in her car. She opened the bathroom door and there he was, his mouth open ready to apologize.

'Adrian,' Zannah spoke quietly. ' I'm afraid I have to be alone for a bit, so I'm going now. I'm taking the car. Do you mind getting the train back to London?'

'But you can't! We've still got a whole day here. Not to mention dinner tonight.'

'I don't care about any of that. I'm leaving. I have to think.'

'Darling, please ...'

'Don't, Adrian. I'm going. Don't try to stop me. Please.'

'Then let me at least come with you. I'll drive you home.'

'No,' she said. Then, more quietly, 'I want to be by myself, okay? Please just leave me alone, Adrian. I have to pack. Go down and have a drink or something.'

When he'd gone, Zannah took her suitcase out of the cupboard and started to throw into it everything she'd brought for the weekend. Like someone in a movie, she thought and nearly smiled. She remembered the standing joke between her and Em, who always said that Zannah was so tidy she'd be folding clothes and layering them with sheets of tissue paper even if she was on the run from the police. See, Em? You're wrong. She couldn't even cry. Somewhere – in her head? Her heart? Her stomach? She had no idea, but somewhere in her body – there was what she imagined as a kind of twisted knot, pumping anguish through her veins, mixing it with her blood.

'Zannah? Is that you? Listen to me, Zannah. Calm down.'

'Cal? Oh, Cal, I'm sorry. I don't know what to do.'

'Take it easy. Where are you? Just tell me where you are.'

'I'm in a service-station car-park. I was coming to find Isis. I wanted . . .'

'Start again, okay? Just put the phone down for a second. Count to ten. Then tell me what's happened. Right? I'll wait. Don't rush.'

Zannah put her mobile on the seat beside her and took a tissue out of her bag. She blew her nose, wiped her eyes and took a few deep breaths. Cal was waiting till she could speak to him. She imagined him in the living room at his mother's house, maybe on the sofa. Sitting forward. I phoned him, she told herself. Not Em, not Ma, not Charlotte, but Cal. I did it without thinking. Maybe because I was driving to his mother's house. She picked up the phone up. 'Cal? Are you still there?'

'Yup. What's going on, Zannah?'

'I ran away. From Adrian.' Saying it made her realize all over again what she'd done and she paused to collect herself. Part of her wanted to scream and bang her head on the steering wheel till the pain stopped her thinking altogether. She took another deep breath and felt a little better. 'We were at a hotel in the Cotswolds,' she went on. 'We were having a lovely time and then we had a row and I left. That's it. Then I started crying in the car and I couldn't see to drive so I turned into a services . . .' Her voice faded away.

'Right. Tell me exactly where you are . . . Okay, I know where that is . . . I'm coming to fetch you. Just lock up the car, go into the café and get yourself a hot drink with something to eat. Promise me, Zannah. A bun. A sticky sweet one, okay? Don't move from there. I'll be with you in about an hour, I think. You'll be okay for that long, won't you?'

'I'm fine. I'll be fine. Thanks, Cal.'

'See you, then.'

Zannah felt anaesthetized. She was still aware that, somewhere, the pain was as bad as ever, but it had been dulled by a thick layer of numbness. Cal had done that: made her think she'd be okay, till he got there.

Made her feel as though she was about to be rescued. Also, he hadn't asked what the quarrel was about. He'd just got on with what needed to be done. That was why I phoned him, she told herself. Because he wouldn't get into a flap. Because he'd know the best thing to do. I'll do exactly what he said.

She got out of the car, locked it, and went into the café. Then she sat waiting in front of a cinnamon Danish and a cup of coffee that was mostly froth. She wasn't doing anything as coherent as thinking, but questions flickered in and out of her head. Why hadn't Adrian driven after her? Tried to stop her more forcefully? You had the car, came the answer. You wouldn't speak to him. What was he meant to do? Something, she thought. He ought to have done something. He hadn't even texted her, let alone tried to phone her. Why? He's angry with you. He reckons you're behaving stupidly. Making a lot of fuss about nothing. He thinks he deserves an apology.

Zannah took a sip of beige froth and sat up straight. If he thinks that, he can go and get stuffed, she thought. I'm the one who needs an apology and he has to take back what he's said about Isis and start all over again. She bit into the cinnamon Danish and didn't taste it. Could she believe him if he did that? There would always, she knew, be the suspicion that he was only pretending to like Isis for Zannah's sake. He can't, she reflected, summon up a store of love out of nowhere. And if he doesn't really feel it, hasn't felt it so far, why should it suddenly come to him now? No way. The whole thing was impossible. Zannah felt something like panic creeping in at the edge of her thoughts. The tears were gathering in her eyes and she blinked hard. I'm not going to cry, she told herself. I'll just sit here and Cal will be with me soon. Less than an hour. She looked at the clock. It wasn't even eleven. There weren't that many people around but those who were here looked washed out, miserable and grey because of the hideous lighting. The fixtures and fittings, the cutlery, the decor, everything, every single thing in this place, was ugly through and through. She closed her eyes and leaned against the wall, willing the time to pass quickly.

Isis woke up suddenly and pushed at the duvet with her toes to see if Hamish was still at the end of her bed. Yes, there he was. He was her favourite of the two cats, even though Isis loved Mister loads as well.

Mister was the shy one. He kept himself to himself, that was what Granny Ford said. Maybe Hamish's snores had woken her up. He was a very loud snorer, but Isis didn't mind. You're honoured, Dad had told her. He never sleeps on anyone else's feet. Isis heard the floorboards squeaking outside her room and sat up in bed.

'Dad?' she called. 'Is that you?'

The door opened and his black shape was outlined against the light. 'How come you're still awake, Icey? It's late.'

'I heard something.'

'Sorry.' He came into the room and sat on her bed. 'It was me. I've got to go out for a bit. I'll be back soon, though. You'll see me when you wake up in the morning. Okay?'

'Okay. Where are you going, though?'

'I'm going to fetch someone. I'm bringing them back here, and you'll see them tomorrow. It'll be a surprise.'

'Nice surprise?' Isis felt her eyelids drooping.

'Pretty good, yup.'

'Okay. I'll go to sleep now.'

Even though her eyes were closed, Isis could tell that Dad had shut the door and now it was quite dark in the room. Hamish, who'd woken up for a bit when the light disturbed him, had uncurled. Now he'd curled up all over again, and was purring. The noise made Isis think of a car engine. Dad's car engine . . . Maybe it was a car engine she could hear and not a purring cat. She fell asleep before she could work this problem out.

Zannah looked at Cal, sitting across the table from her. His hair was sticking up at the back and he was wearing a jacket she recognized from when she'd first met him. Could that be? She'd just told him exactly what had happened. She hadn't left out a single detail. It had poured out of her, and she hadn't realized till she'd finished how angry she was, how hurt, and also how much there was to tell. Part of her was shocked by the ease with which the words had flowed out of her: as though she'd been bottling up resentments for months. That couldn't be true, could it? Only yesterday, she had been in love. She'd been happy. Could something change in such a short time? Or had she been deluding herself? Not seeing things about Adrian that she didn't want to see, not wanting to acknowledge his faults because she was too caught up with the wedding. Was she as idiotic and criminally frivolous as that? Thinking this, Zannah was aware that tears were threatening to overwhelm her again.

'Cal, I feel awful. Everything I've put together over the last few months is disappearing. Sliding away from me and vanishing. I've spent ages getting everything ready, dreaming about it, longing for it and now... I can't bear to be the sort of person whose main worry is stuff like that. Oh, God.'

'You're talking about the wedding, right?'

Zannah nodded. 'I know you think the whole thing's ridiculous, but I wanted it ... I want it still ... so much. How'm I going to tell everyone? Cancel everything? Oh, Cal ...'

'Don't cancel anything, Zannah. This can all change. You mustn't do anything till you've discussed it with Adrian. He deserves that, doesn't he? You can't just ... I mean, you love him, don't you? That's what you have to answer honestly, Zannah. Do you really love him?'

'No!' she said. 'Yes, of course I do ... I don't know. I really don't know. I thought I did but now ... I feel as though he's not the person I loved yesterday. I think he's become a different person. Or I'm different, or looking at him from another place. I don't know.'

She wasn't expressing it well. Adrian was still in possession of all the qualities that she'd fallen in love with, wasn't he? What were they? He was handsome. She loved looking at him. She loved making love to him – he was different from Cal, more demanding, more exhausting. Zannah blushed. It had been some time since she'd thought about what sex with Cal had been like. For a long time after the divorce, she'd obsessed about what they'd had together and now that he was right in front of her, memories of those nights came unbidden into her head and she had to make a real effort to push them away, to think of something else. Adrian. Did she love him? He was generous. He was fun. He loved her. If she married him, she could ask for almost anything she wanted and he'd see that she got it. That was an unworthy reason to love someone, wasn't it? For his money? She had to confess, though she'd never have told a single other person, not even Em, that, yes, the money did come into it. It wasn't the most important thing about her love for Adrian but it counted for something.

She looked up at Cal and said, 'I don't know if I should spend the rest of my life with someone who's admitted, who's actually said, that he doesn't love Isis. That's what's important. I don't know if I can separate that from the rest of what I feel about him. What's going to happen? What about the wedding? So much time and effort – and the invitations have gone out and everything.'

'They don't matter a damn, Zannah. You have to do what you think's right, that's all. You mustn't do anything quickly. Promise?'

Zannah nodded. 'Okay ... I suppose so. But what now, Cal? Who should I tell?'

'No one. Not yet. Come back with me. I'll drive behind you if you feel you're up to it. Otherwise, we can leave your car and fetch it tomorrow ...'

'No, I can drive. I'm okay. A bit shell-shocked, but okay. What's the matter with me, Cal? Why can't I do relationships properly?'

'It's not you, Zannah. You're not to blame. None of this is your fault. If the wedding goes pear-shaped, well, things like that happen. No one's been injured. No one's lost their life, nor their livelihood. It's arrangements, that's all. You might lose money, I suppose, but that's it. It's inconvenient. A lot of boring work, getting in touch with everyone and explaining till you're blue in the face, but nothing you can't do if you have to. And you're not going to do anything for the moment. The pressure's off. My mum's longing to see you. She'll feed you up and take care of you and you don't have to hurry to get back to London, do you? It's half-term.'

He put out a hand to help her to her feet and Zannah held it till she reached her car. She got in and wound down the window, about to say something, though *thank you* was inadequate to convey how she felt: as though someone had lifted a huge burden off her back and left her lighter. Cal reached in and gently moved her hair off her forehead. 'Drive carefully,' he said, and smiled at her. 'I'm right behind you, don't forget.'

She saw him walk back to his car and drive it to where she was. Zannah waved at him as she moved out into the traffic. There he was in her wing-mirror, in his rackety old Fiat, riding shotgun, taking care of her. It was like having a police escort, but much more comforting. For the first time since she'd left the hotel, she began to feel as though she might get through this without falling apart. Her mobile started ringing and she didn't answer. It was probably Adrian. He could leave a message. She wasn't in a fit state to talk to him, and it had nothing to do with the fact that she was driving a car. I can't speak to him yet, she thought. What would I say? Tomorrow. I'll speak to him before his flight. I'll know better what to say to him in the morning. Zannah concentrated on the road spooling out in front of her car like a length of silver ribbon.

'They're asleep,' Cal whispered. 'Come in here for a minute, though, and let's have some tea. I'm freezing.'

They tiptoed into the small living room, where the remains of a coal fire were still burning. Mister was curled up on the hearthrug, and the clock, up on the mantelpiece between the two china creatures who resembled him and Hamish, struck one. Their entrance disturbed the cat to the extent of making him raise his head, but he soon sank back into a purring sleep.

'You sit there,' Cal said. 'I'll bring in the tea.'

Zannah listened to the comforting sounds he was making in the kitchen: crockery being arranged on a tray; the kettle boiling. When he appeared, he put the tray on the coffee table and sat down next to her on the sofa. She took a cup of tea from him. Cal said nothing.

'I feel so safe, Cal,' she said. 'I wish I could stay here for ever. It's warm, and there are cats, and I know Isis is upstairs and you're looking after me . . .' Her voice faded away as she realized that she was describing a scene that would have been routine, normal, everyday if she and Cal were still married. Would he notice? Pick up on what she'd said? He put out a hand and picked up a strand of her hair, twisting it gently and tucking it behind her ear. His hand lingered on her neck and she shivered. It's still there, she thought, what I used to feel about him. What's the matter with me? I'm supposed to love Adrian and now I'm wishing Cal would kiss me. I want him to. What would I do if he pulled me towards him? She bent her head to her teacup and took a sip.

Cal said, 'I can't stop feeling it's my job to look after you and Isis.'

'Isis, of course, but me . . .'

'Never mind, Zannah. It's okay. You're tired. Go and have a bath. I've put towels in my room. You're in my bed tonight.' He laughed.

'That didn't come out right, did it? What I mean is: I'll sleep down here on the sofa.'

'Oh, Cal, I could have slept down here ... I don't mind where I sleep, honestly.'

'Mum would want you to have my room. I wasn't going to fight about it. You go up now. Go on.'

'Thanks,' Zannah put her cup and saucer on the tray and stood up. 'Thanks for everything. I don't know what I'd have done without you. Really.'

He took her hand, brought it to his face and kissed it. The kiss was so gentle, that she was barely aware of it, yet the warmth of his lips on her skin made her feel ... how did it make her feel? Unsettled. Strange. Comforted.

'Good night, Zannah,' he said. 'Sleep well.'

Zannah lay in the narrow bed that had been Cal's since he was a boy. She closed her eyes. The room was completely dark. Thick curtains, no street lamps and a carpet that didn't allow even a glimpse of the landing light made for a blackness that was oddly soothing.

I'm not tired, Zannah thought, and immediately corrected herself. I'm totally exhausted but I can't sleep. She lay flat on her back and wondered whether she was strong enough or brave enough to confront the truth that had, she felt, been growing inside her like a tumour. She didn't love Adrian enough to marry him. She didn't want to spend the rest of her life with him. She sat up in bed at once, turned on the bedside light and whispered, 'I don't want to marry him.'

Once the words were there, in the air, out in the open, Zannah started to cry. She wanted to ring Em and speak to her. Or Ma. Or she could get up and walk downstairs to where Cal was sleeping and tell him ... No. No, of course she couldn't. She wiped her eyes and tried to pull herself together. She was being hasty. Maybe she was just tired. Maybe when Adrian came back from America, she'd see things differently. There was almost two weeks that she could use to get back to normal: to feeling the kind of love for him she'd felt till yesterday. Was it possible to love a man on Saturday and stop loving him on Sunday? Did people really do that? Nothing in the way he behaved towards her had changed, so was she overreacting? Would a more sensible person overlook what he'd said about Isis and muddle through the rest of their lives? Lots of people did. Maureen had done exactly that and it hadn't seemed to worry her. A dull pain somewhere in Zannah's stomach told her that she wasn't capable of it. If she married Adrian, however well he treated Isis, she would know that his irritation was there all the time, whether he showed it or not. He'd start to dislike Isis, she thought, instead of just not liking her, and that dislike could spread to me, because I'll take her side in their quarrels. Everything she'd had with Adrian was now tarnished, spoilt beyond repair. What she now felt about him was muddied, as though ink had been spilt in clear water.

Zannah was filled with a peculiar mixture of terror and embarrassment that she'd never encountered before. What everyone would think, what they'd all say, how she'd be thought of – a flibbertigibbet, a woman who didn't know her own mind, frivolous, unkind – was almost as bad as the dreadful thing she was about to do to Adrian. He loved her. What would he say? What would happen now? She didn't know which awful bit of the situation to concentrate on: telling everyone that the wedding was off; cancelling the arrangements – and what about the dress? I'm keeping that, whether I ever wear it or not. I love it so much. And what about the ring? The ruby on her left hand. She'd have to give it back to Adrian, wouldn't she? What was the right thing to do? The magazines never mentioned the possibility of such an eventuality. Their business was happy marriages following perfect weddings. She wasn't going to be having anything like that in her life.

She had to tell Adrian before she talked to anyone else. But was it fair to do something like that when he was on his way to America? She didn't want to spoil his trip. She'd turned off her phone. By now there would be a few messages from him, she knew. Tomorrow, she thought. Time enough to listen to them then.

Perhaps, she told herself, as she lay down again and switched off the light, I can let Ma and Em know. Just them. I'd make sure they didn't say a word to anyone else, but at least I'd have someone to talk to. Then I can meet Adrian at the airport. Once he knows, it can all begin, the unravelling of everything that's been put together over the last nine months.

Sleep wouldn't come. Do I love Adrian? Zannah wondered. I must still love him a bit. What'll I miss about him? She tried to conjure up his face, his voice. She thought about getting up, finding her phone and listening to him in the dark, then decided not to. She closed her eyes. I'm so tired, she thought. The mess of emotion and anguish in her head subsided a little as her body relaxed, and as she drifted into sleep, an image of Cal came to her, touching her hair, touching her neck. Suddenly she was wide awake again. 'I wish I was still married to Cal,' she said, aloud, and felt worse than ever. She had no right, no right in the world, to wish such a thing. I'm going to forget I even thought it, she told herself. He's been so kind, but it was just kindness, wasn't it? Nothing more than that, surely? Kindness and shared memories of their past together. She turned over and buried her face in the pillow. Oh, God, she thought, *Cal*. Was he going to become another source of pain; something else to contend with, along with everything else?

Tuesday

'Are you sure you don't want a scone?' Joss pushed the plate across the kitchen table to where Zannah was sitting, nursing a mug of Earl Grey tea that had long ago gone cold.

Zannah shook her head. She'd hardly said a word since she arrived yesterday. She'd gone straight to bed and now it was nearly three o'clock. She'd slept for hours and hours.

'Exhausted.' Bob had made this dazzling statement of the obvious on his way out to the university. 'All the wedding stuff getting to her, I shouldn't wonder.'

At first when Zannah had phoned to say she was coming up to Altrincham for the rest of half-term, Joss hadn't known what to think. Adrian, she knew, had flown to America yesterday but Zannah was supposed to be going back to London with Isis. Clearly, the plan had changed. Joss was wary of asking anything in case Zannah clammed up, so she took her time over buttering a scone.

'Ma? Can I tell you something in private?'

Joss nodded.

'I'm not going to marry Adrian. I've decided.'

A pause. 'D'you want to talk about it?'

'Not really, but I will. It's ... Adrian wants to send Isis to boarding school, and any children we may have. I don't want to. I hate the whole idea.'

'Is that all it is? Can't you discuss it? Persuade him that you'd hate it? I'm sure he'd ... Zannah, up till a few days ago, you were madly in love with him. How can that have disappeared so quickly?'

'I don't know, Ma, and that's one reason I feel so awful. What sort of person am I if I can love a man one day and just, well, not love him the next? Do people do that? Fall out of love overnight? I may not love him, but I don't want him hurt and he will be and I'll be the one who's doing it . . . I don't know what to do.'

'I suppose if you can fall in love in a couple of minutes, then you can fall out just as quickly. But he'll be devastated, Zannah.'

'But I'll be devastated if I have to marry him, Ma! And I can't spend the rest of my life being unhappy just so that I can say I did the right thing. I've got to look after myself. And Isis. He's as good as told me he's not fond of Isis. I can't spend the rest of my life torn between the two of them. He's jealous of her. He said so. I can't marry him. But when I think of what everyone's going to say . . . I just can't face it, Ma. I'm so sorry. You've all . . . The money and the work! What's Charlotte going to say? And Maureen . . . I simply don't know where to begin. All those people to be notified . . . There's so much . . .' She put her head into her hands and groaned.

Joss stood up and went to sit on the chair next to her. She put an arm round Zannah's shoulders and squeezed her tight. 'Listen, darling, don't worry about anything, okay? You haven't told anyone else, have you?'

'Only Cal. And Em, of course.'

'Then wait. Stay here as long as you like and rest. You might feel different when you see Adrian again. When you've spoken to him, you'll know better what you want.'

'I can't do it over the phone. He keeps ringing and texting me but we don't say anything about, well, our quarrel. He tries to bring it up and I keep changing the subject. He wants to discuss serious matters and I say we'll deal with it when he returns. But now that I've thought about it, I know what I want and I can't have it. Oh, God, Ma, I've been so stupid! I want Cal and it's too late. I've divorced him and he's moved on and now . . . I feel like going to bed and never getting up again.'

'Don't say that, Zannah.'

'But it's true. That's what I feel.' She reached for a scone and picked it up and began nibbling it, not seeing it, not, Joss was quite sure, tasting it. 'Can I stay here with you and Pa for a few days? Cal's got to work, of course, but Granny Ford's happy to have Isis till the end of half-term. Em says she'll go and pick her up at the weekend.'

'Of course you can stay. We'll look after you.'

'Thanks, Ma. I'm going back to bed, okay?'

Joss stopped herself saying *but you've only just got up*. Instead she nodded and said nothing. This Zannah was one she hadn't seen for years: not since the breakdown after she and Cal split up. Would she be ill again? Not if I can help it, Joss thought.

Once Zannah had gone upstairs, Joss started to wash the coffee cups. Out of the window, she noticed that the camellia was dotted with buds showing pink, almost ready to open. The sun was struggling through a thick bank of grey cloud. It occurred to her that in breaking up with Adrian Zannah was showing strength of mind and determination. She could have compromised, Joss reflected, even to the extent of letting Isis go to boarding school. Many other women, perhaps equally reluctantly, allowed their children to be sent away. She had stopped loving Adrian, and Joss thought she knew why. She still loved Cal. She'd never got over him. Adrian was a kind of substitute. Had she ever loved him? Probably. But if she suddenly had no desire to marry him, how strong had it been all along? Maybe even Zannah didn't know.

Now here she was, ready to cancel the wedding she'd been longing for; ready to inconvenience all sorts of people – ready to risk the wrath of Maureen, which Joss knew would be something to see – in order to do what she felt she had to. That was brave, and it was also right. It would be wrong for her to marry Adrian if she didn't love him.

The contrast between Zannah's courage and her own spinelessness struck Joss with a force that made her stop what she was doing and take her hands out of the sink. She stood there, wondering whether she'd ever be capable of something like that: something that turned what everyone expected on its head. Her daughter wasn't exactly saying: *To hell with the lot of you, I'm doing what I have to do*, because Joss could see that this course of action was going to be hard for her. She hadn't even split up with Adrian yet, and you could see she was suffering; dreading the encounter, and with good reason. How did you tell someone you had loved yesterday that today you didn't love them any longer?

I couldn't do it, she thought, and went to fetch a tea-towel to dry her hands. If I told Bob the truth, if I said I was still in love with Gray, even though I haven't seen him for so long, what would happen? She had a sudden vision of all the separate pieces of her physical life: her dresser, her crockery, her clothes, her laptop, floating by on a swollen stream of muddy water that reminded her of the pictures on TV of the aftermath of those hurricanes in New Orleans and Texas last September. This house, their house, hers and Bob's, broken, the roof smashed in, glass splintered out of the windows, empty. It had been such a terrible year for natural disasters: hurricanes and then the earthquake in Pakistan. The entire world was there, right in front of you, every night, impossible to escape. You could click through the channels with your remote and share the suffering of the starving, the homeless, the bereft, the refugees: a whole planet's worth of misfortune that put what you were feeling into some perspective without making you any happier.

It was ridiculous to think like this. If I were to leave Bob, nothing would be broken. The life I've lived so far with him would disappear, that's all. He'd be . . . what would he be? The truth was that they spoke together in an intimate way so seldom that she had no real idea of how the loss of his wife would affect him. He'd be shocked; outraged, probably, and also hurt. He'd wonder what he'd done to deserve it. I can't do it to him, Joss thought. He's been good to me in many ways. He hasn't given me what I need and want, but that's not his fault. He has never really known what that was and that was partly my doing. Maybe I never made it clear enough what I needed. He's not a bad person, or a bad husband. He's done his best for me, always. I can't fling that back in his face. It's no fault of his that the right person, the man I love, and will always love is someone else and not him. Gray . . . .I promised the girls I'd never see him again and I'm not going to break my word.

Joss went to sit down at the kitchen table, where she picked up the newspaper and held it without reading it. Anyway, she reflected, there's nothing to say that Gray would want me even if I did leave Bob. He'd looked so happy sitting with his arm round Maureen, in that ghastly picture over Christmas, on Adrian's camera phone. How coupleish they'd seemed! He certainly wasn't pining. Probably he'd pushed her to the back of his mind so thoroughly that she'd become nothing more than Zannah's mother. What would he say when he discovered that Zannah had called off the wedding? There's something good that's come out of all this, she thought. I won't have to meet him and make polite conversation at the wedding. Thank God for small mercies.

*

It was midnight when Gray went to his study. Maureen was fast asleep. He'd sat in front of the television like a zombie, not watching something or other that she was keen to see. She'd been pleased that he was there because he so rarely kept her company on the sofa, and he'd felt vaguely guilty, but not guilty enough to concentrate properly on the kind of thing she enjoyed. Tonight someone in the silly play that had flashed across the screen had reminded him of Lydia and he'd spent the rest of the hour in fantasy, counting the minutes till Maureen disappeared into the bedroom and he could be alone.

He'd become like a stalker. Every day he put Lydia's name into Google and sometimes he was rewarded. A few nights ago, he'd come across a fact that had preoccupied him for days. She was giving a reading in London at the end of April. He had rung up and bought a ticket the very next morning and was now living for that day. He hadn't decided what to do. He could sit in the audience and disappear silently or perhaps . . . Would she see him if he came up to her afterwards and invited her for a coffee? Wondering about that took up far too much of his time. You're pathetic, he told himself. Like a schoolboy.

Under this teenage-crush behaviour, something more serious was going on. He'd made up his mind to leave Maureen; to ask her for a divorce. Since Christmas, he'd mentally moved out of the marriage. He simply couldn't go on pretending to be happy. Playacting. He was treating this house as though it were a comfortable hotel and Maureen had become no more to him than a competent housekeeper. It's not fair to her, he thought, and knew he was kidding himself. This wasn't to do with her but with him. With what he wanted, which was out of this house, out of this marriage and out of this town. I can leave everything: the hospital, my job . . . the whole of my life till now. I can find a job in London, he told himself, and when I go to the reading and see Lydia, I can say: *I've left her. I've asked for a divorce. I won't be married any longer. I'm leaving Guildford. I'm going to live in London*. When she saw how serious he was, surely she'd ask for a divorce as well and then they could be together. Wouldn't she? Of course she would. He'd persuade her. He sat in the darkened room, gazed unseeing at the glowing screen in front of him and lost himself in fantasies of how it would be when they were no longer apart. That's what stalkers do, he reflected. Pretend that someone loves them when in reality they don't give a shit. They were demented souls, who didn't recognize the truth when it smacked them in the face. Was that what he was like? Had she stopped loving him? Part of Gray, the rational part, had to admit that this was a possibility but he preferred to indulge the craziness that refused to allow the idea to enter his head.

Monday

Zannah stood at the barrier in Arrivals at Heathrow and wondered whether there was an ideal place to tell someone you had stopped loving them and no longer wanted to marry them. She'd discussed the problem with Emily for hours. Somewhere public, Em had suggested. That, she reckoned, would make it more inhibiting and you'd be less likely to throw things and scream and shout. Zannah hated the idea of other people being anywhere near her while she was doing something so private. A walk through the countryside? Not if you lived in London and the person you were meeting was jet-lagged. There was no alternative: he'd have to be brought back to his flat. Not her flat, because Zannah wanted to be able to leave: to be the one closing the door at the end of the conversation.

Would it be a conversation? A shouting match? She had no idea and was dreading it more than she'd ever dreaded anything in her life. When she'd discovered Cal's infidelity and told him their marriage was over, she'd been hurt, sad and tearful, but now she felt a paralysing mixture of guilt and anxiety that was wrecking her sleep. One of the worst, the most excruciating, things was how this situation made her feel about herself. What sort of person was she if she behaved like this? Surely only a worthless human being fell in love one day and then a few months later, simply stopped. Adrian didn't deserve a wife like that. Zannah hadn't realized that it was possible: that you could go from feeling nothing but passion for someone, to growing impatient with many things about them, and finally (after a very short time) to not loving them. She was shallow, and selfish and all the things that everyone would no doubt call her when she told them what she'd decided.

She thought of the letters she'd have to write to the wedding guests and shuddered. I'll worry about that when I have to, she thought. For the moment, there was the small matter of meeting Adrian and breaking the news. She'd managed to get the day off school by telling her head the truth. Thank God for a kind boss!

Emily had pointed out that it was unnecessary for Zannah to go to Heathrow now that she'd decided they were going back to the flat. Still, Zannah was waiting at the barrier. She'd promised Adrian on the phone that she'd be there and if she was going to disappoint him in the more important matter of their wedding, she had no intention of letting him down when it came to something so small and relatively easy to achieve. Also, the trip to Heathrow had distracted her. She'd had to concentrate on traffic and parking and getting to the right place in Arrivals, which took her mind off what was ahead of her.

There he was. He was waving at her and smiling and he looked so handsome. Zannah waved back and when he reached her, she allowed him to hug her, feeling sick and treacherous, and also acknowledging that she still fancied him like mad, and wanted him to kiss her. She didn't stop him, but allowed herself to kiss him back, perhaps with not as much abandon as she would normally have shown.

All the time they'd been walking to the car, the talk had been inconsequential. Meaningless. When they set off, with Zannah driving, Adrian kept chatting away about the flight, the food, the movies. He asked after his mother. Then he phoned her on his mobile and Zannah was relieved to hear him arranging to go down to Guildford on Saturday. He'll have the perfect person to talk to about how horrible I am, she thought. Maureen'll cheer him up. I'll have to speak to her before then, though. On the phone? In person? Would the head allow me another day off to go and see her? She probably won't want to see me.

'Mum says would you like to come down there on Saturday as well? It'd be great, wouldn't it? I've said I'll go down . . . Hope that's okay?'

Zannah nodded and searched her mind for what to tell Adrian . . . What bits of news could she offer in return for his scraps about New York and how great it was? He chattered on, then turned to her. 'You're very quiet, Zannah. Anything wrong?'

'No . . . Well . . .' Why couldn't she lie convincingly?

'Tell me.'

'At the flat. It's not the kind of thing you talk about when you're driving.'

'God, that sounds ominous. You're the boss. If it's okay with you, I'll just close my eyes. Still the middle of the night for me. Right?'

'Yes, fine.'

He fell asleep at once and Zannah drove on, rehearsing different ways of saying what she had to say.

Once they were in the flat, everything was a little easier. Adrian put down his cases and she went into the kitchen to put the kettle on. What would people do without tea at times like this? When she brought the tray out into the living room, he was sitting on the sofa.

'Can we have it at the table?' Zannah asked. She wanted to avoid the possibility that he'd put his arms round her. 'It's more convenient.'

'Okay. You seem most odd, Zannah. There's definitely something wrong.'

She pushed a cup across to him but he ignored it, and went on: 'I'm not blind, you know. You're unhappy.'

She removed the ruby ring she was wearing and slid it across the table towards him. He frowned and stared at it. 'What's this?'

'Your ring, Adrian. I'm giving it back.'

'Why on earth ...'

'Because. I can't marry you. I'm so sorry. I can't.'

She'd never seen Adrian lost for words before. He turned white, then red, and kept staring at the ring, then at her as though somehow, if he waited long enough, everything would become clearer. She had to say something. 'It's not you. It's me. I ... I've realized while you were away. I don't love you as I should. I mean, I love you, but not ... well, not enough to spend the rest of my life with you.'

He pushed the chair back and stood up. 'This is about Isis, isn't it? Just because I said what I did last time. If it weren't for that, everything would be fine, wouldn't it?'

Was he going to do it? Apologize? Say he'd never meant it? She and Em had gone over what Zannah might say in such a case.

'No,' said Zannah. 'I thought that was it, but it isn't. Not really. Of course Isis comes into it, but ... I've thought about it and I don't think it'd be fair to you. What I feel about you has changed. I don't love you in the same way that I did, Adrian. There's no good way to say this. I'm so sorry.'

He strode over to the window and turned round, shouting at her, 'It's no fucking use being sorry! You're nothing but a spoilt, selfish bitch. As long as everything's going your way it's all wonderful, but the minute someone wants to do something you disapprove of, that's it, you're off. No looking back. No regrets. Nothing. How about me? What am I supposed to do now?'

'I don't know.' Zannah sat at the table and wondered if he was right about her. Perhaps he was, but she couldn't do anything about it. She wasn't going to fall in with what he thought about Isis but even if she did, she'd already admitted to herself that she wanted still to be married to Cal and no amount of adapting herself to Adrian's desires would change that. Should she tell him? Would that make things better or worse? In the end, she decided to shut up and let him think whatever he wanted to about her. She said, 'I know your mother's worked fantastically hard on this wedding . . .'

'And spent a fortune. Don't forget that. What're you going to do about it?'

'I'll deal with it, okay? I'll pay back every penny. I'll speak to your mother.'

'Don't bother. I'll tell her. I'm going down on Saturday as you know.'

'That's days away, Adrian. I'll tell her. It's the least I can do.'

'Thanks for nothing. Over the phone, I presume?'

'I'll go and see her. I'll cope with everything.'

He went back to the sofa and flung himself on to it. 'What d'you expect me to do with that ring?'

'Take it back. It's yours.'

'No, I bought it for you. Keep it. I'm not interested in it.'

Zannah stared down at the ruby. She knew that if she kept it, she would never wear it. She said gently, 'Adrian, it cost you a lot of money. Perhaps you could get some of it back?'

'I don't want the bloody money – can't you understand? I want you and I can't have you so I'd rather not have anything to do with your ring or any other crap you think up, okay? It did cross my mind a second ago to beg you to marry me. To beg you to love me still, but that's pointless. You've made your mind up and you want nothing more to do with me, so as far as I'm concerned you can get stuffed. And I'll tell my mother. I'm going to drive down there right now. You can forget about seeing her. She won't want to speak to you. In fact, once she gets over the shock, she'll probably be quite grateful not to be getting involved with your relatives. She was never entirely happy about having what she called a con in the family, and when I tell her what you've done to me, she'll think she was entirely justified.'

'I'd better go.' Zannah stood up. 'Goodbye, Adrian.' What could she say to make things better? Nothing. Why wasn't there some form of words? She tried, 'I hope we can still be friends.'

'Oh, do me a favour, Zannah. Fuck off with your mealy-mouthed clichés and leave me alone.'

She left quickly, feeling ashamed, sick and relieved all at once. She walked quickly to her car. As she drove towards her flat, she was making a list in her head of who had to be told, what had to be done. Ma would want to come down and see her but she didn't want that . . . She'd only just emerged from a blanket of parental care in Altrincham and the last thing she needed now was someone else to take into account. No, she'd let her know on the phone and say she was absolutely fine. She started to go over the other repercussions, and wondered whether she could still turn round, go back to Adrian and tell him she'd been mad. He'd forgive her, she was sure, if she pleaded with him. They could still have it: the wedding, the flowers, the music, the heavenly food. The day they'd remember throughout their lives. She still wanted it. She longed for it. There must have been something wrong, she decided, with the whole relationship from the beginning if what I'm feeling sad about now is the wedding. Perhaps Adrian's right and I am selfish and spoilt. I must be completely unfeeling as well. How would Adrian manage? Would he be okay? I ought to care more than I do. Why aren't I crying? Am I completely heartless? Zannah knew it wasn't that. She'd done her thinking and her crying when she was up in Altrincham last week. Now, she needed every bit of her energy to deal with everyone she had to tell: Mrs Hayward, Maya, Charlotte, Ma, Pa, and Maureen too, because whatever Adrian said, she'd want to tear a strip off the woman who'd let her son down. I'm ready for her, Zannah thought. I've got to be strong from now on.

*

Cal was the first person she tried to reach. Of course he was out somewhere and all she heard when she rang his mobile was *'Leave a message and I'll get back to you.'* She said, 'Cal? It's me. I just wanted to let you know. The wedding's off. I've split up with Adrian. 'Bye.'

Emily was at work but Zannah reached her on her mobile. Before she'd had a chance to say a word, Emily said, 'You okay, Zan?'

'Fine. Can you talk?'

'Not really. Have you done it? How did he take it?'

'Not well, but better than I expected. He's going down to tell Maureen tonight. I'd better go. Got to phone Ma and Pa. I'll tell you the details tonight.'

'Okay. Sure you're all right? I can come home early, if you like. What about Isis?'

'She's going to Gemma's for a bit after school.'

'Right. See you later, then.'

''Bye.'

She'd just put the phone down when she heard the trilling of her mobile. Adrian. Texting her. Trying to get hold of her. Wanting her back. She fished the phone out of her handbag and looked at the display. It wasn't Adrian, it was Cal. She clicked on 'read'.

Don't cancel anything. Must talk to you. xx.

'I've sent for Graham, darling. He needs to know what's happened.' Maureen felt as though she and her son were the survivors of a natural disaster. She would never, she told herself, understand it as long as she lived. How could someone throw away the chance to be married to Adrian? She'd always had certain reservations about Zannah without knowing exactly what they were, but had put down her hesitation as the natural jealousy a mother felt about the woman who was about to marry her son. Now, however, it looked as though she'd been spot on. Zannah was nothing but a silly little bitch who gave herself airs, and she seemed to Maureen, now that she looked back, to have been ... What was the right word? Stand-offish. Superior. As though she felt she was better than you were. Snobbish. She was not the woman for Adrian. Maureen's duty now was to console her son and persuade him that he'd had a narrow escape, not a devastating loss. She said, 'You're being very brave but I can see it's a shock. I can't believe it. I really, truly can't. How could she throw away the chance of being married to you, that's what I can't understand.'

'She doesn't love me any longer.' Adrian was drinking his third gin and tonic. 'Shit happens.'

'She must be mad. Quite, quite mad.'

The moment she'd opened the door to her son, Maureen could see that he'd been hurt. She'd been right not to allow him to speak till he'd eaten and drunk something. Then it had all come pouring out: the treachery, the underhandedness, the sheer *cruelty* of that Zannah, who looked as though a strong wind would blow her away.

'I'll have to ring Genevieve in the morning. And Roland. Cancel the food and the cake. I'll lose the deposit, of course. What does she propose to do about that?'

'She did say she'd take care of the money stuff. She wanted to come down and see you.'

'I'm not interested in talking to her, thank you very much. Though I might email her. Or, better still, send her a letter with a piece of my mind enclosed, along with the bill. What's happened to the ring?'

'I've got it. I tried to get her to keep it, but she wouldn't.'

'I should think not. Take it back and see if they'll give you anything for it. I'm sure they will. Something, if not the whole lot.'

'Just let me get over it in my own way, Mum, okay? I loved Zannah. I'll need time to recover. She's hurt me.'

Maureen had to stop herself hugging him to her bosom as if he were still a small child. Instead she reached across the sofa cushions and squeezed his hand. 'Of course, darling. Of course you loved her. But you'll be all right. Really you will. You're so handsome. It won't be any time at all before you meet someone else. Someone much more suitable, I hope.'

'Hello,' said Graham, coming into the room. Maureen had been so absorbed with Adrian that she hadn't heard him. She sprang up at once.

'Oh, Graham, thank God you're back. It's off. The wedding's off. Can you believe that girl? I'm still dumbstruck. Poor Adrian. Look at him. Sit down and I'll pour you a drink and tell you about it. What did I say about that family? From the word go? Didn't I point out that no one else we knew had a relation who'd been to jail? Didn't I?'

'You did, Maureen,' Graham said and went to sit down on the chair opposite Adrian. 'But I think Adrian should tell me what's been going on, don't you?'

Adrian sighed and started his story all over again. Maureen only half listened to what he was saying. She began mentally making a list of the people she'd have to contact first thing tomorrow morning. Poor, poor Adrian. He might seem in control and grown up, but Maureen recognized the signs. The darling boy was in agony. Until he was quite recovered, he would be her priority.

Cal was sitting across the table from Zannah in a local Greek taverna he'd always been fond of, and which she privately thought was a bit rough and ready. He'd come round to the flat straight from work and invited her out for a meal. Emily was away for the night in Newcastle.

'I often have dinner in restaurants,' Cal said.

'Then you've changed.' Zannah smiled. 'You used to think going out to restaurants was a waste of time.'

'I still do, a bit. This is a special occasion, though. I want to say something.'

'Which you couldn't do at home?'

Cal shook his head. 'Didn't want Isis to know. Not at this stage.'

'Know what?'

He leaned forward and helped himself to more wine. Then he gazed straight into her eyes in a way that Zannah found disconcerting. He seemed not to know what to say next, which was strange for him. If it had been anyone else sitting opposite her, she'd have said he was nervous. What did Cal have to be nervous about? He said, 'I've been thinking, Zannah, and I want to ask you something, okay?'

As he spoke, he reached for her hand. Don't make too much of this, she told herself, trying to ignore the thrill that ran through her. What you're feeling is no more than ordinary pleasure at Cal's kindness. She knew this was a lie even as she was thinking it. She *was* thrilled. She couldn't help it. She still fancied him, but that was no reason to get carried away.

'Ask me whatever you like,' she said finally. He was being kind, because he knew how she'd be feeling after breaking up with Adrian.

He said, 'Will you marry me, Zannah?'

'What? What did you say?'

'I asked you to marry me.'

'Why?'

'What do you mean, *why*? Isn't it obvious?'

'No, Cal, it isn't. Not a bit obvious. You want to marry me?'

'I was married to you once, and I wish I still was. I've wished it for ages. I love you, Zannah.'

'Oh, Cal, why didn't you say?'

'You were with Adrian.'

'That was only in the last year . . .'

'I know. But that's . . .' He sighed and went on, 'It's been quite hard to live through, Zannah. I didn't say anything because, well, you'd made your mind up and I didn't want to spoil anything, but it's been tough seeing you so happy with him. I used to dread bringing Isis back because your face... You know what I mean.' For almost the first time since she'd known him, Zannah could see naked emotion in his eyes, the kind of emotion he'd always been at pains to cover up with a smile and a jokey remark. The shock made her catch her breath. She turned her hand in his, grasped his fingers and squeezed them tight.

'Go on, Cal . . . tell me,' she whispered, leaning towards him, near enough to smell his skin: a smell she'd have recognized in the dark, in a crowd of people.

'You were in love and it showed, and every time I saw it I wanted to obliterate it. Forget it at once. I couldn't . . . Shit, it sounds corny as hell but I couldn't stop dreaming about you. I thought I'd got over you but I hadn't. Not really. And all the time, as the wedding kept getting closer and closer I wished things could have been different.' He smiled at her. 'And now you've broken up with him. So I'm asking you to marry me again. Will you, Zannah?'

'Yes. Yes, I will.'

He was lost for words, Zannah could see. He looked down at the table, then raised himself a little from his chair and leaned over the space between them. He took her head between his hands and kissed her on the mouth. 'Darling Zannah,' he whispered while his lips were still on hers. She heard her name breathed softly into her mouth, and felt herself melting, dissolving.

Cal sat down again, and smiled at her. 'I've wasted hours imagining this. I have missed you … I've *missed* you so much, Zannah.'

'Me too,' Zannah said, as she sank back into her seat. 'I didn't know I *was* missing you but I was.'

'Really?'

'Yes, really. I can see I was now.'

'So …' He took a deep breath and grinned at her. 'Let's order pudding and I'll tell you something else.'

'Tell me you love me instead, Cal. Tell me again.'

'I love you, Zannah. I love you all there is.'

'And I don't think I've ever stopped loving you. Not deep down. I'm so sorry, Cal. I could have …'

'Never mind that. I want to talk about the wedding. The one you arranged with Adrian.'

'I'll have to cancel everything now. Maureen'll deal with the catering but the rest … I've got to do that.'

'No, you must keep the whole thing exactly as you planned it. I'll fit in with that.'

'With a marquee and flowers and a church ceremony and a traditional wedding dress and bridesmaids? You cannot be serious?'

Cal nodded. 'I am. I'm especially keen on the bridesmaids. Isis says the whole day will be, like, soooo wicked. Her exact words. As far as I can make out, what we've got to do is uninvite Adrian's friends, invite mine instead and find some food from somewhere at quite short notice. And I'll have to hire a proper suit. Piece of cake. Piece of wedding cake.'

Zannah laughed. 'God, Cal, you've always hated that sort of thing. You really must love me.'

'Oh, Zannah, you have no idea how much.' That look was back, the burning gaze she'd seen before. Then he grinned at her, suddenly back to his normal self. 'Right, where's that waiter? Let's see if we can get hold of some baklava. And a bottle of champagne.'

'Daddy, what're you doing? Why are you and Mummy cuddling like that?'

'Isis?' Zannah sprang out of Cal's arms. After the champagne, they had made their way home and relieved Louise, who'd been babysitting.

Now she and Cal were on the sofa, giggling and kissing like teenagers. They were nearly at the stage where . . . well, she was grateful that this interruption was happening now and not later. She patted her hair and tried to sound as though she had control of her breath. 'What're you doing up, Isis? You went to bed ages ago.'

'I had a bad dream. I'm sorry. Daddy, you're still here . . . why haven't you gone home?'

Zannah watched as Cal went over to Isis, who was standing on the stairs. She was carrying one of the toys that had lived on her bed since she was a baby: a pink rabbit that used to be furry but was now totally bald and missing one of its ears. She looked half asleep. He picked her up and brought her over to the sofa. He said, 'We've been talking.'

'It didn't look like talking. It was snogging. I've seen snogging. Mummy does it with Adrian sometimes.'

Zannah sat forward and said, 'Isis? Are you properly awake? Can you listen carefully while I tell you something?'

'Something bad?'

'No . . .' Zannah made a face at Cal over Isis's head and he went on.

'Mummy and Adrian have broken up, Isis. They're not going to be married after all.'

'But what about the wedding? Won't I be a bridesmaid? I wanted to so much. And what about Gemma?'

Zannah almost laughed. Nice to know that Isis had her priorities absolutely clear. She said, 'No, there's going to be a wedding. I won't be marrying Adrian, but you'll still be a bridesmaid. Gemma too.'

'Good.' That seemed to satisfy her until suddenly, as though the thought had only just occurred to her, she said, 'But there's no one to marry, Mummy, if you've split up with Adrian.'

'What about me?' Cal touched Isis on the shoulder, to attract her attention. 'Have you forgotten about me?'

'But . . . you and Mummy split up as well, ages ago. I don't understand. What about Adrian? Who's he going to marry?'

'I don't know about Adrian but your mother's going to marry me again, Isis. We're all going to live together. What d'you think of that?'

Isis looked from Zannah to Cal, then back to Zannah. Her face changed. Her lips began to tremble and soon she was sobbing. She flung herself into Cal's arms.

'Icey, why are you crying? What's the matter?'

Isis pulled away from him and wiped her eyes and nose on the sleeve of her nightie. 'Is it true? Mummy? Daddy? Are you really . . . ? She struggled to speak through her tears. 'Will you come and live here, Daddy? With us?'

'For a bit, I suppose, after the wedding. We'll have to find a house somewhere in the end. But we can think about stuff like that later.'

Zannah said, 'Are you ready to go back to bed? Will you sleep better now?'

'Can I have a drink?' said Isis. 'And a biscuit?'

'Why not?' Cal said. 'We should celebrate. Apple juice and chocolate Hobnobs all round.'

As Cal and Isis went out to the kitchen, Zannah leaned back against the cushions and closed her eyes. Isis is properly happy, she thought. She hasn't been like this all the time I've been with Adrian. She sighed, because there he was, in her mind again, and she had no desire to think about him at this moment when she felt as though her life was suddenly, wonderfully, starting all over again. She, too, like Isis, was happy. The fears she'd had about the rightness of leaving Adrian were gone. Vanished into thin air. Still, a part of her shrank when she thought of what Maureen might be saying to her son at this very moment.

'She's asleep,' Cal said, coming to sit down on the sofa again. 'What did I do with my shoes, Zannah? It's late, isn't it? I ought to go home.'

Zannah watched as he peered down at the carpet. 'They're by the door, Cal, but you shouldn't drive. We've had too much to drink. You can stay the night.'

He sat up and looked at her, saying nothing. Then he took her hand and held it, running a thumb over her palm, raising a kind of delicious gooseflesh on her arms. What would he do? What would he say? I want him not to go, she realized. I want him near me tonight. I want . . .

'Are you sure?' Cal interrupted her thoughts. Zannah stood up and went to the foot of the stairs. Cal came to stand beside her. He put his arms round her and whispered in her ear, 'What about Isis?'

'Fast asleep,' Zannah whispered the words against his lips. 'She won't wake up.'

'What about the morning?'

'What about it? It'll be fine . . . You're her dad.'

'I've got to get going early anyway.' Cal sounded short of breath, as though he'd been running. His hands were inside her blouse, caressing her back, and he was kissing the hollows at the base of her throat. We're wasting time, Zannah thought. His fingers had found the fastening of her bra. 'Let's go up, Zannah,' he murmured.

They stumbled together up the stairs to her bedroom. As soon as the door shut behind them, they moved towards the bed and Zannah sighed with pleasure. She lay on her back and the soft puffiness of the duvet rose up round her. She closed her eyes and let Cal kiss her, and gradually her skin, her flesh, began to remember how it used to be. How it was going to be from now on. She wrapped her arms round him and he buried his face in her long hair and whispered her name, over and over again.

Sunday

Gray lay in bed, aware of Maureen still sleeping beside him. When he had been a more junior member of the hospital hierarchy, he'd been full of admiration for those doctors or surgeons who routinely broke the worst sort of news to the loved ones of their patients. Telling someone that their child had died; their parent, their sibling, their spouse – how did they do it? Where did they find the words? More recently, there had been a couple of occasions when, distraught with grief, someone who'd been recently bereaved had asked to see him, trying to find out the answer to impossible questions like *why* and *how*. He'd always tried to concentrate on explaining the scientific detail as plainly and kindly as he could. If relatives knew precisely what had happened on the operating table, that was something. Very often a death was no one's fault. His words were not a consolation, but at least they were the truth. He dreaded facing anyone who was still raw with grief, whose eyes were red from crying, who was teetering constantly on the verge of hysteria, but he did it when it needed to be done.

And now this: he had to ask Maureen for a divorce. He'd been putting it off for some time and had tried to tell her on a couple of occasions before without success. It wasn't really comparable to breaking the news of a death. Divorce, though it was hard, was far less of a trauma than bereavement, wasn't it? Particularly for someone of Maureen's temperament. She was an optimistic person and had a good opinion of herself. She was confident and efficient: not a candidate, surely for pining? Even though he'd decided on this course of action long ago, the reality was hard. They'd been together for so many years and had so much shared history that the break would be painful. He, too would have regrets, but he loved Lydia and that was the difference. He had the hope that one day they would be together. Maureen would be alone. She would keep the house.

He had agreed, without saying a word to Maureen, to take up a job at the Whittington Hospital in London and intended to give in his notice as soon as he'd done this . . . broken up his life with his wife. Then he would find somewhere to live. He'd already looked up a few estate agents on the Internet. There was this advantage to leaving Guildford, too: he wouldn't risk bumping into Maureen in the street or at parties given by their friends. Her friends. Gray was sure of one thing: most of their friends would become hers. She'd been the one who cultivated people, invited them to parties and meals and they'd support her in the face of what would undoubtedly be seen as his treachery. He couldn't blame them, but he wouldn't miss them. He was pretty sure his colleagues wouldn't react like that. Several had married for a second time and they wouldn't cast him into the outer darkness, even though they might regret the fact that he was moving to another hospital.

She'll have all the money she needs, he thought. I'll see to that. Adrian'll be there to comfort her. The fact that the two of them were going to Barbados on the honeymoon tickets was a bit of luck. In a few weeks, Maureen would be lying in the sun. Gray thought that the sudden, unexpected announcement that Adrian and Zannah wouldn't be getting married after all was a good thing. He wasn't certain how it would affect his plans with Lydia, but surely it ought to make matters easier. They wouldn't be related. They'd be unattached to anyone else, or to any other problems, and able to be together, alone, in a much more satisfactory way. The separation would be more . . . well, more separate. He imagined Maureen recovering quickly from their divorce, getting to know other people, branching out in all sorts of directions, but he realized that this was probably wishful thinking. She'd be hurt, and he was the one who'd be hurting her. He couldn't put it off much longer. I'll tell her at breakfast, he decided. That'll give us the whole day together if she needs to talk to me. Or I can go out if she wants to be alone. Yes, breakfast. He brought to mind again his colleagues, or policemen, or priests breaking bad news. There was only one way to do it: simply and quickly with no hesitation. He'd look her straight in the eye and speak.

Gray slipped out of bed and went to have a shower. As the water poured over his head, he rehearsed what he'd say and everything sounded wrong. Well, it would come to him. He felt uncertain and jittery. Go on, he told himself. Say it. You're terrified. This is what stage-fright must be like. I've got to get it over with. Soon.

When he came into the kitchen, the sun was shining on to the table. We could, he thought as he sat down, be in a Sunday supplement as an advertisement for domestic bliss. Maureen was taking the croissants they always had at weekends out of the oven. She knew it was 'heart-attack food', but was also a great believer in a little bit of what you fancied doing you no harm.

'Maureen?' Gray said tentatively.

'What's the matter?' She must have caught something in his tone, though he was sure he'd sounded perfectly normal. She sat down opposite him and made no move to help herself to anything. 'What's wrong?'

'I have to say this, Maureen. I've thought for days about how to do this and there's no other way. I've got to … I'm in love with someone else. I want … I'm asking you to give me a divorce. I'm so sorry.'

Maureen laughed. There was no mirth in the sound. It was a high-pitched, rather hysterical screech. She said nothing and just sat there, staring at him. Gray could see the colour draining from her face and reached over to take her hand. She pulled it away at once. 'How dare you?' she hissed. 'How dare you say such things and then do that? Take my hand like that? Don't touch me. Don't ever touch me again. Are you waiting for me to cry so you can put your arms round me and make yourself feel better? Well, I'm not going to. I wouldn't give you the satisfaction, you bastard. You're a complete bastard.' Her voice shook a little as it rose into a shout. She was leaning across the table now, red in the face and yelling at him. 'A complete fucking *SHIT*! How can you sit there and just *TELL ME* such a thing? How can you? Who is it? Go on. Who is it? Is it someone I know? A nurse? Is she younger than me? Prettier? Better in bed? What does she let you do? Are you going to tell me? No, don't. I don't want to know. But who is it? You've got to tell me that.'

'Maureen, please …'

'Shut up! Shut up and don't you dare tell me to be calm. I don't want to be calm. I want to kill you. Who is it?'

'You won't like it.'

'Oh, I see. You've chosen the one person I'd object to and anyone else would have been just fine? Is that it? You're mad. You must be mad.'

'It's Ly ... Joss Gratrix.'

Maureen gave a cry like someone being stabbed. A cry halfway between a moan and a shriek. Then she put her head down on the table and started to sob. Her hands ... she was flailing about with her hands and the plate of croissants crashed on to the floor. Gray tried to keep his voice even. 'I met her at Fairford Hall, on a poetry course, long before Adrian got engaged to Zannah. We ... we tried ... but ...'

Maureen looked up. 'What if those two had got married? Had you thought of that?'

'We've thought of little else since the engagement party last year.'

'You've been screwing her all that time? While I ... You ... you ... I haven't got a word that's strong enough.'

'No ... no, that's not how it is, Maureen. I promise you. I haven't ... I mean, I haven't even seen her or spoken to her since November. She ... I'm not doing this very well. She doesn't know about this. It's actually not to do with her, or not really.'

'Crap! You expect me to believe that? You're a fool as well as a bastard. I bet you've been seeing her all the time.'

'I haven't. I swear. Why would I lie to you?'

'Then what's the rush to leave me? Why, if you're not even fucking her at the moment?'

'I think she'll agree to see me again if I'm not married. And, Maureen, I mean it when I say it's not all about Lydia ... I mean Joss. I feel it's not fair to you to stay with you when I'm in love with someone else. That's all.'

'Well, that's hunky-dory for you, then, isn't it? Never mind about Adrian. Never mind about me and the hours and hours I've put in over the last few months arranging the bloody wedding. If it'd been left to Joss Gratrix, her daughter wouldn't have had a wedding at all. That cow's about as much use as a chocolate teapot.'

'Don't say that, Maureen ... it's not like you. You're upset ...'

'It *is* like me and I am upset! I've got every right to be. I told you when Zannah threw Adrian away like a used Kleenex that there was something wrong with that family. The aunt spending time in jail, and even now living with someone who stuck a knife into her husband. I knew nothing good would come of it, but I never said a word because poor Adrian was so much in love. They're all completely horrible. I've got a bloody good mind to pick up the telephone and speak to Bob, or whatever his name is, and wipe the smile off their faces once and for all. Does he know you've been fucking his wife?'

A white mist of rage rose in front of Gray's eyes, obscured his vision. He grabbed Maureen's wrist and she cried out. 'Leave me alone, you bastard. You're hurting me.'

'If you so much as *whisper* a word to anyone in that family, Maureen, I swear you'll live to regret it. I mean to make sure you won't lose out financially in this divorce. This house. I intend to put it in your name at once, but if you start making mischief, well, it's going on the market and we'll divide the proceeds. D'you understand what I'm saying?'

'Only too well, thank you. You've tied my hands there, I see. Never mind. That whole family can go to hell, for all I care. I'm not wasting my time with any of them ever again. You can relax. I shan't mess up your sordid little affair. That's what it is, you know, a hole-in-corner, shabby, sordid, *disgusting* little affair. I expect you think of it as a grand, romantic passion, don't you? Typical!'

Maureen stood up and began to gather the croissants off the floor and on to a plate. She went to the silver bin in the corner and swept them into the rubbish. Then she held the plate crushed against her chest and started to weep. Gray struggled to understand what he was feeling: a peculiar mixture of anger (wanting to hit her, shut her up) and regret over what they'd had that had disappeared. Worse, what they'd had that he'd destroyed, all by himself. Madly, he wondered if there was any way he could go back, undo everything, say he didn't mean it, but then he remembered what he'd decided and knew it was right. The guilt he was feeling was natural after so many years but he couldn't let it change what he knew he wanted to do. He *had* to leave her. He looked at her, about to say something gentle, something conciliatory and as he met her eyes, he flinched at the fury he saw in them.

'That's it,' she said. 'That's what I feel like. Like rubbish. Fine as long as you want me and then chucked out. Pushed into the bin. I don't want to look at you, Graham. Leave now. At once. I'll get your stuff packed up. Tell me an address too, or I'll send every one of your possessions to that bitch. Mrs Butter-wouldn't-melt. Wispy little Joss who writes those oh-so-exquisite poems and wouldn't hurt a soul but didn't mind a bit fucking someone else's husband. I don't want to see you again. And you can find yourself a lawyer because I'm phoning Mr. Bartram as soon as I hear your car going down the drive. Go. Go on! Go and don't come back.'

Her voice was rising, moving towards hysteria. As he left the room, the plate she'd been holding flew past his head and crashed to the floor where it shattered into pieces. It could be worse, he told himself. I'm glad she's filled with anger and not grief. I'm glad she's chucking plates at me. He'd got off rather more lightly than he'd feared. Maureen would calm down. Mr Bartram, their supremely soothing and clever lawyer, would help her. She'd start demanding money, setting conditions. She'll be okay, he thought. She's going to get over this. He went upstairs slowly, looking around him at the house he'd taken for granted for so long. It was beautiful. She'd made it what it was and he'd scarcely noticed. A pang of regret for all the days and nights: for the life he and Maureen had lived together came over him. He felt as though he'd pulled the plug on a huge mass of water which was now swirling down the drain. He couldn't stop it. It was too late now and in a moment of panic he wondered, Am I doing the right thing? Will Lydia want me? He sat down on the top step, just outside his study, and took deep breaths to steady himself. He needed to pack. And leave.

April / May

Tuesday

This time next week he'd be on his way to the South Bank for Lydia's poetry reading. Where had the time gone? Gray walked over to the window and gazed at Highgate Wood. The young man from the estate agents who'd brought him to look at this apartment had been surprisingly tactful and allowed him to walk round it on his own.

In the weeks since he and Maureen had split up, ever since he'd walked out of their house in Guildford, he'd been trying to imagine where he and Lydia might live and this was it, exactly. His job at the Whittington Hospital, though perhaps not as satisfactory as the one he'd left, was fine for the moment. He'd been surprised by how sad he'd been to leave his old hospital, and saying goodbye to his colleagues had been harder in many ways than walking out on Maureen. What did that say about the quality of his marriage? This street was perfect: elegant stuccoed houses, painted white, neat front gardens full of hydrangeas and azaleas and now, in late April, lilac beginning to blossom behind low walls. He saw happy children emerging from sparkling cars in the care of mothers who seemed glossy and prosperous, like the women you saw in advertisements.

The apartment was on three levels, almost as though these rooms were part of a house. Gray had liked it at once. He walked in through the front door, and there was a small bedroom on his left. Then up the stairs to the bathroom (lovely; newly decorated) and the kitchen; up more stairs to the half-landing and then up again to the big bedroom and the surprisingly large and high-ceilinged living room. Best of all was the small but elegant roof terrace that faced south and which he knew Joss would love better than all the other features of the property.

Gray suppressed an impulse to say, 'I'll take it ... Please wrap it up for me,' to the young estate agent. The golden parquet floor was so smooth he wanted to stroke it.

He went to find the young man. 'Can we go back to your office? I want to make an offer.'

'Fantastic,' he said, practically bouncing with suppressed excitement. 'That's great.'

As they left the building and walked out into the spring sunshine, Gray imagined Lydia in that bedroom; that living room. Looking out of that window. What if she hates it? The thought crossed his mind and he dismissed it. She'll love it, he thought. I know she will. And anyway, she might not even want to cross the threshold. This place is mine. I'm the one who's got to live here, so I'm the one who has to be happy with it. And I am. More than happy.

Isis was thrilled to discover that there was such a thing as magic after all. She didn't tell anyone about it, but it had to be true. She'd been wishing for her mother and father to get back together again for ages and ages and now they were going to and it was the best thing that had ever happened in her life. It was better than all her birthdays, Christmases, parties and outings rolled up together. And, best of all, there was still going to be a wedding and she was still going to be a bridesmaid. Dad was going to join in. He did a lot of grumbling about it, but he was doing it anyway to please her and Mum. He groaned every time anyone mentioned how funny it would be to see him in a proper suit with tails and a flower in his buttonhole and everything. Even Em had laughed at that, when Mum and Dad told her about the wedding.

Isis couldn't understand why Dad didn't come and live in Mum's flat now but he didn't want to. They were going to find a house with a garden and, once they were settled in, Isis had made up her mind that she would ask for a kitten. Or maybe two kittens, so that they'd be company for one another. She'd even decided on their names: Holly and Mimi. Now Mum and Em were washing up and Dad was phoning someone called Mattie in New York to see if he would fly over to be the best man.

'It's a long way to come,' Isis said, 'just to go to a wedding. Don't you know anyone who lives here?'

'Lots,' Dad said, 'but Mattie and I were at primary school together and he was my best man last time your mother and I went through this process. I think he'd be hurt if I swapped him for someone else, don't you? Now, just hang on a mo while I try to get him on the phone.'

Isis went to lie down on the sofa and tried to get lost in her book, but there were too many things to think about. Next week they were going to Miss Hayward's again, to see how she was getting on with the dresses. Gemma was coming too. Then the person Mum and Dad called the Rev. Geoff, who was the vicar at the church, wanted to show everyone what they had to do during the service. Mum and Dad had to talk to the organist as well.

When Dad put the phone down, he was smiling. 'Want to hear what Mattie said about the best man thing?'

'Go on, then.'

'He said he'd be thrilled to bits. He kept going on and on about me coming to my senses at last. Sends you a big hug, Zannah, and says he can't wait to see you. He's going to come over a couple of days early, too. Good, eh?'

'Cool,' Isis said, and went back to her book.

The doorbell rang then and Em went to see who it was. A man came into the room and she introduced him to everyone. 'This is Alex Rivera,' she said. 'He's the *best* photographer. Come and sit down, Alex. This is Zannah and Cal. And that's Isis, my niece.'

'And probably a bridesmaid. Right?'

Isis nodded. She liked this man. Em had been telling them about him for days. She'd met him on a fashion shoot and told him about the wedding and she'd gone on and on at Mum, nagging her to choose him to take pictures of everything. He wasn't handsome but he had a nice face. He was very tall and his clothes were quite messy. His jacket had pockets that were bulging with stuff he'd shoved into them and his socks didn't match. Mum was looking a bit doubtful. Em and Dad thought he was okay, you could see. Alex took a sip of coffee from his cup, and spilt some on the saucer when he put it down, then took a big album out of a rucksack he'd brought with him.

'Can I come and see, too?' Isis asked, and Dad pulled her on to his lap because all the chairs were taken.

He whispered in her ear. 'No talking, right? Alex is going to explain what he does.'

'Well,' said Alex. 'I don't do posed wedding photos, everyone lined up in the traditional way. What I like is to be there the whole day, if that's okay with you, from the very early morning. Like this.'

He pushed the album towards Mum. Isis peered over to see it too. Lots of the photographs were black and white, or sort of brownish, but there were some in colour as well. Lots of the pictures had no people in them but were of things like bouquets lying on chairs. Veils and tiaras. Dressing-tables with makeup on them. Pretty shoes and big white dresses hanging on the backs of doors or peeping out of cupboards. The bride having her hair done. Lots of photos of couples coming out of church, dancing, eating, being happy. The groom kissing the bride. The bride with her parents. The bride and groom with both sets of parents, but just chatting, not standing in a row. People smiling. Loads of flowers. A few bridesmaids sitting on the grass with baskets on their laps. Or sitting on window-seats. Isis particularly liked the look of those.

'They're beautiful, Alex. Em, you were quite right.' Mum was smiling now. 'I'd love it if you could take photos at our wedding.'

'Thanks. That'll be great. I'll put the date in my diary. I'll even come beforehand and take some shots of other stuff, if you'd like that ... fittings, rehearsals. Just say the word.'

Mum said, 'I wouldn't mind a photograph of Miss Hayward. She's making my dress. And Maya who does the flowers ... the church being decorated.'

'Okay,' said Alex. 'Just give me their details and I'll sort it with them. I should say that I'm good at being unobtrusive on these occasions. You'll forget I'm there, honestly. Everyone does.'

Mum, Em and Dad laughed at that, and Dad said, 'Aren't you a bit tall to blend in?'

'I melt into the background, believe me. After the first few minutes, no one gives me a second thought.'

Isis left her father's lap and went to have another look at the pictures of bridesmaids. Their dresses weren't as nice as hers was going to be.

'Zannah's quite determined,' said Charlotte. 'No presents on display. I think she's right about that too. Most of the presents aren't the kind of thing that goes on tables anyway. Bob and Joss have bought them a beautiful new computer. And Mrs Ford has apparently arranged a trip to Disneyworld at Christmas. That sort of thing. There are, it seems, a great many vouchers coming in and they'll enjoy spending those once they've found a house. It saves us a lot of trouble too, finding a table and a place to put it. It's also . . . Well, why would you want people looking at vases and towels and whatever else anyone's thought to give you?'

'I suppose so,' Edie said. 'Though I do like that scene in *High Society* where they dance round the gift table singing "Who Wants to be a Millionaire?" But of course, they had silver coffee pots and gold-plated soup tureens and what have you on their table. Celeste Holm. That was her name. The woman who was dancing about with Frank Sinatra.'

Edie smiled at the memory.

'Do you think,' Charlotte asked, interrupting her fantasy, 'we ought to have named places for everyone, or just set out the tables and allow people to find their own seats when they've helped themselves to the buffet? Not counting the top table which seats twelve, there'll be six tables for eight.' She thought for a moment and went on, as though she hadn't asked Edie's advice, 'Yes, I think I'll consult with Zannah and Cal and make a plan . . . We can have it displayed at the entrance to the marquee. That'll prevent any scrabbling around and they'll both know who'd go well with whom. The family of course at the top table: Cal and Zannah, Bob and Joss, Em, Isis and Gemma, Mrs Ford and Mattie, the best man. And, of course, the three of us.'

'Do you mean me and Val, too? We're not really family, Charlotte.'

'Zannah insists. She says you're like fairy godmothers, so you count. And of course I agree.'

'I'm very touched, I must say. Val will be thrilled to bits, too. I must thank Zannah for her kindness.'

'By the way, I've spoken to Mr Marquee,' said Charlotte. That was what they all called Stan Merryweather, whose firm's motto was: *Merry Marquees Whatever the Weather*. He was as jovial as his name suggested: a great barrel of a man who'd loomed over them when he came to look at the garden and who threatened the safety of their china by his very presence in the kitchen.

'He says a slightly smaller tent's not a problem. And apparently Zannah's found a caterer who's willing to do a buffet in time. It'll cost a little less than Maureen was spending, but of course she's had to pay the deposit money back. Still, we should manage.'

Edie said, 'Now, Charlotte, please listen. Val and I have been discussing this. We haven't given Zannah and Cal a proper wedding present yet. Wouldn't paying for the buffet be more sensible than another set of cutlery or some towels? That includes, of course, the cake. In fact, I've been speaking to someone who's happy to make one for four hundred pounds. What d'you think?'

'That's much too kind of you, Edie. I can't allow you to spend all that money. Really ... perhaps just the cake? How about that?'

'No, Charlotte, we've worked it out. We'll afford it. Just living here with you saves us each a great deal of money, you know. Please allow us to do it ... we really want to. I've got the name of the caterer that Maureen was going to use. She'd cancelled of course, so Genevieve was relieved to hear from me, I can tell you. And don't forget, we're down to sixty people ... Maureen wanted over a hundred I believe. Incidentally, Val said the garden would cope much better with that number. Any more and she reckons her best effects might be overlooked.'

'She's only saying so because that's how many are coming. If we had more, she'd have been perfectly happy with that. You know Val.'

They laughed and Charlotte said, 'That's really wonderful of you both. And you can tell Zannah yourselves tomorrow. She's coming to the church to talk to the vicar. They'll be going through the order of service and the music.'

'Excellent,' said Edie. 'I'll let Val know at once. She'll be so pleased.'

Tuesday

It was astonishing to Joss that winning a prize could make such a difference to the kind of reading you were asked to do. For years she'd been going to back rooms in libraries or chilly church halls, and sometimes to schools, trying to enthuse audiences of twenty people at most, but more often groups of six or eight. Now here she was, in a proper small theatre with what seemed like crowds sitting in rows in front of her. The Madrigal Prize was the draw. Everyone was curious to see who had won, and whether she'd deserved it. Increasingly Joss felt that she probably hadn't. She'd written nothing for months: not since her last meeting with Gray. She felt as though there were words, thousands of them, banked up behind a wall, but whenever she tried to hammer her way through to reach them, her brain seized up entirely. Her head felt as though it were full of sand.

She'd not said a word to anyone about this occasion. There was enough to worry about without having her family there in force to see her so exposed. She'd accepted the offer of a hotel room from the organizers and already she was wishing she could be there, watching television by herself, enjoying the toiletries and the fluffy white towels in a bathroom that was luxurious mainly because it wasn't in her own house.

Now her mouth was suddenly dry and she took a sip of the water the organizers had provided. For the last few days, she'd been working out what she was going to read, fretting that anyone who'd already bought *The Shipwreck Café* would come away disappointed. She'd found some early poems and, of course, Russell Blythe was on the platform with her and he'd amuse everyone. Then, perhaps, they wouldn't notice her shortcomings.

She'd opted to go first. The chairperson, a plump, jolly woman called Mona, who wore Edna Everage glasses, was doing the introduction. Saying nice things about the collection, the Madrigal, about her. Joss couldn't see the audience because the spotlight was shining on to the stage. Was she sweating? Would her voice work? She thought of Gray and pretended he was there, sitting in the audience. He'd given her a piece of advice once, when she'd confessed how nervous she became, faced with strangers waiting for her to speak. 'Find a spot at the back of the hall and pretend I'm there. Talk to me.'

Joss stood up and smiled. That was another trick. You had to look as though you were enjoying yourself, even if you felt like dying of embarrassment. She opened her mouth, and for the next fifteen minutes lost all sense of everything except the words on the page; getting them out coherently; addressing the spot at the back of the theatre where the imaginary Gray was sitting. The next thing she was aware of was applause. She sank back into her chair, relieved and suddenly exhausted.

After the reading, the house lights went on and Joss and Russell took their places behind the table. Astonishingly, a line of people were clutching books, waiting to have them signed. She bent her head and wrote her name in each copy that was put in front of her. After a while, Joss realized that the words *Lydia Quentin* had become meaningless to her and she had to concentrate hard to remember that that was what she had to write, over and over again.

'Lydia?'

'Gray ...' It couldn't be! What was he doing here? What could she say? Her heart lurched and thumped and she felt hot and cold, and had no idea what she might do next. Should she get up and run away? No, how would that look to Russell and Mona?

'I was wondering if you had time for a coffee? It's been so long ...'

'Well ...' No. She didn't want coffee. She wanted to be somewhere else altogether. Somewhere far away. 'Okay. Just a quick one.'

'There's a café just opposite. We could go there.'

'I ... I'll be finished in a moment. I'll come over and find you.'

'Right.'

She watched him leave the auditorium. I don't have to go, she thought. I could slip out of the back and disappear. She stood up and said to the others: ' I'm going now, if that's all right. I've promised to have coffee with ... an old friend. You remember Graham Ashton, don't you, Russell? From our course in September?'

'Of course. I was going to tell you he was here. Quite forgot. I had a drink with him before we came in ... nice chap.'

She went through the goodbyes and thank-yous and promises to keep in touch and congratulations on selling so many books, and felt as though she were watching herself from somewhere near the ceiling. Most of her attention was on Gray. She'd forgotten what his physical self was like. She'd made him into a sort of benevolent ghost, a visitor to her imagination and her dreams, but there he had been, in front of her, his hands on the table. His smile. Had she imagined it or had she really smelt him? No, that was impossible. He'd been too far away. All she knew was that her feelings for him hadn't grown weaker with the passage of time. She'd been telling herself she was over him. She'd almost convinced herself that forgetting about him was an option and now here they were again. She sighed and left the theatre. The road in front of the café felt like a dangerous border she was crossing.

He was sitting at a table near the back. As she approached, he stood up.

'Hello,' he said, clearly not knowing what to do: should he hug her, shake her hand? In the end, he said, 'I expect you're hungry. I'll go and get us some food. What would you like?'

'Anything. Really. You choose. A panini sandwich or something ... and coffee.'

She watched as he chose the food from the display on the counter and brought it over to their table. Then he put the tray back on the stack, and came to sit down again. He said, 'Lydia, before I say anything else, I just want you to know how sorry I am about the wedding being cancelled. I know Zannah was set on the occasion, and even though she's the one who broke it off, I really do sympathise with how she must be feeling.'

'How's Adrian taking it? Is he okay?'

'He's sore, but he'll be all right, I'm sure. Maureen's going to Barbados with him on the honeymoon tickets.'

'That's a good idea. But you're out of date, Gray. The wedding's going ahead as planned.'

'Really? That's impossible, surely?'

'Cal's asked Zannah to marry him again. It's like something in a movie.'

'Did Adrian know about that when they split up?'

Joss smiled. As long as they were talking about Zannah and Adrian she was okay. She wouldn't say anything wrong. 'No, he didn't. I think she must have told him now, though. She had no idea that was in Cal's mind when she and Adrian broke up. None at all. She'd simply decided she didn't love Adrian enough to marry him. I reckon it was brave of her to admit she'd made a mistake.'

'That's not how Maureen sees it. She feels Adrian's had a lucky escape from a girl – and a family – who were nowhere near good enough for him. Her words not mine.'

Joss looked down at her plate in embarrassment. 'I know she must feel terrible. I did too, when Zannah first told me. I . . . I had nothing against Adrian, Gray, but I can't pretend I'm not pleased that she and Cal are getting back together. I'm sorry.'

'No need to be.'

Silence fell between them. What should she say now? Would he speak first? He took a sip of his coffee. He said, 'I've rehearsed a meeting like this a thousand times. I didn't think it'd ever happen.'

'I didn't either.'

'Maureen and I are divorcing, Lydia. I told her in March that I wanted to leave her. Shortly after Zannah called off the wedding.'

The red and white squares on the tablecloth swam in front of Joss's eyes. She felt slightly nauseous. 'What reason did you give?'

'I told her I didn't want to live with her any longer.'

'Did you tell her about me?'

'Yes. But I said we hadn't seen one another for months. She didn't . . . doesn't believe me. She thinks . . . Well, you can imagine.'

'I don't know what to say, Gray. Those pictures at Christmas . . . the ones she sent Adrian on the camera phone . . . they upset me.'

'I'm sorry. Part of me wanted you to be upset. I wanted you to be feeling as bad as I was...'

'You and Maureen looked so happy together, like a holiday brochure.'

'I was … never mind. It wasn't like that, I swear. Every day was endless. I haven't stopped thinking about you. I've left home. I've got a job in London. This is where I'm living now.' He pushed a piece of paper across the table. 'I've written down my new address and phone number for you. It's in Muswell Hill … a lovely apartment. Everything's changed, Lydia.'

She knew what he expected her to say. He wanted her to follow his example. Ask Bob for a divorce. Leave home. Start a life with him. She folded the paper in half without looking at it, and put it into her handbag. Then she said, 'Zannah and Cal's wedding is less than a month away. I promised my daughters, Gray. I promised Bob, too, but that's … Well, I can't. I can't start it all again. I'm sorry.'

He leaned forward and glared at her. Joss flinched. 'Let me get this quite right, so that I make sure I'm not twisting what you say. You're not going to leave your husband. Is that right? Even though I've left Maureen?'

Joss nodded. She knew no words would convey what she wanted to say, so she kept quiet. Gray was white with fury. 'I can't believe this. You're trotting out the whole fucking promises thing all over again. Haven't you had enough time to think better of that crap? This is just a rerun of what you said in November. I cannot believe you're going to throw away what we have again … I just can't believe it.'

'Nothing's changed, Gray. I'm still bound. You know I am.'

'What I know is that you're selfish and cowardly. I've broken up my marriage and my career and you're not prepared to do anything. Nothing at all. Oh, no, your cosy little life has to go on exactly as it always has and I've just been an inconvenience that tripped you up for a bit but which you've now got sorted out to your satisfaction.' He stood up suddenly. 'D'you want to know something, Lydia? I've just this second realized and, okay, I'm a bit slow on the uptake, but it's clear to me now. You don't love me. You're absolutely okay without me. I saw you at the reading. You were completely self-possessed. Perfectly poised. You weren't tormented or upset in any way that I could see and that's the bottom line. I can tell you're fine without me because you're not prepared to give up one single thing. You're not going to try to bend even one of those completely pathetic principles of yours. Not for me. Okay. Goodbye. That's it. There's only so much shit I'm prepared to take. Stay and finish your sandwich. I'm going.' He flung a ten-pound note on to the table and rushed out of the café.

Joss sat there after he'd gone, paralysed. All the time he'd been talking, she'd wanted to interrupt him and explain, tell him why, beg him to wait just a little longer, but he'd given her no chance. How could he have misunderstood her so completely? Has she really seemed composed? Happy? I'm not, she wanted to shout. Really, I'm not. She could text him. She could phone him and say it was all a huge mistake and of course she'd leave Bob and come to him. She'd been mad, stupid, ridiculous. She loved him. She took her mobile out of her bag and stared at it, blinking back the tears. What would I say? she asked herself. The wedding ... I can't tell Zannah all this now. Not after what she's been through with Adrian. And Bob ... if I couldn't leave him before, what's changed? Nothing, except that Gray's even more furious than he was in November. He's left Maureen. Joss knew he'd expected her to fall into his arms and she hadn't. She couldn't, not yet. Would she ever be ready? She had no idea. She felt as though the scab on a wound that had been healing quite well had suddenly been torn off. She was bleeding and in pain all over again.

Friday

Maureen looked at the calendar. Just over a week to go to the wedding that ought to have been Adrian's. For a few days after that announcement from her Fucking Bastard Husband – and that was how she'd always think of him from now on: she used all three words every time he came into her head – Maureen had been ablaze with rage and fury. She'd simmered for ages after he'd told her, walking round the house and swearing to itemize every single object in every single room and lay claim to the whole lot. He'd told her that woman wasn't in touch with him, and if you believed that you'd believe anything. No, she had her claws into Graham all right. Now that Mr Bartram had sorted out the legal side of things, she felt safer. Nothing she did now could change the fact that the house was hers and a sizeable settlement as well, but Maureen was damned if the Prize Bitch was going to lay her fingers on so much as a teaspoon from her kitchen. Fucking Bastard Husband was rich enough to start all over again and the last she'd heard was a card with his bloody new address and phone number on it. And a note telling her about his new job, as if she gave a shit. He'd obviously gone and found a love-nest that was just the thing for creeps with no morals who ditched wives they'd been living with for more than three decades in favour of wispy poets with no tits to speak of. And what's more, she thought, that daughter of hers has inherited both her titlessness and her homewrecking capacities.

Much of Maureen's time over the past couple of months had been spent doing things with Adrian to cheer him up and she thought she'd almost convinced him that a move to Guildford, at least to live, wasn't completely out of the question. He was feeling better already, she could tell, even though he did still go into deep glooms and miseries occasionally, moaning on about Zannah and how unhappy he was. When he was in that mood, it was up to Maureen to emphasize the positive, to bolster his confidence. Once they were on that plane and off to Barbados, all would be well, she was sure.

Today, she was the one in need of bolstering. As what was to have been her son's wedding day approached, she felt worse and worse about missing out on the wonderful, no, the perfectly beautiful arrangements she'd made. She regretted things that she knew were completely ridiculous, like seeing the cake she'd designed actually there on the table. She was even cross, at some level she didn't understand, that she wouldn't now be able to assess how Zannah's wedding dress had turned out. Even worse, she'd never have the satisfaction of all those people seeing how much better-looking, how much more expensively dressed she herself was than that Gratrix mouse. Now, she was sitting at the computer feeling a little woozy. She hadn't slept well, although she'd swallowed a couple of pills last night – and who could blame her? Even after liberal applications of Estée Lauder concealer, her eyes still weren't up to scratch. She couldn't help it. She was crying altogether too much. She looked like a cartoon character with red lines drawn in squiggles all over the whites of their eyes. This usually meant they'd been hit over the head and flattened by an iron frying pan. Like me, she thought. I've been hit over the head. That's what it feels like.

She squared her shoulders and turned on her computer. Zannah had already written letters to the guests who were now no longer welcome at the wedding. Mercifully, no one had sent any gifts yet so there had been none to return. She'd received a cheque for Genevieve's deposit from Zannah, and it gave her some pleasure to think of the ghastly Gratrixes having to tighten their belts. As she stared at the screen, an idea came into her mind. It was so startlingly simple, so beautiful and so devastating that she wondered why it had only just occurred to her. She thought about it for a few seconds. She hadn't been in touch with anyone from that family since Graham had told her his intentions, because she was damned if she was going to lose her house as well as her husband, but all that was taken care of now and she could do what she wanted. Fucking Bastard Husband swore blind that

that woman and her husband hadn't discussed divorce. Well perhaps, Maureen thought, it was time they did. Why should that bloody woman be sitting there looking forward to a divine wedding next week, when Maureen herself was in this turmoil? Let her have a little turmoil of her own. At first, Maureen thought of writing directly to Prize Bitch but she could delete the email and pretend it had never arrived. No, she'd got something much more effective up her sleeve . . . something quite deliciously nasty. Here was a chance to make that woman wish she'd never laid eyes on Graham, and at the same time her message would in all probability wreck the wedding. Fantastic. Better than her wildest imaginings of revenge. She intended to write the kind of words it would be impossible to ignore and she knew exactly who would be getting them. Brilliant. Terrific. A revenge that would be all the more pleasant for having been delayed a few weeks.

Maureen felt suddenly hot and sweaty, as though she'd been running. She clicked on *compose* in her email and stretched her hands before hitting the keys. She typed quickly, stabbing each letter with her scarlet-tipped fingers. Then she pressed SEND without reading through what she'd written. Maybe that last bit was rather OTT but what the hell? How often did you learn that your entire life was in ruins? Serve the whole lot of them bloody well right, Maureen thought. I don't give a twopenny damn what happens to any of them.

'Joss? Are you busy?'

She looked up from her desk and saw Bob standing in the doorway. He was holding a piece of paper in his hand. Joss was so surprised to see him there that she started to get up.

'No, it's okay,' he said. 'If you're working, this'll wait. But I wanted to show you something.'

'What is it?'

'An email. I printed it out. I thought you should see it.'

Joss did get up then. 'Come in, Bob. Take the chair. You look . . . I'll sit on the bed.'

He gazed at the piece of paper and didn't say anything for what seemed a long time. Joss found that her heart was pounding. It occurred to her that this was the first time in years that he'd even crossed the threshold of this room and she pushed that thought to the back of her mind. Bob said, 'It's from Maureen. I think you should read it yourself. I'm sorry to have to show you such a thing.'

Joss took the sheet of paper from him and started to read:

I feel you should know that my bastard of a husband is divorcing me. He claims to be in love with your wife and I know for a fact she's been screwing him for years. Adrian has had a lucky escape from your family and I hope that the whole lot of you rot. Maureen.

'You're not saying anything, Joss.'

'What d'you expect me to say? She's a vicious woman and I wish you'd deleted the message without bothering to print it out.'

'Is there any truth in it?'

Joss looked down at her hands. 'No. No truth at all. You know our history, mine and Graham Ashton's. I promised you I wouldn't sleep with him again. I've not seen him since November. Or been in touch with him. He did come to my reading in London a couple of weeks ago, but there were other people around in the theatre. Nothing happened.'

She covered her face with her hands. Surely in these circumstances it was okay to lie a bit. She didn't know what to think. She wanted to scream abuse at Maureen. How could she do this? How could she hurt them so, simply because their daughter had broken up with her son? But it's not only that, she told herself. It's me and Gray. She can't bear it that he doesn't love her any more. She thinks we're together. He hasn't told her the truth. She thinks we're still lovers.

'Joss? Joss, look at me, please.'

She took her hands away from her face and sat up a little straighter. 'What are we going to do about it?'

'I don't know. I'm not sure whether I believe you.'

'You'd rather believe a harridan who's clearly demented with rage, is that it?'

'She's lying, is she? About you and her husband?'

'Yes. What she says there is a lie. We have not been, as she puts it, "screwing for years". I told you. Before he turned up at my reading – unexpectedly, I should say – we'd not even been in touch by email since November. I promise you that's the truth, Bob.'

'Ah, but is it the whole truth?'

'What do you mean?'

'Please think carefully before you answer, Joss. I mean it. And don't lie to me. You implied, when we discussed this, that the whole matter was nothing very much. A storm in a teacup and easily overlooked. Is it possible ... Do you love this man?'

She opened her mouth to deny it. She was surely a good enough liar to carry such a thing off. Then the word came out, almost in spite of what she'd planned to say. 'Yes,' she whispered. 'I do love him. Desperately. It's not going anywhere, but I can't seem to stop myself. I'm so sorry, Bob.'

She got up and went to the window. She could feel Bob's silence growing behind her. What would he say? How could this conversation continue?

'*Desperately,*' he whispered, and Joss cringed. How could she have let that word slip out? He went on, 'What about me? D'you love me?'

'Yes. Of course I do, but ...'

'But what? Clearly not *desperately*. I want to know what's in your mind, Joss. We've been married for more than thirty years, for God's sake. Can't you tell me what you feel? Explain things to me? I'm begging you ...'

'Okay,' Joss said. 'Okay.' She came to sit on the edge of the bed again and took her husband's hand. 'It's hard, but I'll try. I've loved you for years. I'm used to you. We get on well. We have Zannah and Em and Isis to bind us together. You've looked after me from the very first day we met. You've provided a home and money and comfort and companionship, and all those things that are so important. That's why I promised you I wouldn't see Gray again. I didn't want to hurt you. I didn't want to ... well, to disregard what we've always had. And I thought that if I didn't see him then the kind of feelings I have for him might fade. Or go away altogether. But they haven't. I'm sorry, Bob. I'm not going to do anything about it ... Perhaps over time ...'

'And how is what you feel for this man different from your feeling for me? Where does the desperation come from? I want to know. I'd like to be able to understand.'

'He's more ... interested in things I'm interested in. My work. He reads my poems. He writes poetry. He's more involved in my thought processes.' She could have added, but didn't: he sees me. He thinks I'm beautiful. He notices my clothes. He tells me he loves me all the time. Or he used to.

'It's the sex, isn't it?' Bob was frowning. 'The *desperation* has to do with sex . . .'

'Oh for the love of God, stop it! I don't want to hear one more word about "*desperation*," all right?' She was shouting and forced herself to be calmer, to speak more quietly. 'I don't want to talk about that, if you don't mind.'

'I'm not enough for you. I don't satisfy you. Probably never have. Go on, deny it.'

'Don't be so stupid. Of course you've "satisfied" me. I refuse to discuss this, okay?'

'Not really but I suppose you're right. Especially if you're not seeing him.'

'Exactly.' Joss nodded.

'Your reticence on the subject speaks volumes, however.'

' I don't know what you're saying.'

'You could have told me, reassured me . . . Oh, never mind, Joss. You're right. The whole topic's unseemly. I won't mention it again.'

'Thank you,' Joss said, under her breath.

Bob stood up and went over to the door. 'It's just over a week till the wedding. Not a word to the girls about this, d'you understand? It was that woman's intention to put the kibosh on Zannah's wedding and I'm not allowing her to do that. D'you promise? Not a single word?'

'I promise . . . But what . . . ?'

'I'm going downstairs now. There's the conference in Birmingham starting tomorrow. I'll think about what's best to do. Good night.'

Joss stood staring out of the window for a long time after he had gone. Why was he the one to make the decisions? Why shouldn't she? Maybe, she reflected, because I don't know what to do. She sat on the divan bed and tried to imagine what was going through his mind. Maybe tomorrow she'd be able to gather what his thoughts were before he went off to his conference. How troubled could he be by all this if he could even contemplate driving to Birmingham to sit in seminars and lectures? No, that wasn't fair. Bob had always used his work to bury any worries he may have had. It was one of the things that irritated her about him. He never came to her to pour out his fears, his dreams. Would she have felt differently about him if he had? Joss had no idea. She wondered what the chances were of her getting a good night's sleep.

Saturday

'Tea?'

'Thanks . . . yes.'

Joss filled the kettle and waited for it to boil. For the last few months she'd been planning to buy a new one because the noise this one made was getting on her nerves. Now she was grateful for the screeching and high-pitched gurgling that went on till the water boiled. Talking was out of the question. Joss made the tea and brought it to the table, where she deliberately took longer than usual to pour it and add milk.

'There you are,' she said. Bob was trying to hide behind the *Guardian*, which was harder now, since it had become smaller. Perhaps broadsheets could advertise themselves as being just the ticket for a tense breakfast table. She sat down and waited for Bob to say something. She could have spoken. She could have said, *I haven't slept a wink. I don't know what to do. What's going to become of us?* but she was waiting to see what would happen if she didn't. It had always been her task in the marriage to bring up awkward matters for discussion. And he, all through the years, had generally fled to the safety of his work, leaving her to deal with whatever it was. Not this time, Joss thought. Let him say what he's decided. I'm not going to prompt him.

She'd just buttered a piece of toast when he spoke.

'I've thought about our situation, Joss, and I've decided that this isn't the right time to make major decisions about our life together . . . if we're to have one. The wedding is a week from now and I don't want *anything* to disturb the happiness of that day. I'm determined it will be wonderful for Zannah, Isis and Cal and therefore I'd ask you not to mention any of our . . .' He waved a hand. 'You know what I mean.'

'But you must *know* what you intend to do!' Joss nearly hit him. How could he extend the uncertainty over a whole week? 'I see you're not bothered about whether I have a happy day at the wedding.'

'To tell you the truth, Joss, I don't care whether you do or not. I intend to enjoy myself as much as I can. I can't deny that this . . . this development . . . has been a bit of a shock.'

'But I've explained to you that it's over. I haven't seen Gray since November. It's over, as far as you're concerned.'

'Ah!' He bent forward over the table and banged his fist down so hard that the butter dish jumped. 'Condemned out of your own mouth!'

'What are you talking about? What have I said?'

'You said: "as far as you're concerned". Now, call me pedantic if you like, but that means to me that it's not over as far as you, Joss, are concerned. Am I right?'

What could she say? Should she lie? As she looked at Bob, red in the face with anger, a kind of stiff cold took hold of her. I don't care any longer whether it's what he wants to hear. She said, 'Yes, you're quite right. I'm not going to hide it from you. But I'm not going to act on it, so you don't have to worry about that.'

'I'm not worrying. But I'll let you know in the next day or so what I've decided to do.'

'Why not now? What's the matter with right now?' For God's sake, she thought, let's get this over with.

'I've got to go. In case you've forgotten I'm giving a lecture at the conference.'

'Nice to see that your domestic troubles won't be interfering with that. I won't be here when you get back. I'm going to London. I'll phone Charlotte in a minute. There are rehearsals and fittings going on next week. Just let me know when you intend to get to Clapham. We're sharing a room before the wedding, but that can't be helped.'

'I'll ask Cal to book me in with him and Mattie. They're in a hotel, aren't they? Don't want to embarrass you.'

Joss got up and left the room.

'You've not finished your toast,' he called after her.

She didn't answer because if she had she'd have sworn at him in terms he'd never heard her use before. How did he dare to be so bossy, so calm, so unconcerned about everything? It was an act, she knew, but that didn't make it any less irritating. He didn't want to show her how hurt he was so she ought, perhaps, to be more indulgent towards him, but what she felt was something like rage. He knew she wanted, needed, to know what his intentions were. The possibility of a future with Gray was like a mirage, shining somewhere on a distant horizon. I won't think that far ahead. I'll put Gray out of my mind till the wedding is over. She wondered how she could concentrate on Zannah and Cal when everything she'd thought of as her life was in the process of being broken up and rearranged.

The Paradise Spa deserved its name. Zannah, Claire and Louise were lolling in the Jacuzzi. Tropical plants grew up to the blue-glass dome of the roof, and loungers covered with white towels of complete and utter mega-fluffiness were placed round the perimeter of the main pool. Emily slipped in next to the others, loving the foam, the warmth, the effervescence. 'This is like sitting in a giant glass of Alka-Selzer,' she said, 'only hot. And always fizzy. Fantastic.' She sank down and rested her head on the curved marble edge of the small pool.

'We've driven everyone else away,' said Louise. 'D'you think they can tell we're a hen party?'

'It's Em's fault. She forgot to bring the little hats with *Hen Night* written on them in sparkly letters,' said Zannah. 'But we're not pissed. No one would ever guess.'

'I think,' said Claire, 'that the first toast at lunch ... You did say champagne at lunch, didn't you, Em?'

Emily nodded. Claire went on, 'The first toast will be to Em who found this marvellous spa for us and showed us what a hen night can be if you forget about the night part of it. All-day pleasure, lovely food ... Brilliant.'

'I just thought,' said Emily 'that if I had to suffer yet another pub crawl, I'd rather stay at home. This is my idea of Paradise, which was how I found it. I put Paradise Spa into Google.'

'How many other kinds of pool do we still have to go in?'

'Only three. Plunge pool, ordinary swimming-pool and Japanese pool with hot stone massage, and lunch of course. Don't forget that ...'

'Shame about the naked men,' said Louise, 'but even without them, it's worth every penny.'

'Don't talk about money,' said Zannah. 'This must have cost you lot an absolute fortune.'

'Yup. Thin soup for a month. My children'll have to go without shoes till at least Christmas,' said Claire.

'This time next week,' said Louise, 'we'll be in church, singing "Love Divine All Loves Excelling". You nervous, Zan?'

'Not really. I've been well rehearsed. I've got the dress at home and it's better than I ever dreamed of. The food's sorted and I'm not telling you what you're getting. You'll have to wait and see. Flowers'll be okay. The photographer's great and I'm secretly working on him to fall in love with you, Em.'

'He's not my type,' Emily said. 'And, anyway, he's married. With a baby. So think again.' She was surprised by how genuinely happy she felt for Zannah and Cal now. Any last hope she might have had of herself and Cal coming together in a blissful distant future had long ago disappeared.

'Damn!' Zannah laughed. 'Never mind. But no, I'm not a bit nervous. Excited, yes, but I think the nerves went out of weddings when the wedding night stopped being a terrifying ordeal. Can you imagine what that must have been like? Horrible. You've never seen a willy. You don't know if it's going to hurt. Will you do the things you're supposed to do? Will he? I'd just die, if it was me. That's the best thing about the sexual revolution, I reckon. The fact that you know what you're doing. No alarms and no surprises.'

'Speaking of which,' said Claire, 'do we assume that you and Cal … ?'

'Me and Cal what?' Zannah had started to giggle before she'd even heard the question.

'Well,' Claire hesitated.

'She wants to know,' said Louise, 'if you and Cal have made love since you got together again. She's a nosy bitch.'

'I don't think I'm going to answer that.' Zannah whooshed her hands through the water.

'Ah, go on!' said Louise. 'We haven't got naked men on this hen night, but we can at least hear about your passionate reunion with your ex. Can't we?'

'I don't think so,' Zannah said. 'Sorry.'

'But it was passionate, wasn't it?' Claire asked.

'Of course it was. What do you think? Use your imagination, for God's sake. I'm not going to spell it out.'

'And was it everything you'd hoped for?' Louise was giggling.

'More than. Now shut up, please.' Zannah looked at her sister. 'Can't you make them behave a bit better, Em? I don't want to talk about this, really.'

'You're not supposed to be well behaved on a hen night, you know,' Emily said. 'Still, as you're my only sister, I'll see what I can do.' She had no desire to hear details. Just thinking about it embarrassed her. Being over Cal is one thing, Emily told herself. Dwelling on him and Zannah in one another's arms is quite another.

Thursday

Zannah had a good idea of what was going on, but she pretended not to. It had been quite hard, over the last couple of weeks, to ignore the whispering and giggling and hiding of things behind backs whenever she came into a room. Today was her last day of teaching her classes. She'd been met at the school entrance by Claire and Louise who had taken her to the staffroom and told her to stay there till she was called. She sat down and looked at her wedding notebook, which was now so full of bits of paper Sellotaped to the pages that it no longer closed properly. Bills and letters were forever slipping into it and getting lost among the wedding stuff.

The head had been super-kind and given her tomorrow off to do things like going to the church to see the flowers were in order. Like talking to Genevieve the caterer about last-minute things. Like transporting the dresses and the rest of the paraphernalia to Clapham. Like reminding Cal to pick up his wedding suit. Zannah hoped very much she wouldn't burst out laughing as she walked down the aisle towards him. When she'd gone with him to try it on, she didn't quite recognize the man who stood in front of her, and she'd gasped to see him so respectable. He'd even arranged to have a haircut without being nagged. They'd fixed up accommodation for Cal's mum and her cousin from St Ives and Cal's childhood friends. Now they'd arrived, she had to check they were okay with where they were staying. Finding them beds had been a major operation. Cal had arranged it, rung up friends, booked b-and-bs, sorted them all out brilliantly. Still, however well organized you were, there was always the possibility of something going wrong.

Something was up already. Pa had decided to stay the night with

Cal and Mattie at their hotel instead of at Charlotte's. Why was that? Had he and Ma quarrelled? What about? She wanted to know but dreaded the answer, so she hadn't mentioned it when she'd spoken to him. He'd sounded okay, but he was good at hiding things. I must speak to Ma tonight, she thought. She'd been at Charlotte's since the weekend, but things had been so frantic that they hadn't had more than a couple of hurried conversations and Ma was always hard to make out on the phone. You could never tell what sort of mood she was in.

Someone was knocking at the staff-room door.

'Come in,' Zannah said. Marcella and Colm from Year Six were standing there. Marcella said, 'Please, Miss, can you come with us?'

They made their way to the hall and the children held open the doors for her. Zannah stepped in and there was the whole school, clapping and whooping. Everyone was dressed up in party clothes. The head said, 'Ready, children?' and then came the sound of the piano plinking out a few notes. Suddenly, they were all singing: *'Happy Wedding to you!'* to the tune of *Happy Birthday*. . . . *'Happy wedding, Mrs Ford, happy wedding to you!'*

Everyone, Zannah could see instantly, had worked tremendously hard. All round the hall paper flowers in shades of pink, mauve and fuchsia were taped to the walls and to every bit of furniture. There were thousands and Zannah wondered how long ago they had started to make them. The girls had pink bows in their hair and the boys had mauve ribbons worn as ties. Someone had been doing things with the office shredder and confetti in large quantities was being thrown at her, and when the singing was over, some of the little ones came running towards her and hugged her legs.

'Thank you!' she started to say.

'We've got a present for you, Miss,' That was Finn, one of Isis's friends, almost hidden behind a bunch of pink and white roses. Marcella gave her an envelope, curtsying as she did so. Zannah's eyes were full of tears. 'I had no idea,' she said. 'This'll be my best present, I know. You're all . . . Well, it's lovely of you to do this for me and I'm very grateful.'

'You have to open it, Miss,' Colm said. 'You have to see what it is.'

She tore open the envelope. Inside, there was a voucher for four people to go on the London Eye and a music token for twenty-five pounds.

'That is fantastic! I've been longing to go on the Eye . . . and I don't know what I'll buy with the token, but I bet you'll all have your suggestions. Thank you so much. I'm … I'm so surprised by this!'

The head clapped her hands. 'Now, children, line up please. The dinner ladies have made us a special wedding lunch. Mrs Ford? Will you lead the way, as you're the bride?'

Zannah handed her flowers to Claire, who bore them off to the cloakroom, and set off for the school canteen, with Isis, Gemma, Finn, Marcella and Colm following close behind her. The confetti, it seemed, was never-ending. Pieces of coloured paper were still falling into her hair and all over her clothes.

The Wedding

Joss was so deep in thought that she didn't see Zannah till she was standing next to her. She leaped to her feet, and Zannah said, 'Ma? Is anything the matter? What on earth are you doing in the marquee at this hour of the night?'

'I could ask you the same thing. You're the bride, supposed to be getting your beauty sleep. I didn't think anyone else would be awake. I couldn't sleep and I wanted to have a look before ... well, before tomorrow.'

'Today. It's after two. I'm the same. I wanted to see it while it was ... I don't know. Untouched. I'll always remember it like this. It's beautiful, isn't it, Ma?'

'Yes it is. I want everything to be perfect for you.'

'But, Ma, what's the matter with *you*? I'm not so selfish that I haven't noticed you've been ... well, not yourself. You're not ill, are you? Please tell me it's nothing like that.'

'No, no, nothing like that at all.' Joss put out a hand and touched her daughter's shoulder, to comfort her. Even in this light, she could see that Zannah had turned white. 'Let's sit down. I did promise your father I wouldn't say anything before the wedding but I think ...'

'Say anything about what?'

'Let's sit down, darling.'

Zannah pulled out two of the chairs that had been brought in by the marquee men. The cloths were piled up on the buffet tables, waiting to be unfolded; the crockery and cutlery were lined up under muslin and there were baskets of sugared almonds beautifully wrapped in ribbon-tied bundles of silvery tulle waiting to be set out beside each plate.

The flowers would be arriving at dawn. Joss sat down opposite her daughter. 'I like the way this marquee looks in the dark,' she said. 'I like the emptiness and all this cream and gold. Tomorrow it's going to be decorated and full of chattering people and noise and ... Well, it's good to see it before that happens.'

'You're making small-talk, Ma. Just tell me, okay?'

'Your father had an email from Maureen. A horrible, horrible email.'

'What did it say?'

'Among other things, that I'd been *screwing her husband for years*. Which isn't true. I didn't ... I haven't ... I promised you girls. I've not been in touch with him since November. Then he turned up at a reading I did and ...'

'You've started seeing him again.'

'No. I haven't. He wanted to, but I said I couldn't ... I couldn't do it to Bob and you and Em. I didn't tell you the whole truth, back in November. I didn't want to hurt you. I didn't want you to think badly of me. I'm so sorry ... it was cowardly. I simply ... well, I didn't want to rock the boat. Not then. I feel differently now.'

Zannah said, 'Oh, Ma, how awful! For both of you. I feel so bad now. Guilty. It's our fault. We hadn't any right to tell you what we wanted you to do. It's your life and we were just thinking of ourselves: how our lives would be affected by what you and Pa did. I think we're the ones to apologize. And I never said anything, not even to Em, but I always sort of suspected that there was more to it than you told us. I allowed myself to be deluded because there was so much going on. I'm sorry, Ma, that you've had to go through this alone. And I'm sorry for Pa too. What happened when he got the email?'

'We had a row. I told him I was still in love with Gray .... He's left Maureen, you know. They're getting a divorce. The email, I think, was her way of hurting me because she was hurt. And also getting back at all of us, for what happened with you and Adrian.'

'Are you and Pa going to get a divorce?'

'God, Zannah, you don't need this now! I truly didn't want to spoil tomorrow. I was going to tell you later, after the wedding. I can't live with him any longer.'

'But Ma, don't you love him? Not even a bit? Poor old Pa!'

'Of course I do! You can't live with someone for more than thirty years and have children with them and not love them. He's been good to me, but he's been ... Well, you know your father. He's in his own world for much of the time. He doesn't ... he doesn't really *see* me any longer. He doesn't ... Oh, God, I'm not telling you all this, Zannah. You're his daughter. I don't want to come between the two of you. I know I'll be hurting him, but I can't...'

'I understand, Ma. Really. If you stay with him, then *you'll* be miserable. You have to go for what'll make you happy. I believe that. I don't think *anyone* ought to sacrifice herself. Or himself.' Zannah leaned forward and put her arms around her mother. 'He'll be all right, you know. Em's going to Egypt with him, and Cal and I will take Isis up there lots and lots. Isis adores him and he'll always be her grandpa. He'll get over it. And you should tell Em about this too. She might think Pa's being hard done by, but she'll be okay with everything in the end, I promise. Don't worry, Ma.'

'I *am* worried, Zannah. I can't help it. I don't know how I'll tell Bob. Or when. I only know I'm going to do it. Very soon. I'm determined about that.'

'Have you spoken to Graham?'

'I don't know if he'll even want to speak to me after the last time we met. You see why I couldn't sleep, don't you?'

Zannah laughed. 'I suppose so. But we should both try, don't you reckon?'

'Yes. I'll be okay, I think. I wish I'd spoken to you earlier.'

'Me too. Still, I'm glad you have now.'

Zannah stood up and took her mother's hand as they walked into the house together. Joss turned to lock the French windows behind her, glancing at the marquee which loomed ghost-white against the dark sky. She closed her eyes and made the sort of wish she used to make as a child: Please. Please let Zannah be happy and let me be happy too.

'Good morning! I hope I'm not too early?' Alex, the photographer, was standing on the doorstep. Charlotte was ready for him. Even after the disturbed night she'd had, she was up before six. She'd dressed in a respectable house-coat, determined not to put on her wedding outfit till the last possible moment. The breakfast things were laid out in the kitchen, and the agreement was that everyone would help themselves when it suited them.

'No, not at all,' she said. 'We're all up. The flowers arrived a few moments ago. Maya's in the marquee, setting out the table decorations. The bouquet and the bridesmaids' posies and the buttonholes for the men are in the larder. Do just look around wherever you like. I'll tell Zannah you're here. She'll be down for a bite of breakfast in a moment, I'm sure.'

'I'll go out to the marquee, then. Take some shots of the tables and so on. Please try to forget I'm here. Really. I don't need any looking after.'

'Good. That's excellent. And do help yourself to breakfast or coffee or anything else you'd like.'

'Thanks. The house is beautiful and so's the front garden. I bet the back's even better. I'm going to have a look.' He disappeared out of the French windows.

Isis came into the hall, still in her pyjamas. 'Hello, Charlotte. Isn't it a lovely day? I'm so excited. Can I go and look in the marquee? Alex is here. I saw him.'

'He won't want you getting in his way, dear. Why don't you come with me and I'll get you some breakfast? Where's Gemma?'

'Still in bed. She's coming in a minute, she says.'

Charlotte led the way to the kitchen. 'Sit down, Isis,' she said. 'You'll need something inside you or your tummy will rumble all through the service.' She put a bowl of cereal on the table and handed Isis a spoon.

'Will it?' Isis asked. 'Really?'

'Yes, indeed. Eat up.'

'Can't I wait for Gemma? Or Grandma?'

'No,' said Charlotte. 'You'd better eat up now. It's going to get very crowded and busy in here later on. Lots to be done before we set out for church.'

Joss looked out of the window in Edie's room from which she could see most of the garden. She'd gone back to sleep for a couple of hours after her conversation with Zannah, but her eyes felt as though they were made of lead. Thank goodness a professional makeup artist was doing their faces this morning. Bright sunshine slanted across the grass, which Val must have brushed and combed for days to make it so smooth and green and velvety. The azaleas, the wisteria, the ceanothus: every shrub and flower looked as though it had been put in place by a set-decorator. The leaves fluttered a little in the small breezes that blew through the trees. Seven o'clock. Only four and a half hours to go to the service. Just over three and a half hours till the procession. Joss hadn't been too keen on that idea, imagining everyone soaked and dripping, under umbrellas. That's my pessimism, she thought. Zannah had been quite sure that the weather would do what she wanted it to, and it had.

She turned to look at her outfit for the day, hanging on the back of the bedroom door. Back in March, when she bought it, she'd thought perhaps it might be too severe, too plain for a wedding, but last night, when she tried it on to show the girls, they'd both said she looked wonderful and she'd decided to believe them. The dress was a sleeveless silk sheath in the most beautiful dark peacock blue, and there was a collarless edge-to-edge jacket to go over it. With it, she intended to wear the pearls that had belonged to her mother: three long strands, joined together in a clasp at the back. Her hat, more of a decoration really, was small and black and Joss intended to take it off at the first opportunity. And there was her bag, lying innocuously on the chair by the door: a velvet envelope in the same colour as the dress. She thought of the piece of paper with Gray's handwriting on it, hidden in one of the inner pockets. It's like a small grenade, she thought. I don't have to pull the pin, but if I do . . . She pushed the thought away, unwilling to consider it with so much else going on. Later. There would be time enough.

Now she found herself wondering what Maureen had meant to wear for the wedding. She would definitely have eclipsed me, Joss thought. She'd have made it her business to do that. Was she thinking about them now? Joss was prepared to bet that she was. And Gray, what was he doing at this minute? He was probably fast asleep.

Where was Bob? Zannah said he'd told her he'd be here at eight and he was always punctual. She wasn't worried about avoiding him. She was sure he would go out of his way not to speak to her if he could help it. The hairdresser was coming at eight-thirty. The marquee looked quite different in the light of day. Joss had enjoyed watching it being put up last week, then filled with tables and chairs, cream linen and glass vases. She picked up her towel and went to see if the shower was free. With so many people in the house, you had to get into a bathroom whenever you could.

Zannah sat in an armchair and watched Pat, the makeup artist, who was about to start on Emily's face. 'I do *not*,' her sister was saying, 'want to look like something you'd find as a prize in a fairground, okay?'

'Sssh,' Pat said. She was a chubby, cheerful young woman with a no-nonsense approach and she was wearing no makeup at all, as far as Zannah could see. 'You chose me, didn't you, out of all the other makeup artists you could have picked? Just trust me, okay?'

Isis and Gemma were sitting on the bed, waiting for their turn. They were next and then Zannah would be the last to be transformed. The girls had been stunned into open-mouthed silence at the array of jars, bottles, tubes, brushes, tissues, combs, hair ornaments and cotton-wool spread out on the dressing-table. The bedroom in which she'd slept last night had become a theatrical dressing room. She was in her new dressing-gown, more of a *peignoir,* really, waiting to take her place on the chair. Then the hairdresser would do his stuff and at last, she'd be putting on the dress. It was hanging up, swathed in a sheet, and her shoes – satin, high-heeled, dyed to match the dress – were in the cupboard. They were comfortable, but Zannah wondered whether the comfort would last all the way from the house to the church and back. The weather was perfect, which was lucky. She'd been very upbeat about what they'd do if it was pelting down, but thank Heavens she hadn't had to start arranging for cars at this unearthly hour of the morning. The beautiful handbag embroidered with a pattern of tiny butterflies and dotted with pearls that Edie had given her, was *something old* and it contained the *something blue*, a handkerchief trimmed with lace that Val had produced last night. She'd be wearing Em's pearl earrings *(something borrowed)* and the *something new* was a set of flesh-coloured satin underwear that she hadn't been able to resist. Briefly, she thought of tonight: of what Cal would say when he saw it. She shivered with longing, and tried to erase the images that had suddenly appeared in her head. There was too much else to think about before the ceremony.

Someone was knocking at the door. Zannah went to open it and there was Alex.

'Can I come in, ladies?'

'Take a picture of us!' Isis called. 'Take a picture of us getting our makeup on. I'm going to have blusher. And lipstick. Pat said I could.'

'Sit down, Isis,' said Zannah. 'Just let Alex do his thing, okay?'

Isis subsided on to the bed again. Alex stood near the window. As far as Zannah could see, he was pointing his camera straight at the messy dressing-table. Then at the shoes, and the dress, swathed in its white sheet.

Isis and Gemma stood in the doorway of the marquee. Charlotte had told them they could go and have a look, as long as they didn't get in anyone's way. Grandpa had come, just a few minutes ago, and he, Grandma and Charlotte were in the kitchen with Em. Mum was still upstairs, getting her hair done and putting on the wedding dress.

There were lots of people in the marquee, including Alex, who was walking about taking pictures of the flower arrangements, the glasses, the piles of plates and the cakestand. The cake wasn't on it yet, but the caterers had already started to bring out some of the food and put it on the tables, covered with thin cloths. Most of it, Mum had explained, would be arranged while they were at the church, but Isis still hoped to see the cake before they left. It was supposed to be ready at ten o'clock.

Maya, the flower lady, beckoned the girls to where she was. Isis liked Maya. She was quite old, about as old as Grandma, but very pretty, with long red hair in a plait down her back. She was wearing an overall, like the ones they put on at school when they did painting.

'Hello, Isis ... and this must be Gemma. Well, don't you both look beautiful? Lovely. *Really* lovely. Your posies are in the larder, next to Zannah's bouquet. Have you seen them?'

Isis nodded. She was glad Maya had noticed how pretty they looked. When she had put on the bridesmaid's dress and gone to stand in front of the mirror, she had felt like jumping up and down for joy, only she didn't dare, because that might spoil it. The rosebuds on the sleeves, the ribbons and the swishy, silky sound of the skirt when she moved about made her feel so happy that she thought she'd burst. She knew she looked pretty, because Gemma did, too, and the two of them did a little dance together when they were dressed. They couldn't help it. They'd been sent to wait quietly downstairs till it was time to walk to church, but Charlotte had said it was okay to sneak into the marquee, for a bit, to see the flowers.

'The tables look really, really pretty,' said Gemma. The vases were like little boxes made of shining clear glass. Each one was full of red and cream rosebuds and dark green leaves, like the ones in Mum's bouquet. Some people had started to lay the tables with silver knives, forks and spoons. A lady with a big basket was putting little bags of sweets next to each place. There were flowers hanging in enormous bunches from the roof of the tent and all round the walls, the same colour as the table flowers, but bigger, and Isis didn't know what they were called but they were gorgeous. 'I can see a butterfly,' she said to Maya. 'Up there in the roof flowers.'

'Lisianthus, those are called, and there's a few other things as well, but mainly it's foliage with lisianthus and roses. The butterflies were your mother's idea and a very good one. Look, here's one I've not put in yet ...'

The butterfly was silver and Isis thought it was the most beautiful thing she'd ever seen. 'You can keep it,' said Maya. 'I've got plenty more. Why don't you put it in with your roses? There's a little pin thing here, can you see? Just stick it among the flowers.'

'Oh, yes,' said Isis 'I'd love that!'

'And here's one for Gemma too.' Maya smiled. 'I should have thought of that myself. Well done, girls. They're just the right finishing touch.'

So far, Emily thought, so good. Or maybe not. There'd been a sticky moment back there in the kitchen. Pa came in and sat down and almost as soon as he did, Ma had got up, rather pointedly, and gone to do something that was probably entirely unnecessary. She and Zannah had discussed it a bit last night and agreed that they must have had a row, or Pa wouldn't have spent the night in a hotel. He claimed that Cal needed moral support, but that was rubbish. Cal was fine, and anyway, Mattie was with him and supposed to be looking after him. They'd had their version of a stag night which wasn't a stag night at all, as far as Emily could see. They'd gone out together to a movie and had a meal, which they'd been doing regularly since they were twelve. When she'd asked Cal about stag nights, he'd smiled and said, 'Can't bear them. As Jack Nicholson said in *Terms of Endearment*, "I'd rather stick needles in my eyes".'

Now everyone was ready to set off for the church. They were lined up in the hall. Zannah would go first, once she came downstairs in the dress that everyone couldn't wait to see. She'd gone into Zannah's room to help her but had come downstairs while her sister's hair was being done. Alex had finished taking pictures of her in the dressing gown she called a *peignoir* (Pretentious? Moi?) and now he was here in the hall, standing next to the grandfather clock, snapping at everything: the bridesmaids sitting together on the bottom step, peering at their posies; Charlotte, very smart in a coffee-coloured crêpe suit and a rose-pink hat, checking her lipstick in the mirror near the front door, Ma obviously miles away, thinking about something else, Pa adjusting his tie. He looked, Emily thought, very handsome. She went over to him. 'You ready, young Em?' he asked. 'You look a treat, I must say.'

'Oh, this old thing!' Emily laughed. 'Just something I had lying about in my cupboard! But I'm glad you like it. I thought I'd never find something to wear. This is not, as you know, my kind of occasion.'

'Never mind, we're off in a couple of days to Egypt. Keep that in mind when the going gets tough.'

The dress Emily had found after much searching was a dull mauve and she'd fallen in love with it the minute she saw it and paid the exorbitant price without a second thought. Devoré velvet was possibly not completely suitable for a May wedding, but the dress was loose and floaty and the fabric fell in smooth lines from her shoulders to mid-calf and made her look like a princess. She'd borrowed Zannah's amethyst earrings – a swap for the pearl ones she'd lent her – and she'd even found a handbag in a slightly darker velvet, sewn with sequins in a flower pattern.

'She's here . . . the bride . . .' That was Alex, from his vantage point. Isis and Gemma jumped and ran to stand next to Ma. Zannah came downstairs and paused for a moment on the bottom step. Emily blinked. She hadn't expected this. She'd been to fittings, and to rehearsals, but this . . . this was amazing. Her sister was completely beautiful. The dress was like something out of a fairy tale, every pearl catching the light; the cream lace draped exactly right, the headdress held by hair that had been swept up to reveal Zannah's long neck and radiant face. *Radiant*, for God's sake. You can't help it, Emily thought. When you try to describe it, you fall at once into clichés. The whole wedding thing was a thicket of clichés, but Zannah was glorious: the very best she'd ever, ever looked. Emily glanced at Ma and saw tears in her eyes. Pa went up to Zannah and kissed her cheek: gingerly, so as not to disturb the makeup. Pat was worth her weight in gold, Emily thought. No one would know that the bride was wearing anything other than lipstick but she knew better. There were layers and layers on both their faces: primer and foundation and concealer and powder and final spritz of Evian spray to fix the whole lot. Fantastic, Emily thought. I might go in for makeup more often in future.

Isis broke the spell and shattered the awed silence that had fallen. 'Mum!' she shrieked. 'Oh, Mum, you're so pretty! Is it time to go now?'

'Yes,' said Zannah. 'It's time.'

She took her place at the head of the line and Pa went to stand next to her. The bridesmaids walked behind them, carrying their posies carefully. Then came Ma and Em and Charlotte, walking together. Cal would be waiting in the church, where the guests were no doubt already in their seats. This was the moment. They were about to step on to the stage. The show's about to begin, Emily thought, feeling as though a movie camera was recording everything, as though she was part of a performance, which, of course, she was. It wouldn't have surprised her to find that music was playing outside, like a kind of overture, but no. Passers-by, and there were quite a few of them, waved and smiled. Alex must have left the house before them because there he was, next to a convenient tree. Emily stuck her tongue out at him. She couldn't help it and, sure enough, he took a photo of her as she did it.

One of her better decisions, Maureen thought, when Adrian's dreams had melted away like snowflakes on a hotplate, was to insist that he didn't cancel the booking he'd made for himself and his bride to spend their wedding night at the Savoy. Once the dust had settled, she'd been on to the hotel with tears in her voice, explaining everything to the really lovely girl in Reservations, and here they were, after she'd altered the booking to two nights and two single rooms, sitting in the hotel dining room enjoying a heavenly late breakfast. Adrian looked better, to Maureen's eye, than he had for ages, but it was best to check.

'You're not brooding today, darling, are you? Or fretting?' She broke off a piece of croissant and buttered it. Heavenly bliss!

'No, I'm okay. I'm trying not to think of what's going on in Clapham, but most of the time I can do that, no problem.'

Maureen leaned forward. 'I'll tell you what's going on down there! I've worked it out. Since I cancelled Genevieve, they'll have had to fall back on any old person who could manage to do a wedding at short notice and what they'll have is' – she ticked off the offending items on perfectly manicured fingers – 'Vol-au-vents with pastry the consistency of Play-doh. Not properly heated up. Very little champagne. The rest of the wine at rock-bottom prices, probably from Tesco. Canapés that have stood around too long and got dried out. Terribly stodgy wedding cake. Maybe the columns that hold the tiers apart will collapse. Wouldn't that be a hoot? In any case, it's sure to be a cut-price, economy affair. You're lucky not to be associated with it.'

'Yes, well ... The dress'll be beautiful. And Zannah ... I can't pretend I don't miss her.'

'But not Isis.'

'No, not Isis. Not really.'

'And not that old jailbird, Charlotte.'

'I liked Charlotte,' Adrian objected. 'She was always very nice to me.'

'Ah, that's just a front. When push comes to shove, I don't think you can trust someone who's been in jail, can you? I always felt I never knew where I was with her. Never knew what she was thinking.'

'Well, there's no point dwelling on that now. I'm getting used to the idea.'

'Tomorrow early we'll be off to the sun, darling. There'll be crowds of pretty young girls everywhere you look, I'm quite sure.'

'Hope you're right, Mum. But don't worry about me. To quote the Kaiser Chiefs, "Every day I love her less and less".'

'Are they a pop group? I've never heard of them.'

'Never mind ... They're not your sort of thing, really. But you see what I'm saying? I'll live.'

'Have another cup of coffee, darling. Then we'll go and look round Harvey Nicks. I could do with another swimsuit for when the one I have is drying. And perhaps another cover-up. I don't want to catch the sun. Not with my colouring.'

Zannah wasn't going to be late for her wedding. They'd all walked to the church together, in the warm May sunshine, and when they reached the porch, she and Bob had simply stood aside till everyone else had found their places. Joss was relieved that because he was giving Zannah away he would only sit beside her for part of the service. She'd greeted Cal's mother and some of his friends. Granny Ford – it was hard to remember to call her Grace – hugged her and promised that they'd get together for a proper chat after the ceremony and wasn't this a turn-up for the books and she was so pleased that they were going to be properly related all over again.

Joss walked down to the front pew and picked up the printed order of service. She was pleased with how it looked: an elegant font, quite good paper. Fortunately, she'd been able to get in touch with the printer in time to change the name of the bridegroom. She glanced at Cal, looking quite unlike himself in morning dress, but handsomer than she'd ever seen him. Standing next to Mattie, his fair-haired, bouncy-looking best man, he was clearly not a bit nervous in these surroundings, but completely relaxed and smiley. He grinned at her, for instance, as she sat waiting for the service to begin, and Joss smiled back.

The church had been transformed. Near the door where the bride would appear stood two small ornamental bay trees, with cream ribbons tied in bows scattered among their branches, and Joss smiled. How prettily Maya had adapted the trees-in-church idea which Maureen had admired when Prince Charles had married Camilla! The end of each pew was decorated with roses and trailing foliage and the lectern, too, had flowers twined round it. Roses, lisianthus, peonies and ivy spilled out of two enormous vases on either side of the altar. The organist was playing Bach ... a toccata ... and the music filled the vaulted roof and Joss felt its glorious vibrations passing through her body. She glanced behind her and saw a kaleidoscope of smiling faces and hands raised in greeting and nodding heads and hats heavy with flowers and banded with ribbons and dresses in pastel colours and the grey and navy and black of the men's suits. The Bach piece had ended. Joss heard the drawn-in breath of nearly seventy people as Zannah's entry music, Jeremiah Clarke's *Voluntary,* swelled and soared in the church, and looked towards the huge doors, like everyone else. She had to turn back quickly, opening her tiny handbag to find a tissue because the impulse to weep – which she'd always thought was ridiculous ... why weep at a happy event? – was nearly irresistible. It's her beauty, Joss thought, the beauty of this woman, my daughter. The congregation, you could hear them, were sighing with amazement at the dress, but for Joss, this Zannah was like a palimpsest: she could see all the other Zannahs there behind her, or perhaps *through* her ... the baby taking her very first steps and falling head first into a bed of tulips; the schoolgirl with her skirt turned up at the waistband so that far too much leg was on display. Joss had shouted at her then, and her anger had had no effect whatsoever. She remembered, too, the young bride in the register office when she married Cal the first time: up-to-date, fashionable, and wearing, in Joss's opinion, far too much blusher. All those Zannahs had become *this* one: poised, elegant, and looking as though she wanted to be *here* and nowhere else. About to marry this man and no one else. Knowing her mind and knowing this was going to be for ever. Joss touched a tissue to the corner of each eye. That's what's making me cry, she thought. Her hope. Her belief. Her faith that her dreams are about to come true.

'Dearly beloved, we are gathered here today in the presence of God and of this congregation to join together this man and this woman in holy matrimony, which is an honourable estate.'

The Rev. Geoff has a gorgeous voice, Emily thought, and now that he was doing his intoning bit, she could see why Zannah liked the traditional words. In a minute, they'd be at the 'for richer, for poorer, in sickness and in health and till death us do part' bit which was the highlight of the service.

Emily felt quite surprised by how much she was enjoying things. Pat was amazing. Everyone she'd had a hand in making-up looked fabulous. Even Charlotte hadn't been able to resist and the result knocked at least ten years off her age. Some of the hats in the audience – oops, congregation – were ridiculous. Why didn't people *think?* Several women, wives of some of Pa's colleagues who should have known better, were in headgear that wouldn't have been out of place at Ascot but which prevented anyone sitting behind them seeing a thing.

Cal's face, when he saw Zannah walking up the aisle, was something Emily would always remember. Gobsmacked would have been the word, but that was too crude. He was gobsmacked but in a sort of awed, church-suitable way. He gazed at Zannah and smiled. Emily could see how much he loved her. His eyes were shining with it. You felt you could almost put out a hand and feel its warmth. Zannah smiled demurely back, but Emily could tell that she was controlling herself. For two pins, she knew, her sister would have grinned as widely and enthusiastically as the groom.

'Who giveth this woman to be married to this man?'

That was Pa's cue. He stepped forward and sort of handed Zannah over to stand next to Cal, and he himself went to sit next to Ma. What a load of nonsense, this giving away of someone. No one belonged to anyone else, but if you went with the antique gorgeous words, you had to go along at least a bit with what they said. Even if you didn't believe it. What about 'till death us do part,' for example? That might have made some sense when you didn't live much beyond forty and then only if you were very, very healthy. Nowadays, when you could reckon to live for more than eighty years, was it fair to ask someone never to shag anyone else *ever*? Emily didn't know what she thought about that, but Zannah seemed happy to sign up for this life-sentence. She realized, with something of a pang, that she'd never again be able to fantasize about Cal falling in love with her one day. He was obviously fine with the idea of a lifetime with Zannah.

Ma was pale. Why, Emily wondered, watching her pretend to sing 'Love Divine All Loves Excelling'? Even though it was one of her favourite hymns, she wasn't making much of a noise. She could even have been lip-synching to the tune everyone else was belting out. Edie's choral society pals made a difference. They were obviously enjoying every minute. Ma's face, even with Pat's efforts, was drawn and pale. She seemed exhausted. Isis and Gemma, whose entrance behind Zannah was accompanied by a collective 'Aaah!' were behaving like little angels, sitting quite still with their flowers on their laps. Isis was also holding Zannah's bouquet and her task was to hand it back to her in time to go back down the aisle. You could see that this responsibility was on her mind. She kept casting her eyes down to check that the arrangement hadn't fallen to bits while she wasn't looking.

When the Rev. Geoff finished speaking, Cal bent forward. Before he kissed Zannah, he whispered in her ear, 'God, Zannah, I love you so much. But I feel like a complete prat. Can I change into jeans when we get back to the house?'

His lips touched hers briefly and she could hear Isis, somewhere off to her left, having a fit of the giggles suppressed by Ma.

'Don't be silly. You look great.' And he did. He was just as handsome now as he had been ten years ago, and she loved him even more now than she had then.

'And you're the most beautiful, my darling. The most, most beautiful.'

After signing the register, they turned to walk down the aisle. Zannah smiled, and went on smiling as they passed everyone waving to them from the pews. The doors stood open. She closed her eyes briefly, fixing the moment in her mind: she and Cal, together again, her hand on his sleeve, the bay trees looking glorious, the organ filling every corner of the space with music that lifted the heart, and a wide band of sunlight spread like a gold carpet over the flagstones; sunlight which was there for her and Cal to walk in all the way home. As they stepped out of the doorway, Isis and Gemma threw a shower of confetti over them. They'd walked out of the church ahead of the bridal couple and had been waiting to ambush them. Zannah laughed as she brushed a thousand pink and white rose petals off her shoulders.

That young photographer was charming, Charlotte decided. She, for one, was much relieved that he'd decided to do away with stiff formations of assorted relatives standing in the church porch. She, Edie and Val watched as he slipped between the knots of people waiting on the grass in front of the church for the wedding party to move towards the house.

'She looks,' Edie said, 'perfectly lovely, doesn't she?' Charlotte and Val nodded and Charlotte glanced to where Bob and Joss were standing together. It looked to her as though they were involved in a conversation that might easily turn into a quarrel. Joss was frowning. Charlotte managed to catch Isis as she ran about among the guests.

'Isis, I think you should go over and see if your grandfather is ready to set off for the house. We ought to get there before the other guests. Will you do that?'

Isis nodded and went off happily towards Bob. When she grabbed his hand, he smiled at her and they walked off together.

Isis thought she'd never seen anything half as beautiful as the wedding cake. She and Gemma had come up to the house with Charlotte and Grandpa, Edie and Val. Brian, who was the main person in charge of the food, gave them his special permission to go into the marquee before anyone else and have a look at the cake.

'Don't touch it, though, girls, will you?'

They shook their heads. There were ladies in black dresses with white aprons getting ready to take trays of drinks round to everyone while they milled about on the lawn.

Lots of food was already spread out on the long white table. There were two enormous whole pinkish fish, decorated with lemon slices like scales and surrounded with little flowers made of radishes. Glass bowls full of salad and baskets of rolls were on the table too and Isis felt hungry. It was ages since the bowl of cereal she'd had at breakfast. As well as the cold food, there would be lots of hot things but they'd only come out when everyone was there, ready to eat.

The cake was like three huge squares, one on top of another. The icing was so white that it made your eyes feel funny, like when you stared at snow. On the very top, there was a little pile of rosebuds that looked as though someone had dropped them on to the cake by accident, because some had fallen off and were sort of scattered round the other layers. They were exactly the same dark red rosebuds that she and Gemma had in their posies. Charlotte had taken those away to put in some water, in the larder, so that they stayed fresh. It was a shame, Isis thought, that they were going to spoil the cake by cutting it.

'Hello,' said Alex. 'I'm just going to take a picture...Isn't this cake grand? Why don't you two stand next to it, and pretend to pinch one of the roses off the top.'

'Did Brian say you could come in here?' Isis asked. 'He said no one but us was allowed to look before the guests arrived.'

'Oh, I'm allowed,' said Alex. 'I've got a free pass to go everywhere today.'

He took a few more pictures and wandered off to find something else to point his camera at: someone polishing a glass. A waitress chatting to Brian.

The speeches were over and no one had said or done anything embarrassing. Charlotte felt relieved. Cal had been charming about cutting the cake, and even though he was out of his natural element, he had dealt well with being in the limelight. Most of the guests had moved out on to the lawn with their drinks and the catering staff were circulating among them with more wine. The food had been delicious and she wished, briefly, that Maureen had been here to taste it. Surely even she would have approved of the wild mushroom and smoked mozzarella tart, the chargrilled butterflied leg of lamb with *salsa verde*, the wonderful oriental duck-breast salad and the cinnamon pavlova with berries and ginger cream. Here in the marquee, the staff had already cleared away most of the detritus, and a few people were still sitting at the tables, eating wedding cake and drinking coffee.

She went out to look for Joss and Bob and at first couldn't see them anywhere. Then she spotted them standing together near the hawthorn bushes. She frowned. They had their backs to her, and a stiffness about the way Joss was standing convinced Charlotte that they weren't exchanging happy wedding chit-chat.

'I thought we'd agreed,' Bob said. 'You promised you'd wait till after the wedding.'

'I've changed my mind,' said Joss.

'I can see that. Very well, then, spit it out. I think I know what you're going to say.'

'I want a divorce, Bob. I'm sorry. Really. I can't go on like this. It's not fair on you, for one thing.'

'Oh, you're worrying about me. How touching! Well, I can't say I'm all that keen to stay married to you, so you might say it's all worked out for the best.' He didn't sound as though he believed what he was saying. There was a note of bitterness in his voice that she'd never heard before, but then, the circumstances were out of the ordinary. I can't, she thought, expect him to sound pleased.

'I shall consult a lawyer,' she said. 'That's what you're supposed to do, isn't it?'

'Not my business really. I'll be in Egypt in any case. Just get on with it, and leave me in peace.'

'But, Bob ...' Now that she'd spoken, Joss was overwhelmed by the enormity of what she'd done. Was this it? Really? 'We'll see one another, won't we? At family birthdays and so forth ...'

'Not going to bother about things like that now, frankly. I shan't forgive you for fucking up my day, though. You could have waited. As we agreed.'

'And if I'd waited it would have fucked up *my* day!' Joss noticed that her voice was dangerously wobbly and took a deep breath to steady herself. 'If I'd waited, I'd have been sitting here for six weeks while you swanned off to Luxor. I'm not prepared to do that, Bob. I'm going to take care of myself from now on. I have to do this. I hope one day you'll be able to see that I really had no choice.'

Joss waited to see whether he would say anything. Would he plead with her to stay with him? He might point out that she did have a choice: she could give up Gray for ever and stay with him till they were ancient. She could stay with him till the very end of her life. He said nothing. As Joss was racking her brain for a formula that would take her away from this place, from this situation in a graceful way, he turned suddenly and strode off briskly towards a group of his colleagues who were standing near the rose-trellis laughing at something. She watched him get straight in there with a remark that made them all chortle even more enthusiastically and she thought, okay. He's going to pretend he doesn't give a damn. Fine. So will I. She felt as she imagined a baby would feel, if it emerged into the world already grown: excited, overwhelmed by possibilities and nearly paralysed with terror of what might happen next. She also felt very light and detached, as though suddenly she'd floated free of her own life, and was drifting over the physical world that had defined her for years. She squared her shoulders and made her way into the house.

*

Emily and Zannah were up in the bedroom. The wedding dress was hanging up on the back of the door, already hidden in its muslin shroud. Zannah had just stepped into a chiffony floral skirt and top of supreme prettiness and now looked a bit like someone in a Botticelli painting.

'I didn't think you were going to have a honeymoon,' Emily said. 'Are you? I thought Cal had to be at work on Monday.'

Zannah giggled. 'Apparently the hotel was so fabulous that he's booked us a couple of nights there. Isis is going to Gemma's till Monday. We'll do some of the things people never do when they live in London. I'm not going to use my London Eye voucher, though, because I've promised to take Isis and Gemma on that. Someone's knocking, Em . . . Who on earth can it be?'

'Probably Isis,' Emily said. 'Shall I let her in?'

Zannah nodded and Emily opened the door.

'It's me,' said Joss. 'Do you mind if I join you?'

'Yes, do come in, Ma. She's got something to say to you, Em,' said Zannah, over her shoulder from where she was sitting at the dressing-table.

'Really? To me? What have I done wrong?'

Ma was frowning. What on earth was the matter? She said, 'Nothing. Nothing at all. It's me. I've got to tell you something.'

'Sounds serious, Ma. Are you okay? You look a bit pale.'

'I *am* okay, Em, but I'll be more okay when I've told you this. Not telling you has been awful, but I didn't want to spoil your day. It's nearly over now, though, isn't it? I told Zannah last night but only because she caught me skulking about in the marquee in the early hours.'

'The suspense is killing me. Go on. Spit it out. I can take it. I'm a big girl.'

Joss sat down on the edge of the bed and began to speak.

Isis and Gemma were standing together. They'd been admiring the beautiful pearl bracelets Mattie had given them as their official bridesmaids' presents. Tiny silvery bits between the pearls caught the light and glittered. Isis looked at the guests gathered round Mum and Dad. They were all clapping and cheering. Grandpa and Em were next to one another, and Grandma was talking to Charlotte. Alex was still taking photographs. There would be thousands and thousands of pictures to look at. Edie and Val were laughing together and talking to Granny Ford, who was red in the face.

'I'd like to thank all of you for coming to celebrate our wedding,' Mum said. 'And especially I'd like to say a big thank-you to my parents, to Charlotte, to Edie and Val. It's been like a dream come true. And now I'm going to close my eyes and throw my bouquet and I hope the person who catches it lives happily ever after with the man of her dreams.'

Mum looked at Grandma and smiled at her. Grandma smiled back and waved at Mum. Then Mum threw the bouquet up and up, nearly as high as the top of the marquee. Everyone watched it flying through the air and when it came down, they all looked round to see who'd caught it.

From where she was standing, Joss realized, the marquee was like the kind of pretty tent you saw in picture books illustrating medieval jousts: white and gathered into a point at the top. She lifted her eyes above it to follow the trajectory – was that the word? Arc, maybe, or parabola, she couldn't remember – of the bouquet that Zannah had just thrown into the air. It seemed to be moving very slowly. She could make out each flower and leaf as it came closer: dark velvety roses, and freesias and ranunculus and vibernum and trailing ivy. The sky was dotted with white clouds now. What had Zannah said? *Happily ever after with the man of her dreams* . . . Even though she knew Zannah had meant the bouquet to be for her, Joss had no real intention of reaching out and trying to catch it. The whole thing, she'd told herself, was nothing but a silly superstition. At the last moment, though, some reflex over which she had no control made her open her hands and the flowers dropped into them as though that was where they belonged. As though they were hers by right.

Joss sat in the car looking at the front door for a long time. On the seat beside her, the piece of paper with Gray's address on it was lying under the A-Z. The house was very pretty: square, on three floors, with a neat front garden. White stucco. White paintwork. Lovely curtains in the ground-floor front room. Which window was his? She could see the buttons to the left of the front door. I just have to go and press one, she thought. It's no more difficult than that. I have to do it. I have to know.

She got out of the car and walked up the front path. At the door, her courage almost failed her but she pushed the button marked *'Ashton'* and waited for Gray's echoey voice to speak to her from the intercom. Nothing. I should go, she thought. He's not here. I can leave a note. Should I leave a note? No ... I'll come again. Another time. Maybe I ought to go away and think for a bit longer. Make sure I'm doing the right thing.

'Joss?' He was standing on the doorstep. She couldn't speak. Her whole head was suddenly full of white space: silence and more silence with not a word in the world that she could have articulated. She looked down, terrified all at once, and Gray stepped out and took her by the hand. 'Come in,' he said. 'Come home, my darling Joss.'

She took a step over the threshold and heard, somewhere in the far distance, over the clamour of her own heartbeat drumming in her ears, the beautiful, heart-lifting sound of the white front door clicking shut behind them.